The SWORD of Hannibal

TERRY McCARTHY

WARNER BOOKS

NEW YORK   BOSTON

Cover design by Diane Luger
Cover art by Steve Stone
Typography by David Gatti
Book design Charles A. Sutherland

Warner Books

Time Warner Book Group
1271 Avenue of the Americas
New York, NY 10020
Visit our Web site at www.twbookmark.com

Printed in the United States of America

First Paperback Printing: June 2005

10 9 8 7 6 5 4 3 2 1

***STRABO SURGED FORWARD,
DRIVING HIS HORSE DIRECTLY
INTO THE CARTHAGINIANS' MIDST.***

The river erupted in a flurry of shouts and hooves and clashing metal. Three of the elite Falcon soldiers raised their swords high to swing at Strabo as his horse slammed into them. They swung at air. Strabo had thrust his horse into them as a diversion and leapt from the saddle.

The first Falcon stabbed at him, but Strabo stepped to the side and yanked the soldier from his saddle. He drove his blade through the man's throat, pulled the sword away and in the same motion brought its backswing through the exposed hamstring of the second Falcon. The man's blade met Strabo's with a loud *clang*, and Strabo used the opportunity to dive beneath the horse's legs, emerge on the other side, and plunge his sword through the Falcon's stomach before he could react. The soldier's face was wide with shock, but Strabo did not see it. He was already upon the third Falcon . . .

For
Therese

Acknowledgments

Many thanks to the indefatigable Jacques de Spoelberch— UberMensch! And to Les Pockell (master of the classic story), Beth de Guzman, Andie Avila, and Stephanie Finnegan at Warner who were of great help to me. I also owe a debt to the following:

Mrs. Berles
Mrs. Packard
Miss Cartright
Mrs. Biggs
Mrs. O'Rourke
Mrs. Hoos
Mr. Stewart
Mrs. Smalligan
Mr. Froyslund
David Meyer
Debbie Invaluable Hyde
Leslie Rundell
Sandy McClure
Dan McNulty
The Osters
Justin McCarthy
Jeannie McCarthy
Francis McCarthy
Tim McCarthy
Jeff Hyde

Linda Aikens
Rick Kra niak
Paul Lacasse
Annette Lacasse
Steve Wilson
Tom Lynch
Sue Aiello
Jo Bourgeaulais
Bill Hainey
Barbara D'amato
Jeannie Bratschie
William O. Steele
The Gang at Kinko's
The Orrs
Pat McCarthy
Joan McCarthy
Maureen McCarthy
Tobin McCarthy
Eve Walsh
Bob and Jeanne Temmerman

Author's Note

When Western civilization was still young, every nation, city-state, and tribe was dominated by two superpowers: Carthage and Rome. The two military behemoths squared off and the bloody struggle raged for years across the Mediterranean.

The
SWORD
of
Hannibal

Chapter 1

*S*trabo couldn't have seen the soldiers coming, not in his condition.

His only thoughts were that if this was earth, it was earth that rose and fell like the sea and bright light bathed him when he thought it should still be night.

It must be daylight. He could feel the warmth of the sun on his back, a back once scarred by fire and now ever wary of the sun. He couldn't prevent a salty slurry of seawater from rising up his throat and rushing out of his mouth onto the sand. He rolled over painfully. His left side bore the wound of an unmistakable sword slash four fingers long. Cleaned by the sea, he noticed dimly, it didn't bleed much. Not too deep.

The beach was stained with wide plumes of blackened sand and a stench hung over the surf. He lay drenched, nudged by an ebbing tide. The sea was gentle now with morning and the passing of the high winds that beset the hellish night before. He struggled to gather his wits and they came to him in a jumble.

A routine trading fleet, they had been thirty-seven ships

and now they were none. The hostile Carthaginian navy had appeared unexpectedly behind them at midday. The merchant fleet had run before them with the rising wind for as long as they could. The Carthaginian commander must have known the approaching storm would overtake them eventually, though the wind held to the fleeing fleet's advantage for hours before they were caught.

The storm had hit them all, pursuer and pursued. Then the pursued had run out of sea at the Majorca points, those jutting promontories that protected shallower waters from the heavy seas to the west. The merchant fleet had to curtail sail just to stay afloat, and when they did so, they were cornered.

Fat with lumber and tin from the Moroccan inland, their boats wallowed helplessly before the nimble galleys of the Carthaginians. Boat after boat was boarded and put to the torch by flevaum, those long-range flaming arrows favored by the Carthaginian navy. A navy that had no need for lumber—only destruction. They ruled this end of the Mediterranean Sea with time-honored violence.

Clutching his side, Strabo managed to pull himself up and survey the immediate landscape. He was reminded of all those swimming lessons at the hands of his older brothers along the riverfront, upstream from his father's fishing fleet and the floating detritus of cleaned fish drifting in wide beds out to sea. His young arms had churned furiously, desperate to escape, his lungs screaming and his limbs struggling as his older brothers forced him beneath the surface. He would slip away, only to be accosted again, and in this way his experience with water was well practiced. *Thank you, brothers, long gone that you must be.*

What of Nabulam and of Ozgul? Ozgul had leaped over the side just as the enemy's boarding platform shuddered wickedly onto their deck. He looked resolute one moment and then panicked in an instant and leaped with a wide-eyed glance over his shoulder. His leather shoulder armor flapped behind him like powerless wings and he vanished into the sea. He must be gone. He could not survive those heavy seas, for he was no swimmer. And Nabulam. He was . . . Where was he? He was last seen on the quarterdeck extending those useless prevention poles that the attackers snapped easily as they came within range. Nabulam and those he labored futilely with; they must all be lost.

Strabo could not know that, in truth, the Carthaginians had left six ships floating. But only those with ivory; these they towed away.

The beach was a landscape of charred destruction. Blackened spurs from burned keels lay scattered about, some pieces only a span in length, others as tall as three men. Littered over the sand were burned oar pieces and rigging, blackened hull sections and wagon chassis, and shattered Phoenician cargo boxes. Nothing on the beach stirred unless rocked by the storm's lingering surf.

The broken skeleton of Strabo's doomed fleet surrounded him. As did the bodies. Blackened bodies and blackened limbs, bloated by the sea. The sea had its fill of humanity that night and so regurgitated hundreds of corpses up and down the beach. Probably fifteen hundred lives lost all told, Strabo thought.

The soldier in Strabo took stock of his situation first, his weapons second, his body third, and his resources last. The situation was obvious. He was alive. As to weapons, he had none. He was injured and weak, but felt stronger than might be expected after hours in a storm-tossed sea. And what resources did he have at his disposal? Only himself.

His weapons were lost in the attack, but not before his favorite sword saved him when the deck was overrun by howling Carthaginians. He killed three of them in his escape. The first charged clumsily with pylum upraised and Strabo simply stepped aside, wrenching the man's spear away and using it to pull the man off balance and onto Strabo's out-thrust sword. Though the man's mouth opened wide and his eyes bulged beneath arching brows, he made no sound save for the thud of his body striking the deck.

He encountered the next man on his way down to the foredeck. The man stabbed at Strabo but missed. Strabo cut him down in an instant and muscled on through the shrieking throng, all swinging limbs and weapons and bodies lunging frantically and slipping on the bloody deck.

He made it nearly to the bow when he saw another war galley coming, its ramming equipment raised and bearing down on his ship from one hundred paces away, its prow pawing the waves like a mad bull. He had no time!

The storm threw pellets of rain into his eyes as he turned back and sprinted along the high rail line toward the stern. There were fewer men here, most now fallen or forced to the center of the ship. Over his shoulder he glimpsed the new galley accelerating terribly toward them. Sixty paces, fifty paces. Strabo heard the pounding of the warship's drum. Ribbons of tattered sail glanced off his face as he ran along the rail line, the sea only spans below him as the boat heaved unnaturally in the gale.

Forty paces, thirty. Then a man on the rear deck spotted him. The man stood nearly two spans high, tall for a Carthaginian. He bore a leather and bronze breastplate, forearm shields strapped tightly to his thick wrists, and a hip thong with bronze leggings. The man positioned himself in Strabo's path and waited patiently, twisting an Attican long sword in his hands with practiced familiarity and blessing his luck that he would trip across such an easy kill this far from the delirious fray on the main deck below.

With nowhere else to go, Strabo continued straight at him. The man raised his sword as Strabo approached, intending to cleave Strabo in two like a standing log. As the man's sword reached the top of its arc, Strabo surprised the soldier by diving headfirst toward the man's feet! The soldier brought the sword down in a flashing arc.

But Strabo was sliding on the wet rail deck with his short sword drawn.

He slid into the man's legs and, with a desperate slash, sliced one of them off clean below the knee. The man's sword came down off balance and sliced into Strabo's side, hacking off a chunk of flesh and taking a piece of his rib before thudding into the wet wooden deck with little sound, so sharp was the man's weapon. His severed leg separating from the rest of him, the tall man toppled like a broken pole. Strabo was doused in his blood as he slid beneath him and past.

Twenty paces. Ten. The war galley closed on its prey with a roar. There was no time for Strabo to contemplate the now legless soldier's undoing as the new galley closed on the ship and crushed into it at all speed.

Strabo rolled to his feet, surged forward, and charged off the stern of the ship into midair.

The iron-plated prow of the attacking ship took them directly in the side and the shudder reverberated through both boats. The impact was of forty tons of matériels natural and man-made; iron and wood, heavy canvas sail and clay provisioning containers, leather rigging and stone tables, mahogany sparring, and thousands of stones' worth of lumber and tin. All colliding at speed in the middle of the night with nothing but ninety fathoms of angry salt water between the collision and the floor of the Mediterranean Sea.

The shock of the impact rocketed past Strabo as he seemed to hover, if only briefly, his sword swinging above him in a futile bid for ba'ince in the space where man was not meant to balance, here above the hungry sea like black marble below him, the sea that yanked him from the air and into the coldness of its belly below.

Ripped as he was from a burning cargo vessel teeming with the grunts and cries that come only from hand-to-hand combat, the plunge into the sea insulated him from the din above. Now he had only the wind and the waves to contend with. And the wound in his ribs.

Ships were sinking all around him, but he was able to swim free of the confusion. The cargo fleet had tried to hug the coast in the hopes of anchoring in if the wind grew too much for their heavy ships and overburdened sails. They had not gotten close enough. Strabo squinted through the waves, and after he rode the top of a dozen swells, he guessed he was within three leagues of shore.

Not an easy swim, but he thought he might make it with the wind at his back. If not for his side, screaming now after the initial numbness. Each wave launched a cascade of needlelike mist before it as the heavy wind caught the crest. Between gasps Strabo caught an occasional glimpse of a distant shoreline far off in the darkness.

His arm smacked painfully into something hard in the water, a harboring oar. Now the wind bore him and the oar toward the shore far away. He struggled to keep his head up and his mouth clear of the sea, and when each moment was right, he would gulp for breath in throaty gasps.

Three leagues is a long way, a half a day's trip over land on horseback. And this was a bellowing sea. After several hours of struggle, he forgot about the trading fleet and the fat fee owed for his services. He forgot the men he had killed to escape and the men he knew on board.

After several more hours, he gave no thought even to who he was. His own identity held little importance out here. He seemed only to be along for the ride as the body of a man clung to a hunk of ship and struggled to breathe through the spray of the wind and the waves. There was no sky, no light, no boats. Just water and wind and spray. And noise. The wind howled at him and water assaulted his ears incessantly, loudly spattering him when his head was above water and grinding his ears with salty froth when his head was submerged. The dull roar of it all deadened him.

The waves ground his tunic over the harbor oar until the cloth disintegrated, feeding the sea just as surely as his ship had.

Strabo's sense of time left him. All was water and kicking and trying to breathe. There was no shore in this world. There were no people or families or livestock. No love, no courage, no faith. He was an insect, with an insect's mindless mind. Clutch. Kick. Gulp air. Endlessly.

Anesthetized by the ceaseless water, he would proceed until his body sacrificed everything a living thing could— then finally give out. He would be unaware of this happening and would drown with no thoughts. In a vacuum. Gone.

This seemed as sure a fate as any when the seabed suddenly reared up to peel from the water at last and become a shoreline, then to stretch into a plateau beyond that. The plateau crouched between the sea and the ancient foothills that lined the east coast of the vast Spanish Peninsula. The sea coughed Strabo up onto a beach studded with high rock formations leaping from the sand in jagged fountains of granite.

And now here he lay, just another scattered remnant of a dead fleet.

Foggy as his thoughts were, he knew he had lost his sword. He didn't like being exposed out here on the beach, weaponless. He tried to stand up only to crumple over on his injured side.

He winced and tried again. He rose to a wobbly knee and knew he could not stand. He thought he would lie down for a while and regain his strength.

Then he heard them. He swiveled around, exhaling painfully. There, fifty paces away, was a Carthaginian shore party. Three soldiers of lower rank and a fourth sporting the armlets and leather shoulder wings of a field officer. Strabo wasn't sure, but that thing off in the distance bobbing at the water's edge must be their dinghy. Strabo knew there would be other shore parties up and down the coast. They were here strictly for surveillance, to see what had washed up on these remote shores. They were shuffling across the sand, kicking at pieces of burned tinder and tiny masked crabs as the creatures skittered by.

With a sigh, Strabo eyed a craggy assemblage of rocks towering nearby. A choice defensive position, he thought. He could scramble into those rocks, climb high, and keep those tons of granite between him and danger. He could lob stones from up there and maybe escape to higher ground or simply hide and never be discovered in the first place. If only he could get there.

The safety of that rocky outcropping was only paces away, but it might as well have been a league. He spat, or tried to spit, but there was no saliva left in his drained body. The shore party had him.

Strabo knelt unsteadily in the sand and swayed as the men reached him. They were dirty, muscular, and bristling with weapons. One grinned at him from beneath a helmet of cheap bronze, beaten to crude shape by some drunken forger at camp. His few remaining teeth were brown and broken. The soldier was typical of the desperate mercenary types in the Carthaginian army. The man asked his commanding officer, "Can I take his nose?"

The man spoke Greek, which was no surprise to Strabo as the Carthaginians favored the tribes and allies that could speak Greek, the closest thing to a common language in the Mediterranean world. Good communication was an asset to an army, as Strabo knew well.

The officer was impatiently scanning the beach, ignoring Strabo. "No time for that, kill him. We have ground to cover here."

Strabo knelt helplessly before them, his neck vulnerable to the inevitable deathblow. But he could hold himself up no longer and dropped heavily to the sand, face first.

"See how the condemned man bows before me!" The soldier with the rotten teeth laughed. The others enjoyed the joke with assorted grins and smirks.

"Look at me!" the soldier shouted at Strabo, and kicked him heavily in his wounded side. Strabo grunted from the pain of it, delirious now through his fog of exhaustion and loss of blood. He rolled over on his side. What little strength remained, he used to clutch his ribs.

Down in the sand, Strabo's last thought was of a man blocking out the sun, his hand on his sword hilt. Strabo's state of mind was such that he could only manage the thought that his shirt of armored mail still clung to his shoulders. Strabo's mind swirled upside down and then fainted to nothing.

In the real world above him, his executioner's commanding officer barked, "Finish him. Let's be off." With that, the soldier with the brown teeth unsheathed his sword with a ring and raised the shining weapon above his head. His comrades stepped back to give him swinging room. Strabo's executioner flexed his muscles and drew in a large breath, preparing to bring the sword down with steadied force, when his companions suddenly regarded him curiously. The heavy metal point of a long-iron Spanish war arrow had appeared jutting from his throat, spitting a fine mist of red that rained down over the man's armored neck cowling.

The executioner's eyes bulged and he stumbled forward to fall next to Strabo in the sand, still gripping his weapon with both hands. An arrow shaft the length of a man's arm was strung through his neck. The others spun quickly, reaching for their weapons as the whir and hiss of feathered, spinning shafts filled the air around them. *Thunk! Thunk! Thunk!* The arrows found their marks with the sound of shafts piercing flesh and skidding to a halt at the first bones they met.

Porcupined with arrows, the entire shore party dropped as one to the sand. Dead.

From the outcropping of rock that Strabo had deliriously considered, ten wiry men appeared from where there had been none. They wore pants with leather panels stitched inside each thigh. Their hands were callused from a lifetime of holding the reins—for they were first and foremost horsemen. Their hair ran long and dark into small braids that dangled down their necks.

They descended on the dead Carthaginians with short daggers and made quick work of them, efficiently lifting their heads and slitting the soldiers' throats for good measure. Working in twos, they dragged each corpse down the beach and flung the dead into the surf and the retreating tide.

Two of the men quickly fashioned a stretcher from the shore party's spears and cloaks. They heaved Strabo's limp body onto the stretcher and disappeared with him into the safety of the rocks.

The beach lay quiet now in the morning sun except for the lapping of the weakening waves. Minutes later, a line of horsemen appeared on the ridge high above the beach. They led two extra horses rigged with the loaded stretcher suspended between them. The troop dropped out of sight over the ridgeline, heading west. Heading inland.

———

Hostilities between Carthage and Rome were escalating rapidly, resulting in an unambiguous directive to the Carthaginian navy from headquarters: Clear the sea-lanes and sweep the east coast of the Spanish Peninsula clean. The navy ranged up and down the coast patrolling ports and accosting any shipping associated with Roman interests. And they weren't being subtle about it.

Chapter 2

"You are certain you were not discovered?"

"Yes, sir. The beach was clear for a league."

"The prisoner?"

"Still out cold."

"And the dead?"

"The tide took them."

Nargonne of Asturias clasped his substantial chin with one hand while the other rested on his sword hilt. He was furious at these dim-witted youngsters. He needed information, not corpses! But he only had a few men at his disposal now and was reluctant to chastise them too severely over their misstep on the beach.

They had returned to this windswept makeshift camp jubilant with their small victory. Nargonne knew it was just that: a small victory and probably a dangerous one. So far, the Carthaginians were unaware of his presence and of his intentions. Though the Carthaginians had many troops in the Spanish Peninsula, they were mostly far south in their home port of Cartagena.

The fact that their fleets were ranging this far north disturbed Nargonne. There was nothing of interest up here, only poor coastal fishing villages barely scraping up a living. And inland? A few desperate farmers.

Which was precisely why he was here. This was rocky, hilly country, crisscrossed by streams and rivers and flush with heavy forest and bush. It was easy for a small force to disappear here, as Nargonne's men had done. It would be very difficult for a larger force to make their way around. And for the professional soldier, a Roman or a Carthaginian, not much room to fight. Not in the way they preferred, anyway.

He turned his attention back to his men standing before him.

"Bring me the prisoner when he can speak." He dismissed them with a wave and they spun on their corkheeled sandals and were gone.

Nargonne instinctively surveyed the camp. He had nearly one hundred men here and employed a traditional military tactic to disguise their numbers: bivouac beneath trees with the lion's share of the men out of sight.

The horses, too, were kept under cover and only lightly equipped. Nargonne disliked heavy armor and heavy tack. Not that they could afford such equipment. In any event, he wished to be fast and light on his feet. His was not some great army with the advantage of size that could throw its weight around. Nargonne had banned heavy saddle; only light leather "speed pads" were allowed. With such little armor and their horses' habit of roaming free without the benefit of a stockade, they looked like an itinerant band of horse-herdsmen. Which was perfectly fine with Nargonne.

His men were scattered over this hill and the next, but

all within earshot of the warning horn should need be. There were no fires—they had been put out as soon as the beach party had entered camp with the news of their encounter with the Carthaginians. They would eat cold food today.

There was the sudden sound of hooves behind Nargonne and he turned as a man rode up on a blue-black stallion and came to a stop. The two men nodded at each other. It was Ribas, Nargonne's right-hand man on this expedition.

Nargonne hailed him. "Good riding, Ribas."

"Good riding," said Ribas in reply.

Ribas was followed closely by two others on mountain ponies. The two men were dirt-covered, their hair worn loose, not tied as usual, and dust ringed their nostrils. Although they wore the broad ponchos of the Tardet people, they were Nargonne's men. Scouts. They kept a careful distance from Ribas.

Ribas was one of only a few in their group with military experience. The reasons why he appeared from the eastern hills one day to settle in their province were known only to him. And everyone kept it that way. The citizens of Asturias were a private people.

But one could not misinterpret the nature of this man. He gave his name as Sukor Ribas and wore his hair greased in the manner of a maritime brigand from the lawless Mediterranean ports of Algiers or Bou Ismail. Nargonne and his people recognized that Ribas was cut from different cloth than they. More than two sword lengths tall, he was as quick as a cat. Easy with a saber, it was said. Easy with a lance. He was strong, big-boned, and cruel-looking.

Nargonne smiled at the men. "Good riding," he said. "Good riding," they returned.

Ribas stirred in his saddle, nodding at the two scouts.

"They tell me the smelting works in Andorra have delivered copper war kettles to Cartagena."

The two scouts nodded in affirmation.

Ribas watched Nargonne raise his eyebrows at this and smiled in satisfaction. The Carthaginian capital here on the Spanish Peninsula, Cartagena was a wealthy, sun-washed city on the southern coast of the mainland, staring watchfully out over the Mediterranean Sea. It was from here that their renowned general, Hannibal, had vowed to wage war on Rome, the sworn enemy of Carthage. Although he had yet to make good on that threat, it was well known that Hannibal had one hundred thousand troops there, maybe more. Rome had left Hannibal alone as long as he confined himself to the sprawling Spanish continent, and this had gone on for years. And while he had been gathering allies for some time, Hannibal had never mounted a much anticipated campaign against his Roman enemy in Italy.

It was also common knowledge that Hannibal had been constructing a huge fleet. As ship after ship was completed, they were secreted to ports up and down the coast from Benidorm to Málaga. Who knew how many ships he had by now? Isn't that what he needed to attack Rome? A great fleet. Had the day come at last?

"How large are these kettles?" asked Nargonne.

"Roughly fifty jars each, as far as we can tell," one of the scouts said.

"They are planning for two oxen each just to pull them," the other quickly added.

"How many kettles total?" asked Nargonne.

The two scouts swallowed and Ribas answered for them.

"One hundred," he said.

A low whistle escaped Nargonne's lips. One of Hannibal's secrets of success was an extraordinary attention to the care of his troops. He knew well-fed soldiers fought with strength and rarely mutinied. Many mercenaries joined his army for the daily meals alone.

Nargonne quickly did the math. Each Carthaginian soldier ate one meal per day. Under their war kitchen protocol, a kettle went to fire five times each day, producing one hundred meals per kettle at each cooking. One hundred kettles meant some fifty thousand meals per day.

It was as Nargonne had brashly predicted and he rubbed his hands. Hannibal was on the move.

Strabo winced as he came to. His hands were bound behind him and his legs were tied as well. Even lifting his head from the dirt seemed a great effort.

The ground around him was littered with leaves and twigs. Through squinted eyes, he could see a form watching him from just an arm's length away. A boy squatted and stared at him nervously, his eyes wide. His long hair was tied behind his head and he had no beard yet. He wore leather pants and an oversize loose tunic that nearly covered his legs as he hunched there on his calves.

Behind the boy was a wall of thin, coarse fabric, glowing with the light of day outside. Strabo realized he was in a small field tent. He heard the *yip* of a dog from the other side of the cloth. The boy leaped up soundlessly and darted outside.

Strabo allowed his head to drop again and it hit the dirt more painfully than he had intended. He shut his eyes briefly, begging for sleep, but yanked them open again. *Where am I? The mainland? The Balearic Isles?*

Without moving his head, he could make out the shapes of two reed bowls and a leather flask. The remains of a meal. He had eaten. He remembered now. Someone had propped him up roughly and forced a milky gruel in his mouth, rubbing his throat and making him swallow as if he were an ailing puppy. He could only remember vague shapes of light and shadow moving about him, as if it had happened when he were a newborn with undeveloped eyes. It seemed they had barked loudly at him and poured water down his throat.

They were keeping him alive, but they weren't being particularly gentle about it. That boy was no Carthaginian. A slave? Was the boy tattooed like Carthaginian slaves? Strabo couldn't remember and his mind faded to blackness once again.

He first heard the whispering through a deep, dull sleep. Then he was turned onto his side. Strabo pulled his eyelids open and they were in there with him in the small tent, the boy again and two armed men. They were dressed like the boy and their beards were full, though trimmed short. They held daggers. Strabo noticed the metal was poor. There was almost no curve to them and they bore no engraving. One edge of each knife was scalloped. A skinning knife. What kind of warriors were these?

The men spoke to each other and Strabo blinked in recognition. Was that a Biscayne dialect? Then one of the men spoke to him. In Greek.

"Sit up," the man said.

Strabo stared at them a moment, then struggled to comply, only to topple over as pain lurched through his left side. His ribs. The sword slash on the ship. He was wrapped in some kind of rough hewn tunic and couldn't see his wound, though he could feel it well enough. He still wore his thin mail shirt beneath the tunic. The mail was strong, constructed of fingernail-size links of bronze chain woven together with hardy cord. It had not been destroyed by the sea and that gave Strabo hope. The sea had not destroyed him either. The men lifted him to a sitting position, exchanging a look between them.

"You speak Greek," one of them said.

Strabo nodded weakly.

"How long were you in the water?" the man asked.

The water. The fleet, the endless waves, the beach, the Carthaginian beach party. Strabo could only shake his head.

One of the men stood and ordered the other man and the boy to feed Strabo again, then slipped out of the tent.

They fed Strabo wordlessly. The food had little taste, but Strabo found this time he was actually hungry. After a while, they laid him down and he groaned as they cleaned his wound and stuffed it with leaves and herbs. Again he slept.

When they came in again, he awoke more clearheaded. They looked into his eyes, apparently gauging whether or not he was coherent. The same man that spoke before asked him, "Can you speak?"

"Yes," Strabo managed.

The boy stood clear as the two men lifted a dizzy Strabo to his feet and dragged him outside. One man produced a dagger and hacked away the leather cord binding his ankles. They left his hands bound.

It was dark and they were on a rocky, forested hillside. A dozen more men like his captors surrounded him. Strabo could see that they all bore long swords, but in those leather sheaths he could not discern the nature of their blades. Everything was shadowy and gray, and though the breeze was cool, the heat of the late-summer days still emanated from the numerous boulders that labeled the landscape.

He could see by the moonlight that the brush was thick beneath the trees. Good cover everywhere, he thought. He turned and regarded his tent. Suspended low to the ground by two immature daphne bushes, it was nothing more than a worn, sheer fabric, colored like the surrounding rocks. Whoever these men were, they were adept at camouflage.

He was led along a ridgeline and at first he stumbled over the rocks, struggling against the darkness and his bonds. He wondered why the men didn't blindfold him as well. He would have, had he been in charge of a prisoner. He would have added a gag. Strabo felt his legs returning. Good. Whatever they fed him, it made him stronger.

Strabo felt the eyes of others watching them, though he could make out no one in the darkness. He noticed strings of rabbits and game birds hanging along the path. The men had been trapping their own food. Strabo counted several hundred paces before they came to a steep cliffside that rose before them. Set against the base of the cliff was a tent, designed and deployed like the other one, only much larger. It glowed faintly from a small fire inside.

His escorts halted here and two of them went inside. Strabo could smell no sea on the breeze, so it was either an offshore wind or he was simply far from the coast. He looked up to read the sky. Archnid's star was over the moon—if that was Archnid's star. Then the shoreline would be west of him if he had washed up along the Balearic Sea coast, and he was sure now that he had. He knew the sea and felt he was still close to it. Suddenly he wanted to be back in the water at the mercy of the waves, not men.

A man poked his head out of the tent and motioned for the guards to bring him in.

They ushered him in where he was confronted by a semicircle of four men sitting cross-legged on the floor. They were all bare headed with close-cropped beards like the others outside.

Then he spotted them. Slings. How could he have missed those? He could make out the twin leather straps hanging from their waists. The men outside had them too, he realized now, as well as quivers and bows on their backs. These men were slingers!

Straight daggers and slings and long, dark hair. Balearics were renowned for the sling. Many a battle had been swayed by the power of such a weapon in skilled hands. Strabo had seen slings in action only once, but that had been enough. Nothing in this world matched the range of a skilled slinger. He had watched one day as his Achaean captors had been cut down by slingers from a nearby wood, slingers that had never even been seen, before or after the attack! The Achaeans' arrows were useless against the range of the slings. But these men weren't Balearics. Balearics scorn swords and, anyway, they prefer a curved dagger. So he hadn't washed up on the Balearic Islands but the mainland after all.

These men here were heavily armed. Swords for short fighting, bows for close range, and slings for long range. He had seen no spears yet. Why not? Were they not part of an army?

Everyone was quiet and a few men watched the man in the center, waiting for him to speak. The man regarded Strabo calmly, then spoke to him in a tongue he did not understand. Strabo did not answer. Then the man addressed him again, this time in the Punic tongue, which Strabo recognized but did not know. Finally the man addressed him in Greek. The man was Nargonne.

"Are you a professional sailor?" Nargonne asked.

Unsure of his situation, Strabo didn't answer. He was a prisoner. Did that mean one wrong answer and he was a dead man? Did that mean . . . a blow to his back sent him doubling over in pain! He fell to one knee, gasping for air.

"No," Strabo finally answered.

"How long have you sailed for the Carthaginians?" Nargonne asked. Strabo's voice was hoarse from disuse.

"I did not sail for them."

"You are not in the Carthaginian military?"

"No," said Strabo.

"Why was your fleet attacked?"

"I don't know," said Strabo.

Nargonne paused, thinking. He watched as the prisoner rose uncertainly to his feet again. This one was strong, thought Nargonne. He had been badly wounded but already was healing fast. Nargonne felt the eyes of his townsmen on him. How could this prisoner help them? If he had knowledge of Carthaginian ways and methods, that would be a great asset to their cause. Think.

"Are you Carthaginian?" asked Nargonne.

This was the question of the day, not just for him, but for everyone in the whole accursed world, thought Strabo. Carthage perched on the North Coast of Africa at a point where it lunged north. Rome was on the Italian Peninsula that lunged aggressively south through the belly of the Mediterranean toward Africa. Geography had decreed the two empires straddle this thinnest part of the Mediterranean Sea and stare each other down over less than a hundred leagues of shallow, easily navigable water.

Carthage was a great power and master of the rich coasts of Africa and Spain. Rome was master of the northern Mediterranean and all points east. There were other kingdoms and mighty tribes, but if one could not stay out of the way of the two preeminent powers, one was forced to choose.

Rome was the more ambitious of the two. An insatiable "Republic" dominated by military bureaucrats. All of Rome was based on reward. More, more, more—it did not matter more of what. It did not matter who must fall. More.

By contrast, decidedly undemocratic Carthage was run by the noble mercantile families whose lineage ran back generations. Their interests were in accumulating wealth and maintaining order. And where Carthage revered ancestral gods, Rome revered nothing but power. Yes, the Romans had their stolen Greek gods, but the attention paid to them was hardly sincere.

The Romans were an unstoppable, godless realm and the Carthaginians were an immovable ancient force. They had been at odds for over two hundred years now.

As to the wild Spanish Peninsula, as far as Rome was concerned, they had "given" it to Carthage. Spain was considered too far away and contained too little to be worth the effort. But the Carthaginians under Hannibal's father, Hamilcar, had discovered vast deposits of silver and much gold in the Spanish hills. Their mines here had grown to staggering proportions producing obscene profits for their masters. Rome now turned greedy eyes toward these riches.

As Strabo's hair was dark and his eyes green, he could have passed for many different peoples. This had served him well in and out of ports up and down the coast. He remembered the arrows on the beach and decided these men were no friends to Carthage.

"I am not Carthaginian," he said at last.

Nargonne intertwined his fingers and rested his chin on his hands.

To Nargonne's right sat two men. The brothers Souk Mallouse and Souk Tourek. They were identical twins but easily distinguishable: Souk Mallouse was missing an eye. Their father had been the reigning elder before his death. But that was before recent events. The events that landed the people of Asturias here on this foreign mountainside. The house of Souk and the house of Castaine were the two most influential families in Asturias. Nargonne was a Castaine. The twins simply looked at him expectantly.

Nargonne looked sideways to Ribas, who sat on his left. Ribas just shrugged his shoulders.

"Lift his shirt," said Nargonne.

Two men behind Strabo grabbed him by the arms and spun him around. They yanked his tunic up over his shoulders and Nargonne and the others noticed only two things. One was the sheet of bronze mail that clung to the man's shoulders beneath his shirt. The other was the burn. Strabo's back was covered by ridges of angry scar tissue. The men could see the burn was an ancient one.

Many Carthaginian regulars proudly bore the tattoo, ironically, of a dove. There was no place for such a tattoo on this man's back. The sight dislodged a special memory for Ribas, but he held his tongue. The men let Strabo's shirt fall back in place and turned him around to face Nargonne.

"What are you, then?" Nargonne said.

Strabo took a deep breath. What difference did it make? He was from nowhere. His life had been spent up and down the Mediterranean from the Adriatic to the Barbary Coast of North Africa.

"I am a sailor," lied Strabo. "But not from Carthage." That much was true.

What would they think of him if they knew the truth? It was common Thracian fleet practice to hire a third party to look out for the owners' interests on each voyage. This "security chief" would be unknown and unrelated to the captain and crew in any way. Although the security chief was given tacit consent to keep order on the ship, his primary, if unspoken duty, was to ensure that the captain didn't abscond with the cargo.

Needless to say, many a security chief had fallen overboard, succumbed to a poisoned meal, died in his sleep, or suffered some other fatal mishap during the course of the voyage, all chalked up to dangerous seas by the captain and his loyal crew. The security chief slept little during a trip.

Strabo had previously acquitted himself well in such a role and had been hired by the Thracians. They could take a chance on one so young for a routine shipment such as this. Ozgul and Nabulam had worked under him.

Nargonne spoke, turning his head and addressing the entire room as well as Strabo. "We have no quarrel with Carthage."

Nargonne turned his attention back to Strabo. "What is your name?"

His name. There was a mystery. He only knew that he was called Strabo from a young age and that his family may have hailed from the Macedonian Coast.

"Strabo," he answered.

"Strabo," Nargonne repeated, and he looked at this man, this man with his long, dark hair, his wide eyes. Alert and capable eyes.

"Whose trading fleet was ambushed by the Carthaginians?"

Strabo considered his circumstances. They hadn't killed him yet. They seemed only concerned about the Carthaginians, and who wouldn't be?

"They were Thracian, mostly," Strabo said. "There were some Africans, some Thebans, and some Turks too."

"What was the cargo?"

"Lumber. Some tin, some ivory," said Strabo.

"And your ship?"

"Lumber."

"They sailed together for safety?" asked Nargonne.

Strabo nodded. A lot of good it did them in the end, he thought.

"Any soldiers?" asked Nargonne.

Strabo hesitated and hoped they didn't notice. Technically, he was not a soldier. He was not a regular of any nation's army.

Strabo shook his head.

Nargonne continued. "Were you hired or pressed into service?"

"Hired," answered Strabo.

"In what capacity?"

Strabo hesitated again before his answer.

"Oar."

Ribas sneered openly at the lie and Strabo winced at his mistake. He should have told them he was a tender or a linesman or even a deck foreman. Not the unimaginative lie of the oar.

Ribas scowled at him and adjusted his tunic in contempt. Nargonne and the others watched Ribas look Strabo up and down. Ribas could see Strabo had no manacle marks on his neck that would indicate involuntary servitude and no shaved head common to those low in a fleet's pecking order. But what Ribas recognized most was that Strabo was here, wounded, yet alive. His wounds meant he had either fought back, or survived a direct attack. Either was an accomplishment for a mere oarsman under trader employ and facing an attack by an experienced military fleet.

Ribas nodded at Nargonne as if to say "May I?" and Nargonne nodded his assent. The warrior Ribas rose with a wicked grin and approached Strabo. Strabo did not respond. Instead, he concentrated on staring straight into space, not wanting this confrontation, not with his hands bound, not at this disadvantage. He could kill this man, maybe, only to be set upon by the rest. Surely they would kill him quickly. But the survival instinct was strong in Strabo. He always thought he still had a chance and that was why he was alive when many others weren't.

Ribas brought his scarred brow up to Strabo's. It was outrageous and insulting how close he was. Strabo could taste the very moisture in the warrior's breath.

"Tell me, *sailor,* from what tree would one construct a stern lowen lock?" asked Ribas.

Any sailor would know that only natural oils of teak would properly lubricate the oars and protect the tricky steering mechanism.

Strabo did not even know what a lowen lock was.

Ribas's grin widened as he struggled to suppress a laugh.

Strabo's eyes tightened.

"Answer him," said Nargonne.

Strabo ushered as much dignity as he could. "My specialties lie on the foredeck," he said.

Ribas bristled and with a flick of his forearm produced a straight dagger, which was instantly pressed against Strabo's throat. Strabo noticed the blade was warm from where Ribas had stashed it close. The two Souk twins straightened in alarm.

Ribas hissed, "Your specialty is stuck pig!"

"Ribas!"

It was Nargonne, his eyes fixed firmly on his lieutenant.

"He is of no use to us," said Ribas. "He lies like a viper."

The animosity dripped from his words and his blade stayed pressed into Strabo's trachea, just short of breaking the skin and plunging in.

Nargonne rose casually and stepped to the two men—attacker and prisoner.

Ribas kept his eye on Strabo.

Strabo waited for the thrust. He noted absently that his side no longer hurt. He noted that just over Ribas's shoulder, the tent lay low over everyone's heads. He noticed the small fire in the corner and how it ventilated smokelessly out the corner. He noted the tiny branches dispersed on the ground.

Strabo noted one more thing; Ribas wore no greaves, those armored shin guards favored by soldiers across the Mediterranean. Strabo decided that if he were to die, he would at least take the shin of his executioner with him with a practiced kick. He readied himself for the strike when Nargonne spoke quietly to him.

"You say you are not currently a member of the Carthaginian military. This I believe to be true. But my question is: Have you ever served with them in the past?"

Ribas held the blade steady and looked questioningly at Nargonne. Nargonne ignored him.

Strabo hesitated again, then turned to Nargonne. Strabo had made up his mind to die fighting.

"Yes," Strabo answered.

"I see," said Nargonne.

Nargonne looked away and the hint of a sly smile slipped across his face. Strabo swayed and adjusted his shoulders against his bonds. So far, he seemed to have succeeded in only one thing; he had convinced them he could not be trusted.

Strabo clenched his teeth in anticipation of the violence to come.

Nargonne turned to Ribas and shook his head. "Not now, Ribas," Nargonne said.

Ribas pulled his knife away from Strabo but not his eyes. Strabo stared back at him warily, careful not to challenge. Not yet. But that challenge would come, Strabo promised himself.

Suddenly there was a commotion outside the tent and two men rushed in, breathless and frightened.

"Soldiers!" one of them said.

Every man in the tent either leaped up or spun on their heels. Only one man instinctively drew his sword as well. Ribas.

They all looked to Nargonne, who remained composed.

"How many?"

The two men looked at each other in confusion. It was clear to Strabo that they had not bothered to count their adversaries and he thought this an outrageous slipup. Nargonne simply moved on to the next bit of information.

"Where?" he asked.

"Coming up the gully. From the lake."

Nargonne rubbed his beard thoughtfully before he spoke.

"Take to the rear escape routes. Quickly. Quietly. Walk the horses until we're clear of the camp." He turned to Strabo's guards. "Don't lose him." With that, Nargonne hurriedly slipped from the tent.

Strabo started to object, but Ribas kicked him forward and the others grabbed him roughly and hustled him out. At the tent opening, Ribas paused and took Strabo by the neck.

"Make a sound and I'll slit your throat," he hissed. As quickly as a man could put a bit to a horse, Ribas spun a damp bend of cloth around Strabo's head, yanked it tight through his mouth, and tied it fast. Then he rushed out into the darkness. The guards seemed frightened of Ribas. For good reason, Strabo thought. But they gathered their wits and shoved Strabo along.

Strabo was stunned at what he saw. The wooded hillside was suddenly alive with activity. Everywhere, men were running, gathering up the campsite and quickly leading horses away. In their rush, some were actually tripping over their swords and Strabo noticed that some had abandoned them altogether. Instead of practiced deployment for a defense and counterattack, these men were sprinting hither and yon with anxious looks on their faces. *Prepare your weapons!* thought Strabo. *Draw your swords!*

These men were preparing to ride instead. Fully saddled and bridled in seconds, they appeared from behind trees, bushes, and boulders. They were all hurrying uphill, toward the even heavier woods and rocky crags that populated the mountainside above them.

But Strabo thought something was odd. What was it? Sound. There was very little! These men were quiet, even with their horses and gear.

This clearing was an expansive patchwork of barren rock and dusty grass that, in the gritty moonlight, might have been the surface of the moon itself. Ringed by trees, it sloped away steeply at one end.

There was no sign of Ribas, but Nargonne was near the edge of the gully tending to his own horse and whispering orders. Men responded by quietly trotting their mounts uphill and disappearing into the trees. Everyone was making for higher ground and Strabo heard the men speaking a hushed mix of their language and Greek. He heard, "Who are they?" and "Are they Carthage?"

Strabo's guards dragged him tripping and stumbling down to Nargonne. Strabo knew Nargonne must have given some orders after the failure of the two scouts in the tent because two men ran up to Nargonne and gave him the number of approaching soldiers as twenty or thirty. Strabo was appalled. Twenty or thirty? All of this commotion over thirty men? There must be nearly one hundred men in Nargonne's party. What was the problem? Deploy and dispatch the enemy! This Nargonne was very cautious indeed, thought Strabo. Either that, or these men were cowards of the highest order.

The news apparently mattered little to Nargonne, for he gave no different orders. He only turned to one of the men who had just run up from farther down the mountain.

"Where is Molena?" Nargonne asked.

The man pointed over Nargonne's shoulder to the far edge of the clearing, where a group of four had just broken through the trees and were leading their mounts uphill. "There she is," he said.

"Get her to safety."

"Yes, sir."

The man sprinted off in that direction.

She? thought Strabo. *What "she"? They have women with them? Isn't this a warring party?*

Nargonne turned to Strabo's guards, who stood there obviously unsure what to do with their prisoner.

"Strap the prisoner to a horse and bring him along," said Nargonne; then he raced away uphill.

Strabo and his guards were now the last in the clearing.

One of the guards barked at the other, "Go get a horse, quickly!" The man ran uphill to catch a group leading horses away while the first guard turned to Strabo.

"Can you ride?" he asked.

Can I ride? Strabo was well trained in the workings of

war. He had served in infantry both heavy and light and had seen training, campaigning, and battle in most types of climate and terrain. He knew his way around lawless port towns and was as handy with a knife in a street fight as any man. His teen years had been spent with belligerent Greek, Carthaginian, and Macedonian infantry, and thus he had more military experience than men twice his age. He had been a party to only one major loss, the Battle of Ipsala, where Macedonians routed the Lydian forces he had been pressed into serving. He was very young then and in the middle lines, but escaped when the Macedonian cavalry got hung up in the Maritsa River. Water had saved him then, he remembered.

But Strabo's primary fighting experience was in skirmishing with sword where hand-to-hand combat skills ruled the day. While the occasional major battles become the stuff of song and legend, it is the countless skirmishes where the work is done. And where soldiers are forged.

But of all the experience he had, he had never served with cavalry. Horses were big and fast and strong and, to Strabo, mindless. He could not understand the great animals and avoided them whenever he could. Could he ride? No, but under the circumstances, Strabo thought it a good idea to learn.

He nodded to the guard.

But the man suddenly looked wide eyed over Strabo's shoulder, turned, and, without a word, sprinted up the hill toward the safety of the trees. Strabo heard it too, something crashing up the hillside!

Strabo whirled around just as two armed cavalrymen burst through the trees below only five hundred paces away. Their horses were armored and their weighty breastplates crashed over the brush like breakers over a storm-tossed beach.

He recognized the warriors' bronze armor immediately. They were Saguntum, a fierce people. They favored the Sumar war ax and both warriors swung them handily above their heads. They were chasing a short man, who was far ahead of them, although the man's lead couldn't possibly last. A wolflike dog ran just before the man and the two raced directly toward Strabo, who stood there helpless. Too far to run to the trees, he thought, not with his hands bound behind him.

The dog outdistanced everyone and flew past Strabo to the trees. The short man sprinted closer. He moved like a cheetah, thought Strabo. And he was running uphill! But now Strabo saw this was not a man but a boy. The boy from the tent. His unruly hair managed to hang in his big brown eyes even as he ran full speed. He had that child-like look of determination on his face, and as he ran, he unwound a well-worn triangle of leather attached to two long leather straps and quickly inserted a palm-size throwing stone.

The boy raced past Strabo and then slid to a stop some twenty paces behind him, his cork sandals spraying gravel in the moonlight.

The first horseman was nearly on both Strabo and the boy now, and for the first time, Strabo realized he had been dressed in the same dark garb as the others. The pain in his side forgotten, Strabo could see the man meant to run him down en route to the boy. Such a maneuver would be no problem for a skilled cavalryman. All in a day's work. And a horseman was armed literally from head to hoof. His iron and leather helmet was equipped with head-butting spikes and iron spurs protruded from the bottom of his riding boots. They would be deadly sharp and useful for more than spurring horses.

A warhorse weighed in at ten times that of a man. Add the warrior and another thirty stone of armor and a warhorse at gallop covering fifteen paces per second would shatter a man, pulverizing bones and flesh on impact, and charge on without missing a step. The victim would be kicked aside like an old straw broom.

How Strabo wished that his hands were free! He focused on the figures fast approaching. Two cavalrymen on horseback, the first a few strides ahead of the second. The first cavalryman seemed hewn to his mount. Very skilled. Murky gray in the moonlight, he was not two creatures but one. All was motion now, and sound. The pounding of the hooves. Strabo crouched, preparing to spring to safety at the last second.

Behind him, the boy dipped his right shoulder and whipped his arm once in a circular motion. From his arm extended a leather sling and from the pocket of the sling flung a bullet—a spinning, jagged, black projectile thrown in speed and terror. It whirred past Strabo's head toward the horseman just as the armored chest of the raging animal closed on Strabo.

Strabo sprang to his left as well as a man can spring with his hands tied behind his back. He couldn't avoid all of the horse but his quick legs avoided most of the blow. Still, he was launched sideways, as if yanked by an invisible string. He noticed as he flew through the air that the warrior's helmet jerked unnaturally in that last second.

Strabo tumbled to the ground, knowing the young

slinger had found his target. He rolled and fought to his feet.

There was a fresh dent in the first horseman's helmet and he hung sideways in his saddle as his horse decelerated to a confused canter. The second horseman passed him by without a glance and pressed with thundering hooves toward the boy, who, with no time to reload for another sling, was running again. He would never make it, thought Strabo. In the distance, Strabo could see three or four men emerging from the woods above them, bows in hand and running fast but they were too far away to save the boy in time. The boy had one chance. All Strabo needed was something sharp.

Strabo lunged toward the disabled first horseman. His eyes were on one thing. Those razor-sharp spurs.

The man moaned in the saddle, but upon seeing Strabo suddenly next to him, he reached desperately for his sword. Strabo spun and draped his arms behind him, wrapped his bonds over the man's riding boot, and yanked hard on the spurs. Strabo felt the spurs slice cleanly through and he was free. Out of the corner of his eye, he saw the second horseman reach the boy and swing the glistening ax round toward the boy's head. He was preparing for a clean neck cut, and why not? The boy was a toy, a practice thing for this man. The ax whirled in the moonlight and Strabo heard the *whoosh* of its speed, but the boy dodged his head just beyond the blow and the ax found only air where the young man's neck had been a fraction of a second earlier. The boy had been saved by his short stature and Strabo felt an unexpected surge of pride at this as the attacker cursed and reined into a wide turn, preparing for another run. The man wouldn't make the same mistake twice, that Strabo knew. He would go for the body and the boy would be sliced in half.

For the moment, Strabo had problems of his own. His horseman had suddenly retrieved a short sword. This was a good idea from the perspective that a short sword is ideal for close-quarters killing. Unfortunately for the horseman, the short sword was Strabo's specialty. Strabo wheeled around and grabbed the bottom of the man's sword hilt with both hands and thrust it upward, sending the blade clashing through the man's chin plate. The man cried out as he fell from his horse and Strabo jerked the sword away. The man landed heavily on the ground, the hard rock of the mountainside knocked the wind from his lungs at once, and he lay there rolled up in a ball, gasping and clutching his head. He was out of the fight and Strabo ignored him, instantly turning his attention to the other horseman.

The second horseman had completed his turn and was closing on the boy, who was running madly for the edge of the clearing just paces away. Strabo dashed across the clearing. The boy was too far from cover and the horseman closed in for the kill, raising his ax for the finishing blow—and the finishing blow came. But it was not the horseman's.

Strabo leaped forward. He let fly the short sword in a practiced two-fisted overhand throw that took the horseman in the side and knocked him from his saddle. He fell with a thud, quivered for a moment, and then was still. The short sword was buried deep just below his armpit.

Both riderless horses neighed loudly and trotted in wide circles. The boy hovered in the heavy brush at the edge of the clearing, panting heavily. Strabo retrieved the sword and cleaned it against the man's cloak. The blade was not perfect, but it was well cared for and well balanced. Then he reached down and relieved the dead man of a short knife; not a very high quality blade either, but it would have to do, Strabo thought. He quickly sliced the heavy leather body straps and yanked the man's chest armor from his body. He freed the man of his round striking shield but left the Sumar axes. They were a weapon best suited for horse and speed.

Strabo put the knife to his ear and sliced his gag free.

More pounding, more horsemen entering the clearing below. They milled about but would soon see the bodies of their comrades in the moonlight. And when they did, they would not be taken by surprise like the first two. Strabo followed the boy to his hiding place in the brush.

The boy was hunched there, scolding his dog. "Some friend you are, Cabo!" the boy said, but the dog just licked him on the face in return. The boy then turned on Strabo. "You didn't have to kill him."

Strabo looked at the boy in astonishment.

"I think I did have to kill him."

With that, he grabbed the boy by the arm and the two escaped with the dog at their heels into the shadows of the mountain above.

———

Years of diligent preparations had come to fruition: Carthage had painstakingly arranged treaties and business agreements until nearly every tribe in Spain was allied with her cause. Then, from the Atlantic Ocean to the

Mediterranean Sea, the Spanish Peninsula's mines were emptied of gold and the provinces emptied of military recruits of all colors. When all was ready, Hannibal's vast army had assembled and begun marching north under the strictest of secrecy.

Chapter 3

*I*t was dawn the next day before the scattered men had begun to reorganize. The Saguntum warriors had chased them but found the rocky terrain rough going for their armored horses. Armored horses were weapons better suited for the open plain. One dead cavalryman and one wounded also dampened their enthusiasm for charging around the mountainside in the dark after a handful of poachers.

For that was indeed what the whole affair was about. Some of Nargonne's men, the boy included, had been poaching the low meadows for days before local soldiers were finally sent out to investigate. Nargonne's men foolishly led the soldiers to the encampment high in the hills, an act of amateurism that appalled Strabo.

He and the boy had joined up with a group of twenty, who were unsure what to do with Strabo now that he was armed. But he had saved the boy. Should they put him under guard again? Two had decided to approach him. They reminded him he was their prisoner and offered him leather bands, meekly suggesting he should be restrained again.

When he scoffed at them, they dropped the whole issue in embarrassment.

Two of the men in the group were the twins he had seen in the tent. The twin with one eye seemed to be in charge. Strabo listened to them discuss the poaching incident and that "Santandar and Cabo" had been involved; the young slinger and his dog.

Several men rode up around noon and told them that Nargonne was in the valley to the north and assembling everyone once again. The group set off immediately and after a few hours their line of horses was stretched out over a half a league. The others ignored Strabo and seemed content to let him bring up the rear. He was alone with his thoughts when he came around a bend in the trail and froze.

The twin with one eye was five paces away with his bow drawn back tightly, a heavy long-iron arrow poised on the bowline pointing coldly at Strabo. Souk Mallouse was one bowman who had no need to close an eye to aim. His good eye stared true while the lost one pressed firmly into his bowline.

Mallouse said nothing. He let the bowline fly and Strabo had not even the time to drop his jaw as the arrow rocketed past his ear. He instinctively dodged, but too late, for the arrow was already past and he heard a thud just a few paces away.

In that instant, Strabo's eyes followed the path of the arrow just as a woodland deer jerked silently in the shadows and toppled head over heels, its momentum carrying it crashing into the brush before the body came to rest. Mallouse's arrow jutted from the animal's chest.

He put his bow back over his shoulder and Strabo narrowed his eyes at him as the man stood there stone-faced. Then Mallouse grinned. His single eye winked at Strabo and Strabo glared at him as he walked past toward his quarry.

Strabo studied the shaft of the man's arrow when they retrieved it from the dead deer. Two long grooves had been routed down the length of the wooden shaft on either side and thin rods of iron embedded there. Strabo was no bowman, but he recognized the "long iron" construction. Long irons were the deadliest of shafts, carefully crafted for accuracy and distance. Good for killing, Strabo knew. Mallouse took the shaft from Strabo, cleaned it carefully, and slid it noiselessly back in his quiver.

They fieldstripped the deer, where it lay, and Mallouse had two of the men return to cut steaks and stuff them into sacks for the journey ahead.

Souk Mallouse was a broad man and fit. He was thirty years old with eyebrows that sat high on his forehead. He nodded to the shield Strabo had left lying nearby, the one Strabo had lifted from the dead Saguntum horseman. He pointed at the runes stamped in a semicircle along the edge of the shield.

"Do you know what that says?" asked Mallouse.

It was an old saying, written in Sumarian and not the Greek that Strabo was most familiar with, but he could read it well enough. It was a favorite Saguntum battle cry.

" 'I am the wind of death,' " Strabo said.

Mallouse nodded, wondering if it was true.

When they had returned to the others, fires were blazing and Strabo could see there was no shortage of food at this campsite. The men had foraged for roots and wild beets and had steamed them over hot coals. They were cooking haunches of venison and everywhere they were bringing in rabbit and game birds on snares they had laid just hours earlier. Strabo watched the young Santandar string a snare at the base of a gnarled gum tree in just seconds. Minutes later, he had a stout rabbit. It was field-stripped, skewered, and dripping over the coals in no time at all.

A big man with a bushy beard was already asleep, a pile of stripped rabbit bone next to him on the ground.

Strabo watched with interest as Mallouse's twin brother, Tourek, dug in and out of a number of bags dangling from his saddle pad like a cluster of grapes. He tossed some orange powder on one of the fires and studied the black smoke the smoldering powder sent skyward. The man fiddled with burned branches on the ground and rolled some polished stones among them. Then he studied some alien markings on the stones and tasted the air. He broke the branches into pieces and spread them randomly around the ground between the fires. Finally the man ate.

Souk Mallouse had one of the men give Strabo a generous portion of venison steak. Mallouse alone knew Nargonne wanted the newcomer alive and well, so he added a foul smelling tea he promised would heal Strabo's wound quickly. Strabo objected at first, but Mallouse revealed that Strabo had already been ingesting the brew the three days they nursed him in the tent, so Strabo relented and drank the bitter concoction. Three days, thought Strabo, and now it's been another day more. He should have been safely to port on the Italian Coast by now. Or dead on the beach if these men hadn't saved him, he reminded himself.

The men now treated Strabo casually. He had not run

away and, more important, hadn't run anyone through with his newfound weapons. Strabo wondered if they had ever wanted a prisoner in the first place.

Mallouse busied himself inspecting the horses, assisted by a man who appeared to be the horse doctor of the group. He was a short man with thick arms and far more hair on his chin than on his head. But his most stunning feature was his face. One side was swollen and discolored and his jaw swelled on that side into a hideous bulge. One of his legs was shorter than the other and ended in a club-foot, so that he limped heavily, though it did not appear to pain him. He moved easily among the big animals. He spent all of his time tending to the mounts while others brought him food and water. He ate as he worked. When he spoke to one of the men or to one of the horses, he spoke in halting sentences and the words struggled their way clumsily from his mouth.

The disfigured man was tireless. He applied grass and mud poultices to many of the horses' fetlocks. He wrapped leather strapping around legs that looked to be faltering. He probed necks and backs and hindquarters. He peered into slimy nostrils. He inspected teeth and gums. Strabo noticed he even examined the droppings of each animal. This he did with assiduous care, sniffing and crumbling the droppings in his hands before wiping his fingers on his tunic and then carelessly taking another bite of venison jerky.

Strabo took stock of the horses. They were as big as the Persian breeds the Macedonians were so fond of. They looked strong and healthy. And not one of them was tied! A single rein on each horse's neck hung to the ground and the horses more or less stayed in place, as if hitched.

The group rested until nightfall, then packed up and gathered behind Souk Mallouse. They waited patiently as Souk Tourek rolled his carved stones and muttered a few inaudible chants before they set off down the mountain into the summer night.

Like on the evening before, the moon shone their way. Strabo heard the nocturnal howling of wolves over the dark distance. Again he watched the trail of horsemen stretch out before him and again he wondered about these men.

They were good with the bow, but they carried no spear. They carried swords but either wouldn't or, worse, *couldn't* use them. They had no shields, no armor, and their horses were unarmored. There were boys among them! They knew no hand signals, couldn't organize a simple defense of their camp, and had no idea how to handle prisoners.

Only one man ever reached for a sword, Strabo remembered. Ribas. He wasn't like the others.

Still, these men could live off the land like no soldiers he had ever seen. They were strangers to these hills, yet they had no trouble finding their way around. They had run from a handful of attackers, yet Mallouse had felled a running deer through the heart in the dark from thirty paces with a single shot of his bow.

These men weren't soldiers. They were hunters. But this was obviously no hunting expedition. *Where, then, are they going?* thought Strabo. *And why?*

———

The Carthaginians controlled the rich port of Saguntum and assembled their navy there. Roman intelligence re-

ported Hannibal's land force was also there: five thousand campfires were observed burning nightly in the hills surrounding the busy port. Experience told them each campfire served a dozen soldiers or more. But what the Romans did not know was that there was no army here, but rather a skeleton crew of crafty Carthaginians who ran from fire to fire each night, tending them and keeping the phony bonfires blazing.

Hannibal's army was elsewhere.

Chapter 4

They reached the bottom of the mountain just after dawn and made their way to a wide meadow bounded by a swiftly churning river. Although morning had arrived, the river still crouched in the shadow of the steep hills at their backs.

The hundred men of Nargonne were all here now. They milled about in small groups around morning campfires. There were many "Good ridings," much hushed conversation about their flight across the mountain, and much staring at Strabo.

A canvas covering stretched over a group of saplings and Strabo recognized Nargonne and Ribas standing beneath it. There was Mallouse's strange twin brother already talking and pointing at Strabo as he entered the camp. Souk Mallouse glanced at Strabo, rubbed the night's fatigue from his one eye, then dismounted and went to talk with Nargonne.

The disfigured horse doctor limped over to Strabo and offered a helping hand, but Strabo ignored it and dismounted awkwardly. The man smiled crookedly and limped away with Strabo's horse, talking quietly to the animal and leading it to the river, where many other horses were wading and drinking.

The big man with the bushy beard was already asleep again. He dozed heavily on the grass as men and horses tiptoed past.

Strabo retreated to a patch of soft grass near the river and sat by himself, sipping lukewarm water from a goatskin and resting his muscles.

He looked up to see the horse doctor above him with his hand outstretched. Strabo found it uncomfortable to look at the man's freakish face so near. The man plucked Strabo's goatskin from his hand and emptied it as he limped into the river shallows. The man checked to see that neither horse nor man bathed or did otherwise upstream, then refilled Strabo's water bag. He returned, handed the bag to Strabo, dropped a pair of new sandals at his feet, and walked wordlessly off. Strabo watched him go and then took a sip from the bag. The water was fresh and brisk and he felt its crispness expand down his chest. He looked down at the sandals. The strapping was made of horsehair.

He probed his side through his tunic and mail—it was feeling better.

He took out the knife he had removed from the Saguntum warrior and regarded it carefully, rotating it in the morning light. He could tell by its weight it was mostly iron. It would be a brittle, unreliable blade. From the color of the metal, Strabo knew it needed more tin and lead in the mix, maybe some nickel. The baking of the material was critical too, and Strabo recalled with affection his "magic" blade, the blade he had made for himself at the armory long ago. The one he perfected with Kabal, the foundryman who owned him for a time. That blade had the right mix, nearly four percent tin and lead, Strabo recalled, and he had baked it red-hot, not twice but three times over three nights. Strabo had fused a strip of pure bronze to the spine of the blade so that the small sword was, at least to the young boy who created it, a thing of beauty.

Kabal's operation had been a small armory, but a good one, and Strabo had never seen one better. It employed some twenty forgemen and another twenty slaves. Strabo was the youngest of the crew, for Kabal wasn't in the habit of working children. "Too weak," the man had claimed. But Strabo was only about six when he had been given to Kabal, the circumstances of which Kabal never fully explained and circumstances that became less important to Strabo over time. He could only guess at his years based on what he was told by Kabal.

And he could only guess at where he was from. Somewhere along the Adriatic Coast was all he knew. He remembered little of the day his young life changed. He thought he must have been playing in the fields above the river delta with the older boys and was trailing them as they returned to their village. They saw the smoke from far away and the boys began to run. So did he, but he could not keep up and so reached the village far behind them.

No one was there but soldiers on horseback. Where was his house? He could not tell. Where was his mother? His father? He wasn't frightened, just confused and surprised. And then he was lifted from his feet by a dark soldier with angry eyebrows and foul breath. Breath like a rotting corpse.

He remembered being given scraps of stale bread and some nuts on the back of a cart and sleeping outside for the first time in his life with a group of strangers. Mostly they were men and injured soldiers with only a few boys like himself. No women, no girls. They followed oxen and horses for weeks and he never got to play. Not once.

And then he was on a boat, but he was sick, so sick. He slept and cried and they only gave him water and he thought he was dead and in another world. And then he was in Sigeum at the Hellespont. He had landed in the port city, where he would live for the next seven years. Sigeum, the busy Aegean port city whose business was trading in arms and weaponry, had been supplying the means of war to all comers for generations.

It soon seemed natural that he had been delivered to Kabal and put to work in the belching weapons foundries that lined the shady streets along the harbor. Here men labored into the night (summer days were far too hot to work in front of a furnace), and the red glow of furnaces and crucibles emanated from every building behind the wharf. In the winter, men congregated in these narrow streets, for it was warmer here than anywhere else in the city.

Here they made the blades for those Sumar war axes. They poured the points of spears and arrows. They poured and struck countless blades of every type: short swords, fighting swords, the curved blades for the men in the east, daggers, and knives of every type.

They poured armor pieces of a dizzying variety and every kind of shield imaginable: Square Turbetine siege shields. Oval Turkish infantry shields. Macedonian attack shields. African cavalry shields.

They also poured wagon parts, chain mail, and armor pieces. Fasteners, pins, buckles, bolts, and nails. They poured hilts for weapons and odd parts for siege engines. And, of course, every kind of armor a battle horse would require.

They poured chain. Millions of links of these. Light chain and heavy. Large and small. All metals, all lengths. Even in slow times, the armory could always turn to chain for a profit. And Strabo knew in his cruelest thoughts that this was something that would never change. And he, enslaved himself, had heated and poured and pounded chain. Bent it, linked it, cooled it, and rolled it up on heavy wooden spools that would carry misery up and down the Mediterranean for years to come.

Enslavement was a normal thing. A necessary thing. What else should be done with the vanquished? Was not slavery a sensible alternative to execution? Of course it was. But still it stung Strabo.

Then each spring during Parade Days, all the city would turn out to display their handiwork. Visitors came from all over the Ionian and Aegean Seas, and from as far as the western coast of Africa and the Indian mountains in the east. The narrow streets would be alive with color and people in different clothes. There were competitions and demonstrations. There were feasts and plays and gambling tournaments. There was an unending line of unusual-looking people in and out of Kabal's foundry works day and night for nearly a fortnight. Many placed orders that would keep the crews working through late winter.

It was during Parade Days one year that Strabo vanquished his first foe and learned that no victory comes without cost.

Most of the foundrymen had military experience and they would train others in the rudiments of fighting. The boys especially enjoyed this, though it was rough sport. They played with the real thing, mostly, except they padded sharp edges and wound balls of fabric around any surface designed to cause fatal damage.

The other boy was Strabo's age, twelve at the time, but far more savvy and possessed of an exceptionally vicious streak. He would have made a great wolf, Strabo thought. Bargaa was his name, and though he was indentured in the foundries like Strabo and hundreds of other boys, Bargaa was a master manipulator and managed to get other boys to do most of his work as well as his bidding.

And he made up his mind that he didn't like Strabo, and Strabo, because of one particular habit, made himself an easy target. Bargaa had learned of Strabo's knowledge of what they called "alphabetix."

The mistress of Kabal's house, Bala, a quiet and frightened woman, took a liking to Strabo and shared with him a secret: She possessed a rare treasure, more precious than any metal that passed through the town. It was a battered Greek manuscript featuring an extended full-chorus play by Aeschylus and a treatise on numbers described as "geometry."

Bala would warn Strabo to keep this business just between the two of them, and though Kabal knew of it, he didn't approve. It wasn't wise to advertise the alphabetix to just anyone, as many considered such practices a form of black magic.

She would unveil the manuscript with exaggerated fanfare and sit with Strabo, taking the young boy carefully through the pages. Strabo was as fascinated as she and they took the joy of the pages together.

Strabo would sneak off to the foundry, where he could read by the glow of an ebbing furnace. It was sweating hot and uncomfortable, but worth it for the restless boy with no others to keep him company. No one but Aeschylus.

Strabo would never fully master geometry, but he would learn well the alphabetix, the letters and thoughts of men.

His young mind was astonished that one man could scrawl his words onto a parchment and another man could read aloud those words and know the other's thoughts from miles away and maybe even days or weeks away, or even, as this text taught him, centuries.

This seemed unworldly to Strabo, yet it was true. And it was simple. He grew to love the text and thought that it would prove important some day, although he didn't know how.

One night he gathered up some ocher oven chalk and scrawled a few words near the entrance of the foundry for all to see.

The markings caused quite a stir and Kabal was quick to sponge away the markings before many townspeople had seen them. He did not know that he was erasing the word "horses" from the hitching rails and the word "water" from the cooling barrels.

Kabal had acted fast, but not fast enough. Some of the boys had seen the runes, including Bargaa. He made wild and noisy accusations that Strabo was a young sorcerer, and Strabo soon found himself across from Bargaa in the weapons practice area.

At first, Bargaa battered the uncertain Strabo back and forth across the dirt, drawing blood from Strabo's forehead, his hand, and his mouth. But it wasn't until Bargaa struck him hard in the nose that Strabo learned to fight. A heavy jolt of pain stunned him and blood spurted from his face. The pain taught him a little. The fear taught him a lot.

For he was suddenly afraid of losing. Afraid even of dying. The fear lifted him and surged through his veins and then the fight was decided as Strabo was both patient and fast and Bargaa was neither. The other boy was much stronger, but brute strength, Strabo learned, had its limits; it was easily defeated by speed and brain. Strabo bore down and parried with the other boy until the time was right and then Strabo suddenly overwhelmed his opponent, bouncing his wooden sword over Bargaa's head in a flurry of blows so furious even the men had difficulty getting him off the boy.

Strabo learned controlled violence from Bargaa that day. It was discipline, discipline, discipline, and then a finishing savagery of bone-breaking intensity.

Ignoring the other boys' praise, he had left Bargaa in the dirt with others tending to him. He wanted to be alone. For Strabo, the praise was empty and without joy. It only mattered that he walk away and not Bargaa. Strabo had survived.

It would be less than a week before he received his final lesson from Bargaa.

Bargaa and a mob of other boys ambushed Strabo one morning as he pulled an old cart of dyes and mold pieces behind the low, sooty buildings of the foundry. The boys had a bucket of red-hot scraps of sizzling, near-molten iron. They cried out, "Witch doctor!" and tackled Strabo. Then they held him down while Bargaa poured the red-hot contents of the crucible onto his back.

Strabo unleashed an inhuman shriek of pain when the hot metal pieces bore through his light tunic and melted into the fair skin on his back. The cry frightened the boys, even Bargaa, and they ran off immediately. Strabo's back arched in agony and the smell of burning flesh filled his nostrils. And the smell of hot iron. He would forever know iron.

Strabo fainted in shock and confusion. He emerged to a world of pain and Bala tending him. He didn't enter the foundry again for nearly two months. His shoulders, his back, his right buttock, forever smothered with the painful scars of the liquid metal. And he would always feel the heat thereafter, his back ultrasensitive to fire and heat and flame.

Fire and water and metal, Strabo thought. They are in me. They have wounded me and saved me and nearly killed me. Metal from earth, water above, and fire in the air.

Strabo plucked a twig from the riverbank and flicked it absently into the river. *My back is more freakish than any horse doctor,* he thought. He turned his head to watch the current carry the twig away. *This water must someday reach the sea,* he thought. *Just like me.*

He saw the girl. She and Santandar looked on as the horse doctor tended to the feet of a tall horse mottled the colors of the brown leaves of autumn. The horse lay on the ground and nodded his head lazily, tolerating both the procedure and Cabo the dog, who sniffed around his mane. When the horse doctor stood, the girl poked him playfully and then hugged and kissed the hideous man. He only shrugged, and when she turned, Strabo saw her face clearly for the first time. Her dark hair was cropped short, not long and braided as it should have been. Even from this distance, he could discern almond eyes peering from beneath the long eyelashes of a woman.

She turned those eyes on him and he diverted his own away in a start. The woman unnerved him. What was she doing here?

Down the bank of the river, he could see Nargonne and his captains convened in a conference, occasionally glancing his way. Nargonne, Ribas, Souk Mallouse, and Souk Tourek stood purposefully out of earshot of everyone else. Nargonne listened carefully to Mallouse, as he always did. And as Mallouse talked, his brother, Tourek, nodded supportively, as he always did. Mallouse described for Nargonne the attack of the cavalrymen on Santandar and the boy's rescue by Strabo. He told of Strabo's competence in weaponry and his lack of riding skills. He told of the nights in the hills, the questions Strabo asked, he even told of the incident with the deer he had shot over Strabo's shoulder and they all chuckled, even Ribas.

The river ran swift and clear and rolled small pebbles along the water's edge.

"He could have run at any time," Mallouse said.

"He could have given us away," said Ribas.

"He's no friend of the Carthaginians."

"He's no friend of ours either."

"He saved the boy."

Ribas was unimpressed. "Maybe he did. But he could have turned on any one of you," he said.

"But he didn't."

"He could have, you fool!"

Ribas pleaded with Nargonne. "The man should be stripped of weapons."

"He hasn't killed anyone yet," said Mallouse.

"Maybe you'll be the first." Ribas scowled.

Nargonne listened patiently, fingering his necklace, which bore the image of a horse head in blue enamel. He stared blankly into the moving water.

"Bring him to me at sunset," said Nargonne.

Nargonne sent them all away and rubbed his thick belly absently. *I'd rather be home,* he thought, *where the food is always hot and within easy reach, thanks to the skills and kindness of my daughters.* He was a little overweight, the way he liked it. "I'm wasting away out here," he said aloud to no one. His daughters were no longer children but grown to young women. How he missed them now. They were round and curvy and bright, and they still hugged him incessantly. He sighed. *How much we love our girls,* he thought.

I will find her, he knew, *and bring her home.*

But how exactly? Certainly most of his men were in grave danger. They had been lucky so far, but enough was enough. He was liable to get them all killed. The council had quickly approved his request for so many men, but now he realized he had made a mistake. It was obvious the troop was too big. They needed to be more discreet, to travel even more lightly than this.

They needed an edge and this "prisoner" and his military experience might just be the edge Nargonne was looking for.

By afternoon's end, Nargonne had finished a light dinner of fire roasted rabbit and ground meal biscuits washed down by the cool water of the mountain streams that trickled through these low hills. He was full, but not as full as he wanted to be. He was never as full as he wanted to be.

He had reviewed the horses with the handlers and had heard from everyone about their various exploits escaping from the soldiers on the mountain. But sooner or later, Nargonne knew, he would require sword against sword.

His men were hunters and herdsmen, villagers, tradesmen, horsemen, and farmers. Good men all, and all exceptional riders. But this was a job for professional soldiers. For Ribas. Ribas had agreed to this mission for a price. Maybe this newcomer Strabo could be convinced as well. Surely he was a professional. Any doubts about that had been erased on the mountainside in the dark two nights ago. What would it take or, more to the point, how much would it take?

Nargonne gathered his captains around him and had Strabo brought to sit nearby. He looked them over. Only Ribas and the Souks knew the sword well, as did Nargonne. Only they had experience at war. And one more. The big, bearded Barbestro. He would stay.

"Gather the men," he told them.

Soon all one hundred men gathered on the grassy beach that curved its way along the river. Nargonne kept one person from attendance. His niece, Molena, was the only woman he had brought on this expedition. Did he not fear for her life? Of course he did. He did not choose it to be this way. Under the circumstances, she was as dangerous as she was beautiful.

A fine horseman in her own right, she had her father in her and the memory of his brother pleased Nargonne. But she was a distraction to the men and Ribas had complained bitterly until Nargonne forced her to cut her hair close and wear the clothing of men from the top of her head to the whites of her feet. She had complied. Too enthusiastically for Nargonne's taste. The blood of his family ran true in her.

Nargonne sat comfortably on a boulder facing the stream, the mountains forming a high backdrop behind him. Ribas stood nearby.

Nargonne asked for quiet and began by telling them that all but a few of them were going home. There were murmurs of protest, but Nargonne raised his hand and silenced them.

As Nargonne spoke, Ribas casually nodded his approval. He knew they had no chance. Not with this crew of farmers and herders. By the gods, he thought, he was better off alone. These amateurs were likely to get him killed.

The men were somber at the news. Nargonne thanked them for their efforts and praised them for their courage and sacrifice. But, he explained, the situation had changed. Now, instead of sheer numbers, they were more in need of stealth. He did not elaborate and ordered the men home immediately, to ride within the hour. This urgency, Ribas realized, was to allow little time for dissent. He knew how clever Nargonne could be.

He urged the men to return as safely as they had journeyed here, that is, by night travel. He warned them to stay alert for they might be called upon to return to these parts.

"You must restore a normal life for our women and our children until this unfortunate episode is past. You must return to our lands to prepare us all for the future."

Strabo wondered what unfortunate episode Nargonne could be referring to. Plague? Siege?

Nargonne dismissed them with a few final words. "You have been an able force, a formidable force, and I have been proud to lead you. Should anyone have opposed us, they would have found they had made a poor judgment indeed."

The audience cheered at this implied understatement and men smiled in satisfaction. Strabo had seen firsthand these men in action and he recognized this last bit from Nargonne as a morale-boosting hyperbole. No wonder he was in charge.

Strabo was surprised and embarrassed to be standing so close among them, but Nargonne ignored him. Strabo watched him hug the disfigured horse doctor and kiss him good-bye. Then Santandar appeared and Nargonne hugged him so hard he lifted the boy from his feet. He tousled the boy's hair and kissed him too. So here was the boy's father, thought Strabo. He heard Nargonne tell the two to stay together. He pointed to each in turn and said, "You watch out for your uncle and you watch out for your nephew." The two nodded and looked grim.

Nargonne scolded them. "Am I a child? I know what I am doing, now go!" Uncle and nephew turned to their horses with shoulders slumped. Santandar chanced a long look back at his father, but Nargonne shooed him off with a wave. The two finally mounted and left, Cabo trotting dutifully behind.

Strabo again marveled at how lightly these men traveled. Within a quarter of an hour, they were all on horseback and filing away across the shallows, crossing the river and disappearing into the thick trees beyond. Goodbyes were many but brief. In another few minutes, they had all crossed the river and were gone. The meadow where they had spent the day was empty.

Only a handful remained: Nargonne, Ribas, the twin Souks, the big, bearded man, the girl Molena, and Strabo.

They had stood in a group by the water's edge, watching until the last of their comrades faded into the shadows. Strabo didn't like being down this low, surrounded by hills. By definition, the water's edge is as deep as one can get in a river valley and that meant they were on the lowest ground available. *In hostile country, I want the high ground,* Strabo thought.

Nargonne and the others went about breaking camp and preparing their horses. Nargonne nodded with satisfaction as the sun edged lower in the sky and touched the ridges in the west.

"We leave at full sunset," he said.

Strabo's naturally nervous eyes wandered up toward the ridges that lined the eastern side of the valley. He could see high up on their peaks the late-afternoon sun catching the tops of the pines.

Up there, along the same rocky trails they had come down the night before, the sun caught something more. Hundreds of orange glitters of light flickered like stars in an evening sky.

Strabo's heart lurched. Only one thing reflected sunlight like that: spear tips of polished bronze! Whoever they were, they weren't bothering to shroud their weapons from reflection, which meant they were moving fast.

The girl hadn't yet heard the stranger speak, now she was surprised to hear him, and in perfect Greek, no less. Strabo pointed to the reflections descending their way.

"Sunset will be too late," he said.

———

Carthaginian Command was wary of any threat that might come from within the Spanish Peninsula itself. They policed it thoroughly, casting a wide net in front of the advancing army. Uncooperative tribes were crushed, bandits were run off or executed, and suitable recruits were pressed into service. News of Hannibal's gathering horde was kept in close check.

Chapter 5

They raced along the streambed, careful to keep their hooves in the water. When they came to wide shallows, they crossed and recrossed the river a dozen times to "wash" their trail, as Ribas put it. Their only handicap was Strabo. He scowled and struggled with his mount while the others rode with seasoned skill. More than once they had to retrieve him from the riverbed, soaked and cursing. The horse he rode was the mottled one with the lazy look and it seemed to regard Strabo with contempt.

No one was more appalled at Strabo's lack of horse sense than Molena. What kind of a warrior was he? In truth, their pace was fast even for riders of their experience and they kept it up all through the night, dismounting and walking the horses every two hours. Walking, Strabo regained his strength. He groaned every time they mounted again. Ribas grinned at his suffering and nodded happily to the Souk twins. He barked at the man to keep moving and was careful to keep Strabo in front of him.

The sun rose, ushering in an overcast day, the first truly

cool day of autumn, and still they kept riding, following the river on what appeared to Strabo to be a northerly course. Finally at noon they stopped at the mouth of a deep canyon, where Nargonne instructed the big, bearded man, Barbestro, to ride ahead and reconnoiter. Molena dismounted and led the horses to grass and fetched snakeroot with which to tend to the horses' legs. The others attended to tack, adjusting bridles and reins.

Nargonne and Ribas huddled together, scratched lines in the dirt, and glanced occasionally over at Strabo.

Strabo had dismounted clumsily and collapsed to the ground in a heap. The pain in his side was all but forgotten now for the growing pain in his groin. The skin on his inner thighs glowed swollen and red beneath the leather pants they had given him.

He looked at the horse, but the animal simply lay down in a lazy heap and dozed. The thing seemed more dog than horse.

"Worthless beast!" Strabo called to it.

"His name is Castaine. It means blue ocean in the tongue of the South."

Strabo looked up. It was the girl, hands on her hips and looking down on him with unmasked disapproval. Without another word, she turned from him and crouched to rub the shins of the horse. The girl was filthy from the ride. Strabo had never seen a woman with short hair. Such hair didn't seem right on a woman. Besides, it made her look like a man from behind in her cloak. She rode like a man too, he thought.

"I can think of a more appropriate name," snorted Strabo.

She looked sideways at Strabo but spoke to the horse.

"He's a lunkard, Castaine, I'm sorry, but you get the tough jobs because you are a great horse, a steed of legend, a steed of magnificent—"

"You mock me," Strabo interrupted.

The girl only smiled wickedly at him, and for the first time, Strabo noticed greenish bruises around her eye and cheek, bruises that had yellowed with time. But fairly recent, Strabo thought. She saw him take note of the marks and looked away.

"You should be ashamed of yourself," she said. "You will hurt Castaine with your foul ways."

"Foul ways!" Strabo leaped up and then paused, wincing as the pain in his legs caught up to him. He was momentarily without words.

"Maybe you should go back to where you came from," she continued. "You washed up on the beach, didn't you? Like a dead fish."

What nerve has this girl! Then Nargonne and Ribas appeared. The girl suddenly smiled sweetly. "Remember, his name is Castaine," she said to Strabo.

Nargonne eyed her suspiciously, but she merely grinned, dropped Castaine's reins, and left. Strabo glared after her for a moment before turning to the two men before him. Nargonne was direct.

"Who were they?" he asked.

Ribas was silent, cautiously eyeing Strabo's weapons, his own hand on the hilt of his blade. He didn't like being so close to the stranger. *Let him draw his sword,* Ribas thought, *and we shall see what we shall see.*

"Spears and speed," Strabo answered, "can only mean Carthaginians. Probably Numidian javelin and horse."

"Couldn't be," argued Ribas. "Inland? This far north?"

The three of them were silent as Strabo looked Ribas over again. Ribas had been unaffected by the forced ride all night. Indefatigable, thought Strabo. He looked fit and he looked fierce.

"They were Carthage, I'm sure of it," Strabo said again.

They were out of earshot of the others. Nargonne held out a stick of jerky to Strabo, and Strabo had the fleeting thought that he was being fattened up for the kill.

"Take it," Nargonne said.

Strabo took it and chewed some. Nargonne and Ribas did the same. Nargonne motioned for Strabo to sit. Ribas did not bother to disguise his pleasure at the obvious pain Strabo was in as he lowered his aching body to the ground. Ribas and Nargonne sat.

Nargonne offered Strabo water from a goatskin and Strabo drank.

"Are they following us?" Nargonne asked.

"I think so," said Strabo.

"After you?"

"After you, I would think. Maybe your bowmen killed an officer on the beach. The Carthaginians don't care much for rank and file, but officers are sacred."

Strabo noticed that Ribas and Nargonne exchanged a lingering look upon hearing this. What were these two up to?

"Why do you not run from us?" asked Nargonne.

"He is safer with us, he thinks," said Ribas, smiling in a thoroughly unfriendly manner at Strabo, taunting him.

Strabo said nothing. He was poor at hiding himself, poor at disguise and guile. His skills lay elsewhere and he knew it.

Nargonne pointed his jerky at Strabo in mock accusation. "You are no oarsman," he said. "You are no oarsman and you are no sailor."

"A mercenary," hissed Ribas. Strabo did not deny it. Why bother? He did what he pleased and the rest could be damned.

"I do what it takes to survive," said Strabo.

"So we have seen," said Nargonne.

There was another long pause in the conversation, which Strabo tried to ignore. *Damn these two,* he thought, *they have more patience than I!* But it was Nargonne who finally broke the silence with a question for Strabo.

"What should we do about the Carthaginians?"

"You can't fight them," Strabo answered.

"No. We can't."

"But you can run. They'll let you go. If it serves little tactical purpose they will call off the hunt sooner or later."

"Yes. We could run," said Nargonne.

Again the silence. Nargonne chewed and spat jerky juice onto the ground. His head was bowed low and he absently drew a line in the dirt.

"But we won't," he said. Nargonne brought his face up to smile broadly at Strabo. "Maybe we will join them." Ribas smiled just as broadly. Strabo was extremely unhappy that he wasn't in on the joke.

Nargonne grew serious. "We'll pay you."

Strabo said nothing.

"Handsomely," Nargonne added.

"For what?"

"To join the Carthaginian army with us." Strabo could not conceal the look of dismay on his face. Nargonne continued. "It's only temporary, of course."

"For how long?"

"That depends on how successful we are."

"How successful at what?" asked Strabo.

Just then, the big Barbestro rode up to them and reined his horse expertly to a stop. "It's all clear ahead."

Nargonne nodded. "Good, Barbestro. We'll take to our mounts."

Barbestro turned and shouted to everyone to take to their horses and move out.

Nargonne stood up, tired of the conversation with this arrogant mercenary. He turned to his horse. Strabo followed him and asked, "How much?"

"How much do you want?"

"A talent." It was an outrageous amount.

"Of silver?"

"Of gold."

Ribas gasped. A talent was as much as a man could carry, nearly forty stones' worth. But Nargonne surprised him and laughed as he got on his horse. "If we are successful, I'll give you two," he said.

Ribas smirked but said nothing and lifted himself to the saddle. Nargonne stared down at Strabo.

"Two talents it is then. Are you with us?"

"I need some time to consider it."

Nargonne nodded. Only Ribas detected the sly grin he wore.

"That sounds reasonable," said Nargonne. He and Ribas turned their horses to join the others, leaving Strabo standing by himself. He watched the men go and then turned his eyes to Castaine. The horse was on the ground, sound asleep again. Strabo wondered if the horse and the big man Barbestro could possibly be related.

The twin Souks conferred briefly with Nargonne, a direction was decided on, and the group gathered and began moving out of the canyon mouth, single file. Strabo painfully climbed onto his horse and followed.

This time, Nargonne motioned for Ribas to abandon the rear and move ahead, leaving Strabo last in line for the first time. The line of horses began to stretch out as they wound northward into steep canyon country.

No more than an hour passed when Nargonne came galloping back to the rear, pulled his horse rudely in front of Strabo, and blocked his way. The others looked furtively over their shoulders.

"Keep moving!" Nargonne shouted at them. They did.

Nargonne held Strabo and his horse at bay. Strabo didn't know what to make of this man. He did not know what to make of any of these people.

Nargonne stared at him. Finally he spoke.

"Time is up."

"What?"

"This is a rescue mission, Strabo, and you will know only what you need to know, and no more. Understand?"

Nargonne's horse shied, but Nargonne held him in check.

"Are you in or are you out?" said Nargonne.

"I need to know more details."

Nargonne angrily pointed to the east and Strabo got a taste of the man's temper for the first time.

"The sea is that way! Back where you came from. You are free to go there. You, unlike me, and unlike the rest of us here, are free to do anything that you want. Do you understand, Strabo from the sea?" Nargonne spat the words with contempt. "Anything you want!"

Again Strabo said nothing and Nargonne's voice rose even higher.

"Do you think I would take my people halfway across the accursed world for nothing? Put them in harm's way? Put them where they should not be and pit them against those more capable than they in the ways of war? In the ways of death?"

As a rule, Strabo was unaffected by tongue-lashings. But these people were different from the ones he knew so well. Different from officers and soldiers and merchants and fleet managers. Different from slaves and foundry-men. He knew there must be good reason indeed for Nargonne and his people to be here. The promised money might never come, but they had saved him on the beach. He gazed off toward the east and sniffed. He smelled water on the air.

"Now choose!" Nargonne said.

Strabo said nothing. Then, as competently as he could manage, he nudged Castaine around Nargonne's horse and followed the others, trotting to catch the back of the line. Castaine behaved himself and Strabo didn't look back.

Thinking of warriors and gold and death, Nargonne glared after him before settling into his saddle pad and smiling to himself. *Wise choice,* he thought. *So I will have my revenge. And more.*

———

The northern provinces of Italy had already been chafing beneath Roman rule when word spread that Carthage was openly threatening Rome. Emboldened, the provinces rebelled and now Rome faced a double challenge: potential invasion from afar, insurrection from within. There was much debate within the Roman military elite as to how best to meet the dual threat. The danger from the notorious Hannibal seemed more dire. It was decided that one of their more capable generals, Scipio, would charge up the western Italian coastline, the only possible avenue of land attack, and position his legions in the Carthaginians' path.

Chapter 6

*F*or the next three days, they rode their way north beneath threatening skies. Strabo noticed the woman mostly kept to herself, riding in silence.

At one point, Strabo mentioned to the Souks he thought he could smell the sea on the wind and Souk Tourek scratched a map in the sand. They were heading north and east, toward a wide gulf along the Mediterranean that sat in the lee of the Spanish Peninsula. So they would reach the sea, thought Strabo.

"Why there?" he asked.

"You shall see," said Tourek, and Molena smiled mischievously.

Nargonne and Ribas decided they were no longer being followed. Strabo suggested the troops following them probably cut off and followed the rest of his people as they made their way home. Nargonne laughed happily at this. "Excellent. They will never catch them. Not one." And Strabo figured he was correct. On horseback, these people were without peer. They could make a six-hundred-stone horse dodge through the trees as nimbly as a rabbit.

They moved primarily in the day now and Strabo saw a lot of the girl, though they talked but little. She was much more woman than girl. Though they all wore similar tunics, it was hard to mistake the contrasting contours of gender. Strabo thought of her and was afraid to think of her.

Ribas and Nargonne left Strabo alone, but Mallouse spent much time riding with him. Strabo even picked up a few tips on riding, though he still looked forward to the horse breaks when they would walk their mounts for a half a league at a time. The two Souks rode jet black horses they called Tundra and Corcell. "They are cousins," Mallouse told Strabo.

To pass the time, Strabo taught the Souks some basic Carthaginian hand signals. The sign of the bird: Proceed. Sign of the wolf: Stop. Sign of the snail: Go cautiously. A closed fist: Quiet. Nargonne and Ribas watched and Strabo noticed they mastered the signals instantly.

They ate handsomely along the river trails and Strabo was glad they were so adept with the bow. The Asturians felled many game birds and even relieved some nests of their eggs. And from the one-eyed Mallouse, Strabo learned more of Nargonne's people and of their objective.

"A rescue mission," Nargonne had said.

They were a peaceful and productive people, Mallouse told him. Their villages hugged the northwestern coast and the weather was brisk in winter but the coastal lands fruitful. They hunted, farmed, herded, and traded. And raised horses. The finest horses in all of Spain. They had a burgeoning fishing industry whose nets grew fatter every year and poured affluence into Asturias by the boat-load.

"You would like it there, Strabo. Our villages are clean and happy. We are very civilized."

They were newly organized under the protectorate of the regional Carthaginian governor in Leonas, although they had little contact with that outside governmental authority. Leonas was far from their land.

They had not one, but two schools, Mallouse boasted.

"Like in Greece?" Strabo asked.

"Yes, so that all who want may learn the letters. I have learned many of them myself." Mallouse smiled proudly.

Strabo had thought such organizations were exclusive to Greece and territories of the Ptolemaic Empire. Or only in the great cities. Like Rome. Or Carthage.

Mallouse's face darkened.

"But now the Carthaginians have taken control of the provinces, and things are"—he paused—". . . different."

A Carthaginian colonel, Machoba was his name, had visited their land. They feted him and entertained him generously. But he took a liking to one of their women, and his soldiers kidnapped her the next day.

A kidnapping, thought Strabo. Not an uncommon occurrence. The military did what it pleased.

"The fiend took *two* women. Her sister too," Mallouse elaborated. "They are twins. We have many twins amongst our people, Strabo." His single eye lowered at Strabo. "This Machoba is an evil man, not worthy of Carthage."

All tribes in this part of the world had great respect for Carthage and the prosperity they had brought to the entire peninsula. But their influence could be harsh and cruel, as Nargonne's people learned.

Strabo was told Machoba's men had killed the girls' parents in the episode. Not twenty four hours later, while the elders debated what to do, one of the girls escaped and returned to the village wholly on her own. A tough girl, Strabo thought.

She had been beaten and raped by Machoba and his chief lieutenant, Akdar, a thug every bit as foul as Machoba himself. Akdar had mutilated the girl, Mallouse said. This last bit of information struck home and disturbed Strabo. Mutilated. What did that mean? But Mallouse declined to elaborate on that point.

The governor was outraged, not at the kidnapping, but at the escape of the girl. He ordered her returned to Machoba and sent five hundred soldiers to enforce the command. Though many in the town argued vociferously for her to be sent back to preserve their peace and safety, the furious elders refused to deliver her.

"The girl is of the house of Castaine, Strabo," Mallouse offered. "She is Nargonne's niece and Sargonne's niece as well. Her murdered father was their brother."

In retribution, the governor ordered the Asturians' fishing fleet confiscated and a fine of twenty talents levied upon the village. They had a single year to pay the fine—or else. And it was widely understood that "or else" would mean destruction of their lands at the hands of the Carthaginians. But without their fleet, the payment was impossible.

Twenty talents? thought Strabo. Not even a big city could afford a fine so steep.

He had heard enough. He indignantly asked Mallouse, "Anyone consider fighting back?"

"Strabo," Mallouse said as if to a child, "the governor has over five thousand professionals under arms and we are a people of only a few hundred able-bodied men. Surely you can see we are no match for them."

It was true. He had seen these men in action and he knew they were no fighters. They did possess a respectable determination, Strabo thought. Still, it was clear they would not have stood a chance.

Mallouse added that he left out many details, which Strabo would learn in good time.

But Strabo could guess much for himself.

The girl who escaped could only be Molena. That would explain why she was here with them. Surely Nargonne feared for her safety at home with so many wanting her returned to the colonel Machoba. Now Strabo knew they were going after her sister.

"Nargonne intends to rescue the girl," Strabo said.

Mallouse nodded.

"And pay the fine?"

Mallouse nodded again.

"How?" Strabo had to laugh.

"As you will find, Nargonne keeps very closemouthed about such things, but he has a scheme in his head."

It had better be a good one, Strabo thought.

They spent the better part of two more days scouring the riverbanks for a suitable crossing point, for now the river ran fast and full. Along its banks, they had to shout to each other to be heard.

Souk Tourek rolled his stones and studied the flight paths of the birds high above them.

"What do you see, brother?" Mallouse asked him.

Tourek would only shake his head grimly.

Castaine continued to toy with Strabo, and Strabo lost his composure at last and slapped the horse across its jaw, which only resulted in stinging pain in his hand and another display of temper from Nargonne.

"Be good to the animal or I will arrange a lesser mount for you," he warned.

"Worse than this?" Strabo protested.

Nargonne ignored him and moved on, but Molena did not. Her eyes fixed upon Strabo as if they would slice him in half. For his part, Castaine seemed unaffected. Strabo's blow had no more impact upon the horse than anything else the man did.

Strabo tried to ignore Molena's icy look. But she would have her say.

"If Nargonne allowed, I would release Castaine from your servitude and send him racing to the wind. Away from you forever!"

"The wind?" Strabo laughed. "This horse couldn't run downhill."

Molena harrumphed and turned her back on him, cantering off. Mallouse grinned at Strabo. Strabo glared at him, but the man kept grinning as if he held a secret. Strabo was growing tired of horses and tired of horsemen.

"Yes, Souk?" sighed Strabo.

"He is the fastest horse, faster than Tundra and Corcell together," Souk Mallouse whispered. "Of course, not while you sit on his back."

Strabo didn't believe it. Who wouldn't have noticed the ungainly gait of the horse and the way its shoulders stooped lower than the others? The horse was as lazy as a mutt in summer. Maybe one of these riders could make the creature run but certainly not fast.

"And who might the fastest rider be?" Strabo asked.

Mallouse nodded his head toward the girl trotting away.

"No," said Strabo.

Mallouse only nodded with glee.

Strabo didn't believe that either.

He began to wonder if two talents of gold were worth torment such as this. He comforted himself with the thought that when he had riches in his grasp, he would walk away, not ride.

The river eventually descended into steeper country, where the water howled through high granite walls. From here, they couldn't even get to the water, let alone cross it.

Finally a passable crossing point did appear: a narrow beach that mirrored another beach on the other side, where they could discern an easy climb out. No dangerous eddies were apparent, and while the river ran fast here, there were neither difficult rocks nor boulders for the horses to negotiate.

Downstream, things quickly turned treacherous. The river dived through pillars of sheer rock face on either side to boil away down the canyon. The surging water formed a raging torrent there as the steep canyon walls pinched it and threw the water noisily around a blind corner. Beyond the corner, Strabo could tell by the muffled roar, heavy white water awaited—or worse, falls. Had someone been on the other side with a stout rope, the crossing would have been a simple matter, but such was not the case.

Barbestro explained they would leapfrog their way across the river, using the combined weight of the horses against the current.

Like Strabo, Molena was doubtful, and she suggested

they backtrack upriver, where they might find a kinder passage. But Nargonne vetoed that. "We're running out of time," he said. "We'll cross here and now."

Above them, river ospreys rode the thermals that rose from between the canyon walls. The huge Barbestro went first, edging his horse carefully into the river. The horse appeared appropriately nervous and Strabo wondered if maybe, in this instance, the horses didn't have a little more sense than their riders.

Nonetheless, the horses began their way cautiously forward as the water surged over the thick calves of Barbestro and up to his waist. Ribas followed him. The current ran over the horses backs at the deepest point and threatened to swamp them, but the animals held firm.

Molena went next followed by the Souks. The horses proved more than capable after all. But their legs were so spindly, Strabo thought. He chalked it up to the neverending mystery of these animals, and when his turn came, he entered without fear. *If I fall, I'll swim for the bank,* he thought.

"Easy, Castaine," urged Strabo, employing the horse's name at last out of sheer desperation. He noticed Molena watching him carefully. Strabo thought briefly that her look was one of concern, but he quickly deduced she was most likely expecting him to go under at any moment and didn't want to miss the show. Any concern from her would be for Castaine, not him. But the horse did not panic; in fact, Castaine seemed to take his time crossing. At the deepest point of the crossing, the horse even slowed to sip at the water surging by.

"Move!" Strabo urged, and suddenly Castaine stopped altogether.

So this is it, thought Strabo. *Here he tosses me for good.* Strabo readied himself for the cold water, but the horse just continued lazily forward. By the time Castaine climbed the bank on the other side, Strabo had to stuff his stomach back down his throat.

Nargonne was the last to cross. When he finally waded ashore from the deep, they all breathed a sigh of relief. An unusually big sigh of relief, thought Strabo.

"Barbestro, I thought we might be going home without you." Nargonne chuckled. The entire group laughed nervously and Strabo was struck by a sudden thought that horrified him.

"You can swim, can't you? You live by the sea."

No one said anything. They just exchanged uneasy glances. Nargonne said, "Strabo, there are skilled fishermen and seamen in our lands, but we here, we are horsemen. Why would I take a troop of fishermen into the mountains on horseback?" He laughed at this, as did everyone else, leaving Strabo questioning the wisdom of hooking up with such an incautious crew.

They began spurring their horses up the steep slope when Ribas suddenly halted his horse and pointed back over the water.

There on the opposite bank was another horseman. Even from this distance, he looked trail beaten and exhausted. The group couldn't believe their eyes. It was Santandar! Behind him followed the horse doctor and the boy's dog.

Nargonne was the first to whip his horse forward and gallop back to the shore. The others followed and Strabo could not help noticing that Nargonne's customary reserve had momentarily vanished. Strabo had discovered Nargonne's Achilles' heel—his son, Santandar.

"Barbestro, the rope!" Nargonne shouted, waving his hand wildly. The rush of the river drowned out his voice and Santandar must have thought he meant for him to cross because he gamely spurred his horse forward into the water and Cabo followed.

"No!" they all cried, but the exhausted boy and his horse were soon in the deep, the horse impatiently surging toward his fellows on the other side. Barbestro dispatched Mallouse down the riverbank and Tourek followed. Nargonne charged blindly into the river bent only on the boy.

But the river soon overwhelmed the boy and his mount. The dog Cabo swam futilely upstream of the horse, but the current shoved him into Santandar's legs. The horse, wild-eyed and snorting water from its nostrils, bucked, then slipped; boy and beasts were carried kicking downstream in an instant!

Nargonne bellowed and whipped his protesting horse into the river when he was cut off by Strabo on Castaine. "Down the beach!" Strabo shouted. "With the rope!" Castaine slid to a halt and Nargonne watched Strabo leap from the horse's back into the surging waters and disappear in a torrent of froth.

Nargonne understood at once. He reared his horse and leaped from the river, racing down the beach. Riderless, Castaine surged after them. For Nargonne, there was no seeing or hearing, no grasping of reins, no gulping of air in ungodly exertion and fright. There was only his son, swirling like a twig in a merciless maelstrom of mountain water. To Nargonne, death was suddenly everywhere. In the water. In his throat.

The others spurred downriver. Molena had lost sight of Santandar but could still see the river flipping Strabo end over end like a leaf in the wind.

He's a dead man, she thought. *Brave and stupid are the dead.* Then he disappeared around the blind corner and their horses came to a wall of rock. They were forced to work their way up the ravine to a place where they could make their way downriver.

Barbestro grabbed Mallouse by the shoulder and pointed across the river to the horse doctor still hesitating there in confusion.

"Get him across," he said as he thrust a coil of rope at Mallouse and galloped away.

The current had seized Strabo and shot him forward like a slingshot. The shock of instant submersion in the cold mountain water was nothing compared to its tremendous noise and the power of its grip.

Nargonne and the rest drove their horses to the top of the ravine, and as they crested the ridge, they could make out three black forms tumbling through the rapids in the distance.

"Ride!" thundered Nargonne, and they rode at a dangerous gallop across the rocky ground, paralleling the river below.

Far behind them, Mallouse held a rope for the horse doctor and guided him from the water. The man was stuttering in fear.

"He make me come. He m-make me. H-he is a troublemaker; he make me. . . ."

"Later!" barked Mallouse, and set him upon dry ground. He instructed the man to stay put and then leaped to his saddle to follow the others.

The howling water flung Strabo and spun him, tumbling him through a zigzag sluice that cut through the cliffs, and then he was on the other side, where the water ran wider as it broke into white rapids. Strabo longed for a lungful of air but couldn't figure out which way was up.

Just when the force of the water lessened with the widening of the river, the hungry rocks of the rapids set in. The first rocks struck his shins and he instinctively covered his head with his hands just as his fingers absorbed the painful jolt of a boulder meant for his skull.

He hoped the boy's lighter weight would carry him higher in the water, avoiding most of the rocks. The boy! He was ahead, but not far, Strabo knew.

Strabo pulled himself above the writhing surface at last and heard the sound of his lungs gulping for air over the din of the angry river. The sound of the rapids reverberated off the canyon walls. It was a welcome noise. Crushing as it was, at least it was the sound of the surface.

Strabo righted himself and caught a glimpse of a pair of bony legs flailing about in front of him. The boy was alive and kicking madly. Strabo caught a glimpse of the boy's horse swimming to the bank, scrambling to shallow water and safety. Between him and the boy, Santandar's dog, Cabo, struggled. *What a mess this is,* thought Strabo.

He pulled himself forward, choking for air and managing a glance downriver. Up ahead, the river pinched in again and disappeared with a low roar that was unmistakable—only falls roared like that. And the canyon mouth was closing fast.

Strabo pulled harder, but now two new enemies loomed: fatigue and time. Fatigue would not be a gradual thing in rushing water of this magnitude. It would be a sudden thing. The three of them—man, dog, and boy— would struggle until their muscles finally protested in sweeping arcs of pain and, shortly thereafter, quit altogether. They would sink and the current would drag their drowning bodies over the falls and beyond until some random rock finally claimed their lifeless bodies.

Time. There wasn't much. Strabo pulled harder and drew closer . . . the dog an arm's length away now . . . and the boy just beyond that. Strabo's lungs burned and his chest muscles ached.

But wait, something was following on the riverbank, then receding . . . only to reappear. They were there, on horseback! The going must be difficult because they weren't keeping up. But they were there.

A few more pulls. His arms were weak and slow. Everything was slow. The boy had stopped kicking and his head was barely above the current. Strabo reached for the boy and felt claws raking across his chest! Panicked, feverishly frantic, scratching claws. Cabo pawed at Strabo and scrambled on top of him, sending the man underwater again. Strabo cursed him and bobbed to the surface with the dog on his back.

Nargonne and Ribas had raced over the ridge, only to encounter thick brush and impassable rocks. Finally they could see a narrow beach just big enough to run their horses along.

"There!" they both shouted at once. Nargonne negotiated the rocks and eyed the river that swirled with three rapidly moving specks. The river that had his son.

In the water, the dog yelped in Strabo's ear. He seemed to be barking to get Santandar's attention. But Santandar barely had strength to get his face above water. The river had him. *I love you, Father,* he thought. *I'm sorry, Father. I'm sorry I'm dead. . . .*

Whack! Something pulled him around on his back.

"Pull!" he heard. *Pull what? Pull where?*

"Swim!" and then a thick "Whoof!" in his ear, and Santandar reacted without knowing, paddling in the direction he was pulled. The sky whirled past above them, the walls of the canyon a gray blur.

"Pull!"

High above, black kestrels watched the scene in the river far below. A dog, a boy, a man.

Strabo could see the end now. The gray walls of the canyon loomed before them and the sound of the approaching falls grew deafening. Strabo pulled frantically toward the bank. *They're there,* he thought. *I saw them.* The dog clawed at his neck and the boy flopped gamely, but the two of them were of little use.

Then Strabo began to lose to the river too. His arms failed to respond and his legs kicked lamely in disobeying jerks. His hearing still worked—the roar of the falls filled the canyon.

His thinking was muddled. *I'm swimming* was all he could muster. *No, wait, I'm near the coast with the riders. Wasn't the bank near now? The boy, the dog . . .*

The riders, where are they?

"Nargonne!" he cried, and then his strength fell away and he slipped beneath the churning water. *Take a breath, breathe. . . .*

But there was nowhere to breathe, no way to breathe, not anymore. He was sinking. Away from the blurry sky and the air above. *The falls have us,* he thought. *The dog, the boy, the man.*

He gulped for air and his lungs screamed for the life-giving stuff, but he choked down solid water instead, and the pain of it struck him like a blow to the chest as the air evacuated his lungs. Something snagged him around the armpit and squeezed tight. *Rocks,* he thought. *Blackness coming; here it comes,* he thought. It was nearly his last thought when the blackness was dashed away by a wrenching pain in his shoulder and the noise was suddenly different, the roar of the falls replaced by a scraping of sand and stone and then the breaking of the surface of the water and air. Air! His body convulsed for it!

He was being dragged painfully across sand and stone, the water shallow now, the bank coming at him fast. A rope ran from a horse in front of him galloping through the shallows kicking up spray.

He slid to a stop in shallow water, the river still moving fast past his nose as he lay there choking. The river had little strength in the shallows. He rolled over and vomited water. An impossible volume of river to swallow, he thought.

Santandar lay nearby, the dog licking his head, and Nargonne unraveling a rope from the boy's neck. Like Strabo, the boy was choking and spitting and gulping for breath.

Strabo felt the rope loosen and someone help him to his feet. His vision was blurry and his legs wobbled, then held. His chest and shoulders were scratched and red with his own blood. Barbestro and Tourek were there. And Molena. They peered at him curiously. Just paces away, Ribas rewound a coil of rope and watched the dripping man.

Strabo's new sandals were gone and, with Tourek's assistance, he stumbled out of the water, where the boy and the dog sat with Nargonne. The group was gathered there on the bank, everyone catching their breath.

Strabo wiped water from his eyes and blinked at the boy. "You owe me a pair of sandals," Strabo said.

———

Carthaginian naval activity suddenly picked up dramatically. Warships and military cargo vessels swarmed along the East Coast of Spain. Intelligence in Rome was skeptical. They knew the Carthaginians were bold, but would they contemplate invading by sea? If so, the Romans were unworried. Their own navy was powerful, and in the event the naval invasion was a feint, their vaunted general Scipio waited at the mouth of the Rhône River poised to intercept any Carthaginian force that might invade over land.

Chapter 7

*M*allouse retrieved the disfigured horse doctor from upriver and introduced him to Strabo.

"This is Sargonne," he said. "Nargonne's brother." Strabo nodded, but the strange-looking man said nothing. His eyes askew, he seemed to look both at and away from Strabo at the same time, like a lizard.

"I lost your sandals," Strabo apologized.

The man shrugged. "Nothing," he said.

But "nothing" is not what Santandar got. Nargonne had dragged him to where he thought they were out of earshot but failed miserably, and all could hear the shouting and berating that went on for nearly an hour. This was rare temper, even for Nargonne. Temper borne of a father's fear.

The boy returned in tears and Nargonne's round face glowed red for hours. Even Cabo kept his muzzle to the ground and darted out of Nargonne's way. The group traveled quietly the rest of the day. Nargonne was incensed. Of all his people, the last one he wanted here was Santandar and it was too dangerous now to send the boy back.

Nargonne only looked at Strabo once, and then only at the man's bare feet.

But Strabo never needed the sandals, for soon they were to trade their familiar riding gear for a whole new identity.

After another day of riding, the group found themselves waiting on a hilltop as Nargonne and Molena, who spoke a few words of the local tongues, visited the camp of some nomads who inhabited this craggy terrain. The Souks brought Strabo over to the edge of a bluff and bade him look down. He did and saw a circle of hide covered tents far below. There were many horses and Strabo could see Molena's and Nargonne's horses among them. Ribas was on edge, but the Souks assured everyone things were under control. Nargonne knew these people, or at least how to deal with them.

At long last, the two came riding back up the hillside with large bundles draped over the back of each horse. Molena let the bundles fall to the ground, where they broke open to reveal a pile of coarse gray tunics wrapped in black leather belts. There were low boots also, of poor leather. She grinned.

"Tomorrow, we are Usson. Anyone for goat's milk and squirrel?"

She laughed, for she had just described the primary diet of the Usson, the wandering hill people that herded goats up and down these hilly ranges along the coast.

Nargonne was on the sterner side.

"Only Greek from here on out, understand?"

They all nodded and regarded the rough clothing with undisguised distaste.

They made camp beneath the lee of a rocky outcropping and settled in. After they had eaten a dinner of rabbit and carrots foraged from the ground just paces from their fire, Nargonne motioned for Strabo to follow him. Accompanied by Ribas, the three of them mounted their horses and rode east.

Nargonne was particularly relaxed. He felt at home on the move and on the march. For the thousandth time, he wondered if the sedentary life back in Asturias was right for him. He let the thought pass.

Nargonne led Ribas and Strabo up a steep rise. The wind stiffened at this high elevation, yet the air reeked of salt water and Strabo knew what lay on the other side. They reached the top and looked over. Thousands of feet below, the evening sea spread out before them. They had no trouble making out nearly one hundred ships anchored along the sandbars stretching far to the east.

Each counted to himself, estimating the size of the fleet below.

"It's the whole Carthaginian navy," gasped Ribas.

"Close to it," answered Nargonne. "If this bunch is to meet up with more ships, reinforcements perhaps from Carthaginian bastions in Corsica or Sardinia, Rome will have its hands full indeed."

"The invasion," said Strabo.

"Oh yes," said Nargonne. "It is my intention that we make way with them. To be on those ships when they heave oar and head east."

Strabo didn't have to ask why. If Nargonne knew of the existence of the invasion force, when he, Strabo, at sea just ten days ago, surrounded by the buzz and bustle of the entire jabbering sailing community, had heard nothing, then Nargonne knew something more. He knew that a certain Carthaginian cavalry colonel was sailing with the force. Machoba. And with Machoba, Molena's sister.

"What is her name?" Strabo asked.

Nargonne regarded him thoughtfully.

"Marinne," he said.

Marinne. Strabo hoped she was of kinder heart than her sister. Not that he gave them much chance of ever seeing her, let alone making off with her safely. Nargonne let Strabo think for a minute, then slapped Strabo on the back.

"Tomorrow you join the Carthaginian army, Strabo. Maybe they'll make you an officer. Look cheerful! For when the fleet leaves, we leave with them. And we'll all get to see Italy!" With that, he and Ribas laughed and headed back toward camp, but Strabo lingered, studying the fleet carefully.

Strabo couldn't be sure from this distance, but to him the fleet looked heavy in the water, which would mean they were fully loaded.

That was curious. If they were fully loaded, then why were they still here? Ships didn't load until the last minute and then they launched at once. Perhaps they were loaded with an unusual amount of provisions. This was, after all, an invasion fleet bound for mighty Rome, was it not? To fight for domination and glory. Load up, sail east, fight Rome. So simple. So complicated.

The ships look heavy. The light was fading and Strabo followed Ribas and Nargonne.

That night, Nargonne was confident. Patience, he told himself. He knew there was always great confusion at sea and at the many port changes, especially with the disparate fighting forces Hannibal had assembled from tribes as far away as Africa. Different peoples, different tongues—chaos. They would join Hannibal's army in the guise of Usson tribesmen and look for their chance to free Marinne. And then go for the prize.

All was as Nargonne predicted. Or so he thought.

———

Rome dispatched most of its navy to the eastern ports of Sardinia. From here, they made preparations to intercept the Carthaginian invasion fleet so obviously assembling. Word came from Roman provinces in East Africa that the Carthaginians had attacked Roman garrisons there. Roman Command accurately concluded that those attacks were an obvious decoy. The real thrust would come elsewhere.

Chapter 8

*T*he Usson told Nargonne the Carthaginians had assembled a forward recruiting command at the Crossroads, a shambles of an outpost fully two leagues inland from the bay where the ships of Carthage were anchored. Nargonne could only assume the cagey Carthaginian command was just being cautious and staying well clear of Roman eyes at sea.

He and Ribas set off at first light for the recruiting camp. They would return before nightfall, their trip a productive one. As Nargonne had planned, the Carthaginian recruiters easily accepted them into the army, if only for their horses. Beneath a makeshift lean-to, the recruiting officer had pulled a bronze stamping stick from a smoldering brazier and burned a seal onto a square of leather. Nargonne informed him he had nine riders, so the man produced cold stamps and a mallet from beneath his field bench and whacked the number 9 on the leather over a horse symbol. Welcome to the Carthaginian cavalry, Nargonne thought.

But the day was not without surprises.

Nargonne had struck up a conversation with a provisioning officer and learned the ships in the bay were not
loading up for Italy.

"Those ships are *unloading*," the officer had said.
"Heavy cavalry from Sardinia. Those poor bastards will
be headed inland and north like the rest of us."

"North?" asked Nargonne.

The man nodded slyly.

Nargonne knew his geography well. *North* to Italy?
That would require crossing the Alps.

And that was impossible. The towering Alps were an
impenetrable barrier that soared over the north of Italy; a
defensive bulwark that had protected Italy from the beginning of time. It was impossible to bring a force of any
size over that steep and dangerous range. It was madness
to think otherwise. The Alps were unforgiving, even in
summer months. Cold and cruel, they were the very roof
of the Mediterranean.

"Hannibal is invading Italy over the Alps," the officer
then said matter-of-factly. He waited patiently for Nargonne's reaction and wasn't disappointed. The look on the
new recruit's face made the officer laugh out loud.

Around their fire, the Asturians camped as the Usson.
Nargonne had ordered everyone to wear the Usson clothing and adopt their ways as much as possible. The group
gamely donned their stiff leather boots and long tunics.
Souk Mallouse glared his single eye at the Usson boots
and busily sawed at the heels, modifying them. They had
been hurting his feet already.

Nargonne took Molena and Barbestro aside and lowered his voice.

"It is important," Nargonne told Molena, "that Strabo

gains . . . how can I say this? . . . a *modicum* of skill on horseback."

"Hitting the ground hard is as good as he is going to get." Molena laughed.

"It is important, Molena, for your sister."

The grin vanished from her face. And from Barbestro's. The big man instinctively touched the betrothal band on his right hand at the mention of Marinne while Molena protested.

"But, Uncle . . ."

Nargonne held up his hand to silence her and turned to the others.

"Everyone, pay attention. We are now soldiers, official allies of the Carthaginian army. We will meet up with the main force at Andorra. Andorra is a three-day ride. We leave in the morning, and, Molena, Strabo's training begins then. Good luck."

Strabo raised an eyebrow, but Molena only stood there, a look of dread on her face. Her uncle turned away, smiling to himself.

That evening by the fire, Nargonne gathered everyone to brief them for the days and weeks ahead. His people were not seasoned veterans at this deception business. Few people were. He knew they would need to keep their wits about them. Even so, they had given themselves a healthy advantage by masquerading as Usson. The Usson were a tribe small in number that kept to themselves, and so it was unlikely any of the other mercenaries in the army would be familiar with them and their ways.

The group listened quietly as Nargonne reiterated for everyone their first order of business: Locate Marinne. They would have to be cautious. "Let us not be obvious,"

Nargonne had said. Their spirits rose when they spoke of her again, but Molena swallowed to fend off tears. Strabo noticed that she was successful at this. *She is a tough one,* he thought again.

The second order of business? Locate Machoba, although Nargonne guessed that was not going to be difficult.

"He would recognize only me," Nargonne told them, "but you should all keep your distance anyway." He didn't have to tell them what a dangerous man Machoba was. Or his vicious lieutenant, Akdar.

Nargonne instructed everyone to say as little as possible and to speak nothing but Greek, like the rest of the army. He told Strabo that he would undergo horse training on the trail to Andorra and that Molena would be his instructor. Strabo sighed heavily but reluctantly nodded his agreement. "You must learn to ride well, Strabo," Nargonne had said seriously. "You will need to know the ways of the horse, believe me."

Wonderful, thought Strabo.

Finally Nargonne told them to get a good night's sleep and they all went to bed, excited about their prospects. All but Strabo. The closer they got to the Carthaginians, the more questions he had about this entire enterprise.

How? he thought. *How do we spirit away a concubine from the armed camp of one of the most powerful armies on earth?* The whole idea seemed more outlandish with every passing moment.

And how, Strabo wondered, did Nargonne intend to pay the huge fine? Strabo knew there was only one way to raise the sum required. Kidnapping for ransom. A time honored tradition. But in this case, kidnap whom? The

Carthaginians cared not for a single tribal chieftain in all of the peninsula. No one was important to them, save their officers. So an officer it must be then, thought Strabo.

They would top off this dangerous undertaking by kidnapping an officer of the Carthaginian army? The mere thought of that! And then hold him ransom, and trade him for a jaw-dropping sum of Hannibal's gold? None of them would live through the exchange. Even if they did, how would they get away in one piece? And to bring a girl into this? She should be sent home at once on their most capable horse. This could only end in disaster, Strabo was sure of it. So why should he stay?

The gold was only *promised* gold, after all.

Was it the kidnapped girl? Her fate would be a cruel one, if she wasn't dead already. Or was it Molena? Strabo tried to dismiss the thought.

Why not leave these people to their fate? Wasn't the warrior Ribas capable? And the Souk twins too? But Strabo knew Nargonne needed all the help he could get.

Besides, I can leave at any time, Strabo told himself.

The next day broke with bright sunshine and a cool breeze coming in from the Pyrenees mountain range just to the north. Sargonne spent more than the usual amount of time checking the horses but found no trouble. The group headed out looking for all the world like an assemblage of Usson. Strabo was the last to mount. Nargonne rode up to him. "You've more lives than a mountain cat," Nargonne said. Strabo said nothing, he only shifted uncomfortably on his saddle pad.

Nargonne cleared his throat. "Thank you for saving my son. Again. He is courageous, but a fool sometimes."

"Like his father?" said Strabo.

Nargonne let the insult pass, and after a moment, he released a long, patient sigh.

"What's on your mind, Strabo?"

Strabo nodded toward their line of horses setting out toward Andorra.

"You're sending a bunch of amateurs to break a prisoner out of a military camp."

"You knew that already."

"Maybe I thought you weren't serious."

"Now you know that I am."

Strabo shook his head.

"Maybe I thought you'd change your mind, that some of you would run off, that something would happen. . . ."

Nargonne laughed. "That *something would happen*? Like what? What would happen, Strabo? Magic? There is no magic, Strabo. There is only us."

Nargonne smirked at him. An arrogant warrior's smirk, Strabo thought. And many an arrogant warrior was dead.

"You'll never get her out of there alive, Nargonne."

"Maybe she'll be alive, maybe she'll be dead. But we will get her out." He trotted away. *The accursed man speaks in riddles,* thought Strabo.

Nargonne yelled over his shoulder, "Your riding instructor is waiting for you, Strabo. We all have high hopes!"

The rest of the day was a long one for Strabo. He secured his sword to his saddle pad and the lessons began. As the band wound their way through the low hills, Nargonne ordered the rest of the group to leave them alone, save for Barbestro. He left that hulking man to ride nearby so that Strabo and Molena didn't have to bring up the rear alone. The boy also stayed close, mostly because his dog kept running back to check on all of the commotion.

Strabo envied the Asturians their skills on horseback. They were utterly comfortable with each horse and traded mounts with ease; Tundra, Corcell—all were the same to the Asturians. But he was to ride only Castaine. Molena rode a thick black horse called Archon. Archon looked elegant and sturdy. His shoulders did not droop like Castaine's and Archon stayed on his feet, even when sleeping. He never misbehaved and seemed the perfect horse.

"He and Castaine are brothers," Molena told Strabo. *I doubt it,* Strabo thought.

Like her uncle, Molena was a stern taskmaster. She held out a long switch and made Strabo keep it right on top of Castaine's nose for hundreds of strides at a time. The concentration alone was a challenge for both man and horse.

She had him speak to Castaine constantly. "He must know you completely and be comfortable with your voice," Molena insisted. Strabo spoke to the horse so much he thought the horse might soon speak back.

She had him trot and canter and gallop. She had him canter "off center" so that Castaine danced nearly sideways. She had him ride sidesaddle and feign the launching of arrows. She had him jump.

But mostly, she had him execute sharp turns and this was the most painful part of the lesson plan. He would go one way and Castaine the other and then Strabo would plunge to the ground. Sometimes he popped off unexpectedly. Sometimes he lost his grip gradually, desperately clutching at the horse's short coat only to slip slowly down the haunches of the huge animal and ride it sideways until he lost his strength and tumbled to the ground.

All this while they kept up with the group, more or less. They were never out of sight. If they lagged too far behind, Molena would announce "trail training" and off they would go on a galloping exercise.

Molena finally called off the lessons for the day when Castaine abruptly slid to a stop from a full canter, catapulting Strabo into the air in a somersault that ended in a painful *whoompf* in the tall saw grass of the mountain meadow. Better to end now, thought Molena. She did not wish to kill the man. He was a fighter and they would be needing him soon.

She had never seen someone fall so much or try so hard. He listened, he cursed, he argued and shouted. But he didn't quit.

At this last fall, Strabo crawled up slowly and leveled a burning glare at Castaine, who ignored him completely, absently tugging at pieces of grass.

Strabo retrieved his sword and struggled to pull himself back up on the horse. It wasn't just the muscles pounded by the falling, it was muscles sore from hoisting his weight back onto the horse again and again.

No sooner was he back in the saddle pad when Castaine unexpectedly reared high with a loud whinny, wheeling backward!

"Castaine!" shouted Molena, and she dismounted to control him.

Strabo was flung off again and hit the ground, rolled, and came up seething as the horse pranced nervously nearby. Strabo snarled at Castaine.

Then he saw at once the reason for the horse's shying.

A mountain adder as long as a man's leg slithered through the grass toward Molena, the bright yellow stripe on its back a blur of motion. Strabo's sword was already in his hand as he dived.

Molena screamed. "Strab . . . !"

There was a flash of yellow light, of the late-afternoon sun reflecting off the blade of a sword slicing through the air, the movement of it creating a sweeping plane of metal.

That plane passed through the snake in a blink. The snake's distended jaw continued its path to its target, yellow teeth outstretched. But its head had been separated from its body and the inert head of the snake bounced harmlessly off Molena's calf. She jumped away in panic, falling backward as the snake's body flopped to the ground, where it briefly quivered and jerked.

Strabo got to his knees and sheathed his weapon. Castaine pawed cautiously at the impotent head of the snake. Molena sat on the ground.

The impact of the moment of fear and then the release of it made them both giddy and it suddenly struck Molena that Strabo looked very silly. He was dirty from countless encounters with the ground. Dressed in the ungainly long tunics and leggings of the Usson, his hair pressed sideways by the day's sweat and the dirt and the ground, he looked like a disheveled child come home from a day of unsupervised play.

Despite herself, she broke into a grin.

"Castaine really likes you, you know. He only threw you because of the snake," she said.

"Then these hills must be covered with snakes."

Strabo smiled too and picked up the head of the snake like a puppet and shook it playfully in his hands.

"Hissss," he mimicked, and they both laughed breathlessly before Strabo tossed the snake's jerking body away, careful to throw it away from Castaine, though he briefly thought otherwise.

"Are we done?" he asked Molena.

"Yes," she said. "For today."

For once, she assisted Strabo back on Castaine, and as she did, she touched his left thigh and felt a large knot through his skin there.

"What's this from?" she asked.

"Some battle," he said. "I don't know how it happened. Someone hit me with something. It never healed."

He said no more about it and she thought of the snake and the man who had struck like lightning. Exhausted and alone with their thoughts, they made their way back to the group and helped make camp for the night.

There, Strabo again marveled at the Asturians' hunting skill. They didn't bother with bows tonight, they simply fanned out and began stringing snares.

Strabo watched them work. Santandar was particularly adept at this business. He would descend on a copse of trees or a thicket of bushes. Then he would reconnoiter the small area thoroughly, painstakingly examining the ground for rabbit tracks and the claw scratchings of game birds. He deftly set the snares while carefully keeping his body downwind so as not to contaminate the trapping area. Then he would be off to another likely trapping spot and do the same there. By the time he finished the second setup, he went back to the first to find a catch. Then he returned to the second only to find another. All of which went a long way in explaining how Nargonne maintained his distinctive girth even out here in the field.

Strabo was in charge of the fire, which he put together with practiced efficiency. He said little to the group and they little to him. Souk Tourek scattered broken twigs about the camp and examined the entrails of a slaughtered rabbit at great length. He rolled his stones and consulted the night sky. Cabo sniffed at the rabbit's innards, but Tourek shooed him away.

Strabo was handed a haunch of roast rabbit, which he brought back to his blanket and devoured while the rest of the band sat around the fire and talked. None paid Strabo any attention except for Ribas, who picked his teeth with a slender tooth bone and unabashedly checked on Strabo now and then, as if Strabo were still suspect.

Strabo finished his rabbit and lay down. He looked over at Castaine, who seemed to be eyeing him occasionally, just like Ribas. *Why don't you two ride together?* he thought. And then he was asleep. He would have dreamed of Castaine and Molena and the adder, had he the strength.

Around the campfire, there was no shortage of suggestions for Molena to aid her in making Strabo's learning all the more entertaining.

"Tell him put fingers in horse's mouth to steer." Sargonne laughed.

"No, use his ears to steer, his ears!" Santandar giggled.

And while he was not impartial to such sport himself, Nargonne did take Molena aside. "I need the man in one piece," he reminded her.

For Strabo, the next day was more of the same, except colder. One would expect Molena to be kinder after the snake incident, but he had no such luck. Another morning of following the switch at close range. More cantering and trotting and galloping. The falls, while painful, were mercifully fewer.

By midday, they stopped to water the horses at a mountain spring. Molena had just said to Strabo, "We'll practice turns this afternoon" when there was a hail from Tourek, who rode the vanguard of their line a half a league in front. He was galloping back, and when he pulled up in a cloud of dust, they all gathered around him.

"There are horsemen in front of us. I saw them an hour ago and thought they were moving faster, but they're slow. We'll catch them by midafternoon."

"How many?" asked Ribas.

"Five."

Nargonne was silent.

"Who do they look like?" asked Ribas, looking at Nargonne.

"I don't know. Long cloaks. Celtiberians maybe. They look weak on their mounts, though. Poor horsemen."

"Recruits like us?" asked Barbestro.

They all looked to Nargonne and he shrugged his shoulders. "We should be running into more and more people as we get closer to Andorra. Stay close for the rest of the day."

So they rode in close order and caught up to the men in the late afternoon.

The strangers' mounts were a disgrace. Malnourished and sickly, they could scarcely carry their riders. What's more, the poor animals were weighted down with chest armor crudely constructed of leather straps reinforced with studs of iron. Further weighting them were coarse sacks tied to their saddles bulging with clanking pots and tools.

Ribas and Nargonne went ahead to speak with them, and when they returned, Nargonne explained that the men were indeed Celtiberians and they had enlisted with the Carthaginians as well. There were many brigands in the hills, their leader had said, and suggested they ride together. Nargonne had agreed.

The two groups converged with polite nods, now that their respective leaders gave them the go-ahead. The Celtiberians rode slowly but were well armed with short swords, leather breastplates, and round skirmishing shields. None of their matériel matched, but that was not unusual, and not once did they refer to their animals by name.

Strabo took the unusual step of concealing his sword beneath his tunic. He got the feeling he and the rest of Nargonne's party were being sized up.

As they rode, Nargonne talked at length with their leader and learned there were many Celtiberians converging on Andorra and that Hannibal's army was marching in a line so long it might take a day to pass through a single village. Fifty thousand, maybe a hundred thousand men, they said. They did not know. But Nargonne was sure of one thing. When they reached the valley of Andorra, the place would be teeming with people. All that confusion would work to his advantage and he smiled at the thought.

The leader of the Celtiberians called himself Hochmoor. From the Singuine Valley, he said. His beard was thick and black and his eyes darted beneath a weather-beaten copper skullcap. Some skirmish trophy, no doubt. With Hannibal, he explained, they would march for food and then fight for treasure. Hochmoor grinned. "We will return to Singuine the richest men in the province!" He was charming and pleasant and offered to help Nargonne in any way he could. The rest of his party stayed quiet. Hochmoor explained they knew no Greek. There were only Hochmoor, three men, and a young one who barely looked older than Santandar. Hochmoor asked about the girl and Nargonne said only that they were delivering her. "I see" was all Hochmoor said.

Although Hochmoor said nothing of it, anyone could see the horses of the Asturians were outstanding. They were a strong and healthy breed, well cared for and well trained. So Hochmoor proceeded to regale Nargonne with tales of the Numidians, the famous African horsemen Hannibal employed to such great success. "There are thousands of them and they are as fast as forest cats on those animals of theirs. Their African breeds are like yours. Fast and strong. Perhaps you will get along well with the Numidians."

The Numidians rode horses bred from the descendants of the hardy Akhal-Teke breed, Nargonne knew, the finest of the African equine lines. "What manner of horse are these?" Hochmoor asked him.

"I don't know," Nargonne lied. Asturian horses were Barbs, themselves descended from ancient Spanish stock and bred for strength, brains, and speed. Mostly the latter.

When night fell, Nargonne prudently offered to help the Celtiberians with their own fire farther along the ridge. He did not want to share close ground with the strangers. He was careful to keep Santandar close to their own circle, close to Strabo. The Asturians offered the Celtiberians food, which they accepted gladly. Apologizing for having nothing in return, they rode down a ravine and fetched fresh water for all. Still, Nargonne had his group bed down in a tighter ring than usual.

Strabo watched Santandar play with the fire, his cousin Molena idly looking on. He looked unhappy. He is homesick, Strabo thought. He sat by Santandar at the fire's edge and caught the boy's eye.

"You will be home soon," Strabo said.

The boy just nodded and poked at the fire, his ear to the quiet night. There was only the faint baying of wolves very far off.

"The crickets are gone," he said.

So they were. Summer was over. Then Strabo remembered one of his favorite childhood tricks. Santandar and Molena watched in surprise as Strabo put his pinkie finger in his mouth and stretched his cheek wide. Then he stuck his tongue to his teeth and warbled a whistle that rattled ridiculously through his cheeks. The sound made Santandar and Molena laugh out loud.

"That's not a cricket," yelped Santandar.

"Yes it is. A fat one," replied Strabo, and he did it again.

The boy laughed. Molena rolled her eyes at their playing but couldn't help but laugh again.

"Watch this," Strabo said. He then put two fingers to his cheek and inserted a finger from his other hand. He yanked the fingers apart and a loud *pop* leaped off his cheek. The boy shrieked in delight.

"Show me how," he said. Strabo did, but the boy could not master the trick.

"It takes practice," said Strabo, though he was looking at Molena. "Everything takes practice."

"Like the sword," said Santandar.

Molena looked at Strabo and he at her.

"And horses," Strabo said.

Santandar jumped up and grabbed a long branch from their woodpile. He swung it into a log there and it bounced back in his face. Molena and Strabo laughed. The boy struck again and again, but the thin branch had no effect on the log.

"Try this," Strabo said. He handed the boy his Saguntum blade and the boy took it in awe. Molena raised a brow at Strabo, but he shrugged off the look.

"It's only a sword," he said.

"The deathblow!" Santandar shouted. He swung the heavy blade into the log and it shuddered to a stop.

Strabo walked over and withdrew the blade from the log. He raised it over his head, his back heaved, and he brought the weapon down. The sword blasted loudly through the log, splintering it in two and sending the pieces spinning away.

The shock of the impact sent Santandar jumping back with a start and Molena stiffened. Strabo looked at them in the moonlight.

"There's no such thing as a halfhearted deathblow," he said.

The boy giggled, but Molena did not. The sudden fury of the man's sword startled her. *What is such a man capable of?* she thought. Nargonne interrupted them with a stern look. "Practice tomorrow. Sleep tonight," he said. It was an order.

When everyone was asleep, Ribas slipped from his bedding and stepped some forty paces from the perimeter of their sleeping area. There, he bent low and silently shoved a small stick in the ground. He tied a snare to it, then stealthily crept a few more paces, inserted another stick and tied it to the string, and so on until he had encircled their entire sleeping area with a makeshift trip wire. He figured the Celtiberians were not much of a threat, but one couldn't be too cautious. Satisfied, he rolled himself back in his bedding and slept with one eye open.

The only other member of the party who was awake was Strabo. He crept away from the glow of the fire and shielded his eyes from the moon and starlight, the better to keep his night vision sharp. He lay there resting like a wary dog: First one eye open, then the other, so that at least his eyes got some rest for the night.

He and Ribas glanced at each other but once, acknowledging a temporary truce in favor of the perceived threat from the strangers.

Nargonne, for his part, slept soundly. He had spoken with both Ribas and Strabo privately. They wouldn't sleep, he knew. That meant he could and he did. As did the rest.

The Celtiberians came in the darkest hour of the night and the coarse sacks that had so burdened their horses revealed their true cargo: armor and weapons. They had donned bronze greaves to protect their legs and heavy bronze breastplates above. They wore helmets of thick copper. They had no spears, no throwing darts, no bows— just two short swords each. They were prepared for close killing.

Five figures charged Nargonne's sleeping people in the dark. There was no sound save the brush of their leather sandals on the dirt and the clinking of their armor as they rushed their victims.

As capable as they may have been in ambush, this time they had seriously underestimated their prey. They presumed them to be simple mountain people, simple Usson, off to join the army and in over their heads. They would make short work of these simpletons. But this particular group of simpletons had two weapons named Ribas and Strabo, and so tonight, the ambushers would become the ambushed.

They stumbled across the trip wire and ran into a flurry of bedrolls flung in their faces. Ribas rolled to his feet and swung his sword through the side of the first attacker and he howled in pain and staggered to the ground. Ribas finished him in the back before he could turn.

Strabo darted up behind the second one as he passed and cut him down with a ferocious blast below the man's helmet, separating much of his neck from his torso in a flash. That man was dead before he hit the ground.

Cabo erupted into barking and everyone leaped out of bed at the commotion, hearts thumping fast. Strabo immediately dipped his shoulder and then lifted his sword in an upper-cutting thrust into the next man, and his sword drove right through the surprised man before the man could step aside. In fact, the man had not even seen Strabo in the darkness, had barely had the time to register that there was someone else up and on his feet already. Someone who wasn't one of his. That was his last thought.

Strabo kicked him off his sword and he slid to the ground. It was Hochmoor.

Barbestro and Souk Mallouse were the first of the others with weapons and they lunged at the man nearest Ribas. He dodged, but Ribas parried him back and he fell against Barbestro, who rather than stabbing, simply shoved the man back toward Ribas where Ribas slid his sword noisily through the man's chest plate and the man fell.

There was one left and he stopped now on the edge of the fire ring, wild-eyed and frantic. He had both short swords in front of him and he squared off with Nargonne, who had appeared on the other side of the fire with sword in hand. Molena crouched bravely next to her uncle, wielding a short sword with both hands.

It was the young one.

"Drop them and you live," hissed Nargonne.

The young man hesitated, afraid to lose his advantage. Molena pleaded with him.

"Do as he says!"

The boy feinted and parried with Nargonne and stutter-stepped as if he would attack but delivered no blow. He was terrified. Too terrified to do anything, perhaps, but at that instant a warrior lunged from the darkness and cut the young man down in a ferocious arc of unforgiving metal. He crumpled lifeless to the ground.

Strabo.

He whirled over the body and crouched low, still on high alert and wary of more threats.

Then Ribas's voice. "There were five and I count five."

It was over.

Now the only sound in their camp was that of heavy breathing. Santandar knelt beside his bedroll with a short sword at the ready, although he hadn't moved very far and seemed only dimly aware of what had just transpired, the heavy sleep of youth still upon him.

Ribas roamed the perimeter, staring out into the darkness. Strabo and the Souks checked each body for signs of life and found none.

"Sargonne, check the horses," Nargonne said. Sargonne hobbled over to where the horses stamped nervously.

"Safe," Sargonne announced.

Molena was dumbfounded. It had all happened so quickly and it was finished nearly before it began. Nargonne gave a satisfied nod at Strabo and Strabo graciously nodded in turn toward Ribas, still patrolling the perimeter.

"We were ready for them," Strabo said.

But Molena would have nothing to do with congratulations. Not after what she had just seen. Her temper would have been even higher had the nighttime not muted the broad arcs of blood that besmirched Strabo's tunic. She confronted Strabo and pointed at the dead teenager on the ground.

"The young one. He was going to give up."

Ribas interjected from the darkness. "Necessary" was all he said.

"No it wasn't." Molena glared at Strabo.

Strabo's mouth pursed in fury. The intensity of the attack was still fresh upon him. All of the frustrations of the last few days, all of the uncertainty, all of the newness and his newfound ignorance in the ways of horses and mountains and snares, it all boiled over and rose up his throat at once. These horsemen with their jokes and careless ways. The confounded casual attitude of these people! It would get them all killed.

"He didn't even see you. You murdered him," Molena said.

Strabo could contain himself no longer and he lost his temper, the spit flying from his mouth as he roared.

"There is no room for quarter in combat! None. He had

a weapon, I had a weapon, and one of us had to die. There is no other way!"

The sheer volume of his voice made Molena take a step back as a hush fell upon them, but Strabo wasn't done.

"He kills, I kill. We all kill until it is done. Until the fight is done! Until they are all dead or you are all dead. This is not playtime. This is not *training*."

They said nothing to him.

He stooped, his muscles finally reacting to the exertion of the fight. He watched blood drip from the end of his sword. It dripped dark in the moonlight, colorless. The man's lifeblood dripped to the dry ground and was sucked into the soil of the earth. A man he had never spoken to and never would. He was gone and Strabo had killed him. He glared at Molena and the others and pointed at the hacked bodies lying in utter stillness behind him.

"They are dead because they were slow, or stupid, or I don't know what, but I do know that I was neither! And we are alive."

He loathed them at this moment. He hated Molena and Nargonne. He hated Ribas. Oh, how he hated Ribas. He had killed with him. As efficiently as he. The two of them together knew how to kill.

The hate and frustration overwhelmed him. These people! He pointed his sword at them.

"You! You know nothing of this and yet you will go into a military camp manned with professional killers, who are not like you. Believe me, they are not like you, not one little bit, brave as you think you are!"

Strabo's eyes settled on Nargonne.

"You have some wild scheme. . . . I don't know what it is or how or what . . . but you will come to a bad end, you will. You will cower and your courage will flee from you like a rat from a ship."

He turned his eyes on Santandar.

"Will you go into battle? You? Will you go where there is only speed and metal and confusion? A screaming fog of men mad with fear? The sound of horns and war cries and the howls of the dying so loud it drowns out everything?"

Strabo scoffed and leveled his glare finally at Molena again.

"And then there is blood and sweat and then more blood and then the fatigue, your arms so tired you can't raise a dagger, let alone a heavy shield to protect yourself. And when your strength is gone, you are gone and you are dead in an instant."

They stared back at him but said nothing. Ribas stood off to the side—silent.

Strabo swept his forearm across his cheek and wiped the blood from his face. With the hilt of his Saguntum sword, he wiped the spittle from his mouth. He was unembarrassed in front of the girl.

He gulped and began to breathe easier. His hand shook, so he couldn't put his sword back in his belt. He didn't know why it shook so. It did not shake from fear. *I'm done with these people,* he thought.

"You will be cut to pieces," he said.

He turned from them and walked away into the night.

At dawn, they buried the dead men together on the side of the hill. Against Ribas's objections, they buried them deep, as was proper. "They deserve nothing," Ribas had said.

They stripped the dead of their valuable weapons and

converted their horses into light-baggage carriers for the whole party. This eased the burden on the Asturian horses, for now they had five more. And more swords and even helmets and greaves. To Santandar's great entertainment, Barbestro clowned around in a helmet for a minute until a look from Molena made him think better of it. Barbestro reluctantly put it away. For all his gruff talk and burly ways, he had never worn a war helmet.

Strabo had not returned.

Sargonne and Nargonne went over the new horses together. Sargonne announced he would have his work cut out for him with these new ones, but he could nurse them back to health with time. Nargonne ordered Santandar to shadow Uncle Sargonne and lend him his constant assistance.

"You are his official assistant from here on out, understand?"

The boy understood.

"Swear by our family."

The boy touched the necklace at his throat and swore. His necklace matched Nargonne's: a horse head enameled in blue on a circle of copper. His father flashed his own necklace at the boy and they smiled together.

Nargonne said nothing of it, but Strabo's outburst the night before had opened his eyes. His son was on this mission and he could see there would be no mercy shown the young. Not from the likes of Strabo. And soon they would be surrounded by men like him. Strabo had taught him this, at least, and for that he was grateful. Nargonne would keep Santandar from battle, that much was certain.

They left the campsite midmorning and their newly enlarged train headed north to Andorra. They would be there by nightfall.

As they made their way out of the valley, Nargonne considered sending Souk Mallouse to find Strabo. Then he considered sending Molena, but he thought that such an encounter could only end in disaster. He even considered sending Ribas. But in the end, he knew it was he who would talk to the man.

He sent the others ahead, telling them he would catch up with them. Ribas objected to him going off alone but reluctantly relented when allowed to cover him, if only at a distance. Nargonne galloped off, pulling Castaine along behind him.

He found Strabo not far from the previous night's campsite, on the gently sloping bank of their drinking stream. Strabo had not left with a horse, which was no surprise to anyone. Two short swords lay on his lap and he was sound asleep, leaning comfortably against a tree.

Nargonne was tempted to wake him, but he didn't. He tied the horses to a tree, found a comfortable position himself, and joined Strabo in a midmorning nap.

When he awoke an hour later, Strabo was watching him.

Nargonne yawned and stretched and gathered himself. He nodded to the two horses tied to the tree next to him.

But Strabo just shook his head.

The two men said nothing for a long time. Nargonne stared into the passing stream. *This man is not like me,* he thought. *I am a strategist, a thinker. I had my chance to be an adventurer, but that was not to be.*

This man Strabo, on the other hand, is the dangerous type. Like an animal—a jungle cat. What made him this way? Nargonne couldn't know. His own parents had been wonderful and disciplined, loving and strong. He warmed at the thought of them. *I am fat now and older, but still fit,* he thought. *I still have work to do. With or without this upstart. Why, then, do I feel a responsibility toward him? He is nothing to us.*

He smiled at length and asked him, "Where will you go, Strabo the magnificent?"

"Away from here."

"We're going away from here too."

Strabo only crossed his arms and grunted.

"Will you go to the sea?" asked Nargonne.

"I might."

"But your horse will miss you." Nargonne grinned.

"I don't think so."

Nargonne's attempt at humor had no effect, but he didn't regret it. One step at a time, he thought. There was silence for a long time while Nargonne pondered what to say to this man. To help him. To help them both.

"The girl is excitable, Strabo."

"The girl is right," Strabo said, staring at nothing. Nargonne was surprised at the blackness in Strabo's response.

"What if she is?" Nargonne asked. He got up and walked over to Strabo and pointed at his swords. "What difference does it make? Still, we do what we must do."

Strabo looked at his weapons.

Nargonne said, "I don't know why things are the way they are. I don't know why some people end up where they do. I only know we all leave something behind us."

Strabo toyed with the swords, twirling them in his hands slowly, watching the light reflect off the imperfections his trained eye detected in the finish.

"What will you leave behind, Strabo?" Nargonne asked him.

What would he leave behind? Only metal and death, Strabo knew. He thought of ships at sea and of the river mouth where he played as a boy, those memories clouded more and more by the haze of time. The ports he had seen, the coastlines he sailed, the bars and the establishments where he stood as sentry and bouncer against drunken sailors. The shipments of booty and gold he had guarded as a paid soldier. The armies he traveled with, the weapons with which he had practiced. The world and his life swirled before him and there was nothing there in all that metal and weaponry for him to grab hold of, for him to follow. What was there for him with these people?

At that moment, Strabo noticed Ribas hunched on his horse, watching them from a prudent distance. *He* is going, and he is in it for the money, isn't he? The thought struck Strabo like a rebuke and he suddenly realized why he disliked and suspected the man, hated him and feared him. For the man was just like him.

Strabo took his eyes from Ribas and looked up blankly at Nargonne, who looked back at him curiously. *He is trying to read my mind,* Strabo thought. *But there is nothing here for you, Nargonne. There is nothing you can say to me to make me go with you. Because there is no reason for me to go with you. To continue with this insane mission of yours that has no chance, no prayer. No reason except one.*

Her. Her eyes were deep and beautiful and hard as stone. She would die for her sister, Strabo knew. What would he die for?

Strabo rose silently to his feet. Sheathing his weapons,

he walked over to Castaine and pulled himself onto the saddle. Castaine obliged him without complaint and he tugged the horse's reins and walked up the hill toward Ribas without saying a word to Nargonne.

The three of them rejoined the group by noon. The reunion, as it were, was a mute one. Molena kicked her horse away from Strabo and to the head of the line, indiscreetly signaling her feelings to all. Only Souk Mallouse caught Strabo's eye directly. He silently threw his hands up before him in a pantomime of mock horror at seeing Strabo, then trotted off grinning at his great humor. No one enjoyed their own jokes as much as Mallouse.

They now looked like a respectable troop with their extra horses as a baggage train. The huge Barbestro took the front of the line with Molena close behind. The Souks followed and then Sargonne with his new charge, Santandar. Cabo ranged freely, checking in with Santandar from time to time. Then Strabo alone, followed by Nargonne and Ribas bringing up the rear.

They entered the southern edge of the wide Roussillon Valley, from where the Têt River flowed lazily to the sea. It was here, where they had a wide view of the hills on all sides and where the whole valley funneled toward their destination, that they first got a glimpse of the magnitude of the task before them.

Tiny black figures dotted the hillsides nearby and into the deep distance, so far away they were no more than specks. Men.

Everywhere in the valley, men trudged to the north, picking their way to the easier traveling of the valley floor or cutting straight across the valley hillsides. There were hundreds of them, mostly in small groups like theirs.

Some were on horseback, but not many. Horses were a luxury for the likes of these. These men were mercenaries of the purest variety. They were the down on their luck, the outcast, the criminal, the lost, and the destitute. What had they to lose by fighting the mighty Romans? They had only to gain: booty, gold, glory. All were promised by the Carthaginian war machine.

There were the occasional families following a troop of men, although they were encouraged to stay clear of the main camp, and if there was a hint of trouble from any of them, they would be sent away. Nargonne was relieved his son and niece would not stand out so blatantly from this crowd. Still, they would need to be made as inconspicuous as possible.

They could distinguish mule trains and teams of oxen pulling carts laden with goods. These would be the inevitable merchants and traders that followed every campaign. They were the savviest breed of all, Strabo knew. They would prosper regardless of which side proved victorious, for profit and blood traveled together.

At one point, he noticed everyone curiously regarding a train of a dozen open carts with cages bolted to them. They were pulled by several mules each, the whole train tended to by the roughest-looking of men. The cages were empty. Santandar commented he thought they looked like animal cages. "For what animals?" he asked his uncle. His uncle didn't know.

But Strabo knew. Those men were slave traders and slaves were prized booty. Defeated soldiers, soldiers' families, captured townspeople, anyone deemed an ally of the enemy, could become a slave depending on the whim of the military commander in the field.

By late afternoon, the traffic began to converge at the valley's end to the north. The Asturians didn't bother to trap for dinner. There was far too much activity in the area and all the game was spooked and gone to ground until the tumult passed. So they munched on venison jerky and dried rabbit. They were a quiet group today. Maybe it was the night before, maybe it was the anticipation of the day ahead. They all knew the hazardous part of their journey was just beginning.

They followed the general traffic up a long, sloping rise. The late sun threw long shadows off to their right, their horses casting elongated shapes, tall and gargantuan, across the grassy landscape.

At the top of the rise, it was Barbestro who saw Andorra first. The remote mountain town known for smelting was normally a sleepy affair, but today it was overrun. The mining settlement was a confused jumble of stone buildings surrounded by rough hewn warehouses and smelting works. These were, in turn, surrounded by hundreds of grass- and mud-roofed houses.

Strabo could identify the smelting works in the center of the settlement even from this distance. They were the low stone buildings lined with numerous chimneys. Some of the shorter chimneys were for the low heat cooling fires, used to seat and settle metal to a formidable hardness without brittling. The fat chimneys belched the black smoke of the hot fires, where the unrefined ore was melted at impossible temperatures into a glowing fluid of primeval fire. The chimneys were many, and they all pumped thick smoke into the air.

Andorra was not as sophisticated as Sigeum, where Strabo was raised, but it did possess the basic capabilities required for equipping an army, and it looked like everyone here had been working double time lately.

Surrounding the settlement was a primitive defensive wall constructed of odd lengths of timbers sunk into the ground. The wall ran only on three sides as the Têt River, wide and slow in these Pyrenees lowlands, ran along the town's northern border. Every two hundred paces, a shabby tower, barely big enough for a pair of archers, stood guard along the wall's length.

There were some fifty thousand men camped in the valley below them, every speck of meadow and hillside occupied in one fashion or another. As far as he could see, the river to the north was lined with campsites.

There must have been grass there, but not a patch of green could be seen. Everything was covered with tents, horses, carts, baggage trains, and men. Everywhere men. Crawling all over each other. Busy. The energetic denizens of a human anthill.

The smoke from countless fires rose from the camps and joined the smoke from the smelters to create a low haze that hung over the valley. Molena's horse whinnied and stamped and she reassured him. "Easy, Archon. All is well." Far off, she could make out people bathing in the river.

She looked at Nargonne. If he was as overwhelmed as the rest of them, he didn't show it. He just smiled and said, "Looks like we don't have to wait for the Carthaginian army. They beat us here."

Everyone smiled nervously and shifted restlessly on their mounts. Everyone, that is, but Molena. She pulled her cloak tighter against the stiff breeze suddenly blowing in from the northern mountains. The first winds of winter were pushing their way south. She squinted purposefully into the cold and regarded the massive grouping of humanity spread out below them.

Her sister was down there. If she was still alive.

"We're coming, Marinne," she whispered.

———

The Carthaginians had years to prepare hundreds of tons of military matériel. From sandal to sword, no detail was ignored. The army organized horse brigades at unprecedented expense. Hundreds of thousands of weapons were forged and war machines were manufactured in unheard-of quantities. Cities were emptied of security forces, which were then redeployed to the invasion force. Every resource available was brought to bear so that Hannibal could field a fighting force that would prove unstoppable against the Romans. Or anyone else.

Chapter 9

*M*ost of the throng had been at Andorra for days, and many of them for weeks. The forest on the edge of town had been stripped bare for firewood, and everywhere the grassy plain had been trampled to mulch by an endless parade of feet, horse hooves, and cart wheels. Wide pits dug hastily for human refuse were filling up and beginning to stink.

The whole area was completely overtaxed and Hannibal knew it. His army lived off the land, which is why he never stayed in one place too long. His army would always be on the march.

Before they descended the hill into town, Nargonne circled the horses and he and Sargonne did some quick work on Molena. They strapped a splint to her left leg and wrapped a makeshift bandage around its entire length. They rubbed dirt into the bandage and roughed it up so that it looked like she had been wrapped that way for some time. They did the same with her hands and, finally, her head.

The entire ruse was designed to prevent Machoba or

his men from recognizing the twin sister of their recent concubine. Her bandaged leg and its resulting forced limp would eliminate any semblance of a feminine gait, and her covered hands would mask those slender, female fingers.

They topped off the disguise by singeing her riding clothes so that it appeared she had been the victim of fire. Strabo shuddered at the memory of the burn at the hands of the boys in Sigeum long ago. Only Santandar noticed him turn away as the burning was done and jokes were made about her being "cooked" or if she was "done for dinner" yet.

When the job was done, it proved convincing and everyone agreed she made a thoroughly pathetic sight. No one was likely to bother her. *Good thinking,* thought Strabo. *But we're going to need a lot more than circus tricks to pull off this grand plot of theirs.* Every attempt to get Nargonne to reveal his plans had so far been met with silence, riddles, and evasion.

Earlier in the day, he had pulled Castaine in front of Nargonne and challenged him straight up.

"You do know what would happen to us if we kidnap a Carthaginian officer," Strabo had said. "They will hunt you down. Until they have found every last one of your people."

But Nargonne revealed nothing. He only listened patiently, as if listening to a child. Maddening, this man, Strabo had thought once again. Would he not listen to reason? Strabo went on to describe at length the horrors that the Carthaginians would bring down upon the people of Asturias.

"You must know this to be true," Strabo said at last.

Nargonne put his feet to his mount, nudging him forward. He put his hand kindly on Strabo's shoulder.

"Strabo," he said, "please don't mention such tales to my people."

And he rode ahead.

They didn't attract as much attention as Nargonne had feared, at least not at first. They were just one more small group out of thousands of bedraggled travelers. As they made their way down, they encountered more and more campsites until the area grew so thick with the crowd they had to pick their way through.

The array of tribes was overwhelming. As expected, there were many Celtiberians, easily identifiable by the tight bronze skullcaps they wore as helmets. There were also Celts from the north, draped in skins and strutting around with their distinctive heavy trousers that ended at the calf. Those mercenaries with the long capelike cloaks wrapped around them were Lusitanians. There were forest Cantabrians and Belli, Sardinians from the islands, Balearics with their famous slings, Ligurians, Citerions. Turdetani, Insubrians, Cisalpine Gauls, Ulterions, Carpetani, Braneus, and Boii. And then there were the Africans: Libyans, Liby Phoenicians, and the fierce-looking Blastophoenicians with their cantilevered armor and teardrop shields.

There were no other Asturians like themselves. And no Usson.

There were thousands of the battle hardened Carthaginian professional elite. Their much-heralded Campaign Escort corps doubled as the world's first military police force and they ran the show. Hannibal would be among them. It was rumored he took to wigs and disguises, but Strabo never believed that. The truth is, one could see him coming from a considerable distance, as he never traveled without a contingent of dozens of bodyguards, even in his own camp.

If anything about the Asturians captured anyone's attention at all, it was their horses, for horses were few in this army. Nargonne warned them all. "Look to your mounts," he said.

He was worried about theft, especially among an unorganized plain full of mercenaries. Had these men been well off already, they wouldn't be here, Nargonne knew. They would be at home earning a living and raising their families.

His worries about crime would not prove unfounded, even though the Carthaginians were getting the word out that their rule was law. Already two executions for weapons theft had taken place in two days. One man told his story, another told his, an officer drew his sword, and one man fell headless to the ground. The process took less than a minute and justice was not the object. The object was order.

Remarkably, tribal feuds and simmering disputes were rarely an issue here. The Spanish Peninsula was sparsely populated and its peoples widely dispersed from coast to coast. The tribes came from so far away from each other that few of them knew much about the others, let alone had had opportunities to clash in the past.

This was in sharp contrast to the hordes of warlike tribes of Gauls to the north. Those tribes were mad for combat. Internecine warfare infected the whole northern European continent. Blood lust and villainy ruled. If they meant to keep people from their territories, it worked. It was one of the most dangerous areas in the world. No one had any interest in even passing through southern Gaul. Until now.

Hannibal's unprecedented invasion force would be marching directly into the teeth of Gaul territory. There would be no subtlety or covert action. None was possible with an army of this size. The Gauls would wake up to see a giant column of armor moving through their lands and their initial reaction would be to fight, to ambush, to loot. But in truth, Carthaginian silver and gold had already made its way there in the form of tolls and bribes, enough to ensure safe passage by some tribes. But only some. Not everyone had reacted kindly to Carthaginian overtures. Just how hostile they were was not altogether clear.

Hannibal's forces would soon find out.

Nargonne and company made their way confidently through the wide-ranging campsites, looking for the famed Numidian horsemen. They had to dodge countless carts and baggage trains, which ferried the mountains of supplies required of any army on the move. There were a thousand food wagons and cooking wagons of every variety: "cold" wagons for fruit and vegetables, "airing" carts for processing large quantities of game into dried meats and jerky for the troops, "catch" vans filled with trapping equipment so that the troops could readily catch as much of their own food as possible.

There were also "harvest" trains: extra long carts for carrying grain, roots, and nuts gathered along the way. The Carthaginians were experienced campaigners and the timing of this invasion was no accident. Although many would wonder why Hannibal would ever conceive of traversing the icy Alps at any time other than the absolute crest of summer, logistics demanded otherwise. This army would march through southern Gaul, home of the most fertile lands of the Mediterranean, exactly at the height of harvest. And there was no one along the way with power enough to deny them their take.

There were the water, bread, and cheese carts. There were metalworking wagons and cobbler wagons for footwear. There were wine wagons. Cooper wagons for container construction and repair. Lumber wagons for building bridges and rafts and siege equipment in the field. There were clothes trains, armor trains, arrow trains, spear trains, blacksmith trains, and even entertainment trains, where for a few pieces of copper or silver rustled up among the men, singers and strummers would put on shows that were both ribald and drunken.

There were countless weapons carts freighting swords, shields, knives, spears, javelins, arrows, and the like. And there were the always intimidating catapults on wheels. These would send missiles rocketing toward the enemy at inescapable speed. The missiles themselves would be oversize iron arrows or spears capable of blasting clear through an enemy warrior, armor and all. Some of these weapons could launch large balls of iron slag or hunks of rock chiseled to a jagged edge for maximum carnage upon impact. The giant lithobolos, constructed of oak and bronze springs, could fling a two-stone projectile a thousand paces. The resulting strike would shatter an iron wagon to fragments or split an armored horse in half.

The carts and wagons were pulled by the usual variety of draft beasts: mules, packhorses, oxen, wormy ponies, and even a few goats and dogs.

All of these support wagons made up the army's always vulnerable baggage train. The baggage train was usually broken into segments during the march so it could be defended more easily. Hostile forces and professional brigands were as bold as wolves and would attack any train carrying the slightest cargo of value. Many a man was slain for the copper in his cooking pot.

When the army was on full march, stray dogs, which followed the baggage train like flies, acted as watchdogs, providing fair warning against ambush and anything else amiss. To encourage their company, they were fed scraps by the baggage train command.

When Nargonne and Ribas encountered hay and granary wagons crisscrossing the fields, they knew they were close and now they could smell horses strong on the wind. The hair and droppings and urine of thousands of horses. Strabo was glad the blasting heat of midsummer was long past or the stench would be overpowering.

Then they saw them.

They were staked out along the river upstream from everyone else and they were a sight to behold. The legendary Numidian cavalry was the most formidable military phenomenon of the day. And here they were in full force. Ten thousand of them.

The Numidians established a camp within a camp. A special breed within Hannibal's army, they were paid well and they earned it. They fought with bundles of short javelins at their sides and would attack in waves, striking, regrouping, striking again. The speed of their horses and their skill at skirmishing made them hard to kill. The dead they left behind could attest to that. No one in this army questioned a Numidian and they acted accordingly.

And their horses. Now, that was a spectacle no one on the plain had witnessed before! Ten thousand horses. So many, it seemed as if they had taken over the world. The animals ranged for more than a league along the river's bank. Many were holed up in hundreds of temporary pens of timber and rope. Some stayed with riders and others roamed freely, close to their masters and their tents. The horses themselves were of all types, but mainly they were desert horses. Like the mountain Barbs of the Asturians, they were strong, nimble, and fast.

Thousands of Numidian tents covered the area so that the place resembled a rambling African marketplace. The Numidians had adopted the typical Iberian dress: white tunics with purple borders and sandals. They were of dark complexion and stocky—a strong people. The Asturians felt a kinship toward them, for they were horsemen like themselves.

Nargonne and his crew came to a cluster of large tents with poles planted out front sporting bright feathers of many colors, which signified that they were the administrative center of the cavalry. Nargonne and Ribas dismounted and went inside.

Sargonne beamed at Strabo. The smell of horses filled the air. Heaven for Sargonne, Hades for Strabo.

Things went smoothly inside and the administrative officer handed Nargonne his credentials. "Report to Commander Hamar. He wears the red of the Falcon Group."

Nargonne nodded officiously but beamed inside. Red was the color of Machoba's regiment. Nargonne rubbed his growing beard. *I hope the arrogant bastard doesn't recognize me,* he thought.

Nargonne and Ribas left the tent and rejoined the group. No one spoke.

"Quiet today, are we?" Nargonne said.

Everyone smiled, but still no one said a thing.

"Nerves," Nargonne said, and he put his hand on his son's shoulder. "Nerves are good. They give you strength when you need it."

He turned his horse. "Look for the red banners."

They walked into the Numidian quarters of camp. Horses from all over the riverside snorted happily and the air spoke a constant purr of the whinnying and nickering of horses at ease. The Asturian mounts were comfortable with all of the other horses. Their herd, their kind.

The Numidians and the Carthaginian officers were recuperating while they had the chance. They had just marched a hundred leagues over the last month and there were only weeks to go now before they reached the foot of the Alps.

Everywhere, men tended to their weapons and their mounts. Saddles were being repaired and rubbed down against the coming cold. Horses were being groomed of a month of trail dust and their bridles and tack were oiled and fixed. Overloaded carts growled throughout the lines ferrying all variety of horse-tending gear and materials.

Ribas was the first to see the line of fluttering red banners clipped to tall poles along the river's edge that marked the Red Falcons' officer corps. Here they would find Hamar. And Machoba.

Nargonne could not help but notice what lay across the river. There, safely separated by water from the rest of the gathering military horde, was a baggage train unto itself. It was composed of twelve strong wagons with sides and roofs of stout oak reinforced by bands of Celtic hard iron. Each wagon was pulled by a pair of healthy oxen of the strongest breed. The wagons were painted blue and red, the colors of Carthage, and decorated with an ironic mix of doves and military frescoes. The military frescoes were an obvious decoration; the doves, not so obvious. But the dove was a favorite symbol of Carthage.

This train was guarded by at least three hundred foot soldiers and one hundred mounted men. The wagons were equipped with three sets each of heavy axles and wheels reinforced with thick metal bands. Each wagon was topped by a short wooden tower sheathed in protective iron plates. The soldiers protecting this train could fire down at any attacker with relative impunity, reload behind the barrier, then rise and fire again.

Many assumed this to be the leader's baggage train, suitable for Hannibal himself, and it is true that some field generals, particularly Roman ones, traveled with such fanfare. But this was Hannibal's operation and he traveled with the rest of the crowd, as a soldier. This heavily fortified wagon train had another purpose.

Nargonne marveled at the Carthaginian way. Hannibal's invasion of Italy was years in the making and cost an unheard-of amount in silver and gold. The Carthaginians would enter a land and buy or bribe their way through it. Then they would buy soldiers. They would buy entire armies. They would buy loyalty and passage. And then they would buy weapons, munitions, supplies, and food for their soldiers. They would even pay the occasional ransom, he thought.

Although the experienced Nargonne could spot a treasure train when he saw one, even he could not have guessed that the riches ferried along on this mission were one of the greatest collections of gold ever mobilized. Or that the gold and silver on this mission consisted entirely of simple, crude bars: another clever tactic employed by Hannibal's treasurers, since some tribes did not want to be caught with Carthaginian gold. The whole game for many in this region was to be neutral and not favor too obviously Carthage over Rome. Thus, the valuable bars carried no markings so that any tribe was free to be bought without being accused of taking sides.

The fortified train carried thousands of talents of these bars. Although he did not know the exact nature of the treasure, Nargonne knew each wagon carried enough wealth to buy an entire naval fleet, if need be. The amount of gold and silver on this campaign would be staggering.

Nargonne and Ribas exchanged looks but said nothing. There was nothing to be said about such an impossible fortune, thought Nargonne. And nothing would be said. Not yet.

———

The legendary Carthaginian work ethic did not neglect training. Combat skills and tactics were being perfected from sunrise to sunset. Cavalry units and foot soldiers drilled in mock war games and in formal attack formation until every possible battle contingency had been addressed. Elephant brigades trained with the infantry. Leaders from diverse tribes conferred often. Weapons practice time was doubled and proficiency rewarded. Promotions were earned by the cartful. For Hannibal, the time for urgency had arrived. When sword met sword in anger, the Carthaginians would be ready.

Chapter 10

*M*ay I go see the elephants, Father?"

Naturally, Santandar was excited about the presence of the elephants. They created a sensation wherever they appeared, including the battlefield. Nargonne leaned close to his son.

"Leave the dog and take Tourek with you. Speak to no one. Do you hear me? If you are spoken to, walk away. Do you understand?"

"Yes, sir!" The boy nodded and skipped off to collar Tourek.

Nargonne had been directed to a rear quarter of the Numidian cavalry camp. There, they staked out some space and waited for orders. Now the smoke from their fire joined thousands of others.

They were surrounded by horsemen like themselves: recently gathered mercenaries, but not members of the Numidian corps. A few had already proved themselves in small skirmishes before reaching the Pyrenees, but most had not. There were several hundred of them from a variety of Spanish tribes. They all seemed pleased, but Ribas and Strabo knew the fate that awaited them all. They would be first wavers, launched to gauge enemy strength. And first wavers suffered heavy losses.

Nargonne had again warned everyone to say little, and if forced to speak at all, speak only Greek. Mallouse helped Sargonne tend to the horses. Cabo's tail lay still for once and he slept on the ground soundly, oblivious to the crowded scene. Molena rested out of sight beneath a cotton canopy. Barbestro hunched next to her and they whispered together. He had been fidgety and restless as soon as they entered the camp. "Stop looking around like a child," Nargonne had snapped.

They would find Marinne soon enough.

The elephants—everyone craned their necks to see the beasts. Even experienced soldiers never got used to these awesome and unpredictable animals. Santandar leaped alongside Tourek like a boy at a fair.

The elephants were unpenned, only a chain attached to a deeply driven stake kept them. The elephant brigade was accustomed to the rest of the army parading by in fascination and so tolerated the crowds. Attendants fed them and brushed them with great care, as they were an extremely valuable element of Hannibal's army. There were thirty-seven of them in all and they occupied a wide area all to themselves. They were fed fat bundles of grasses and buckets of grain. They were gray and intelligent-looking, and Santandar thought them fantastic creatures from another world.

The animals towered over the largest horses. Their ears were the size of blankets and their feet as wide as wine barrels. Their skin was tough and wrinkly. When one of them restlessly stamped the ground with its heavy feet, the earth shook all around.

Aside from the sheer mass of their mighty heads and bodies, it was their trunks and tusks that men found most fascinating. How odd those trunks looked and how strangely the elephants manipulated the snakelike appendages with both strength and agility. Santandar watched as one of the animals lowered its thick trunk and plucked a single stalk of grass from the ground.

Their tusks gleamed a dangerous yellow. Even Tourek sucked in his breath at the sight of the tusks. They stretched longer than a man's leg! Great weighty sabers, which one could only imagine spearing men clean through and then tossing their punctured bodies aside like bothersome rodents.

An elephant occasionally would stand its trunk straight out and trumpet loudly, garnering gasps and cheers from onlookers.

Their handlers were many and a full train of equipment carts supported the all-but-wild animals. A war elephant in full battle gear was a terrifying sight. Their heads would be protected by bronze plating, which wrapped around their foreheads, and by hinged flaps that hung down over their ears. Each tusk would be fitted with a razor sharp iron tip. Broad, spiked leglets circled each leg, to prevent men from getting too close, and great sheets of leather and bronze armor hung at their sides.

Large boxes clad in toughened hide and bronze plates would be affixed to the backs of the beasts, and from here bowmen and spearmen would strike out at the enemy below.

Elephants trumpet loudly when they charge and kill by

trampling and goring. Once enraged, they become difficult to control, ripping into crowds of foot soldiers and scattering them with angry sweeps of trunk and tusk. Vindictive, elephants were known to ignore the battle all around them and concentrate on one poor victim, trampling him relentlessly into the ground, grinding his bones and flesh into a bloody mash on the battlefield.

It was not only men who feared the beasts, but horses. Hannibal's cavalry trained extensively with them so as to familiarize horses with their sound, their smell, their size. The elephant drivers were heavily armored, for enemy troops quickly learned to target them. Kill the driver, take out the beast.

Tourek and Santandar watched the beasts for a long time.

"I wouldn't want to be anywhere near one of those in battle," said Santandar. Tourek winked at him.

"Stay behind the beast and then it can only kill you with its dung."

When Tourek and Santandar made their way back to their campsite, they could see immediately that something was wrong.

"Ribas gone," Sargonne told them.

Cavalry officers had come by recruiting horsemen. It seemed a small tribe of Gauls to the north had rebuffed Hannibal's entreaties for passage through their territory, sending back only the Carthaginian emissaries' heads as their answer.

"No mercy," Hannibal had said, and General Hanno, the cavalry commander, was sending a small force of three hundred men to dispatch the unruly Gauls. Hanno had decided to send slingers and cavalry swordsmen and put a colonel in charge of the operation.

The colonel had assembled the slingers on horseback, and not wanting to waste seasoned veterans on rabble, he selected a number of new recruits to march with the force.

They had asked for volunteers and Strabo, Ribas, and Mallouse had gone. Nargonne made himself scarce so as not to be recognized.

"Why avoid them, Nargonne?" Tourek asked him.

Molena answered for him. "The colonel in charge of the operation is Machoba," she said.

Tourek cursed his luck and declared he should have been there to go along. Nargonne reassured him that everything was going to be fine. Still, for the first time, real worry descended upon the group. It was nothing specific, those three were capable of handling themselves, they all knew that. But they were getting close now.

Machoba . . . Marinne . . . their task.

The anxiety of it quieted them and they slept restlessly in their bedrolls that night, the low din of thousands of campsites enveloping them.

The next morning, things heated up further. The Carthaginian military assemblage in Andorra was complete. Tribes and reinforcements from all over the Spanish Peninsula had arrived and were accounted for. Some laggards were still en route, but Hannibal would not wait. It was the tenth month of the year and the Alps were getting colder by the day. While Hannibal meant to cross them in winter, he did not mean to attempt the impossible. The mountains were virtually impassable in midwinter, the last and first months of each year. A few weeks would make all the difference. Early winter was a stretch—but achievable. Achievable and still a surprise for the Roman garrisons sleeping on the Italian side.

They would be moving out at once.

The order reverberated over the wide plain. Sargonne prepared the horses while Nargonne gathered up his son and the others.

Molena calmed her horse and rubbed his graying withers. "It's an adventure, Archon. You will be a great hero." She kissed his muzzle and smiled bravely, though she didn't feel it. They had not been in camp long enough to locate her sister, though they knew she must be there.

They mounted up and Sargonne created a train to tow the horses they had rescued from the bandits. He had taken a liking to them and decided they were a charity case worthy of his attention. "Horses good," he had said. "Only skinny." He kept their loads light as he was determined to fatten them up.

Nargonne hurried them along. He wanted to be near the front of the advance, near Machoba's Red Falcons.

As they rode out, Molena sidled up to Nargonne.

Nargonne gestured ahead. "She's up in that train somewhere. We'll find her, understand?"

Molena nodded. She looked toward the hills, where Ribas, Souk Mallouse, and Strabo had ridden off with the cavalry.

"I'm worried about him," she said. "He had better come back alive."

"Your riding protégé?"

"No, not him. Castaine."

"Ah, of course. Castaine." Nargonne was smiling to himself. He looked at the girl but couldn't see much beneath all those bandages.

"That horse will probably save Strabo's life," he said.

"I was thinking maybe Castaine would kill him instead."

Now Nargonne could make out the smile in Molena's eyes and they both laughed for the first time in days.

The great horde began filing out of the valley. The elephants trumpeted in the distance and the countless wagons creaked and groaned under the weight of their baggage. It took the entire day for the army to exit Andorra and form up into a line that stretched to the horizon. The ground trembled beneath the feet of men and beast.

When they reached the top of the valley, Nargonne turned and surveyed the army marching behind them. It was an awe-inspiring sight. Certainly no man alive had witnessed an invasion force of this magnitude before. In the middle of the line, Nargonne could just make out the blue-and-red wagons of the treasure train tucked directly behind the bread and kitchen wagons. The treasure guard fanned out on both sides and seemed to be protecting the food as much as the treasure. *Not a bad idea,* thought Nargonne. *There are times when food is treasure itself.*

Farther down the line, he could discern the hulking shapes of the marching elephants. And then the line grew so distant, Nargonne could no longer make out distinct shapes. A haze hung above the throbbing column.

Nargonne shuddered. *I wouldn't want to see this coming my way,* he thought.

Machoba's attack regiment was soon a day ahead of the main force. They followed their forward scouts with as much speed as Machoba dared without exhausting the horses. They had marched the night before and only rested a few hours before starting again.

The air grew cooler and that saved the horses' strength. This was sparsely populated country, poor for farming, so they encountered few people. Only a handful of goat herdsmen watched warily from nearby hillsides.

Mallouse had informed an officer that he was an accomplished slinger and so he had been assigned to the hundred-strong Balearic slinger group. Ribas and Strabo stayed with the sword and shield cavalry, numbering around two hundred. Strabo kept his mouth shut, as ordered by Nargonne. But Strabo noticed Ribas making small talk with Machoba's favorite lieutenant, Akdar. Akdar was big and powerful-looking and he bore a long sword, a weapon so heavy it could smash most other swords to pieces. Few could handle it well. Ribas then rode boldly out in front of the rank and file, as if he were an officer.

They marched for a day and a half before they came upon the Gauls late in the second day among a series of lightly forested hills. They were as described by intelligence: comprised of three hundred men on foot with only a handful of horses. The Gauls spotted the approaching cavalry too; they made a few false rushes, only to retreat over a small stream to an easily defensible position. Behind them was a narrow gully that led into steep rocks and hills behind. Easy country to disperse and disappear into. Ground the Gauls were familiar with. Country difficult for horses.

The Gauls massed there and lit a few fires in defiance. The hardy Gauls were dressed against the chill in the air—earth-colored trousers of heavy cloth and cloaks of animal hides and fur. Some wore head coverings of fox or cat or bear. Some even wore copper helmets studded with horn and antler. They carried short shields of bronze and hide. They banged their swords against them.

Machoba gathered his three hundred horses on a rise lined with evergreens overlooking the Gauls, eight hundred paces away. Machoba asked the leaders of each group of fifty horses to assemble around him. Strabo again noticed Ribas nudging his horse into their midst.

Machoba himself was a big man. His beard was trimmed neatly and his shoulders stretched wide beneath it. His face and arms were pockmarked with scars from years of fighting and skirmish. An accomplished rider, he held his horse comfortably. His armor was polished meticulously and a costly ivory-handled sword stuck from his weapons belt.

Akdar and Machoba's other lieutenants made the usual suggestions. Wait till nightfall. Draw them out with false charges. Send a flanking force behind them. Machoba listened, thinking. Light would be fading soon.

Ribas knew he was on dangerous ground, but here was an opening. He took the gamble and spoke.

"We have one hundred slingers," he said.

The statement hung in the air for a moment.

Machoba's lieutenants stiffened at the gall of the newcomer and Akdar glared at him. He would make an unsolicited suggestion to a Carthaginian officer?

But Machoba said nothing. Instead, he surveyed Ribas from head to toe. His bright eyes burrowed into Ribas with cold amusement. *Usson?* he thought. *Maybe. But that is of little matter. Our mercenary ranks are full of brigands of questionable background and all claim a more legitimate pedigree.*

"What do you have in mind, Usson?" was all he said, a note of derision on the word "Usson." The Usson had no reputation for battle and Akdar snickered, fingering the long sword at his side.

Ribas coolly ignored him and told Machoba his plan. When Ribas had finished, Machoba smiled. He took off his helmet and ran his fingers over his bald scalp.

"If your little stunt fails, I kill you, of course," Machoba said.

"Of course," said Ribas without concern.

"Ha!" Machoba laughed, and he gave the orders to his astonished lieutenants. An hour later, they were ready.

Machoba separated his cavalry into two groups: two hundred on the rise above the wide canyon, and one hundred just below the rise, closer to the Gauls and squaring off with them from six hundred paces. Strabo stayed with the two hundred behind who readied their swords and shields. In front, the one hundred's horses stomped and pranced, anxious for the coming charge. The hundred carried no shields. Only swords could be seen at their hips and long bows slung over each shoulder.

The Gauls were now grouped at the mouth of the ravine, where there was no cover, but they could turn and retreat up the old riverbed. So while the numbers of each force was about the same, the Gauls had the advantage of quick escape.

At Machoba's hand signal, the battle horns blew and the lower one hundred cavalry men shouted as one. While the upper two hundred waited, the one hundred below surged their mounts forward toward the Gauls.

Watching with the two hundred, Machoba leaned forward in his saddle. The man he had selected to lead the charge was naturally the man who suggested it. Ribas. This was a minor skirmish against rabble, so why not? What's more, Machoba liked Ribas's idea. Machoba had not achieved his rank with an inferior head for tactics.

Akdar could see Ribas's greased ponytail and gray tunic flapping as he galloped. He rode in the middle of the line. *Bold, yes, but we'll soon see how smart the upstart is,* thought Akdar.

As the attackers closed the distance on the Gauls, the Gauls began blowing horns and beating their weapons. They shrieked war cries at the top of their lungs. Their yelling may have been good for their morale, but it did nothing to slow down their foe.

As they drew within five hundred paces, Machoba's battle horns signaled three short blasts and Ribas and the one hundred pulled their bows from their backs and shook them above their heads. One hundred galloping horsemen. One hundred bows in one hundred upraised fists.

The Gauls drew their weapons. Short swords, axes, and spiked clubs. They bristled in front of the charge like angry hornets.

Now four blasts from the battle horns and the hundred horsemen yanked on their reins and abruptly pulled to a stop. Each cavalryman just a span apart from the next, they dismounted and knelt in the dirt. Each quickly fitted an arrow to their bow and fired at the mob of Gauls. While the first arrows were still in the air, the men quickly fitted a second arrow and fired a second round. The sky before the Gauls was filled with arrows and they stood transfixed, watching hundreds of arrows arcing their way.

And then the first wave of arrows fell, followed by the second. There was a moment of silence as the Gauls realized what had just happened.

All of the arrows fell short. They dropped to the ground like harmless litter, the nearest still one hundred paces away from them. The Gauls erupted in gales of howling laughter. They brandished their weapons and guffawed loudly, hurling even louder insults at the incompetent archers.

Akdar looked at Machoba, but his colonel only grinned at the sight. They watched Ribas raise his right arm and point it forward. At this signal, the one hundred ran fifty more paces forward, leading their mounts behind them. Then they stopped and knelt in the dirt again.

Again they fitted arrows to their bows, and with a wave from Ribas, they all fired. The arrows flew as before and landed closer, striking the dirt just paces in front of the Gauls this time.

The three hundred Gauls could not contain themselves. They howled with laughter at this second show of ineptitude and shouted new insults, this time generously using Hannibal's name in vain.

Back on the evergreen rise, Machoba barked, "Ready." He looked down the line. The two hundred were indeed ready. The horses champed at their bits.

To the sound of the jeering throng before them, Ribas and the one hundred stood to their feet. Ribas raised his left hand and the bows were all cast to the ground. Each of the one hundred reached into their belts and produced long leather strapping attached to a launching pouch. Slings.

Though the men wore the white and purple of Iberia,

they were all Balearic—the famed Balearic slingers. They had concealed missile bags behind their backs, each bag containing thirty polished metal discs and spheres of a quarter-stone weight each. Plenty of weight to kill.

Even the Gauls knew that slingers have four times the range of archers. The Gauls realized too late they had been duped into allowing slingers to sneak into range. And at this distance, the slingers had slipped well into their kill zone.

A hundred arms whirled above a hundred heads and a hundred stones rocketed in on the Gauls. Then another hundred and then another round, as fast as a man could put his foot to the ground. The sky above the Gauls was dark with polished iron projectiles whistling into their numbers. The missiles found their marks with astonishing accuracy. The chaos was so sudden the Gauls had only time to deploy their shields in panic.

From the hill, Strabo watched and smiled. *Ribas, you are a sneaky one!* he thought.

Machoba gave the order.

"Charge!" he shouted, and two hundred sword and shield thundered down the hill toward the panicking Gauls.

The Gauls never even noticed the new charge. They were drowning in a hailstorm of iron missiles, and the missiles thumped into their targets again and again. A bullet from a sling is not like an arrow. A direct hit is desired, but not required. Even a miss would ricochet off shield or body only to plunge into someone else. The slingers' finely crafted projectiles shattered limbs, punctured torsos, and burst skulls in wide sprays of red as their victims struggled and spun in vain to escape.

The slingers ceased their fusillade as Machoba's second wave of cavalry passed through their ranks en route to the overwhelmed Gauls. Then the slingers drew their swords and followed.

Every Gaul was hit multiple times. They bumped into one another and stumbled over each other in the frenzy to escape as Machoba's second wave of cavalry crashed into what was left of them.

The Gauls collapsed in ragged heaps of broken and bloodied bodies. The cavalry tore through their ranks, swinging their swords and hacking at every man standing. Some Gauls valiantly fought back but were overcome. Less than a handful were able to reach the gully and escape. In a matter of minutes, the Gauls had laughed with each other, tripped over each other, and died on each other.

The few that had escaped in the confusion didn't bother Machoba. They would return to their tribes and report the massacre and there would be fewer of these irritations in the future as a result. Nearly three hundred Gauls had been killed. The Carthaginian regiment suffered only a few wounded and had not lost a man.

Machoba posted sentries for the night and waited until daybreak to clean up the scene. His men collected what useful weapons they could from the dead Gauls, which were few, because the Gauls' swords were in bad repair and their other weapons, the crude axes and clubs, did not fit with Carthaginian tactics. They also collected many baskets' worth of bracelets, amulets, and necklaces, as well as the oversize gold rings and big gaudy buckles popular with these people.

It took two hours to retrieve all salvageable arrows

(many had been crushed beneath the hooves of the charging cavalry) and to locate and reclaim the expensive missiles employed by the slingers. Most were found. Many were imbedded in the bodies of the dead and had to be pried free. The practiced Balearics used their daggers for this.

By early morning, Machoba's cavalry was back through the evergreens and marching northeast to reunite with the main force. The officers invited Ribas to ride with Machoba's lieutenants and slapped him on the back with hearty congratulations, which Ribas accepted with a characteristic absence of enthusiasm. Only Akdar remained aloof. He was never comfortable when another gained the favor of Machoba. Strabo rode nearby and Akdar thought he saw a look pass between the man and Ribas.

Machoba rode up to Ribas and without preamble announced, "It appears I don't get to kill you today."

"Perhaps some other time," said Ribas.

"Perhaps." Machoba rode silently for a moment, then said, "In the meantime, you're a lieutenant."

He spurred his horse and abruptly rode on without another word. *Usson or no, he is a clever bastard,* thought Machoba. *And I can use clever bastards.*

It was two days before Machoba's regiment rejoined the main line. The regiment was ahead of the march by now and the advancing army was not hard to find. They could see the dust kicked up by the oncoming march from several leagues away. They rested their horses and waited for the column to come to them.

The sight they were treated to was similar to the sight Nargonne had seen looking back over his shoulder from the head of the column. But it was different too. At first there was no noise as the giant thing crawled their way. But as the afternoon wore on, the oncoming host began to emit a low, subterranean murmur. Murmur grew to growl and growl grew to roar as the advancing army overtook their position.

Mago, Hannibal's official captain of the march, had wisely broken the interminable column into three lengths to manage it more easily. Strabo, Mallouse, and Ribas made their way separately back to Nargonne, and when the column stopped for the night, the group gathered close around their fire and spoke in low voices.

"She's here," announced Barbestro.

"We *think* she is here," corrected Nargonne.

But Barbestro was sure. He and Tourek had marched ahead under the pretense of selling some of their extra horses. They had come close to the Red Falcons' main party and glimpsed a column of support wagons.

There were several wagons in particular that got their attention. Unlike the others, ribbons and pennants festooned them, and Barbestro swore he smelled sweet perfume and heard women's voices. But most telling, the wagons were guarded. If concubines traveled with the Red Falcons, then this is where they would be.

Barbestro's stomach had leaped and Tourek put out an arm to hold him back.

"Later," he had said.

It was unnecessary. Barbestro was anxious, but not stupid. He wondered for the hundredth time how Nargonne planned to rescue her. The time was approaching.

———

Despite the best efforts of the Campaign Escort corps in charge of supervising logistics, the sprawling line of the advancing army stretched out as the days wore on. Nargonne's group found themselves bunched with a long line of Celts just behind the last of the Numidian cavalry. Nargonne was careful to stay close to Machoba's Red Falcon regiment, but not too close. The Campaign Escort corps was pacing up and down, keeping a close eye on the column, ready to police at a moment's notice.

After the Carthaginian elite and the Numidian cavalry, most men walked. There were assorted carts and pack animals, but horses were at a premium. The extra horses the Asturians towed, weak as they were, still attracted the envious attention of the multitude of Celts on foot.

At one point, the entire train was delayed for several hours. Nargonne wanted a look at the wagons where Marinne might be held, so he left Sargonne alone with the horses and he and the others rode forward. Strabo went off by himself for a look-see at the armory wagons in an effort to secure a suitable blade at last.

But eager eyes had been upon them. No sooner had they left when a gang of four clever Celts moved in on Sargonne. These Celts had assumed the white-and-purple tunics of the rest of the horde and so looked like any number of men. They began with small talk in Celtic, but Sargonne made it clear he could not understand them. "Speak Greek," he said.

But the men would only speak in the Celtic tongue. Sargonne tried to be friendly, but was confused by their foreign words and by the way the men milled closely about him. The men reassured Sargonne with bright smiles and warm slaps on the back. One of the men flashed a small bag of gold coins at Sargonne and pointed at the horses.

They gathered around the animals and rubbed each horse's legs and haunches, conversing in their unintelligible tongue. Thinking Nargonne might want to sell them, Sargonne tried to be helpful.

One of the men maneuvered himself on the other side of the horses while the other three distracted Sargonne. The man discreetly produced a long bronze pin and a tightly woven pig's bladder. The bladder was gorged with fresh pig's blood, but who would know the difference between the blood of a pig and the blood of a man?

The man punctured the bladder and quickly mopped a generous quantity of blood over his face and neck. He discarded the bladder on the ground and plunged the pin into the chest of the horse. The animal's eyes bulged and it shrieked loudly, rearing high and kicking. The man cried out in pain and "fell" to the ground, well clear of the horse. He spun in the dirt in agony for a moment before falling still, his face to the ground. Sargonne and the others quickly leaped to control the kicking horse. They brought it under control and Sargonne rubbed the frightened beast's muzzle, calming it with reassuring words.

The men were chattering wildly in their tongue now and Sargonne turned, horrified to see the man lying motionless on the ground, his head oozing crimson. Sargonne fetched his healing bag and ran to help the fallen man as the others gathered around.

The man was still. Sargonne's heart beat rapidly. *It all happened so fast! I use horse bandages,* Sargonne thought. He competently produced salve and bandaging from his bag.

Although the Celts made a big show of concern over the fallen man, they quickly moved aside so that Sargonne could tend to him.

The horses forgotten, Sargonne knelt in the dirt and began frantically wiping the blood from the man's head. Still, the man did not move. *Dead?* thought Sargonne. Had the horse killed him? He sponged the blood from the man's head, wrung the bandages, and sponged some more. He looked for the wound but could find none.

Then Sargonne heard a shriek of laughter behind him and he turned to see the other three men galloping away bareback on three horses. *What? Where are they going?* To his surprise, the injured man suddenly scrambled to his feet and sprinted away after the retreating horses.

Sargonne leaped up and lunged after the man, but the man was young and fast and gone down the long column in an instant. Sargonne was left standing there, stunned. He turned and gazed dumbly around. Three horses were gone. There was a bloody spot on the ground where the wounded man had fallen. Sargonne's eyes fell on the dusty pig bladder lying in the dirt. He stooped and picked it up, rolling it in his hands. Was the man hurt badly? He still did not understand. All he knew was that a man was hurt and three horses were run off.

Then it dawned on him. The men had fooled him and stolen the horses. This was not the first time he had experienced the cruelty of others. He closed his eyes in shame and a helpless fury grew inside him. Tears welled up behind his eyes. He cried privately there, his shoulders trembling gently against the solid haunches of a silent horse.

When the rest of the group returned, Sargonne explained

in halting words what had happened. They listened in silence. Not much explaining was required. Nargonne cursed himself. Barbestro and the Souks were inflamed at the bold theft. Molena and Santandar seethed at the affront bore upon their helpless uncle, but they reassured him that all was well, nonetheless.

Ribas, too, was furious, but like Nargonne, more at himself than Sargonne. Only Strabo seemed removed. On the one hand, Strabo thought, *The man is slow, what did they expect?* On the other, he felt an anger he could not identify. He had been robbed, it seemed, though the horses were not his. Why should he feel abused when it was Sargonne who suffered?

Strabo watched in astonishment when Ribas dismounted, put an arm around Sargonne, and told him not to worry. Strabo knew Ribas would sooner touch a snake than another human being, yet here he reassured Sargonne with dignity and affection. *It is only because he is Nargonne's brother,* Strabo thought.

Souk Tourek had studied the pig's bladder, wrung bloody droplets from it over the ground and pronounced that it was a bad omen. *Blood is always a bad omen,* Strabo thought.

Still, over Nargonne's objections, the men insisted on retrieving the lost horses. Nargonne only relented when Ribas reminded him the matter was more about restoring the honor of his brother than it was about the horses. And Nargonne knew they would be in need of extra horses soon if his plans came to fruition.

Later, as night fell and the others began to bed down for the night, Strabo approached Nargonne, who sat with Ribas. Nargonne was fiddling with an iron pin, idly etching the tiny figure of a horse head on the blade of his knife. Ribas was sharpening his sword with a Macedonian stone file, polishing the blade in short strokes, the Phoenician method, Strabo thought. *Where have you fought, Ribas, and for whom?* he wondered. *For just anyone? Like me?*

Strabo pushed these thoughts aside and bade Nargonne sit for a talk.

The three of them settled around the fire out of earshot of the others and Strabo cleared his throat. He knew he was not eloquent. How to begin? He would be talking to the man about his own brother. Nargonne and Ribas waited patiently.

Strabo said, "This is a tricky business."

Nargonne and Ribas glanced at each other.

"That it is," said Nargonne.

"It might be too much for some of us."

Strabo let that comment sink in.

"Some of us?" asked Nargonne.

Strabo sighed.

"Your brother," he said at last.

Nargonne bristled as he had a thousand times at this, as if a limb of his own had been disturbed.

"I fear for him," said Strabo.

Ribas said nothing and looked into the fire.

"And I fear for us," added Strabo, completing his argument. "He is a liability and you know it."

The nod from Ribas was nearly imperceptible, but Nargonne knew the man well. Ribas agreed.

Nargonne stared into the fire and tried to relax. He felt tired. *Compose yourself, Nargonne. These men are warriors. Could they understand?*

Nargonne lifted a thick stake and stirred the embers of the fire.

"Have you heard of the Salcians, Strabo?"

Strabo shook his head.

"The Salcians were a proud people, Strabo, proud like us. But not like us. They put to death malformed children." Nargonne looked calmly at Strabo.

"Would you do such a thing, Strabo? Would you put to death a disfigured child?"

Strabo was quiet.

Nargonne went on. "When one was crippled or diseased, or a little slow or incompetent in the head, that one would be put to death, put to the stone, Strabo. To protect the tribe so that the tribe would not be jeopardized by their incapable members. This makes sense to you, doesn't it, Strabo?"

Strabo had to admit that it did.

"And what would you think of a man who would do such a thing? Knowing he would kill your sister if she was a fool. Or kill your son if his legs were bent. Or kill your friend if he had only one eye." Nargonne nodded his head over toward the sleeping Mallouse. "Would you feel comfortable in such a tribe?"

Nargonne scoffed.

"You know about fighting, Strabo. I think you know what makes one army defeat another. Would you fight with such people?"

Strabo did not know what made one army defeat another. He only knew what gave a man or group of men advantage. He was a skirmisher and honestly did not know what Nargonne was getting at. Nargonne looked at Ribas.

"Would you fight with them? Would you stand with them?"

Neither Ribas nor Strabo spoke. Nargonne could feel his anger growing with these two narrow-minded warriors.

"You would not. And you know not why, but I will tell you why. I will educate you, because you are both young and stupid."

Neither Strabo nor Ribas replied. Each prepared himself for the inevitable lecture.

"You would not stand with them because they would abandon you in an instant; yes, they would. Fools. The instant you were injured, became a *liability,* Strabo, you would be abandoned, for now you would have become a threat to *their* survival. You. You who killed for them, risked your life for them. You who loved them and cared for them all your life. They would abandon you, Strabo"—Nargonne snapped his fingers—"in an instant."

Nargonne shook his head and rubbed his forehead. Then he laughed a joyless laugh.

"The Salcians sought perfection, Strabo, but people are not that simple, are they? Perfection is difficult to describe, isn't it? Perhaps perfection comes not one man at a time but many."

The flickering flames cast ghoullike shadows across Nargonne's face.

"Where are the Salcians now, Strabo?"

Strabo did not like Nargonne's threatening tone, but now he was trapped. Discussion and argument were Nargonne's forte.

"I don't know," Strabo said.

"I will tell you."

The dark look on Nargonne's face was one of evil satisfaction, and it disturbed Strabo. He had not seen the man like this before.

"They are all dead," Nargonne said. "Never to return to this earth. They were doomed the day they chose such a shortsighted path, and may the gods damn them."

Nargonne spat into the fire and the fire hissed back.

"Think! Are you so shortsighted to think the strength of a tribe lies only in its strongest? That is the easy answer, the simpleton's path. The truth is not always so obvious. Might you consider that a tribe's true strength lies in how it cares for its weakest?"

Nargonne let his words smolder above the fire.

"Show me a tribe that takes care of its own, *all of them,* and I will show you a tribe that will live forever."

The two younger men stared thickly into the fire.

"Such people," Nargonne continued, "will fight with the power of the gods, for they do not stand alone. They fight for more than themselves and that gives them more strength than just the strength of their own feeble bones."

Nargonne paused and tugged at his chin through his growing beard. He looked grimly at the pair.

"You may lose a hand, Strabo, and then what good are you? You may lose an arm or a leg. You may be impaled and mortally wounded, your lifeblood spilling away."

The thought of losing his sword hand made Strabo shudder involuntarily. Ribas stared into the flames. Nargonne stuck his face close to the two of them and pointed the burning end of the stake at them.

"You may be struck dead, your bloody body left on the field."

The fire crackled and hissed.

"Do you know what your dying thought will be? I will tell you: that your people will come for you. Even for your dead body, they will come. That is the type of tribe we are, Strabo, that is the type of people we are. We will come, Strabo, we will lift you and carry your lifeless body home if it costs us our lives!"

Nargonne drove the stake into the ground and stood up angrily. He did not care how many others around the nearby fires heard him.

"You will not be abandoned."

His eyes bored through Strabo and he thrust a pointed finger in his face.

"You will be carried!" Nargonne thundered. "Do you understand?"

Nargonne gathered himself, straightening his cloak. Then without another word, he spun on his heels and faded into the darkness for his bed.

The two warriors were left to contemplate the fire together.

Strabo thought of all the battles he had seen. All the lands he had visited. All the soldiers and merchants and pay bosses he had known. None was a friend. Not one. He fought for himself, didn't he? That was the only way to survive, it had to be true! For he was here when many others weren't.

He did not know why one army beat another and he was ashamed. For all his experience in combat, for all the men he had cut down and all the ghosts he had left in his wake, he knew he did not understand the larger issues associated with war. How to fight, when to fight, whom to fight. He could be no general, he knew. He felt useless for the first time in his life.

The armory was far away from here in more ways than one. These notions of Nargonne's had no place in a world ruled by weapons, Strabo wanted to think.

He and Ribas avoided looking at each other. Still, Strabo wondered, *Would you carry me, Ribas?*

Ribas was thinking the same of him.

The next morning broke with the first sustained wind of real winter. The Alps were nearing, but they weren't there yet, and if it was cold down here, the snow would be blowing in the mountains already.

Souk Tourek had rolled many stones and even sliced the pig bladder into tiny pieces, squeezing the blood in random patterns across a smoothed-over section of ground. He regarded the spatterings and muttered to himself. Strabo wished he had a gift for such things. What did the man see? Tourek finally announced in disgust that the signs told him nothing today. "The air is disturbed," he said in an explanation that explained nothing.

The march continued, but Ribas, Strabo, Barbestro, and Sargonne stayed behind. *The stolen horses.* Nargonne took the rest of the party forward, comfortable that if push came to shove, his brother would be standing beside Ribas, Strabo, and the big man. Molena had wanted to stay behind also, but Nargonne forbade it. "You keep your head low," he told her. Ribas had suggested they involve the Campaign Escort officers, but Nargonne did not want to draw undue attention to themselves. He also left Barbestro with a short lecture. "No more moping. We need you now."

The four men remaining behind settled themselves on a grassy rise overlooking the march and waited. Two

Campaign Escort officers approached them and asked them what they were doing there. They only told the officers they were "waiting for someone."

"Don't stay long," they were told, and the officers rode off.

They didn't stay long. Their plan was to wait for the guilty parties to pass, but the Asturians grew impatient after an hour or so. Strabo was concerned, as the fast-moving horde all looked the same after a while. He repeatedly asked Sargonne if he was sure he would recognize the thieves. Sargonne kept shrugging his shoulders, but after relentless badgering from Strabo, he finally shut the man up with an uncharacteristic bark. "Recognize horses!" he said. *Shades of his brother,* thought Strabo.

The thousands of Celts they watched did all start to look the same. Trudging group after trudging group. Mostly in off-white tunics, they did not make a colorful crowd. However, they were efficient and moved steadily forward at a brisk pace for an army of this size.

There were very few horses here in the middle of the march. The few animals they did see were pack animals or small herds of goat driven along near the column.

Sargonne spotted them at midday. All three of the horses. The impudent Celts had not even bothered to disguise the beasts; they had simply loaded the animals down with gear. Too much gear, Sargonne could see immediately. The poor horses were struggling again.

The thieves took only the precaution of separating the horses along the line of their troops. But any horses in this crowd were rare enough to stand out.

All day long, the others had looked at Sargonne with each passing animal and Sargonne had nodded no. But now he stiffened in his saddle. He didn't have to say a thing.

Strabo had been watching Sargonne all morning. The man had been wringing his hands with worry and thanking them all profusely for helping retrieve the horses. Strabo thought of those times when he, too, had been powerless and humiliated. This man had been good to him. He had given him sandals, his own as it turned out, and he alone never laughed when he fell from Castaine. It was Sargonne who gave Strabo his first bite to eat when Nargonne's people had rescued him from the beach. That seemed so long ago. Now it seemed like he had known Sargonne for much longer.

Ribas boldly led the group to where the stolen horses marched, ignored the stares of the passing multitude and loudly announced, "Who leads here?"

Sargonne gamely sought out the faces of the thieves, but no one looked familiar. No matter, thought Strabo, if they were here, they would be unlikely to make their presence known.

"Who leads here?" Ribas again demanded, and a tall Celt, with a brown beard nearly down to his fat belt buckle, emerged from the throng. He did not look friendly.

"I. I am Octul," he announced, and the tone of his voice matched the look on his face.

Ribas ignored the man's attitude and stated simply that he had come for his "beasts."

Strabo watched as some sixty of the Celts slowed to a stop around them. So this was their tribe, he thought. There were a few women in the group, as was the way with Celts. Some took their wives on campaign. Some even their children, though Hannibal frowned upon the practice. And of the sixty or so, they had only six pack-horses. Three were Sargonne's.

The Celts clearly took offense at Ribas's demands. Strabo noticed that two large men flanking the Celt leader, Octul, were more ready than the others. Their fingers tapping their sword hilts gave away their intentions. The Celts looked to Octul, who eyed Ribas.

Octul was wrapped in a heavy bearskin. Good for cold-weather fighting, thought Ribas, and plenty of that was coming their way. Around his waist was an ungainly bronze buckle adorned with a pair of poorly engraved stags. A Celtic short handled battle sword dangled from each hip.

Through a set of yellow and broken teeth, he smiled insincerely up at Ribas and Ribas smiled back.

"We have no beasts of yours," Octul said. "Move on."

The smile on his face belied the authoritative snap to his voice. His words were meant as an order.

But Ribas and the others stayed put. Strabo urged Castaine forward, but a subtle wave from Ribas held him back. Ribas just smiled at Octul, as before.

Octul stared at him and then scoffed and turned away, back to his troops, his long coat of bear hide dragging along behind him in the dirt. Strabo saw that the crowd of Celts were ready to move on, as if the whole affair were over.

It wasn't.

Strabo glanced sideways at Sargonne, who sat on his horse stoically, though Strabo knew he was nervous. Strabo scanned the crowd for more signs of preparation but could make out none. Only Octul's two bodyguards.

Some of the Celts in the crowd were grinning and Strabo felt outrage climbing in his throat.

Then Ribas answered Octul: "I say you do."

The large man stopped in his tracks, and as he did so, his guards put their hands on their weapons and the whole crowd hushed.

The rest of the column behind them, uninvolved, simply began moving around them on the other side in orderly fashion. This was none of their business and they weren't about to make it so, though everyone could sense the confrontation and they gawked over their shoulders as they passed.

Octul turned to face Ribas, his right hand on his sword. *Fool,* thought Ribas. *If it was me, I'd have my left hand on my sword, my weak hand, to throw off my opponent.* This man was not that clever. Neither were his two hulking guards. Octul stepped toward Ribas.

"I don't care what you say. I'm giving you a chance to move on." The grotesque smile was gone from Octul's face. "Take it."

"I will take my horses," answered Ribas.

A small contingent of Campaign Escort soldiers had finally taken note of the stoppage and were heading their way.

Octul stood now with the two guards flanking him, staring up at the men on horseback. The guards drew their swords.

Ribas spoke to Strabo without turning his head. "No fighting," he repeated. But Strabo had slipped into war mode, his mind and muscles hunched at the ready.

"We are all of the same army, friend," said Octul.

"This is true," said Ribas.

"We shouldn't quarrel over small things."

"True again."

Octul's smile returned, but only for a moment.

"So hand them over," said Ribas.

Octul laughed. "Hand them over?"

Too late. To the surprise of the Celts, one of the newcomers had dismounted and marched right up to Octul. It was Strabo.

Ribas motioned for the others to be still. Sargonne was frightened but did as he was told, and Barbestro was as motionless as stone. No silver-tongued diplomat, Strabo restated the obvious.

"Leave us our horses, that is all," he said.

Octul towered over Strabo and was unimpressed. He smiled again.

"Or what?" he said.

But Strabo said nothing, a habit tied to his concentration level when preparing to strike—a habit that did little to endear himself to others. Octul waited another moment and then turned on his heel and barked to his guards itching for a fight.

"Take him," he said.

The two guards charged and Ribas's hand went to his sword.

The crowd surged forward as the guards rushed Strabo, but Strabo only crouched, his arms hanging at his sides as if he were ready to jump.

The two men swung their weapons with Celtic cries of "Death!" and death was theirs, for Strabo suddenly spurted forward between them, ducking the blow from the man on his right. Impossibly, Strabo's sword was in his hand and he brought it backhanded through the neck of the man on his left. The man's head spiraled to the ground. Strabo whirled, and as the man who had missed him turned to strike again, the last thing that man saw was a flash of yellow blade and then he saw no more. His head, too, plopped to the ground at Strabo's feet. His body followed it, crumpling to the dirt. A fountain of red pulsed from the top of his torso, where his neck had been just a moment earlier.

The crowd was stilled as if struck by Strabo himself. Strabo crouched, untouched and at the ready, the blade of his fighting sword tinged crimson and dripping with death. *Take the head of the snake.* His eyes were on Octul.

The only sound was that of the endless column trudging by on the other side of the Celts.

"What foolishness is this?"

It was the captain of the Campaign Escort, who had galloped up with a dozen soldiers.

Still, no one spoke.

"Answer me!" the captain demanded, and he looked at Strabo, then Octul, then Ribas.

Ribas cleared his throat.

"There is a dispute," he said, "about horses."

The captain looked at the dead men on the ground and glared at Strabo, Strabo's sword unrepentant. This was the type of thing the Escort had to be careful of—with so many tribes, so many mercenaries.

"We have need of every man," the captain said. "Solve this another way."

"There is no other way," said Strabo, his eyes still on Octul.

Again there was silence until Octul broke it.

"Pankration," he declared. There was a pause and then

the crowd behind him roared its approval, shaking their weapons and beating the ground with their feet.

"How many horses?" asked the captain.

"Three," said Ribas.

The captain wasted no time. "*Pankration* it is. I shall judge, the winner keeps the horses. The yellow flags at sunset. Now disperse!"

Ribas and Octul locked eyes.

"*Pankration,*" said Ribas.

Octul nodded. His smile had returned.

Barbestro tossed Strabo a rag and Strabo cleaned his sword. Warily he sheathed it, stepped over the dead men, and got back on Castaine. Ribas turned his horse and motioned for the others to follow. They rode back up the column.

"We'll see you at the yellow flags," he shouted over his shoulder. Octul spit in the dirt, thinking, *Yes, you will, you swine.*

As they rode away, Sargonne asked, "What just happened?" Ribas explained it to him. "There will be a wrestling match tonight, Sargonne. It will be great fun. And you will get your horses back." Ribas flashed a reassuring smile at Sargonne and then looked at Barbestro.

"Won't he, Barbestro?" Ribas said.

He and Strabo looked at Barbestro, but the big man just shrugged his shoulders and stared into space.

Strabo was glancing over his shoulder, watching the Celts gather the two dead men and depart. He noticed that this tribe had not left their own in the dirt.

Nargonne was incensed. He had not wanted to draw attention to himself in any way and now they were the center attraction at an impromptu *pankration* match. He knew there were likely to be plenty of interested spectators; at this point, any break from the drudgery of the march would be welcomed by all.

The incident with the Celts had forced his hand. Only the presence of Barbestro was a small piece of good fortune. The man could wrestle. Ribas never would have agreed to the match had he not known. They had all seen him in action, but only at home. This was far different. Barbestro would be pitted against a champion Celt about whom they knew nothing.

Nargonne didn't know who might show up for tonight's sport. Even though Machoba alone might recognize him, he and Molena quickly furthered Nargonne's disguise by adding an eye patch and a turbanlike headpiece to his outfit.

What's more, the Red Falcons had come for Ribas. Several officers had ridden up and requested his presence at Machoba's camp. There had been no time for conversation and Nargonne felt it wisest to ignore Ribas as he left. Eyes narrowing, Strabo watched him go. *Now we'll see,* thought Strabo. He detected a passing look exchanged between Ribas and Souk Tourek but dismissed it as a silent good-bye.

Nargonne had stewed all afternoon about their rotten luck, and the rest of the group stayed away from him. Nargonne was rarely in a sour state for hours at a time. But this mood gave him pause to think and think he did. By the end of the afternoon, he seemed to brighten. He called Souk Tourek over for an extended chat. Then he took Strabo aside and gave him his instructions. Strabo was to act as Barbestro's second at the *pankration* match.

Strabo was stunned at Barbestro's nonchalance over the whole affair. Didn't he know what *pankration* was all about? It was the most demanding style of wrestling, where no holds or hits were barred, save three: no biting, no eye gouging, no strikes to the groin. Everything else was fair play. Strabo had seen many matches of the Greek sport in Macedonia. Few soldiers practiced it because most commanders forbade it. It was too dangerous. Soldiers were simply too valuable to be wasted on sport. Many contestants didn't live through the match, and most of the rest were debilitated for months if not for life. Besides, literal hand-to-hand combat rarely occurred in war. A soldier always had a weapon. So why waste valuable training time?

Word spread quickly and passing troops asked Nargonne which of his soldiers would be in the match.

"I haven't decided yet," Nargonne lied.

Strabo began to see coins emerge from people's tunics. The betting had begun. Molena could sense Strabo's concern and teased him.

"You just don't feel comfortable without a weapon," she told him.

"But it is pointless. There is no gain."

"There are the horses."

"They aren't worth it."

"There is Sargonne."

Yes, there is, thought Strabo. And there it was. Barbestro would risk his life for the man. Strabo wondered aloud if there might be another way out.

"Why?" Molena asked.

"He might not live through it."

The thought had never occurred to her and her brow

grew dim. Strabo regaled her with descriptions of the fights he had seen. Broken skulls. Separated limbs. Burst organs. Permanent incapacitation and death.

"Only one kind of man would engage in *pankration* in the first place," he said. "A stupid one."

Hearing all this, she joined Strabo in addressing their concerns to Nargonne, but he waved them off.

"Barbestro's skill will come to the fore," Nargonne assured them.

Strabo wasn't so sure. When the day's march had halted, Barbestro merely lay down and took a nap, snoring contentedly on his bedding. The man was as lazy as Castaine, Strabo thought.

Souk Mallouse waited patiently while his brother rolled stone after stone and scratched forms in the dirt. Tourek broke a bundle of twigs, scattered them on the ground, and studied them for what seemed an eternity. Finally he sighed and stood up. He put his stones away and turned to Mallouse, shaking his head.

"The signs are dark. There is great danger."

"Danger, yes, of course there is danger."

"I see death, brother."

"You always see death."

"I see the death of one of our own."

Mallouse was taken aback by the ashen look on his brother's face, but then a mischievous smile sneaked its way upon Tourek's face. Mallouse grinned back at him. The two chuckled and went about caring for the horses. No one noticed the extra time they spent preparing special packs and stashing them at the horses' feet.

The Campaign Escort arrived an hour before sundown

to escort the *pankrator* to the match. The soldiers were surprised to see Nargonne walk over and wake a man dozing on the ground. Barbestro rose, groggily rubbing the slumber from his eyes.

"He must weigh a hundred fifty stone!" marveled one soldier.

The Asturians mounted up and followed the Escorts, Strabo shaking his head. Nargonne rode close to Barbestro and leaned to his ear, chatting and giving the big man advice, though Barbestro seemed to ignore him.

Barbestro said little, except to Sargonne, who rode along fretting with Santandar. Sargonne knew enough to know Barbestro was going to battle for his horses.

"Horses come home," Barbestro told him with a wide smile and a hearty slap on the back. "Horses miss Sargonne."

Sargonne brightened at this, his thoughts on the animals.

They finally saw yellow flags fluttering in the evening breeze at a line of trees, where the Escorts had created a wide clearing and ringed it with baggage carts of all variety. There was even a food wagon surrounded by a covey of hopefuls trying to barter for yet another piece of bread.

Molena was startled to see hundreds of men milling about, even though Nargonne had warned them this event would attract a crowd. There was not only a huge crowd of Celts, but also Numidians and many Carthaginian officers. The men were jockeying for good places to sit around the ring. They sat on horses and makeshift benches. They crowded on the running boards of wagons and some even perched on the load beams of a catapult. And just when Molena thought the only thing missing was the elephants, she saw one amble up with its handlers just outside the ring. The animal created the usual sensation and people flocked to get a closer look.

The Carthaginian Command apparently had relaxed the drinking rules for the event, because the wine and grain spirits flowed freely and the crowd grew more rambunctious by the minute. Then Molena yanked the reins and stopped Archon in his tracks. There, among the wagons lining the great ring, were the pennants of the Red Falcons. Strabo looked at Molena.

"Things will work out," he whispered. "He's why we're here, right?"

She could see him. He stood with Akdar and several of his men in front of the wagons. Machoba. She could spot that arrogant stance from a league away. He seemed to be supervising something. And then Molena saw what it was.

Two heavy wagons rolled into the ring and men began unloading their contents in a big pile at the center of the ring. Firewood. Strabo looked at Nargonne, who suddenly looked nervous at the sight of the pyre. But if the prospect of a fiery demise bothered Barbestro, the big man didn't show it.

Fire always made Strabo shudder. Fire should be contained, he thought, in a crucible or a furnace. Untamed, it was a dangerous beast indeed. The addition of a fire in the ring had been Machoba's idea. "Makes things interesting," he had said with a grin.

Standing with a group of officers nearby was Ribas. He looked as if he belonged with them, thought Molena. A warrior. Then why had he come to Asturias? His gaze passed hers perfectly, as if he didn't see her. *You are a cold one,* she thought.

"Just do as you are told," Nargonne had said. *I will. For Marinne.*

The soldiers skillfully constructed the fire in just a few minutes and the flames began casually but were soon roaring, stoking the anticipation in the air.

Nargonne kept his distance, but the others made their way to the edge of the ring, where feed carts had been staggered to form a makeshift grandstand. Eight tall poles marked the spot, a yellow flag hanging from each. Standing there was the captain of the Escort, who had arranged the match.

Nargonne disappeared into the crowd, as did Molena with the Souks. Only Sargonne and Strabo approached with Barbestro. The captain recognized them and waved them on.

Already gathered there was a large contingent of Celts. They jeered the Asturians as they approached and this unnerved Sargonne but had no effect on Barbestro. He was stone-faced.

Strabo whispered to him, "Maybe you should start thinking about combat, about fighting, Barbestro. Prepare yourself!"

But Strabo's way was not Barbestro's. The big man ignored him.

The captain waved the crowd to quiet. "Bring in the booty!" he shouted.

The rabble of Celts parted and three horses were led into the ring. "Are these the animals in question?" the captain asked Strabo.

Strabo looked at Sargonne, who nodded.

Strabo nodded at the captain and the captain spoke in a loud voice to all that could hear.

"The winner of the match takes the animals!"

The cheers from the assemblage of Celts were joined by the hundreds of spectators lining the *pankration* ring. To Strabo, the affair had all the flavor of a dark, barbarian celebration. The leaping fire. The ring of unknown, sneering faces. The energy of the crowd.

The captain continued. "Each round shall last the length of a bottle."

Two men brought forth a water clock constructed of wood and ceramic bowls. They filled the top bowl with water from a bottle.

"There shall be no limit to the number of rounds!"

A limitless match usually meant death for the loser; the crowd roared its approval. Ribas cheered with the rest and caught Strabo's eye. He shrugged his shoulders at Strabo. *What are you up to?* Strabo thought. *Who are you with now?*

But Strabo had other things to think about.

The captain announced, "The contest will not end until one of the two contestants' seconds signals capitulation."

The Celts again erupted at this and began pointing at Strabo and Barbestro. They waved their arms and chanted in their tongue, which the Asturians could not understand. Had they, they would have heard, "Surrender! Surrender!"

"Produce your champion," the captain said. The ring of spectators crowded forward. Barbestro stepped up to the captain and some in the crowd cheered for him. Most *pankrators* ignored the crowd, concentrating on the matter at hand. Not so Barbestro. He suddenly broke into a wide grin. He raised his arms above his head, pumping the air. The crowd responded with cheers and the Celts cast forth a shower of unintelligible curses. Barbestro rotated in a slow circle and pumped his arms for the crowd. The fire burned brightly and crackled, though no one could hear it. It launched sparks high into the night.

Strabo was flabbergasted. The man was as shy as a mouse. What was this?

Barbestro then began hopping up and down to the cheers and Strabo could take no more. He put his hand on Barbestro's shoulder. "Save your strength, man."

Barbestro finally nodded, winked at Strabo, and returned to his customary passive state.

"We need a signal. What is your signal to concede?" asked Strabo.

"I won't concede," said Barbestro.

"I know, I know. You are going to win, but in the unlikely event you are bested, there is no need to suffer permanent injury, Barbestro. I will stop the fight."

Barbestro growled at him. "Do not stop the fight."

"We need you, Barbestro, in good health."

"You need me now and I am in perfect health."

"We can find other horses."

"We will take these."

Strabo sighed but Barbestro finally looked earnest, which Strabo took as a welcome sign.

"If he kills you, I will kill him," offered Strabo.

Barbestro smiled at him as if he were his best friend in the world. "From you, I would expect nothing less."

Strabo felt his spirits lift. *Maybe the big farmer will win*, he thought. But that thought would pass in a moment. The Celts suddenly came alive in a cacophony of shouts as their champion entered the ring.

The Celts were a tall people, but this man was taller still. If the hulking Barbestro tipped the scales at a hundred fifty stone, this man was easily two hundred. And as Barbestro towered over others, so the Celt towered over Barbestro. The thought that bets would be changing hands fast and furious now flashed through Strabo's mind.

Where Barbestro had clowned for the crowd, the Celt only glared at Barbestro. He raised his lips not in a smile but a snarl, revealing two rows of oversize, broken teeth that tilted like drunken tombstones in his mouth. Oblivious to everyone around him, he only had eyes for his opponent. He made no gestures. He said not a thing. He simply glowered at Barbestro as if Barbestro had just murdered his only child.

Here was a veteran *pankrator*.

His arms hung from his shoulders at the ready. His massive head was covered with a motley mane that obscured his face. His beard hung to his chest, but not for long.

Two Celts with sharp daggers descended on the great man and lopped off his long hair and cut his beard tight. There would be no advantage by yanking hair tonight.

Strabo felt the energy evacuate his limbs. The only saving grace now was that perhaps the struggle would be brief. He cursed himself. He had killed the two Celts earlier in the day and unleashed this monster on the gentle Barbestro.

The two *pankrators* stripped away their cloaks and tunics to square off bare-chested. The huge Celt handed his clothing to the man who would act as his second. Octul.

The Celt stared at Barbestro and Barbestro ignored him. There wasn't a man in the crowd who gave Barbestro a chance against the big Celt—save two. Sargonne, who assumed in his simplicity that by right they would get their horses back. And Nargonne. From behind several rows of spectators, he watched the two big men. *Good luck, Barbestro,* he thought. *Give me time.*

In the ring, Octul smiled confidently at Strabo and swiped his finger across his throat. He did not doubt the outcome. Neither did Strabo.

"The seconds will stand aside and would the colonel please do the honors!" shouted the captain.

Octul and Strabo stepped to the side of the ring, each with a parting glance at their fighter. Strabo turned to Sargonne, who carried a wad of rags and a leather water bucket. "Keep those ready," Strabo said, and Sargonne nodded vigorously, stealing a glance at the horses nearby. *His* horses.

Machoba stepped forward, looking as he always did: prepared and capable. He was dressed in light armor and a cloak of rank, his ivory-hilted battle sword dangling conspicuously from his hip. As usual, Akdar hovered at his side. Strabo thought of Molena and of a whip and lowered his eyes at Akdar. He told himself to keep his temper.

Machoba drew his sword and pointed to the timer and the water clock.

"Start the clock," he said. Then he raised his sword and twirled it in the air with a flourish. "Begin!" he cried, and he rushed from the ring, a fat grin on his face. Machoba had energy, Strabo had to give him that. Which only made the man more dangerous.

The man acting as timer tipped the top bowl and water began flowing into the lower bowl in a slim stream. It would be several long minutes before the upper bowl was empty and the first round ended.

The crowd roared. In their midst, Santandar plugged his ears and willed his eyes to close, but the excitement was too much for him. He couldn't keep them shut.

Nothing could be heard above the noise of the crowd as the two men began walking around in a wide circle, eyeing each other. Neither man made ready to attack and Barbestro seemed far too casual for Strabo's liking.

Strabo scanned the crowd for friendly faces. Mallouse had stayed behind at their camp, but Tourek stood soberly nearby, rolling stones in his hand and looking particularly grim, even for him, with Santandar at his side. Strabo couldn't see Nargonne or Molena. He only spotted Ribas, who again looked away when Strabo eyed him. Keep your mind on Barbestro, Strabo told himself.

So Strabo did not see Nargonne slip away, and on the other side of the ring, Molena do the same. Nor did he notice Ribas retreating slowly from his place. In another moment, he was gone as well.

Barbestro and the Celt measured each other, matching each other step for step. Neither man made a move toward the other and both disregarded the crowd's entreaties to the contrary. Eventually the Celt quickened his steps and Barbestro retreated, backing out to the perimeter. He was using the whole ring and steering well clear of the inferno in the center.

The entire first round went on this way until Strabo began to think the whole affair would end up a huge disappointment for the entertainment-starved throng. The only action came when an empty wine cask flew from somewhere in the crowd, narrowly missing Barbestro. Instantly a dozen Escort soldiers appeared and descended on that part of the crowd. They isolated a man and beat him senseless with the butts of their swords before dragging him away. Machoba laughed at the sport of it and pounded his fist with glee.

The upper bowl went dry and the timer announced, "Time!"

Barbestro walked calmly back to Strabo and sat peacefully on the ground. He grinned at Strabo.

"Some fight, heh?"

Meanwhile, the Celt in the ring made a great show of standing where he was and raising his arms to the crowd. The crowd responded with more cheers. All the Celt knew was that Barbestro was Usson, as all Barbestro knew about him was that he was Celt. The Celt shouted in Greek above the noise.

"Usson! I am waiting for you! Usson!"

Octul nodded his head in approval.

The Red Falcon camp was not far from the *pankration* ring and Nargonne hurried up the long line of encampments, careful not to run. Many men were still arriving for the *pankration* match, and in their eagerness, they rushed past Nargonne, ignoring him. Up ahead, Nargonne could see a short figure hurriedly limping along, her bandages fluttering in the high-plateau breeze. He sucked in his breath. *Here we go,* he thought. *You must be strong tonight, my nieces. As strong as Barbestro.*

The smaller clock that measured the recesses went dry and the timer announced, *"Pankrate!"*

Round two had begun. Strabo offered Barbestro water, but he turned it down and got to his feet. The Celt waited near the fire.

Barbestro strode confidently toward him, only pulling up short when he got within arm's length. Again the two men began circling each other, but this round would not be like the last.

The Celt circled, then suddenly feinted left, causing Barbestro to react. Then the man lunged back to his right and heaved a hulking fist at Barbestro. Barbestro ducked it easily, but the crowd reacted loudly. Now the action had started!

Barbestro again retreated toward the outer perimeter of the ring and the Celt followed, itching to deliver a blow. Strabo looked at the clock. The water bowls were of spun clay and he couldn't see how much time was left. It didn't matter, he thought. This cat-and-mouse game of Barbestro's couldn't last.

The Celt lunged forward again and swung the same as before with the same result. Now Barbestro had maneuvered to the far side of the ring and Strabo couldn't always see him for the fire. He appeared again just as the Celt lurched at him again, this time with a left. Barbestro dodged and the spectators groaned.

Then the Celt began to box. He led with a fat left fist and waved it at Barbestro's face.

"Match his stance!" Strabo shouted, but he may as well have been talking to the moon. Barbestro could not hear him and would have ignored him if he did.

The Celt poked his left arm at Barbestro again and again, but Barbestro didn't bite. He knew the right hand was waiting to strike. The two men danced and parried and danced again around the entire ring. Perspiration began to ball on their shoulders and sweat dripped down each man's face.

"Time!"

———

Molena slowed to a halt in the shadow of the red flags. The Red Falcons had drawn their baggage train in a broad circle. Surrounding this was a wide field of hitching posts and horses that encircled the camp in a protective girdle. Deep in the circle, the tents of Machoba and his officers were pitched, as well as the tents of the captured.

The wide band of horses ringed the camp for many paces and the animals neighed and stamped when startled. Most people would be uneasy surrounded by thousands of the six-hundred-stone beasts. Molena was not. She disappeared into their midst, their bodies a welcome cover for her mission. She moved slowly, cooing quietly to the animals, letting them know she was there but careful not to excite them.

She stopped here and there and peered beneath their bellies to keep her bearings. The tents were closer. She wove her way through the forest of hitching posts, negotiating around countless piles of droppings. The animals hardly stirred. She stopped and touched a few on their muzzles and whispered comforting words to them.

Suddenly she stopped, held perfectly still, and listened. She turned and thought she detected movement through the horses behind her. She waited only a moment before moving on. *Time is short.*

She had circled close enough to hear conversation on the wind. Female conversation. And she smelled perfume.

She slipped her bandages off and buried them in the dirt. Then she released her cloak to reveal what she had squirmed into underneath: a dress with elegant embroidery and a fine linen weave. It was dirty and wrinkled now beyond repair, but it would have to do. Besides, she had convinced Nargonne that men were unfamiliar with such things and would not notice. Molena pulled two jewel-bespeckled hairpins from the creases of the dress, yanked her short hair up, and expertly cleaved them in place.

"Halt!" It was a man's voice.

She froze. The shadow tailing Molena froze too, then ducked behind the big head of an African mare. Nargonne.

From just twenty paces away, a sentry was marching right toward her.

The second recess saw Barbestro take some water, and the Celt at last returned to Octul, and the two conferred closely, Octul shadowboxing and shuffling his feet as the Celt listened.

Strabo, for lack of anything else to do, dabbed a wet rag to Barbestro's forehead.

"Don't let him hit you," said Strabo.

Barbestro rolled his eyes at him. "Brilliant strategy," he said.

Sargonne shuffled his feet. "You hurt?" he asked.

"Not yet."

"Pankrate!" came the cry from the timer.

This time, the Celt dashed forward, swinging a series of punches at Barbestro. Barbestro avoided him, ducking and bobbing from side to side. The Celt lunged to tackle Barbestro, but Barbestro sidestepped him just in time. The Celt was quick for his size.

He lunged again and Barbestro dodged him but lost his footing just long enough for the Celt to catch him with a mighty right fist to the side of his head. The spank of the blow echoed across the ring and the crowd roared.

Stunned, Barbestro backpedaled as the Celt expertly delivered another right fist and followed it with a left to

Barbestro's stomach. Barbestro doubled over with a grunt heard all around the fire.

Then the Celt kicked Barbestro in the head and Barbestro stumbled back but somehow managed to avoid another punch. The Celt was in full stride now, huffing and puffing and swinging away at Barbestro.

He connected again and the impact sent a spray of sweat off Barbestro's head. The crowd was jumping now and the Celt stepped up for another blow when Barbestro suddenly dived beneath the oncoming fists. He drove his head and shoulders into the Celt's shins, tackling the man to the ground!

Machoba clapped his hands. Good move!

The two leviathans rolled across the dirt in a frantic mass of swirling limbs. Trousers ripped and locks of hair flew as both men struggled for a grip.

Finally Barbestro turtled, folding his limbs in on himself and gluing his body to the ground. The great Celt struggled to upend him. He tried to lift him by his legs, but Barbestro kicked free and held his defensive position. The Celt attempted to roll him over on his back, but again Barbestro slipped free of the ploy. Finally the Celt wrapped both arms beneath Barbestro's shoulders and began dragging Barbestro. Dragging him toward the fire!

The Celt heaved and lugged Barbestro across the ring. Perspiration and dirt muddied his back. The Celt's lungs gulped for air. Barbestro felt the heat of the fire near.

"Time!"

The two exhausted men separated and walked slowly to their seconds.

———

Molena stared wide eyed at the approaching sentry. Just paces away, Nargonne pulled a dagger. *Think, Molena, do something.* Nargonne crept behind the mare and positioned himself so that he would be behind the guard. The sentry never saw him. All he saw was the girl.

"What is this?" the man barked.

Molena's mouth opened, but no words came out. She stuttered.

"I—I . . . oh . . ."

Nargonne took a silent step forward.

The guard was as anxious as Molena.

"Out with it, woman!"

And those were words of desperate inspiration for Molena. She suddenly leaned over and retched loudly.

The man stepped back in surprise. Molena retched again, spittle dangling from her mouth. Little came out, but the effect was there. The sentry took another step back and a worried look replaced the fierce one. He recognized her. By the gods, she was one of Machoba's women!

Molena stood again and appeared to compose herself. She took a dramatic breath and wiped tears from her eyes. She was shaking, though that was not an act. She straightened first her dress, then her hair, and put on as dignified a look as she could muster. The sentry stood dumbly and was unprepared for the girl's next move. The woman was glaring at him!

"I am sick, you fool!" she said.

The sentry nodded his head stupidly.

"Of course, yes, of course you are. Allow me to assist . . ."

"Get out of my way."

Molena brushed past the man toward the tents and Nargonne ducked back behind the mare. The sentry trotted after her.

"Miss . . . the doctor, I will call for the physicians. They will—"

"They will do nothing! Leave me."

"I won't. I mean, I can't. I will see you back to your lodgings, Miss."

She stopped and turned on him. He was young. Nearly as young as she.

"Very well," she said. "Just keep your distance."

"Of course. I will. I will stay nearby. . . ."

"And shut up!"

The sentry followed, terrified that any harm might befall this woman of Machoba's on his watch.

She marched straight toward the tents, where there were more soldiers milling about in the darkness. Her eyes dashed wildly back and forth. *Where is he?*

There were a dozen small tents in a tight circle. *Which is Marinne's?*

Nargonne watched from an agonizing distance. His dagger would do them no good any longer. Molena was on her own. And though his eyes desperately pierced the darkness, Nargonne didn't see him either. *Show, man, show yourself!*

Molena frantically scanned the tents and the darkness, which absorbed them. *Which one is it?* She lurched to a stop, stalling for time. The sentry skidded to a halt behind her, nearly knocking her over in the darkness. She feigned another swoon, bending over and holding her head, but she dared not carry the act too long.

After a moment, she stood up slowly and once again

made a prolonged show of straightening herself. The nervous sentry waited patiently.

From the corner of her eye, she caught the figure of a man emerging from behind a tent on the far side of the circle. He stood there just long enough to nod his head toward a particular tent before his shape retreated to the shadows. *Ribas.*

Invigorated, she moaned painfully for the benefit of her sentry and made for Marinne's tent. Nargonne had seen Ribas too and went for the tent via a circuitous route through the horse field.

Molena strode up to the entrance to the tent, slapped aside the canvas door, and disappeared inside without slowing. The sentry paused outside, gathering his wits before effecting a hasty retreat.

Back at the noisy ring, the Celt was sitting at last. Octul gave him water. Strabo hovered over Barbestro as he sat on the ground, catching his breath. His face glistened with sweat.

"I make the man work, you see, Strabo?"

"He doesn't look tired to me."

"Not just a little?"

"Maybe a little."

"That's good enough for me. Water!"

Strabo poured water into Barbestro's mouth and he eagerly gulped it down.

"That's enough for now," warned Strabo.

"Water!" Barbestro growled and Strabo acquiesced. The man was still in the fight, when Strabo had honestly thought the whole matter would be finished by now. Still, there was no question as to who was commanding the contest.

"Pankrate!" came the shout again, and the two combatants rose unsteadily to their feet.

The cramped tent was dark and still. Molena's heart raced as she peered through the blackness. She could see nothing yet. But raised side by side from birth, she knew her sister's very scent.

"Marinne," she whispered.

She held her breath as shapes materialized from the fog of the dark. Bags of clothing. A small wooden trunk. A cot!

She rushed forward and slid to it on her knees.

It was lifeless, its only occupants two dirty pillows and a thin blanket of Selhen weave. She pulled the blanket to her and buried her face in it. Drawing a huge breath from it, Molena swam in the scent of her sister. She felt tears coming and closed her eyes, then snapped them open again. *Don't mope!*

She rushed back to the door and poked her head out for a look. Everything was quiet and she slipped the opening closed again. *Now what?*

There was a noise behind her, a fluttering of the tent wall followed by a draft of fresh air. Someone was sneaking in the tent. She had no weapon!

She would kick him, she thought. The dark figure squeezed through the rear of the tent between the fabric and the ground. Whoever it was, he was short. Her height. Exactly her height and moving weakly.

"Marinne!" she gasped.

Her sister stared back at her in disbelief.

"Love!" Marinne cried.

"Love!" Molena answered, and they rushed into each other's arms. Suddenly Marinne pushed her sister away, a look of horror on her face.

"You mustn't be here. You must flee, Molena, flee! Please, O the gods, be merciful. Flee, sister!"

"Hush, sister. It is you who are leaving. Are you hurt?"

She had been abused severely down below and her back put to the lash so often she slept on her stomach.

"I am well," she lied.

Molena studied her sister and winced. Gone was the rosy color that once was hers. Her face was washed and gray.

Molena wriggled out of her dress in a flash. "Give me your dress."

"What? Molena, you can't—"

"Shush you now, shush!" Molena put her fingers to her sister's lips. "There is no time. Give me your dress. Now, sister!"

Marinne wordlessly obeyed and the two switched garments.

"Hurry, Marinne!"

The two of them put their stomachs to the floor and poked their heads out the rear of the tent. There was no one about. Marinne put her hand to her chest.

"I have your locket." She began to cry.

"I have yours. Don't cry. Hush."

They both listened in the dark. Then they cocked their heads as one. The cooing of a dove! Marinne looked alarmed. She saw a figure crouching amongst the horses.

"It is Nargonne," said Molena.

"Nargonne?"

"Now go."

"But—"

"Later, sister. Go!"

"Wait, Molena. Ribas! Ribas is with the Carthaginians. *Our* Ribas! He won't be fooled."

"No, he won't be. Now hurry you!"

Marinne's eyes were wide with concern. "Barbestro," she whispered.

"He is near. Go!"

Marinne was confused, but she obeyed her sister as she had always done. She dashed for the cover of the horses and she and Nargonne vanished into the herd.

Molena pulled herself back inside and sat on the cot. She straightened her dress and waited quietly in the solitude of the tent. She let a few minutes pass. Long enough for her sister to be free of this place. They had come. They had found her. *Bless all the gods of this earth and the next, and bless Uncle Nargonne most of all. Bless him, bless him!* she prayed.

The Celt came directly at Barbestro again. Barbestro had hoped to see him weaker by now, but he seemed steady on his feet. He lunged at Barbestro, but Barbestro backed away toward the outer edge of the ring. Then he suddenly lunged forward to catch the Celt in a counterattack, but the Celt was ready. He dodged to the side and brought a thundering two-handed blow to the back of Barbestro's head.

Barbestro faltered and the Celt moved in. He struck Barbestro in the face, Barbestro stumbling blindly away from him. He hit him again. And again.

The concourse of spectators was alive now, hungry for

a kill. Their excited shouts drowned out the crackling of the fire.

Strabo watched helplessly as Barbestro collapsed in pain to the dirt. The Celt kicked him in the ribs. And then again, until Barbestro rolled to the side; then the man stomped on his face, ripping a chunk of beard from his cheek. Barbestro tried to roll over and turtle, but he moved too late and the man stomped him again. Strabo saw a piece of tooth fly from Barbestro's mouth, an arc of blood trailing it.

While Barbestro quivered weakly on the ground beneath him, the Celt paused and raised his arms high above his head in triumph. The spectators took the bait and chanted "Kill! Kill! Kill!"

The Celts were going wild, cheering at the top of their lungs. Machoba had no interest in the Celt's antics. He watched Barbestro with an experienced warrior's eye. The opponent wasn't finished until he was finished, Machoba knew.

The Celt took a preparatory step backward. His lips drew up over his broken teeth. He drew a huge breath. He threw that enormous body forward and pounced at the fallen man with an animal cry, his huge hands outstretched to throttle him and end this match for good.

But Barbestro came to life! He rolled and dived at the bigger man's ankles and toppled him.

"Whoa!" the throng screamed. What turn of events was this?

Everyone at the ring felt the ground shudder when the Celt landed with a crunching *oomph!* Barbestro immediately rolled behind him and placed him in a choke hold. The two struggled together in the dirt, neither gaining more advantage. Barbestro couldn't get his forearms beneath the man's chin.

To the crowd's astonishment, Barbestro released him and rolled ten paces away.

"Time!"

Neither man moved from his place in the dirt. This time, their seconds came to them.

Nargonne pulled Marinne behind him through the horses. He stopped and produced another set of bandages identical to Molena's disguise. Marinne didn't even ask as he quickly covered her in them. When he had finished, they darted from the horse field and walked briskly back toward the ring.

"Limp," Nargonne told her.

"What?"

"You heard me, girl. Limp!" he hissed.

"Which leg?"

"Pick one." They hustled back along the well worn trail.

Would the noise of the crowd ever cease? Strabo's head throbbed from the sound of it. And he was dumbfounded by Barbestro. "Why did you release him? You had him!"

Barbestro's tongue was cut deep and so swollen he could barely speak. He shook his head painfully.

"No goob, Shtrabo. I dib not have him well."

Barbestro's face was bruised and dirtied beyond recognition. He was soaking with sweat, as if he had just emerged from a lake. Blood dripped from his nose and mouth. His left ear was nearly torn off and seemingly clung to the side of his head only by blood and mud. Wide swaths of skin had been scraped from his chest and shoulders, and the tenderness beneath gleamed painfully. Angry red bruises covered his arms and legs, and half of his trousers were gone.

The big man closed his eyes and gulped for air.

Strabo looked at Octul and the Celt. The Celt had hardly a mark on him, but he was bent over, struggling for air like Barbestro. Octul caught Strabo's eye and the man grinned fiendishly at him.

Sargonne dabbed cool water on Barbestro and stared at his face; it was as if he were staring at a ghost.

"They keep horses. Give them horses," he mumbled.

The anxiety of the moment got the best of Strabo and he turned on Sargonne.

"It's too late for that, understand? Too late!"

Sargonne's face sank and Strabo instantly regretted the outburst. He had to get a hold of himself! *It is only pain Barbestro is suffering. It is not the end. Not yet.*

His eyes scanned the crowd yet again. *Is it me or are they not here? Did they not have the stomach even for this?* Strabo felt fury seize him. Where was Nargonne when his man needed him? Where was the bold talk now?

Strabo did not know that at this moment, it was the others that needed Barbestro.

"Pankrate!" The call came again and Strabo helped Barbestro to his feet. He noticed that Octul had to help the big Celt up too.

Tears streamed down Sargonne's face. Strabo spat on the ground and led the frightened man back to their place. He squeezed Sargonne's shoulder.

"Barbestro is a tiger, Sargonne. Big tiger!"

Sargonne nodded meekly. "Tiger," he said.

As the men squared off yet again, the Celt's friends cheered loudly. At least *they* were close by, thought Strabo. They had not left their man in the dirt.

The loud row from the ring could be heard all the way to Hannibal's tent and up into the nearby hills, where two riders galloped through the night with extra horses and packs and a dog at their heels: Santandar and Souk Mallouse. They settled beneath some trees and waited.

The fire burned hot and the shadows it cast grew to impossible size to play upon the leaves of the trees next to the ring. Upon the boughs there, the shadows of the two men grappled in a struggle as tall as the highest oak.

This round went like the one before, except the exhausted fighters now took turns grinding each other into the dirt. The big Celt was still getting the best of things. Once again, Barbestro turtled and the Celt tugged and towed his resisting body toward the fire. He would stop often, catch some breath, and then drag Barbestro some more. Barbestro pawed at the ground and dug in his feet wherever he could, anything to slow the man's progress toward the flames.

Once, the Celt stopped and, to the greatest delight of the crowd yet that night, he thumped Barbestro's head into the hard ground in frustration. Barbestro groaned loudly and the spectators pumped their fists.

"Time!" was called again just as Ribas rejoined the crowd, discreetly taking his place among a group of Carthaginian officers.

Barbestro lay prostrate on the ground and hallucinated: He stared skyward and beheld the reason he endured all this pain. More pain than he knew existed. Marinne. But her face was blurry and soon he lost her. "Marinne!" he whispered.

Strabo hushed him. "Quiet, you big fool."

Sargonne busied himself uselessly mopping the man's head and shoulders, but nothing would soak up the blood that kept coming. Barbestro's breathing was disturbingly labored. Strabo slapped him across the face to no effect. Strabo shook the man's head.

"Are you finished?" asked Strabo.

With great effort, Barbestro slowly lifted an eyelid. "I will bet you know when I am binished," he managed.

Barbestro's pummeled face stared at Strabo.

"Is he here?"

Strabo felt anger spear his gut.

"Of course he is here," Strabo lied.

Barbestro breathed a sigh of relief and closed his eyes again. He concentrated only on gulping huge quantities of air into his lungs.

Strabo looked up at the ring in disgust. The onlookers still clamored. *How can they keep it up for so long?* he wondered. *There are hundreds here, Barbestro, hundreds! But I am sorry, Barbestro, no Nargonne.* Strabo scowled. *Coward!*

Strabo's eyes searched the mass of humanity in vain as the words spilled from his mouth without thought.

"I will carry you, Barbestro. Have no fear."

Then he saw him. Nargonne was looking right at him from over the shoulders of a group of drunken Celts, and when he saw that Strabo knew it was he, he returned to form and nodded that arrogant nod of his. Strabo blinked in surprise.

"He is here, Barbestro!"—though Strabo could hardly believe it.

"Pankrate!" the timer bellowed with more drama than Strabo thought was necessary.

The cry would be heard for the last time.

Machoba and the rest watched the seconds lift the wasted men to their feet. Barbestro swayed drunkenly forward before taking a few short steps to steady himself.

Even the crowd was exhausted now but shouted with gusto once again when the Celt gamely charged Barbestro and took the struggling Asturian to the ground. The two repeated the now familiar ritual: Barbestro turtled and held fast as the Celt labored mightily, dragging the man toward the fire, which leaped and crackled less vigorously at last. Its power was ebbing too.

The Celt was using the last of his strength. He knew only that he must get the man to the fire, for the fire would finish him. The flames were hope itself for the Celt.

He tugged and pulled. Slowly Barbestro was forced to yield, and the embers soon came sizzling within a pace of his head.

No one at the ring could take their eyes from the combatants in their final throes. No one except the timer. He watched the last of the water drip away. But before he could open his mouth, the heavy oaken frame of the water clock shuddered with a violent impact and the bowls shattered to pieces!

A heavy cavalry arrow had thudded into the clock and the substantial tail of the arrow oscillated for seconds with an audible hum.

The timer looked up to see Akdar with his bowstring to his eye and a great smile of satisfaction on his face. He grinned at Machoba and lowered his weighty bow while Machoba issued the final command of the night.

"Let them finish!"

The look on Akdar's face made Strabo reach for the hilt of his sword. He glared at Akdar through the crowd and Akdar glared back, challenging him. Akdar remembered Strabo from the skirmish with the Gauls and he involuntarily glanced over at Ribas, and then back at Strabo again. *Draw your sword, Usson,* Akdar thought, *and my heavy blade will finish you like a child.*

But Strabo gathered himself and turned from Akdar. For now.

Strabo watched as the Celt dug his heels into the earth for a mighty final effort. He strained and groaned silently, for he had no groans left. He yanked at Barbestro when suddenly the man gave way and the two went tumbling together, head over heels, sending hot embers scattering at the edge of the fire. Barbestro spun in midair to land right where he wanted—on the back of the bigger man's neck.

In an instant, he moved his hands around the Celt and up beneath his arms at last. Before the Celt could react, Barbestro clenched his hands together and they snapped as tight as an iron chain below the chin of the giant.

Barbestro had him. His hairy forearms dug into the man's neck and he pulled hard. The heat of the fire so close singed the hair of his beard, but he groaned and strained and the veins bulged on his head and arms. *Pull!* He pulled hard against the man's chin, pulling the man's head back against his own spine. *Back, back,* he willed the Celt's head back. *Pull, Barbestro, pull! Pull! Pull!*

The Celt flailed his arms and kicked his legs. He kicked so wildly that the two spun several times, carving a deep circle in the dirt. But his resistance was short lived. Though the stronger man, his body was simply too exhausted, and Barbestro's choke hold held.

Barbestro did not hear the crowd or the exhortations of Machoba or Strabo or anyone else. He thought not of Marinne or his home by the sea so far away. His world was reduced to two simple elements: his arms and the Celt's chin.

Barbestro squeezed him fast until he felt the Celt's breath escape him and his body go limp. With a last surge of energy, Barbestro lifted himself to his feet and hovered uneasily over the man, swaying like a stout oak in a stiff wind.

The Celt was still.

The collective gasp of a hundred Celts was never heard, for the crowd exploded, pouring noisily over the ring and descending upon the two men by the fire. Strabo had to fight his way to Barbestro, where the spectators instinctively formed a respectful circle around the two men. One victorious, the other fallen.

The crowd parted as Machoba entered the circle. Octul was bent dutifully over his man, poking him and slapping him gently to rouse him. It worked. The Celt emitted a guttural gasp and rolled over on his side. He was breathing, if with difficulty.

A voice shouted, "Finish him!" and many joined the chorus.

Machoba studied Barbestro to see what the man would do. So did Strabo. Octul looked up from his defeated comrade, a beseeching look on his face. But Barbestro could not see it—not through the blood and the sweat and the dirt. He could only see his foe. The fire flickered and fizzled, waiting patiently.

The towering Celt had fought him with dignity and skill. It was a fair fight. Barbestro felt the last of his strength ebbing away and he gazed stupidly at the fallen fighter through a fog of fatigue. Without a word, he turned from the fire and, leaning on Strabo as a crutch, haltingly made his way from the ring.

The crowd was silent as the winner limped off. Then it erupted as one in a final roar of approval over this great show of honor.

Akdar scowled, but Machoba nodded his head knowingly. He understood the psychology of men at war. All would be united from the common experience of this night. *Good. Good! Because they will be fighting for real soon enough.* Death would indeed come to these two who fought so well. But not tonight.

A half a league away, Santandar and Souk Mallouse greeted a horseman in the night, galloping up their hill and depositing his passenger to their safekeeping. Souks Mallouse and Tourek hugged each other and swore on their ancestors they would see each other again soon. Tourek quickly departed, riding back to the column while Santandar, Mallouse, and Marinne set off north for the Rhône River, Cabo following dutifully behind.

The *pankration* ring was soon deserted and Hannibal's column gradually quieted for the night. In the end, as Nargonne had promised, Barbestro's skill did come to the fore. He possessed the one talent prized above all others in the sport: He could take a beating.

———

Beneath the flags of the Red Falcons, Molena stayed awake through the night when all others slept, praying to the spirits of her mother and her mother's mother. Molena sat on the edge of the cot and cradled a small vial of foul liquid in her hands. The vial was of hardened Balt clay and glazed bright red. It was one of Souk Tourek's vials and one of his dark concoctions waited inside. She tried to fill her mind with images of her parents but couldn't prevent the thoughts of *that man* from shoving their way in.

"He is a pest," she said aloud.

And he was. To her and her heart. How could she feel so for such a man? A man of violence and death. He was stubborn and a fool, and she admitted that she loved him. For, behind his impulsive ways, his heart was as true as hers. She knew that now. He was to be with her, she was sure of it. He would care for her and she for him; she knew this must be true, but how? *How now, Nargonne?* she wondered.

"We will come for you," he told me.

When she detected the first rays of the sun, she pried the cork from the vial and took a deep breath. She plugged her nose like a child and swallowed its contents in one long gulp. *My last swallow on this earth?* she thought.

She did as she was told. She ground the vial to dust beneath her feet and scattered the remains about the floor of the tent. She felt dizzy, as Tourek had said she would. *Not long now.*

She lay down on the cot and pulled the blanket over her. The poison worked its way through her veins and soon she could not feel her legs. Then her arms. She fought the urge to panic, and the panic passed and darkness circled in on her.

Completely helpless now, she closed her eyes in peace. *Come for me.*

Then all thought ended.

———

In North Africa, Roman emissaries arrived at Carthage proper, beseeching the Carthaginian Senate there to rein in their bellicose general, Hannibal. The Romans argued that, by mutual treaty, Carthaginian territory was limited to only those lands south of the Ebro River in Spain. Yet Hannibal had seized Saguntum, a neutral city and former Roman ally. In defiance, Carthaginian officials diverted the argument: What about Sicily? They blustered publicly that the Roman province belonged to Carthage by right, and the Roman diplomats were sent packing, their entreaties ignored.

Chapter 11

*S*argonne prepared the horses before dawn. Barbestro, though he was asleep on his feet by the time they returned to their fire, had been tended to by Tourek and Sargonne deep into the night. They cleaned his wounds and bandaged them tightly. He only moaned quietly and snored through it. Tourek stuffed his mouth with a poultice to stem the flow of blood from the gaps where several teeth had been. Barbestro spat the poultice out in his sleep.

By the morning, one of his eyes would be so swollen he could make no use of it. A thick knot would protrude from his calf and another from his opposite thigh. His lips bulged together, so thick were they from injury. Every knuckle on each hand seeped raw.

"Where are the others?" Strabo had demanded of Nargonne as soon as they returned to camp.

"They are safe for now," Nargonne had told him.

"Molena?"

"We shall retrieve her in the morning."

Strabo had tried not to appear too worried, thinking that would be unseemly in some way.

"Where is she?" he finally demanded.

Nargonne put a hand to Strabo's shoulder.

"She is safe. Sleep."

Nargonne would say no more and ushered everyone to sleep.

Strabo then slept little. What in the name of the gods was Nargonne up to this time? He believed the man when he said she was safe. That should be good enough, he thought. But it was not. Not for a man given to Strabo's need for resolution, his blind need to act and to act fast.

The night somehow excused the others' absence. Mallouse and Santandar were gone. So was Molena. Ribas was still at the Red Falcon camp. Just before first light, Nargonne rousted Strabo and handed him a cloak. He bade him put it on. The cloak was black and hooded.

"Keep your face low, Strabo," he told him. "Go with Tourek. Do as you are told." Nargonne looked serious. So did Tourek.

Strabo glanced at the inert, snoring mass that was Barbestro.

"He will be cared for, Strabo," Nargonne said. "You did well."

Tourek was already on a horse, waiting. Strabo pulled the hooded vestment over his head and mounted Castaine. Tourek wore a black cloak like Strabo's and was carefully stowing his stones away.

"What do the signs say?" asked Strabo.

Tourek answered without looking at him. "They are positive."

The two of them made their way through the sleeping

throng. The army would be waking soon, as it did each day on campaign—slowly. Scattered shouts. Then the clattering of chains and the rustling of equipment. But at this early hour, the column yet lay slumbering before them.

A few minutes more and they were within sight of the Red Falcon camp. Tourek seemed to be scouring the hillsides for something. Strabo followed him up to a small copse of trees overlooking the column. Waiting beneath the trees was a crude wagon.

"What is this, Souk?"

"You will know soon, Strabo. It is important you do as I say."

Strabo went along with him. But he was thinking he might not for much longer. Tourek bade him unroll his bedding. Tourek unrolled his and made his bed beneath the wagon.

"Now we sleep," Tourek told him with a wink.

Strabo crawled inside his bedroll and watched the darkness above him slowly disperse. Some stars still shone. So many stars, he thought. A storm of them.

He heard a *snap*. Tourek had arranged an intricate array of small sticks on the ground next to his head. He played idly with one, placed it on the ground, picked up another, and then snapped it in two.

"It rains today," he said, looking at the pieces.

"Is that what the sticks tell you?"

"The sky." He pointed to the east, where the dim light of a still-distant sunrise illuminated a line of dark clouds.

He grinned and closed his eyes.

———

Ribas had slept in the makeshift barracks of the Red Falcons. He was an honorary officer and the soldiers treated him with respect. Any man who could ensure success on the battlefield and save their skins to fight another fight had proved his worth enough for them.

But Ribas was on edge. Last night had been a long night. His head ached from worry. His shoulders ached from digging. Now he rushed to the officers' quarters at first light when he heard the commotion he had worked and waited for. He double-checked his boots to make sure they were free from any telltale soil and bent to enter the officers' tent.

Concern covered the faces of a dozen officers already there: One of Machoba's women had expired during the night. They were all in hushed conversation when Machoba and Akdar entered.

Ribas stood by silently while one of the officers gingerly explained the situation to Machoba. The man explained how the girl had been reported sick, but not so sick that a doctor had been called.

Machoba froze and every man in the tent tensed. The officer who had done most of the talking was the officer of the watch. Beads of sweat broke on the man's brow, though he did not move. Machoba said nothing; turning to all of them, he stared out to the field. He stood that way for a full minute, maybe more. Then he put his hands to his hips. He turned around and looked over all the officers present. To Ribas, it seemed he looked hardest at him, but in truth, the look he received was just as passing as any other.

Machoba glared at them.

"Understand this, all of you. There is no regiment in

Hannibal's corps like ours. The Red Falcons stand above all."

Machoba was determined to make a lesson from this circumstance.

"Nothing shall distract the Falcons from our duty," he said. "And nothing will keep us from war!"

"This *thing*"—he said the word with contempt—"was but a trifle. A recreation and nothing more."

Machoba spat on the ground.

"Assemble the signifiers and the first rank. Post the short spears on first column and let us have archery bring up the rear today. Listen to me, Red Falcons. The Rhône River lies but days ahead. There we will have battle. Look to your swords and shields and leave housekeeping to the help."

He looked proudly at his men. They were well trained. They would do their job and his bidding when the time came. His mind was, as theirs should be, on military matters. Ahead of the column lay the mighty Rhône, and intelligence had informed Hannibal the river would be defended by the Volkai, an organized and formidable Gallic nation. He had no time for incidentals right now. The girl had been troublesome. He had others.

"We move out in thirty minutes. Watch officers, exercises today are on the run."

He spun and left the tent, leaving the officers relieved beyond description. The only thing that remained was a discussion of what should be done with the girl.

"The concubine should be disposed of properly," one man finally said. It was Ribas. "She may be a nothing, but she was a woman of our commander."

Heads nodded in agreement throughout the tent.

"A woman to the Red Falcons."

Again they agreed.

"There is a coroner following the train," offered Ribas.

The arrangement was made and an officer and two soldiers were dispatched to locate the coroner. Ribas was escorted to the tent of the girl. All of the other tents had been packed up and were moving out. Passing soldiers cast nervous glances at the only tent that still stood as they industriously went about their business.

Ribas never even walked inside. He simply sat next to the tent with several other officers and the two guards who had been posted there and waited.

The soldiers found the coroner where Ribas had told them. He was sleeping under his wagon beneath a small copse of trees. The coroner seemed perturbed to be wakened and he barked at his assistant, who, likewise, seemed surly at such treatment. But the coroner quickly harnessed his horses to the wagon, and after a brief discussion regarding payment, he set off for the Red Falcon camp, his assistant by his side.

The soldiers found the somber coroners unnerving and were glad to finally relinquish the dark men and their hooded ways to the officers at the tent.

Ribas insisted two officers supervise the disposal with him.

"We should execute such things properly," he said. They agreed and were happy to have an experienced voice walk them through these unfamiliar proceedings. For his part, Ribas tried his best to look bored and expressed no interest whatsoever in entering the tent and witnessing the corpse himself.

Bouncing along on the uncomfortable cart next to

Tourek, Strabo felt his heart churn with worry. The Carthaginians had come to consult Tourek about a death. That was all he knew. That, and the fact that he was now engaged in some sort of ruse not of his making. A ruse that had all the markings of one man. Nargonne. And, as usual, Nargonne was nowhere in sight.

Who was dead? Machoba? The Celt? Where in all the heavens was Ribas? Were the others involved in this? That was why they weren't in camp this morning!

He ordered himself to keep his wits about him and he followed Tourek's lead, marveling at the acting skill of the man. Tourek was taciturn and wraithlike, not that he wasn't born for such a role. More than once, Tourek reminded Strabo with subtle gestures: Keep your hood down, and keep low.

The rain helped. It came just when the Carthaginians had found them in the trees. Light drops at first, nothing but specks appearing in the dirt. But soon, fat drops burst on the ground in dusty explosions. By the time they reached the single tent standing alone, the rain fell heavy and steadily.

Tourek hopped off the cart without a care. He handed a black leather bag to his "assistant." The Carthaginians stood attentively as he walked up to the tent, followed closely by Strabo. Strabo suppressed his surprise at seeing Ribas here and gamely ignored the man as Ribas stepped aside without so much as a glance at the coroners. Just as Tourek made to go inside, he halted and Strabo nearly bumped into him. Tourek nervously sniffed the air. He looked around him. He looked at the Carthaginian officers and at the guards. He leaned over and sniffed one of the guards' cloaks. The guard slunk back.

Tourek then reached into the bag that Strabo held and produced two swatches of cloth. He tied one around his hood and face and handed the other to Strabo, who took the cue and did the same. The Carthaginians each took a few steps backward. Ribas stepped back even farther. The Carthaginians exchanged a few nervous glances, then followed his lead and stepped back farther as well.

Rain pouring off their backs, the Carthaginians watched in silence as Tourek took a deep breath and entered the tent. Strabo followed him in.

The tent was dim and empty—save for the lone figure lying on the cot, draped from head to toe with a field blanket. Strabo thought the body looked small for a man.

Tourek looked around the interior of the tent. He bent to the ground, looking for something. He pinched some dust and dirt from the floor and ground it between his fingers, smelling it. After a moment, he stepped to the cot. As Strabo leaned forward, Tourek turned to him and pressed a single finger hard to his lips. The man stared hard at him for a very long moment to make sure he got the message. He did. Then the Souk reached down and pulled the blanket away from the corpse's face.

Strabo felt the breath leave his chest. His body shuddered and his legs bent weakly. All thought fled his head. All blood fled his veins. All was white. The world was white.

As white as Molena's face.

The dim tent spun around him and the cot seemed to pulsate toward him, then away again. He felt something clutch his shoulder. A hand seized his face.

Tourek had him by the cheek and all Strabo could see

was the man's wide brown eyes boring into his. Tourek put his finger to his lips again.

It was a needless gesture. Strabo was paralyzed. Tourek's eyes seemed only the eyes of death, this tent an unreal place. A dangerous dream of dread.

Strabo saw now only the green fields where he had first ridden with her. The roll of her bottom in the saddle, the lure of her shoulders before him.

Tourek bent over her closely and put his ear to her parched lips. Her mouth was open slightly. All was still.

The Souk slipped a hand beneath the blanket and pressed a finger to her wrist there. He closed his eyes and looked up into the roof of the tent. Tourek held his breath.

So did Strabo, until Tourek released his hand and quickly covered Molena again. He turned to Strabo and again grabbed the stunned man by the face. Tourek looked in Strabo's eyes again and made no sound. There, in this tent of death, in this place that seemed not of this world, the big brown eyes held Strabo's. Then Strabo saw him wink.

"Quickly," he whispered.

Strabo had no time to think. Tourek yanked Strabo's arm and pulled him from the tent. Outside, Tourek looked over the soldiers there and adopted an air of officialdom. The Carthaginians noticed that the coroner's assistant seemed shaken, which only added to their worry. Were they not coroners? Death was their everyday business. Death would not shake them. No death would shake them—save the death that would shake any man.

Their own.

"She must be burned," Tourek announced, and the Carthaginians stepped back even farther.

Strabo would never remember the next few minutes.

He was dumb. And he acted so, stumbling as he wordlessly followed the Souk's every command.

Tourek pushed his gear aside and the soldiers loaded the body onto the wagon with haste. They could barely wait to get their hands off the bundled corpse. One of the officers ordered two soldiers to commandeer firewood. Tourek requested a sacrifice and another soldier soon returned with a young goat. Strabo followed blindly as Tourek drove the wagon to a hillside nearby. The others followed in silence. They would let the strange man go about his trade. They had no interest in such nasty business. Even the goat was silent in the rain.

The funeral troop, such as they were, arrived at a spot that Tourek declared to be right. Tourek freed Castaine from the cart's harness and handed the reins to Strabo. He cast sticks on the ground and held up his hands to catch some rain, then read the droplets on his palms.

The steady downpour drummed around them. Strabo helped Tourek stack wood both on the wagon and in front of it. Tourek stacked the wood carefully against the rain so that the fire would take. The Carthaginians stood back respectfully. Ribas sat quietly on his horse.

It wasn't until Strabo noticed the way Tourek manipulated the wood on the wagon that he began to come to his senses. Tourek placed the wood tenderly, the fuel meant only to hover over Molena's body—it hardly touched her. Most of it was piled between the wagon and the soldiers in attendance.

What is this? Is she . . . ?

Strabo wanted to leap on the cart, leap to Molena. Nargonne! The man was a fox! This was not a skirmish where the dead lay dead and the victorious walked. This was a struggle where the dead must disappear.

Tourek asked the half-dozen remaining Carthaginians to step back. They hardly needed urging. Tourek had grumbled about a "sickness" more than once. The soldiers said nothing, but each was thinking "plague." *Plague*. A hideous end that the mightiest warriors and the most cunning generals stood powerless before. *Let it not be the plague!* they all prayed.

The Souk scratched arcs in the mud, though they were muddied and washed away within moments. He cast bones on the ground before the cart and bent to his knees. He recited a long incantation and the soldiers watched the man in the hooded cloak sway there on his knees for several minutes, mumbling the strange words in a low, steady voice. Tourek blessed his luck for the rain.

He asked for the goat. He held the animal to the ground before the cart, raised his voice, and produced a long, slim dagger. He raised the dagger and plunged it through the goat's tender neck. The goat's life ended instantly. Tourek held the small goat like a pitcher and poured the thing's lifeblood from its throat, making two large circles in the mud.

He stood and placed the goat on top of the woodpile in front of the wagon, completing the pyre. He then pulled a bladder of powerful-smelling liquid from his bag and sprinkled it over the wood on the wagon and on the ground. Next he took a flint set and sparked the woodpile on the ground to life. Strabo wondered if the fire would take under the downpour. It did. The liquid Tourek used ignited the fire in a *whoosh*.

Tourek began reciting again. Around and around the

wagon he walked, sprinkling more of the liquid over the wagon and forming mysterious signs over the wagon with his hands. The wet wood's burning pumped a generous quantity of smoke into the air, and the rain pushed the smoke to the ground all around, obscuring Tourek from view.

When he was behind the wagon, the volume of his chanting grew. He began bending up and down and throwing his arms, first to the sky and then to the ground again.

Tourek bade Strabo hold the horse who pulled the wagon. Then Tourek employed the flint set again and this time it was the woodpile on the wagon that burst into flame. Tourek's horse shied and neighed, but Strabo held him firm. The horse flicked its tail frantically. It could feel the heat of the fire and began kicking.

Obscured by both fires now, Tourek was rising and falling behind the wagon and chanting loudly. Ribas had to admit it was quite a show. No one could see Tourek unhinge the other side of the wagon and slide the lifeless body into the hole there, which Ribas had dug and disguised in the middle of the night. Tourek slid the wagon's side panel back in place and kicked the mud-covered canvas covering, which had been placed over the hole, back in place. His chanting never missed a beat.

He ordered Strabo to release the horse.

Strabo did and Tourek reached out and slapped the horse on its rear and the horse shot away. The flaming wagon followed in a shower of sparks and smoke as the animal's fear took it at top speed away along the hillside. Ribas spurred after the wagon and the Carthaginians followed, as had been Tourek's intent.

Tourek had only one final order for Strabo.

"Free the horse," he told him.

Strabo mounted up and galloped after the flaming cart. Castaine caught it quickly. Strabo pulled out his sword and with one expert swing he sliced the harnesses from the horse and the horse bolted forward, free from the weight of the cart. Strabo and Castaine gave chase and caught the frightened horse one hundred paces later. The cart rolled to a stop and burned there in the rain, the Carthaginian contingent watching from nearby.

Tourek walked over to the Carthaginians and said, "It is done." Ribas nodded gravely and Tourek walked away to meet up with Strabo, who approached with the other horse. The wagon blazed in the distance.

Ribas turned his horse back toward the main army moving across the plateau behind them. He did not look back. The rest of the Carthaginians followed.

The girl's tent and its contents would be ordered burned. The captain would report to his superiors that the deed had been done, that the contaminated body had been cremated, and that proper honors were given to the woman of a Carthaginian officer.

Tourek and Strabo walked their horses back down the hillside, weaving through the ubiquitous boulders and brush that dotted this terrain. Strabo felt his neck crane round to stare back at the small fire, which still smoldered on the hillside.

"Do not turn your head, Strabo. Allow them to clear away from this place. We will stay close. Don't worry."

Strabo obeyed.

When the Carthaginians disappeared over a rise, Tourek halted. He and Strabo erected a pole covering and hovered beneath it. They watched Hannibal's column move sluggishly through the rain a half a league below them on the plain. Even through the steady rain, they had a clear view of the copse above and the wisps of smoke that marked it.

"We take shifts," Tourek suggested.

One dozed while the other kept his eyes firmly on the lonely cluster of trees. Strabo, in particular, snored heavily, despite a head weighed by worry. His body was young and strong and could take long days of abuse. But his mind was yet untried and the confusion and emotion had taken their toll.

No one bothered the copse and the last of the column dribbled past just after noon. Nargonne and his brother had passed earlier and Tourek flashed him one of Strabo's war signals. The sign of the bird: Proceed. Nargonne nodded and Tourek could only wonder how Barbestro was faring.

What Tourek did not know was that Octul and several other Celts had shown up at Nargonne's camp at daybreak, bearing a heavy cart. One of the men was a doctor. He fussed over Barbestro and together they all lugged him aboard the cart and made him as comfortable against the weather as they could. Already prone and resting in the cart lay the other man. The big Celt.

Nargonne could read Octul and saw that he was genuine. Octul shook Nargonne's hand and assured him no harm would come to Barbestro. The horse thieves had been punished. "How?" asked Nargonne. Octul made his favorite gesture of slashing his finger across his throat and smiled.

"It is our justice, Nargonne," he said. "Your big man will rest today."

"And tomorrow too," the doctor added. He made it clear the two former combatants would rehabilitate side by side. "If the cart doesn't collapse beneath their weight," laughed Octul.

Octul remounted his horse. Again he smiled at Nargonne and patted the horse's neck.

"This beast is ours," he said with a wink. "One needs friends in wartime, don't you think, Usson?"

Nargonne agreed and Octul led the cart away.

When the last carts trailing the army disappeared over the rise, Tourek woke Strabo. The two of them were at the copse inside a minute.

Strabo's heart was racing by the time he rigged the pole covering while Tourek dug up Molena's "grave." Together they lifted her; she was like a child being released from a hole. Strabo felt her skin. It was cold.

"Fire, Strabo. Can you build a hot one?" asked Tourek, and Strabo sprinted off, gathering wood at a furious pace. Could he build a hot fire? He could build a fire hot enough to melt iron and soon the new fire blazed and Strabo found himself blessing Ribas for digging the hole beneath the trees' protective limbs.

Tourek fished more concoctions from his saddlebag and mixed a powder with oil and forced it into the still girl's throat. At first there was no response. Molena's body stayed still. Tourek continued. Then her body suddenly lurched forward and she vomited a great black mass of liquid. Strabo cringed as Tourek forced more potion into her and she vomited again. Less this time. Then Tourek whipped together a different mix and forced this down her throat to no apparent reaction. Her limp body accepted it and he laid her down.

To Strabo's great embarrassment, Tourek removed Molena's clothing and rubbed a tangy-smelling liniment over her body. When Tourek rolled her over, they saw for the first time the recent welts that scored her back. She had escaped from Machoba quickly, but not in time to elude his whip. The welts rose in painful ridges and spread from her shoulder blades to her buttocks. *She will bear those scars to her grave,* Strabo thought.

Strabo didn't want to see her this way. Her breasts white with the cold, the soft covering of her loins dark and still. They wrapped her again in dry blankets. Tourek listened again to her breath and put his ear to her chest. His nimble fingers probed her wrists and the arteries at her neck.

"This will take time," he said.

Tourek ordered Strabo to cradle her close to the flames and keep her dry, while Tourek spread broken twigs and needles of pine about their campsite. Then Tourek settled in a blanket. He left his stones in his bag for once, and for that Strabo was glad. He wanted no part of predictions and soothsayers right now. Tourek rose again each hour and mixed more of his potion and forced it into Molena.

"The poison is an ancient one, Strabo," Tourek said at length. He told Strabo what had transpired and that Marinne was free.

"And I was to know nothing," said Strabo.

Tourek measured him for a moment.

"Each knew what they needed and no more."

Strabo regarded the explanation as simply more misdirection from Nargonne. Strabo knew what Nargonne must have known: Strabo never would have gone along with it. That he would have considered the ploy too reckless, the outcome too uncertain. That he would not have put the girl in such danger.

There was further logic to the escapade that was lost on Strabo. Nargonne had always placed Strabo wherever there was danger from weapons and soldiers. In the *pankration* ring. At the camp of the Red Falcons. At Tourek's staged burial. Nargonne's explanation to Ribas had been simple: "If things go awry, Strabo will kill who he needs to kill, and some of us might yet escape."

Still, it did pain Nargonne that, try as he might, he could think of no safer approach than Tourek's poisons. Molena must soldier for us today, he had thought at the time.

Tourek's face lay shrouded in the shadow of the hooded cloak; rainwater dripped past his eyes in a steady stream.

"The dose had to be just right, Strabo. I pray that it was."

So Mallouse and the boy and Molena's sister had gone ahead. Nargonne had done it, thought Strabo. He had freed Marinne without leaving a trace. But Strabo hardly considered the operation a success—the cost was yet to be determined. Strabo knew Molena would trade her life for her sister's if it came to that. *By the gods, let it not come to that!* He asked Tourek which god he should pray to.

"Pray to the god responsible for our plight, Strabo. Ba'al Shamin." Ba'al Shamin was an ancient god, a Carthaginian god that ruled all others, a powerful god in this part of the world that many worshiped.

Strabo prayed to Ba'al Shamin and promised him eternal devotion. If he delivered.

At nightfall, Molena's breathing was still shallow and her skin still white. Only her body temperature had improved. Unconscious, she managed to swallow some of what Tourek gave her. Tourek also began extracting fully exhausted coals from the blazing fire. He let them cool and then crushed them into a powder, which he mixed with oil and slid down Molena's throat a few times each hour.

Tourek disappeared into the darkness for a time and returned with fresh water and six rabbits. They roasted some of the rabbit and stewed the rest. Alone on the wide plain, the two famished men feasted. Tourek suggested they let Molena sleep uninterrupted, so he gave her one last treatment of the powder and the two men finally slept.

They both woke early. The sky was still overcast with clouds but the rain had given way to heavy mist. To Strabo, Molena seemed little improved, but Tourek was convinced her color was better. He mixed more of the powder and continued to pour it down her throat, but only every other hour now.

In an effort to take his mind off their somber task, Strabo spent the time trying to hone his sword to a fine edge. He had decided he must replace the Saguntum blade at his first opportunity, as it would not take the edge he preferred.

The day of the *pankration* match, Strabo had spent hours dawdling among the forgers at the armory train in search of a more sophisticated sword. A man raised at the hearth of the furnace could tell much from a blade. He inspected Assyrian swords and African, Greek, Macedonian, Gaul, Roman, and Turk. The weapons were mostly crude. Why could no one master a fine iron blade? All of the good ones were bronze based, where the iron ones were heavy and brittle.

Back in Sigeum, Kabal himself had never achieved a suitable iron sword, though he experimented with hundreds of mixtures and plied the iron with every metal known: nickel, tin, lead, copper. Even gold.

Weapons makers everywhere knew the future belonged to some as yet undiscovered iron alloy, but all had failed to unlock the secrets of the mighty ore. The magic formula, if it existed, remained a mystery. Strabo had heard talk of a new type of iron, *steel,* that was both light and strong. But that seemed just another rumor. Strabo had left the armory train in frustration, the bronze Saguntum blade still at his waist.

Now he gathered wood for their fire and tended it ceaselessly. Eventually he made his way to their drinking stream. He squatted by its edge for a long time. Then he took to arranging small rocks in circular patterns on the sandy bank, as he had seen Tourek do. He carved arcs and circles in the sand. He broke sticks and tossed them in random piles to the ground. He stared at the signs he had made, forcing himself to concentrate.

But the signs told him nothing and at length he kicked them in disgust. He stripped his clothing off and stepped into the stream. Here was familiar ground. He immersed himself in its frigid waters. He bobbed his head and kept it under, holding his breath for as long as he could. He swam back and forth and ducked underwater, idly exploring the rocky bottom.

The water cleared his head and healed his spirits. He

felt his energy return, despite the cooling weather. No matter, he thought. The hot fire would dry his clothes and warm his bones. He cleaned his clothes on the rocks, then collected wood all the way back to the fire. When he returned, he could scarcely believe his eyes. Molena was sitting up.

Strabo dropped the wood in a heap and dashed to the fire. Tourek was feeding Molena rabbit stew and grinning ear to ear. Strabo dropped to his haunches and looked at her. She stopped eating and smiled weakly at him. Tourek stayed the bowl he fed her with, waiting.

"Feed her, man, feed her!" said Strabo. He wanted to laugh, to reach out and touch her, to seize her and bring her close. She smiled at him and admiration for her swelled in his chest. The recklessness he had cursed was forgotten.

"I am really here," she said at last, more to herself than anyone else. Her voice was raspy and tentative, but Strabo thought it heavenly.

He was not sure what to do with himself. He stood. He squatted. He shuffled around the fire while Tourek tended to her.

"Sleep now," Tourek told her, and he made her comfortable beneath the blankets. She watched Strabo smile back at her. Then she shut her eyes and slept.

The sleep of the dead, Strabo couldn't help thinking. Tourek let her sleep all night through and she didn't stir until far after sunrise. She was able to put down more stew, seemed disoriented, and was soon asleep again. Strabo was not there to see her rise. He was catching fish in the stream. Lacking the proper tools, he simply constructed a crude rock berm in the shallows and stabbed fish as they became trapped in it. The process occupied him and he was successful. Though the rain had stopped, its effect was to wash many insects into the stream and Strabo had his pick of the fat fish preoccupied with feeding.

The men cooked the fish. In the late afternoon, Molena woke again and ate the rabbit and fish indiscriminately. Tourek was relieved to see her ravenous at last. Finally she belched loudly, taking both men by surprise. She grinned at Strabo and he grinned back, filled with relief.

Molena announced she had to attend to the call of nature. Strabo helped her unsteadily to her feet and the men obliged her privacy. When she finished, she sat by the fire and breathed deeply.

"That is good. You have your lungs back," said Tourek.

Molena suddenly looked serious. "I have my wits back too. We have to go."

Strabo was doubtful. "Can you ride?"

"I'm not a child, Strabo."

"You're not well, Molena. You must care for—"

Tourek interrupted him. "She is right. We must go."

He immediately began packing up without another thought. Molena began weakly pitching in.

Strabo protested further, but the two stubborn Asturians had decided. Their camp was quickly abandoned and Strabo knew he would never forget this hill, this life-giving stand of trees, this most difficult of ordeals for him. An ordeal that was not his own.

They made Molena comfortable on the reliable back of Castaine and set out with the setting sun at their backs.

The blind could have followed the army they followed. Some fifty thousand men and their horses and equipment had beaten a ruddy swath across the plain. For better footing, the three traveled along the edge of the great army's wake and made good time.

They traveled all night beneath the stars before resting at daybreak and releasing the horses to feed. While Molena slept, Tourek and Strabo shared smoked fish and dried rabbit.

Strabo eyed Tourek.

"You saved her."

The Souk smiled. "I sent her there in the first place."

Strabo considered this. At another place and another time, he might have been furious with the Souk for doing so. He had no such thoughts now.

"You are a very different sort of man, Souk Tourek."

"Me? I was going to say the same about you!"

They laughed in the way only men with a mutual understanding could.

Strabo eventually did ride, when Molena was stronger. The three travelers said little and marched hard for two days. They should have known the return journey would not be so simple.

When they made camp at nightfall of the second day, Tourek excused himself and rode back where they had come from. Molena and Strabo shrugged. The Souk had his ways. They made a simple camp under cover of a thick stand of casterberry bush studded with maples.

An hour later, Tourek returned.

"We are tracked," he said.

Molena stiffened.

"Who?" asked Strabo.

"I don't know."

Tourek described how he thought he had smelled

smoke on the wind the night before, but it didn't last and was weak to begin with. The smoke on the wind was heavy tonight, he said. Whoever they were, they were close.

Strabo sniffed. He could smell nothing. Molena, however, could smell it too. She looked at Strabo in alarm.

"Passing armies create many stragglers, Molena. Like us. And then the buzzards come. Bandits and thieves."

"I see."

So they slept in short shifts for a few hours, then rose at midnight to move on. Just as they were mounting up, Tourek sniffed loudly and announced, "They are here."

Strabo told Tourek to get in the underbrush. "Quickly!"

Tourek slapped the horses free and ducked away with his bow. The horses trotted off into the darkness.

Strabo pulled a length of smoldering tree limb from the fire and handed the cold end to Molena. Molena took it and stared at the crude club.

"It's still smoking."

"Good."

"I prefer my dagger."

"Short weapons are for the strong and those with advantage. We have no advantage here and these will be men, Molena. They are stronger than you."

She looked offended.

"But no tougher." He smiled reassuringly at her. *No one's tougher than she,* Strabo thought. *The woman is a lion. So am I.*

Four men emerged from the darkness. Three on foot, one on horseback.

Strabo stood still, his hands on his hips. He had cast away the sheath of his sword and concealed the weapon against the back of his leg. He felt its hilt against his thigh. The only weapon still visible was his knife.

"Stay close to me until I attack," Strabo whispered. "Then get away fast."

"Maybe they are friendly," Molena offered.

They weren't.

They strode up to their fire and stood there, boldly looking them over. The men were dirty and well armed. Even in this cold, they wore short tunics.

Molena looked at the one on horseback. A coarse cloak hung over his shoulders. He was bearded and tall and wore a leather skullcap with unruly earflaps that dangled at his neck. The horse shifted its feet and its tack jangled. Then the hair rose on the back of Molena's neck; she saw the chains. Strabo saw them too.

They were slavers.

The horseman spoke.

"Where is the third?" The man spoke easy Greek and his manner was matter-of-fact, as if the occasion were routine.

Neither Strabo nor Molena answered him. Strabo drew his knife and the men on the ground answered him by drawing their swords. *Good,* thought Strabo. *Attack. Scatter so I can take you!* One of them leered at Molena and it was not difficult for Strabo to read the man's mind. *You will die first,* Strabo thought.

"Where is the third?" the horseman demanded.

They did not answer. Molena held her club high and it smoldered in front of her. She couldn't place their tribe. They looked like they could be Libyans, Molena thought.

The horseman adjusted himself in his saddle.

"Come peacefully," he said, "and no harm will come your way."

The slavers were comfortable that numbers were on their side. But they had never encountered the disciplined patience of a warrior forged as a child among furnaces and combat yards. They were unprepared.

And they still received no answer. In his practiced way, Strabo had taken stock of the men. They seemed handy with their weapons but held them casually, as if they were toys. A mistake. They carried no shields and no armor. Another mistake.

The horseman had a spear, though it was hardly at the ready. His sword was stuck in a clumsy ornamental sheath, the handle a pitted and rusting stock of iron. *Useless*, thought Strabo. *And spears are easy to defeat. Just get close.*

Then Strabo saw something that would seal the course of them all. It was looped through a bronze ring at the back of the horseman's saddle, and though it was just a thing, it may as well have screamed at Strabo.

He made his decision and cried out over his shoulder, "Souk! Can we follow their trail back to their camp?"

The slavers were dumbfounded. The man was calling to the other! He is nearby! They shifted on their feet, but there was no answer from the darkness. Deep in the brush, Tourek couldn't believe Strabo was exposing his position.

"Answer me, man!" The urgency warbled in Strabo's voice and then his answer came from the dark.

"Yes" was all Tourek said and all that Strabo needed.

His sword materialized in his hand and he leaped like a cat for the man on the left, though his target was the man on the right. They reacted to his attack, but when Strabo reversed directions, all three men were caught flat-footed. Strabo took the first man's head in a single, unobstructed blow and was on the middle man before the first man's head hit the ground.

The man on the left darted for Molena, while the man in the middle backpedaled away from Strabo, but Strabo knocked his weapon aside with ease and ran the man through.

Molena had her strength back. She dodged and clubbed her assailant over the head, but the man whirled and came at her again. She fended him off with a flurry of rapid blows, keeping him unbalanced.

The horseman's spear was out and poised to strike Strabo when an arrow from the underbrush whistled through the smoke of the fire and *thunked* into the man's chest. Howling, the man spun in his saddle and Strabo finished him with a swift stab through his unguarded torso as he fell.

Strabo did not wait for the man to die. His knife was in his hand, he spun—the knife flew. The man on Molena took Strabo's knife in his spine, clear to the hilt, just as an arrow ripped through the side of his neck and gushed out the other side. Molena stumbled back, her club still at the ready.

The man swayed and Molena watched him try to speak. But when he opened his mouth, he only disgorged a thick plume of bright blood, which ran down his chin and neck like milk down a baby's face. He fell and was still.

Molena had not even taken a handful of breaths. It was over.

Tourek emerged from the trees with his bow and Strabo

kicked the bodies of the dead. The horseman's horse shied nervously but stayed. One of the horseman's legs twisted unnaturally up the horse's side and hung there, tangled in the reins. A gasp came from the man and Molena winced as Strabo thrust his sword again through the man's mid-section. The body jerked and died. Strabo turned to Tourek.

"Can we track their path at night?"

"Why, Strabo?"

Strabo pointed his dripping sword at the leather band wrapped in bronze wire dangling from the horseman's saddle. Molena gasped.

It was Cabo's dog collar.

Strabo cursed the men and their pitiful weaponry. They had nothing he found useful among the four of them. Ridiculous, he thought. And deadly for them. He made a mental note to strike a deal with the Carthaginian armory when they made it back. By the gods, he required a good blade!

Any thought of sleep had long vanished. They moved quickly now with three horses; the new one was a good mount.

"You shall meet Archon," Molena told the robust mare. She winked at Strabo and he blushed in the dark.

Tourek had apologized to Strabo for the delay in his response from the bushes. "That was a tricky moment, Strabo," he said. Strabo was just happy the Souks were such good shots. He would never be as adept with the bow.

The slavers did leave a painfully obvious trail. In daylight, Strabo himself could have followed it.

The slavers had been traveling along the sandy river fed from a multitude of springs trickling in from the high hills. They crossed and recrossed the shallow river a dozen times. The slavers hunted their quarry along these banks, because the desperate always sought water. Water first, Strabo thought. Had the others been captured here? Were they still alive? The dog, at least, was dead. Of that he was sure. It was only a dog. A barking, slobbering pest. Still, Strabo found himself vowing the slavers would pay for the bighearted animal's life.

Molena was surprisingly unworried. She knew her sister was alive.

They rode for much of the day and rested at last in midafternoon. The slavers' trail had taken them in a wide circle and they were now nearly back to where they had started, with the exception that they were across the river by nearly a league.

And they found Cabo. His dead body, peppered with arrow wounds, lay on the bank of a stream. Flies buzzed over the carcass. Strabo angrily slapped the insects away and carried Cabo's body to higher ground. He and Tourek dug a hole and carefully buried the dog. Little was said. The look on Strabo's face told Molena he was of the same mind as she. She watched him tend to his weapons and they dozed in shifts until the sun slept again.

Then they rose, ate, and prepared the horses for another long night on the trail. But within the hour, they crested a wooded hill and even Strabo could smell the fire. They slowed and crept closer for a look at the slavers' camp.

The slaving party was apparently small, for there was only one tent. Strabo theorized the dead horseman must have been their leader.

No sentries were posted—none that they could see—and they waited nearly an hour. Were they actually asleep in their field beds with no lookouts? Strabo was disgusted with them at this point. The fools apparently had even killed their only dog and so gave themselves not even that chance at an alarm.

The slavers' captives slept in the open without benefit of any coverings whatsoever against the chill of night. Strabo could not see the chains in the dark, but he knew they were there, for he could make out a dozen posts planted firmly in the earth. The captured would be chained to these. He could make out seven inert shapes lying in the dirt amongst the posts. With luck, Mallouse, Marinne, and Santandar would be among them.

His companions watched curiously as Strabo poured the contents of a water bag into the dirt. He removed his cloak and tunic, created a puddle of black mud, and began scooping it up and slathering it all over his face. Then he smeared his bare neck and forearms with it until he was completely covered.

They got the message and he helped them do the same. The moon was a thin crescent and soon they were darker than the night itself. They were three mud wraiths breathing in the shadows.

They discussed their strategy and slunk down the hill through the trees as silent as wolves on the hunt. Strabo drew his sword and, contrary to every ounce of training, covered the bright blade with mud.

Molena's heart thumped. Strabo had insisted that she *stay away from trouble.* He was correct in these things, she now knew. She was still weak. But there would be no stopping her here. Not with her sister so near.

Strabo moved silently to the entrance of the tent and tied a length of horse rein to a nearby post. He pulled the rein across the tent's opening and let it lie on the ground. He waited.

Tourek and Molena tiptoed to the seven figures on the ground. The bodies lay still as stone in the blackness, yet their identities were obvious to them. They both went to their twins.

Mallouse woke first. The man's forehead was bruised and swollen. He had been beaten and Tourek's heart immediately flamed in anger.

Tourek had his finger to his lips. *Is it Tourek?* thought Mallouse. This muddied face looked like a ghoul born in the swamps. But this was no foggy hallucination. His brother had come!

Molena put her cheek close to her sister's and woke her slowly as she had done a thousand times at home. Marinne smiled in her sleep and then woke to her sister close to her, her gentle fingers over her mouth. To her, it was a dream at first. Then she bolted upright, jangling her chains and looking at her sister in utter amazement. But the black and filthy face could not disguise the eyes she saw blinking back at her.

Tourek whispered in his brother's ear, "How many?"

"Five," Mallouse whispered back, pointing to the tent. He saw the black silhouette of mud that hovered next to the tent. When he recognized Strabo's battle crouch, he knew their luck had changed.

"Tourek, there are four more," he whispered. "Out on the hunt."

Mallouse watched his twin brother shake his head

through his earthy camouflage. "Not anymore," Tourek said. "Santandar?"

Mallouse pointed silently to another sleeping form just a few paces away.

Tourek feigned holding reins in his hand and silently mouthed, "Horses?"

Again Mallouse pointed wordlessly. There, nearly two hundred paces away, Tourek could just barely see a group of horses settled beneath the trees.

Someone else stirred behind him. Tourek turned to see one of the other captives leaning up, his eyes open and staring at the earth-encrusted Tourek. The stranger's eyes bulged at the sight. A ghost! A monster! A hellish spirit come to take them!

No one alive could have moved fast enough to stuff the scream of panic that exploded from the man's mouth.

The Souks jumped to their feet and Tourek charged to the tent, pulling his bow from his shoulder.

Strabo had positioned himself so that he might see both the front and the back of the tent, should someone be savvy enough to exit the rear.

The slavers all tried to storm out the front. Strabo sliced the stay lines and the tent collapsed in a dark heap of kicking and screaming. Strabo began jabbing into the tent with his blade, producing cries of pain.

One man burst his way out and Strabo snatched up the rein he had laid down. The man tripped and died on Strabo's blade before realizing a thing. Another two followed. They struggled out together and together they died. The first by Strabo's sword and the other by a direct shot from the bow of Tourek so powerful the arrow went right through the man's throat and out the other side.

Two slavers remained inside, moaning.

Marinne stared at Strabo. She turned to her sister. "Is that him?"

Molena frowned. "Later," she said. She looked for Santandar, who sat rubbing his eyes. The teenager still looked asleep.

"Out!" Strabo kicked whatever moved against the tent walls. "Out, I say!" he kicked a few more times and two men crawled ungracefully from the tent and sprawled on the ground. One bled from the back and twisted in pain. The unlucky other bled from the side of his head and the back of his thigh. Strabo had stuck him twice.

Strabo sliced a long gash in the tent and yanked it hard, splaying the whole thing open. He thrust his dirty hands into two wicker bags and produced a pair of iron crimpons. He threw them to Tourek.

Tourek tore at Mallouse's chains with the crimpons and freed him after a struggle with the iron linkages. Mallouse hugged his brother.

"Souk Mallouse!" called Strabo. "Bring your brother's sword." Tourek handed his sword to his brother, and despite limbs wounded by fighting and stiffened by the irons, Mallouse moved quickly.

"Watch these two." Strabo had watched Tourek struggle with the metal bonds and didn't have the patience to watch him free the rest. He took the crimpons from Tourek and deftly clicked Santandar and Marinne free. Strabo looked hard at Marinne. She was her sister's identical twin, all right. But he would have no trouble telling them apart. Molena had been too long in his thoughts. Molena helped her sister to her feet and Santandar rubbed his ankles and grinned at Strabo. Strabo told him to help his uncle and went to the other four captives. The man who had screamed, an old woman, and two young boys. The two boys were wide-eyed with fear.

"Who are they?" Strabo said over his shoulder.

The man spoke excitedly in a tongue unknown to Strabo.

"They are herdsmen," Marinne interrupted. "These are his sons and his mother. The boys are hungry."

Strabo clicked the man and his family free. The man pulled the boys close and wrapped his arms around them. The old woman joined them.

Strabo looked at the two sisters standing together: the muddy version and the clean. He grinned. They looked at each other and grinned too. Mallouse, never one to miss an opportunity, stepped next to his brother and gestured to Tourek's mud-covered body and then gestured at his own. Then he held his nose to his brother, as if he stank.

The two little boys laughed.

Strabo walked over to the two surviving slavers.

"What do we do with them?" asked Mallouse.

Strabo thought for a moment. "Santandar, bring me some irons." The slavers swore in colorful Greek and began arguing, each blaming the other for his predicament.

One of them spat at Strabo and Strabo kicked him again, harder, and the man groaned and was quiet. Santandar brought the leg and arm irons. Strabo patted the men down, and when he was satisfied they were unarmed, he crimped the irons fast with practiced efficiency.

Molena looked on with disapproval. "You are good with the irons, Strabo." She didn't mean it as a compliment.

"I am."

He dragged each man to a post and crimped a set of chains to each of their bonds.

"This isn't civilized," said Molena.

"No, it isn't."

The angry one let loose a string of what could only be expletives in a foreign tongue. Strabo drew his sword in an instant and butted the man in the face and the slaver collapsed in pain, fresh blood dripping from his nose.

"Leave them, Strabo. That is enough," Molena said.

But it wasn't enough for Strabo. He made them naked. Cutting the clothes from their bodies, he threw their garments on the heap that was their tent.

He looked at Marinne. "Ask the herdsman if they can make it home."

She did and the man nodded vigorously.

"Ask him if the slavers have any horses of his."

Again she spoke to the herdsman and he shook his head no.

"Go," Strabo said to the herdsman. The man nodded and herded his family away in the dark.

Strabo turned to the Souks. "Any more of these?" He held up the crimpons. They searched the wicker bags and found none. Strabo nodded.

"Take the bags. Fire the tent."

Strabo turned back to the two naked slavers and let them watch him slip the iron crimpons beneath his tunic. They looked unhappy indeed.

"Santandar." Tourek ripped something from the horseman's saddle and approached the boy. He handed him Cabo's leather collar. Santandar made a grim face, then cradled the collar carefully and stowed it safely away.

They gathered the horses. Their own and two more of the slavers'. Santandar fetched Castaine and the other two horses from the woods. Together again, they all set off without looking back. They left the slavers choking on the smoke of their belongings and shivering in their chains.

The weather stayed cool and wet and the rain fell hard at times. Tales of their respective exploits were traded along the way. The slavers had surprised them in the night and Mallouse was furious with himself.

"It is no matter now," his brother told him.

It would be three more days before they caught up to Hannibal's great column. Though the ride was wearying, the horses proved more than worthy. Marinne doted on her recovering sister and soon Molena's health was restored.

Molena said little to Strabo, less than he would have liked.

The journey gave Strabo time to think. He thought of Tourek and the man's mysterious ways. He thought of the army they would soon rejoin at the Rhône River. He thought of Nargonne.

The man had rescued Marinne. And Tourek had brought Molena back. Impossible, thought Strabo. But Nargonne's intentions were clear: The girl. Machoba. The fine. And the girl was done.

Machoba was next.

The Carthaginian navy brazenly sailed two hundred ships off the southern coast of Sardinia and then retreated. The Romans were incensed and declared the foray an act of war. Though no direct hostilities resulted, the Roman Senate instantly approved measures for ship-building. Since Carthage refused to bring Hannibal to heel, Rome publicly offered the Carthaginians a choice: war or peace. Without hesitation, the senate in Carthage chose war.

Chapter 12

*H*annibal's teeming host ran up against the flat western bank of the mighty Rhône River and dispersed along the shore for a league.

The Rhône was a formidable force in these parts. Its network of tributaries spread across the European continent and channeled the land's waters to the waiting Mediterranean Sea, a hundred leagues to the south. Its girth delineated lands, fiefdoms, and tribal territories.

If the shoreline to the south, where the Rhône poured to the sea, had been more hospitable, Hannibal would have chosen to enter Italy along the coast and thus avoid the anticipated path through the freezing Alps. However, that narrow course would deprive him of the element of surprise and would leave him open to attack.

This section of river was true wilderness. There were some settlements nearby, but Hannibal had purposely intended his crossing to occur in the middle of nowhere.

Hannibal's engineers had the final say on the crossing itself, of course, insisting on a section of river with a wide turn, where the bottom was hard and the depths ran shallow along the river's outer reaches. The banks here sloped gently on Hannibal's side and provided sound purchase for heavy carts laden with an army's worth of invasion support gear.

The slope on the opposite side, however, was steep and heavily wooded, the forest there as thick and healthy as an autumn crop: ideal ground to mount a defense.

It seemed Hannibal was taunting the uncooperative Volkai tribes, who had vowed to oppose him. And so he was.

"They will come," he told his Command corps.

At first, there was no sign of the Volkai, so Hannibal's forces spread out along the river unopposed and regained their strength, making full use of the time without travel. Weapons were refurbished. Local tribes on the western side of the river, friendly to Carthage, enjoyed great trade selling all manner of beast and foodstuffs, and Hannibal opened the coffers.

Ore and wood, fabric and leather, herbs and grain and crops—all were purchased from eager sellers with the unmarked gold from the Carthaginian treasure train. The locals flocked from leagues away to hawk their wares.

Hannibal's forward emissaries had done their jobs well and arranged for a multitude of watercraft for purchase and lease. The denizens of the river region provided boats of all kinds: canoes, rafts, fishing boats, and river scows.

The meal wagons worked nonstop, producing an endless line of feasts and also preparing for a march over mountains, where food would be scarce for weeks. "We fight fat," Machoba was heard to say with a smile.

A great amount of construction began immediately. Rafts had to be built to get the army's unprecedented mass of equipment and supplies across the river. The rafts also had to be prepared for defense. The Volkai had not yet shown themselves, but the experienced Carthaginians fully expected resistance. They would be ready one way or another.

Trees were felled and the lumber hacked into shape and assembled under the direction of the engineers. Precision was not a priority, as the rafts would be abandoned as soon as they reached the other side. The priorities were speed and efficacy. All varieties of war machines, animals, carts, and wagons must be accommodated. Inventory was tallied and checked until the engineers were satisfied all could be shipped across in a manageable number of trips.

The elephants posed the most ticklish task. They crossed minor streams without complaint but protested in terror when confronted with wider water. Each weighed as much as a hundred men. They were skittish beasts and prone to panic. Most believed that no army had ever sent them over water the likes of the Rhône, which explains why the Romans would never anticipate their presence. What was not widely known was that one army *had* previously performed the feat—Hannibal's.

His resourceful engineers covered the floor of large rafts with soil and brush, disguising them as pieces of land. They went so far as to install small trees around each raft's perimeter to screen the animals' view of the water and to aid in penning them in.

They moored the rafts to shore and the animals were held there for days so that they might be acclimated to the uneasy feeling of the ground swaying beneath their barrel-size feet. They coaxed the nervous younger animals on board first; then their parents, slaves to instinct, followed.

But the army's initial trip across the Rhône would involve no elephants. The first trip would be an all-out assault: horsemen, swords, arrows, and shields. The warriors must cross the river and then emerge as a storm of angry blade and shaft and point. Top officers conferred deep into the night along the Rhône's banks to refine their strategy.

The army made sure everyone along the waterfront was busy. Nargonne might have been the busiest, though he didn't look it. He and Sargonne fashioned a crude crutch from hickory, scarring and staining it until the shaft looked like it had seen years of hard service. Crutch securely wedged into armpit, Nargonne feigned injury and limped and plodded his way up and down the camp a dozen times—an obvious cripple was rarely bothered.

He took in everything and learned much about the preparations for the crossing and for battle. He eyed the Numidian cavalry and the Red Falcons. From a distance, he watched Machoba and Akdar drill their troops. He studied the Balearics, the Celts, the Iberians, the Africans, the Libyans, the Carthaginian proper, the engineering corps, the provisioning corps, the elephants, and the armories.

He found himself drawn again to the treasure train. It was backed up to the water. A defensive position. As usual, it was adjacent to the bread train and kitchen wagons. The bread train itself consisted of over thirty heavy wagons. Sentries guarded the bread train night and day, though only a few, as might be expected. The treasure train sentries were far more numerous and added horse security, as well as foot soldiers.

There was constant activity at the treasure wagons.

Gold was carefully inventoried and payments monitored and cataloged in great detail. Nargonne knew the army's gold stock dwarfed the amount anyone might demand for ransom.

The Carthaginians were paying out gold bars to the locals in great plenty, gearing up for more than a river crossing. They were stocking up for a major excursion through the mountains—in winter.

Small military expeditions had passed through the Alps in the past, but only in midsummer, and even then the dangerous peaks were barely negotiable. No army of any substantial size had ever passed. A crossing as ambitious as this in winter was unthinkable. Unthinkable, Nargonne mused. Not anymore.

He stared at the line of thirty bread wagons. In contrast to the decorated treasure wagons, they were rough-hewn, bare, and dilapidated; tattered canvas clung to their oaken sides. Each was virtually indistinguishable from the other.

At length, Nargonne limped away, past the construction gangs, past the horse yards, past the crews of men casting fishing nets in the river. He watched the nets fly high over the water, bloom like flowers, and then fall, whistling softly to the surface with hardly a ripple. He went back to where he and Sargonne and Barbestro had camped, near Octul's Celts.

Nargonne had allowed Sargonne to fall in with a smithy, a man who needed assistance as he worked his way through the throng each day. The smithy was kind and genuinely appreciated Sargonne's skills. His specialty was beasts of burden and he looked after cart horses and mules, oxen and donkey. Sargonne had asked him, "Work elephants?" The man had laughed, saying, "Not if I have anything to do with it!" Sargonne was busy and his talent with animals put to good use. The creatures needed his hand. The Carthaginians drove a ferocious pace and brooked no quarter for pack animals.

Barbestro had healed, more or less, though one could easily discern the remnants of the *pankration* match. A knot on his calf had solidified into a dark purple mass. His knuckles were healing fast and so were his bruises, though in places his skin was still colored yellow and blue. One eye was still black, the other still swollen at the brow, and his ribs still hurt on both sides. His mouth bled occasionally and his lower lip would bear the scar of the match for life. He had lost two teeth and injured another, a molar deep in his mouth, and that caused him the most discomfort of all. He bore it all as he bore everything—with long naps. And he thought of his Marinne, who was soon to be safely at home.

To Nargonne's surprise, and Octul's, Barbestro had become familiar with his giant *pankration* opponent. The two had been carted side by side and recuperated together on the march to the Rhône. Barbestro learned the big Celt's given name, but it was unpronounceable to him, so he referred to the man as his Celtic comrades did: Ox. A logistics officer had taken one look at the two huge men and immediately assigned them to heavy raft construction, a stroke of serendipity lost on Nargonne. Until later.

Ribas was with the Falcons, and Nargonne had not seen him, although he had received two notes scribbled on leather tucked beneath his saddle pad. Both notes read simply, "All is well."

Nargonne finally neared his campsite and discovered a small group gathered around Sargonne. He limped closer then stopped as surely as if he had hit a stone wall—a man could always recognize his son without seeing his face.

Nargonne's "limp" miraculously healed as he hurried toward them. Santandar, Tourek, and Strabo. Nargonne's spirits leaped at the sight of them, for he had just been thinking the men were overdue. But his son? What was *he* doing here? Santandar threw his arms around his father before composing himself. Nargonne withheld a smile until they told him about the slavers and that the girls were safely in the hills with Mallouse.

Reunions were not uncommon in camp. Comrades who fell behind still trickled in. So the talk and the back-slapping that surrounded the reunion of the Asturians went unnoticed.

General Hamar finally made his appearance. He was the Carthaginian commander in charge of "foreign" troops, as the Carthaginians referred to their mercenaries and Nargonne's troop fell under his command. Hamar's entry was a certain sign that battle would soon be afoot. The man could be seen on horseback meandering with his entourage through the troops.

For the Asturians, the remainder of the afternoon was spent in a close circle and Nargonne asked many questions of them all. Sargonne was beside himself with relief and sat beaming.

"You are certain she is in good health?" Nargonne repeatedly asked Tourek of Molena. She is, he was assured time and again. Nargonne told them of Barbestro and Ox and of their new friendship with Octul. Strabo was skeptical. It was he who had killed two of Octul's personal guards.

"We are all quite safe with them," Nargonne said. Then he paused. "Well, maybe not you, Strabo." He held a straight face for as long as he could, then burst out laughing. They all laughed.

Eventually Strabo broke their reverie.

"Where is Ribas?"

Nargonne paused and the group went quiet.

"He is with the Red Falcons, as he should be. I need him there."

"I see" was all Strabo said, a look of disapproval on his face. Nargonne decided not to let him off the hook, plus he wanted everyone to be clear on this point.

"It is evident, Strabo, you do not see the value of having friends in high places."

"As long as they are friends."

"Don't be a simpleton!" Nargonne barked at him. "I have told you to think, now think! Do you not trust my judgment? Do you not trust your own?"

Strabo soured. "I only want to be paid." He regretted the comment immediately.

"Is that so, Strabo?" The man's pouting irritated Nargonne. He needed men of firm frame of mind, not children. Had the upstart not delivered his people to safety yet again, Nargonne would have run him out of camp.

"I only question his capabilities." Strabo offered the excuse weakly.

"He is a smarter man than you, Strabo. You would do well to pay some heed."

Patience with a sword, Strabo had. It was discipline of a different sort he lacked.

Tourek helpfully changed the subject. "Nargonne, we

have fixed a rendezvous point with my brother. You can meet with him if you like."

"There is no need." Nargonne frowned. "I know *he* will use his head."

Then they heard the shouting.

Troops from all around began running toward the river. Within minutes, Nargonne and the others crowded on the riverbank with over thirty thousand men. A buzz hung over the crowd and numerous Carthaginian officers on horseback joined them. The officers calmly watched the opposite side of the river with the rest. They had expected this. They were not fools and had sent many an experienced scout to reconnoiter the other side.

The army watched as a mass of foliage rustled its way through the imposing forest on the other side. Thousands of bunches of branches and leaves shook and rattled their way down to the opposite riverbank. It looked as if the forest itself was marching toward them.

The Volkai had come. Thousands of them.

The scouts were consistent in their counts and Hannibal's commanders knew there to be some seventy-five thousand of them in the area.

So the Volkai substantially outnumbered Hannibal and they had an option the Carthaginians did not: This was their home country and they could recruit more bodies if need be. Both sides knew they held another tremendous advantage. The Volkai simply needed to hold. They had no need to fight their way over one of the largest rivers in the world against an entrenched enemy with the unforgiving steepness of the hills at their back. Such an enterprise would be folly, of course, and everyone knew it. Still,

Hannibal went to pains to make it clear to his officers and the enemy alike that that is exactly what he intended to do.

The Volkai were a warlike breed, much more so than their Celtic cousins in the area. They were big and tall and given to ruthless marauding. They fought without mercy or remorse. There were no prisoners in a Volkai victory.

The Volkai operated out of camps in hilltop clearings, a half a league back from the river's edge. Now they had come to the river with nearly all their number, each bearing an unwieldy bunch of leaf-festooned tree limbs.

It was an old trick, designed to intimidate through exaggerated size and to disguise the Volkai's number. The illusion of a moving forest also spooked the uninitiated. The spectacle made for an unnatural show and gave many an opponent pause.

The mass of foliage bristled and shook along the opposite bank's entirety. Then branches were dropped, and every one hundred paces, a Volkai warrior emerged from the sprawling, man-made thicket.

They were far on the other side and they knew their voices would hardly carry to the invading Carthaginians and their tongue was foreign, but that did not matter. Their point would be made. This was not a random affair. Each man had been rewarded this honor courtesy of some previous feat.

The Volkai warriors wore short skirts of heavy cloth and their upper tunics were cut short to match. Many came bare-chested to war, without armor of any sort. The message was clear: Men mad enough to fight this way would make dangerous opponents indeed. They were experienced woodlands fighters and preferred their legs clear so as not to get caught up in the unruly brush that covered the forest floor. They were fond of compact shields and short swords. And although there was a great wealth of worthy metal in the hills of their lands, their metalworking remained unsophisticated, as their weapons showed.

Like the Celts, they wore broad leather bands that stretched from wrist to elbow on their arms. Their swords dangled from fat leather baldrics, which stretched from one shoulder to the opposite waist. Huge bronze buckles adorned their belts. The Carthaginians could make out the occasional chief by the set of white swan feathers that hung from their helmets.

The Volkai were also fond of the spear, an aging weapon that Hannibal and other military minds with a contemporary bent were defeating with modern battle tactics. As for the bow, they had a few, but the bow was only useful in well-organized tactical strikes, and the Volkai were hardly organized, as events would show. Some wore helmets of rough bronze, but most headgear was of heavy pelt and hide and sported some animal's head or tail. Hill cat. Boar. Bear. Intimidating they were, but actual protection was slight.

One by one, each Volkai warrior that had stepped out began beating his chest. Each launched into a loud harangue, shaking his sword and spear at the enemy that faced him on the other side of *his* Rhône. As they spoke, they punctuated their delivery with occasional thrusts of spear and wobbling of shield. Their comrades responded with timely cheers, and thousands of jeers flew across the surface of the water toward the invaders from Carthage.

The Volkai had honed the Celtic practice of intimidation to a high art. Their war horns filled the air with earsplitting blasts that reverberated up and down the river. The Volkai warriors pranced up and down and gesticulated wildly, banging and bashing their weapons together to create a frightening clamor.

The Carthaginian contingent could not make out much of the Volkai's haughty speeches, but had they heard them clearly and had they understood the Volkai tongue, they would have heard speeches like this:

"Meet me, cowards! Women! I am Auch, son of Dodonac, and I mark my line back to the invincible Mazemet! We rule the lands of Sothath and Giron. What do you rule? Goats and monkeys!"

This was the type of insult that brought a roar from his Volkai brethren.

"I have murdered a man just this morning and he cried like a baby. I alone have killed a thousand men in battle and I will take a thousand of you to your grave. Your organs shall swamp our blades. Your heads will adorn our houses. You will choke on your own blood and the Rhône will flow red with your foolishness. You are fish food! Fools! Ask the Romans of the Volkai! The Romans were no match for our might. Our dogs fed on their carcasses and grew so fat they can no longer walk. The Romans ran home and hid beneath their beds and put on women's undergarments!"

It was true enough. Even the sophisticated power of the Romans had been unable to subdue these lands.

"Come fight me, children! I will smile and eat your livers! Why don't you fall on your own swords this moment and save me the trouble!"

They kept it up for hours, many men stepping forward

and seizing their chance in the sun with gusto. There seemed to be no limit to their blustering.

A few Libyans and Celtiberians stepped to the bank and waved their arms and shouted, bidding the Volkai to come on over. Everyone laughed at this. Neither side was crossing the river today and all present knew it.

As darkness fell, the Volkai retreated into the safety of their forest as quickly as they had come, but the sound of pounding continued throughout the night. The Volkai were fortifying their beachhead with stakes driven into the sand and sharpened to fine points.

Nargonne had studied the Volkai and the same striking thought occurred to him as had to Hannibal. The Volkai had few horses. Nargonne noted something else. On the Carthaginian side, though much of Hannibal's army had shown up to watch the Volkai performance, the Numidian horsemen were absent and the cavalry of the Red Falcons were nowhere to be seen.

Nargonne pondered this. He now recognized that Hannibal had one critical weakness, though few who opposed him ever possessed the savvy to figure it out, let alone exploit it.

Hannibal could not afford to lose men.

His army had been forged from the sparsely populated Spanish Peninsula. Where the Romans could field a million men, Hannibal could barely manage a hundred thousand, and that on his own soil. His tactical skill was thus born of necessity and honed by the cleverest mind of his generation. His resources limited, he composed his battle plans accordingly, and thus stealth and deception guided his every move.

The Campaign Escort urged everyone to bed down for the night, so Nargonne and the others returned to their fire.

Barbestro was waiting for them there, and when he saw the newcomers returned, his spirit soared. He was assured Marinne was safe and the news of his betrothed filled him with energy.

He told the group of his work on the big rafts and of yet another competition between him and Ox, this one entirely friendly. It seems the man challenged Barbestro to an impromptu log-lifting contest. Each hoisted logs heavier than the one before and a small crowd had gathered to cheer them on.

"The lifting was the easy part, Santandar. Dropping the cursed things nearly crushed my tiny toes!"

Santandar laughed.

Ox had eventually won. Barbestro described it without malice. The construction crews slapped them on their backs and congratulated the huge Celt.

"Tomorrow we lift chickens!" Ox had joked.

Unnoticed by the others, Nargonne slipped his fingers beneath his saddle pad and produced another of Ribas's notes. "Night ride" was all it said. Nargonne took Tourek and Strabo aside. "Sleep now. It promises to be a short night."

Barbestro, Sargonne, and Santandar would stay, Nargonne decided. He, Strabo, and Tourek prepared their weapons and horses. They clothed their weapons in swatches of cloak and made sure no metal was free to make telltale sounds as they rode. Strabo watched Nargonne attach two stout coils of rope to his saddlebags. Though the rest of the army was not yet close to sleep, they made to their beds.

Tourek paused long enough to roll his rune-covered stones and he studied them intently. Nargonne came over to him and urged him to bed.

"The future is uncertain," Tourek said.

Nargonne's eyes gleamed like black marble. "No it isn't," he said.

Santandar made his bed next to his father's. Despite the threat of the Volkai, Santandar felt eminently safe with his father, as a son would. The two chatted aimlessly beneath the stars and enjoyed an easy conversation as father and son. But Nargonne's mind was racing. How? he wondered. How?

Santandar spun Cabo's collar between his fingers beneath his blanket. The boy deigned to offer his opinion of Strabo.

"He is a great warrior, Father."

Nargonne soured at the thought of him.

"The man is a worthy weapon. That is all." Nargonne sighed. "A great warrior is something else entirely. Strabo can't see beyond the edge of his sword, Santandar. All the world is not so . . . straightforward. Not all things can be resolved with the blade."

Nargonne smiled at his son in the dark and tapped him on the top of his head. "Use this. It is greater than any sword. Even Strabo's."

They slept.

At three hours after midnight, Ribas appeared in their midst. He had made his face black with soot.

"Come," he whispered. The urgency in his voice brushed the sleep from their heads. Strabo, Nargonne, and Souk Tourek followed him into the night.

They walked their horses at first, exiting through the

rear of the camp before mounting up, Castaine making not a sound. When they reached the cover of the woods, they veered north. Within a league, they were joined by others: Numidians. Like Nargonne's men, their swords and bundles of short javelins were swathed in cloth. Wads of leather and twine muffled the armor of their mounts. As the hours wore on, more joined the soundless procession: Machoba's Red Falcons. All the creatures of the night hunkered down and huddled close to their burrows and nests, still and silent as the nocturnal cavalry rustled like a black wind through their heavy wood.

This night cavalry was spearheaded by none other than Hanno himself, Hannibal's most trusted general. That fact alone emphasized the critical nature of their mission.

Man and horse melded together seamlessly. Soon, there were nearly eight thousand men on horseback combing silently north through the forest, paralleling the sleeping Rhône below. If the forest had seemed to advance when the Volkai had made their grand entrance in the afternoon, it was the shadows themselves that marched tonight.

Tourek broke off at one point, only to return to the silent force two hours later. He gave Nargonne no more than a nod and it was not hard for Strabo to guess the man's purpose.

Deep in the hills, after Hanno's noiseless, ghostly parade passed, three dark riders struck out undetected. They followed the midnight horde at a prudent distance.

————

Roman Command determined that Hannibal had only two options for attack. He must come either by sea or over the rugged land that separated Spain from Italy, the coast of Gaul. So Roman scouting parties scoured all the coasts from Italy to Spain for signs of an invading army. They found none. Far to the south of Volkai territory, the Roman general Scipio and his legions were camped at the mouth of the Rhône, the very center of the Gaul coast. They could find no sign of Hannibal either. Learning of this, Roman Command grew convinced the invasion would come by sea and transferred garrison after garrison to the south—away from North Italy.

Chapter 13

*M*orning found the Carthaginians at the river in full-scale war preparations in every department. The engineers struggled to complete nearly one hundred rafts, wide but nimble, that would each ferry sixty troops across. Heavy raft construction for the elephants and for the weighty treasure train was halted for now, and those laborers, Barbestro and Ox among them, were deployed toward the troops. The bigger rafts would have to wait until the Volkai were repulsed.

Artillery was moved into the shallow waters of the beach and secured there. As a rule, Hannibal was not fond of heavy catapults and lithoboli, those bulky contraptions designed to hurl colossal iron arrows. They were siege weapons, he reasoned, and not appropriate for a fast-moving invasion force. Still, two dozen of the pieces were put to use and their support regiment stocked mounds of projectiles to be at the ready: stone, iron shot, heavy iron bolts. The missiles would terrify the enemy if nothing else.

The Carthaginians required no extra motivation, but

the Volkai managed to provide some anyway. A dozen Carthaginian scouts had been busy on the Volkai side of the river all through the night. Only four returned. The missing scouts showed up at first light, their bloody heads impaled on the defensive stakes laid out on the Volkai beach. Their dead eyes stared across the water at their living cohorts. The Carthaginian troops exhorted each other to avenge their valiant souls.

Now that only two thousand cavalry actually remained in camp, they spent much of their time galloping up and down the Rhône's banks accentuating their presence and exaggerating their numbers.

The Volkai appeared again by early afternoon. Bright yellow war stripes were smeared across their faces and they shouted challenges across the river, daring Carthaginian champions to come and fight for glory, one on one. They presented their own champions in a long succession, which went on into the evening.

As darkness fell, the Volkai dragged an endless quantity of brush and logs into a huge pyre. They sacrificed a number of goats and pigs, slitting the animals' throats and holding the bleeding carcasses aloft, entreating their enemy and their gods alike. They lit the great bonfire and brought forth a sickly-looking cow and sacrificed it as well. They hacked the carcass into pieces and cast it to the flames. The fire roared high for hours and threw hulking Volkai shadows against the trees and over the water.

Then their war drums began. The Carthaginians heard them thumping steadily all through the night. At midnight, the Volkai commenced chanting. It was a low, eerie chanting that rode over the waves and wafted over the

Carthaginian camp. Many an invader had been unnerved by the Volkai rituals and many a fight had been avoided.

Not this time.

Far to the north, Hanno's deadly night cavalry made excellent time. The thick woodlands up there were uninhabited and their passing made no notice. They had ridden hard the first night, and on through the next day, before they rested their horses in the protection of heavy pine along the river's edge. The horses feasted on the tall, juicy grass that lined the Rhône there, and all drank heartily from the river. There was no fire and would be none on this trip until the very last, when the fire would be a very special one indeed.

Advance scouts discovered a suitable place to ford the river where it shallowed and forked to form a broad island. The bottom was mucky on one side but passable, as the scouts had proved, crossing and then recrossing to assure themselves the way was fair. They marked the place with cloth flags mottled the color of the forest and returned to the main group.

When night came again, the cavalry efficiently made their way there, located the flags, and crossed easily in the darkness, aided by animal skins they inflated to help buoy their way. No one saw Tourek affix his own marker to the branch of a bush that had bravely grown in the crack of a man-size boulder at the water's edge. Buried in the sand there, he left a leather note composed by Nargonne.

Now on the Volkai side of the river, the cavalry rode back south in the same fashion they had come—with speed and stealth. Welcomed by all but Akdar, Ribas had been called to Machoba's circle, thanks to the skill he had demonstrated dispatching the hapless Gauls. Machoba welcomed talent and ferocity, and Ribas had both. Machoba would need the best to carry the Red Falcons' mission to success. They had a lot of ground yet to cover and the operation itself would be a delicate one, relying on pinpoint timing.

Strabo, for his part, had a difficult time. His riding skills had improved, but he was with men who had ridden for years and seemed fused to the saddle. Fortunately, they traveled mostly at night, so his amateurish ways were disguised. There was no ignoring the pain in his back and thighs, however, despite the best efforts and easy gait of Castaine.

On this ride, Nargonne looked like a different man. He wore an eye patch, and before they left camp, he and Tourek had split his beard and tied it into two stubby tails secured by tiny leather loops. He had also greased his hair in the manner of the Carthaginians but topped his head with a Celtic helmet. The effect was as intended; no one from Asturias would recognize him, let alone Machoba.

The night cavalry again traveled all night and another day before resting and setting out once again after dark. Command officers began circulating orders. They were closing in on their target.

Eventually General Hanno took them away from the river for more than two leagues and soon they were configured in a wide tactical arc around their prey. They were ordered to eat heartily from their packs, prepare for battle, and sleep well, for they would be up again before the sun.

Hanno's signal crew devised two fire pits. One pit was piled with aged maple and lit. The aged wood burned smokelessly and they tended it in shifts until they had a sizable amount of char. The other pit consisted of pine and assorted softwoods chosen for their proclivity for heavy smoke—white smoke, when hot and doused with water. That fire would not be lit until the time was right. They placed many leather buckets of water at the ready and anxiously checked and rechecked the direction of the wind. They murmured among themselves and prayed to Melquart, their war god, to hold the eastern breeze light and steady.

The night cavalry was in position. Hanno waited.

By morning, the Volkai bonfire at the river had shrunk to smoldering ash and not a Volkai warrior stirred in their woods.

But the Carthaginian side had been rousted by Attack Command three hours after midnight and made ready. Orders were given and repeated. Barbestro, Santandar, and Sargonne ate a fat breakfast, as did the entire army. Hannibal never sent an army into battle without properly preparing them, and that included well-fed troops.

Barbestro gulped his down without chewing, for his injured tooth had abscessed angrily. His entire lower lip had swollen into a hideous grimace. He was ordered to the skirmishers. The smithy took Sargonne and Santandar away among the pack animals, a safe-enough position.

An hour before dawn, all were at their places.

Hannibal's scouts stationed up and down the river had their eyes on the high ridge on the opposite side of the Rhône. In camp, Carthaginian command officers patiently scanned the night-shrouded sky. The camp's signal crew had fabricated two signal fires identical to the fires of Hanno's cavalry, now presumably less than a league away. The signal crew waited.

Hanno's eight-thousand-strong night cavalry had been

gone nearly three days. Their return, such as it was, was heralded by two distant puffs of white smoke that lifted over the horizon, nearly invisible in the dim light of near dawn.

The northern scouts saw them first and launched into a series of shrill wolf calls, echoing along the river gorge to finally fall on the ears of high command. The officers narrowed their eyes and scoured the sky. There they were! Now every officer saw them and every officer knew the code.

Two small puffs. *In position.*

Three more quickly followed, larger than the first two. Bird and wolf calls suddenly echoed in, this time from the south, and then all was quiet again.

Three fat puffs. *Surprise achieved.*

There was a long pause as the shadowy puffs sailed toward the waning stars and drifted drowsily apart. Every officer scanned the sky, as did Hannibal himself.

Finally a single fat puff succeeded the others, floating above the ridge in confident isolation. The ghostly puffs were a league away, but it may as well have been General Hanno whispering directly in his leader's ear. Hannibal surely smiled.

One fat puff. *Ready.*

Hanno and his night cavalry's three-day forced march had outflanked the Volkai far to the rear, behind the enemy's base camps.

Hannibal might be outnumbered, but not outfoxed.

His camp signalmen leaped into action. Competently exchanging logs and char from fire to fire, they returned a signal. But their signal differed from Hanno's.

First, a single fat puff. *Ready.* Next, one small puff, one fat, one small. *Wait.*

Hannibal was fanatical when it came to organization in battle; his disciplined attention to detail was responsible for victory after victory over opposing forces much larger in number.

There were over three hundred men in his signal corps. The largest signal corps in the world, it was an elite group and troops employed there won the position through achievement and mettle.

The Volkai employed none. They didn't bother much with scouts either, as this was their territory. They were completely unaware that eight thousand of the world's finest military cavalry crouched in wait at their rear.

Even the regulars in Hannibal's army expected an all-out surprise attack across the river. Hadn't Hannibal obviously been preparing them for just such an assault? Why give the Volkai any warning?

Instead, Hannibal ordered the war horns of Carthage to life and the Volkai trees trembled from the noise. Among the support wagons, Santandar clapped his hands over his ears against the drone. The elephants, stationed far behind the action, could be heard trumpeting in response above the din.

To the blasting of the horns, sixty wide rafts suddenly pushed off from the Carthaginian side of the river. Each was loaded with one hundred troops, archers all. The rafts were secured to stout ropes on shore manned by hundreds of support troops and they strained to prevent them from being swept downriver, while the pole crews on the rafts sweated their way across.

Suddenly the Volkai appeared. They streamed howling

out of the woods, and within minutes, the bank swarmed with their angry and disorganized mass.

Flanking the Carthaginian rafts were thousands of swimming troops. Spearmen. They were to emerge under the cover of fire and rush directly into the enemy's belly.

The screaming Volkai saw another sixty rafts follow the first wave into the water. The rafts slipped off the banks like crocodiles to hunt. In the growing light, the Volkai could make out the shields and swords of the second wave—swordsmen.

Or so it seemed, though the Volkai would not realize the deception until it was too late. This wave was the Balearic slingers again. They hugged behind the archers by just a few paces.

Downriver, the Numidian cavalry made to cross en masse and Volkai poured from the woods there to oppose them. Many Volkai were still rubbing the sleep from their eyes. Like their comrades up and down the gorge, and unlike the Carthaginians, they had not yet had their breakfast.

But the Volkai had wakened enough to begin blaring their own war horns as well and the sounds of war that bellowed from the gorge could be heard for many leagues. The bedlam was complete.

The river now teemed with activity, crowded with rafts and men. Carthaginian signalmen perched on makeshift towers to keep them visible above the fray and flashed their formation flags as each regiment executed its assigned function with deadly precision.

Far from the river, Hanno and his eight thousand horse saw the smoke signals rise from the Carthaginian camp beyond the ridge. They heard the call of their native horns, distant as they were, and the sound seized them with pride and purpose.

The battle had begun.

Machoba was one of many anxious officers who gathered close to Hanno. It was Machoba's habit to stay close to important men. He turned to Hanno. "Another good day," he said. Hanno simply nodded his head. No new orders were given. Not a single horseman stirred. They remained concealed in their positions.

At the river, the archery rafts drew close and the Volkai began firing long arrows at them, but the volleys fell in the water, just shy of the rafts. Thousands of Volkai archers materialized from the dense wood and knelt in stable positions on the beach. Nearly twenty thousand swordsmen lined the trees behind them, shouting encouragement. It looked certain they would annihilate their slowly advancing, raft-borne foes.

Then came the familiar trick. Thousands upon thousands of razor-sharp iron pellets suddenly arced over the archery rafts and rained down upon the surprised Volkai. The Balearic slingers had struck. The rafts wobbled as the Balearics swung again and again and showered the beach with an unending rain of bullets. The air above the river grew dark with their finely honed stones, and like the Gauls, the Volkai were helpless against the onslaught. Cut down by the thousand and spinning from multiple impacts, they struggled back to the trees. Not many made it.

The Volkai swordsmen at the trees were caught too, though they suffered fewer losses. None of the Volkai had experience against the Balearics. How could they have known that they were so accurate? Then the raft archers came into range and they launched cloud after cloud of whistling arrow. The Volkai fell in waves.

Downriver, the Numidians waded their horses across and drew many Volkai toward them. But the Numidians stopped short of the opposite bank and instead of storming ashore steadied their mounts in the rushing water and fired arrows at the Volkai beach. The Volkai fired arrows in return, but the Numidians backed out of range, then shot ahead again to fire and then retreated again. Then the Numidians surged forward again with their javelins and launched the dangerous barbs at their enemy, only to retreat once more. The frustrated arrows of the Volkai plunked into the Rhône by the thousand and sank harmlessly to the bottom.

On the Carthaginian beach, reconnaissance and logistics groups assembled and compared counts. The enemy had shown less than thirty-five thousand men. Not enough. Carthaginian command ordered withdrawal.

Raft support heaved mightily and ten thousand muscles strained to pull the rafts back. The Numidians withdrew. The entire attack had lasted less than an hour.

As the Carthaginians regrouped up and down their beach, thousands more Volkai appeared and stood over their dead and wounded and shook their weapons, cursing the Carthaginians, who had suffered hardly a scratch. Two attack rafts had foundered and hundreds of archers had been swept downriver. Some drowned, but the rest were assisted from the river by the waiting Numidians. Carthaginian losses were less than two hundred. Though they held every advantage, Volkai losses were nearly three thousand.

The archers and the Balearics reloaded. The signal corps on the beach tended its fires and waited.

Within an hour, the scene was repeated. Horns blew; rafts launched; the Numidians entered the water. This time, the rafts were spread out to cover more river.

Even with their losses, the Volkai still far outnumbered the Carthaginians. The Volkai had now doubled their number to over sixty thousand men to face the attack and all had shields at the ready. There were many spears. They crowded the beach and the trees that guarded it. What orders they had were clear. *Hold the beach at all costs.* They did, after all, still hold the advantage of their own forest at their back.

The east bank of the Rhône teemed with their number as far as the eye could see. Thousands of their weapons gleamed in the sun. Many carried the intimidating double-edged battle-ax. They looked an impassable barrier of shining metal.

Hannibal's second attack had less impact than the first, but still many Volkai were cut down. The beach was so littered with bodies the Volkai had a difficult time just getting around. Again Hannibal withdrew.

The Carthaginians continued this way for three more waves, varying the formation of the rafts and sending the Numidians upriver to the north and then back again to the south.

As expected, the attacks had less and less effect and reconnaissance squads compared notes. By noon, they estimated five thousand Volkai were dead and thousands more wounded.

Command was pleased with the extent of Volkai casualties, and though Volkai losses were not unimportant, casualties were not their aim. The continuous assaults were designed to empty the enemy's main camps from far behind the river and draw nearly all the Volkai down the steep woods to the river.

Though the two thousand Numidian horses were absent, the Carthaginians actually paused for lunch before preparing for another assault. This one would be the last. The signal crews on the beach prepared their fires, and when command was confident all was ready, their signal climbed into the sky. Two fat puffs.

All of Hanno's thousands of horses stood at the ready, save one—Castaine. He was lying down with eyes closed and Strabo dozing peacefully against his back. Nargonne hunched nearby, unable to relax. His mind was working overtime now. The time was near. How much luck would they need? he wondered.

In midafternoon, a stir went through Hanno's cavalry and officers began gesturing with hand signals that were passed on down through the ranks. Nargonne joined everyone in looking up at the sky above the river. Two large balls of smoke floated over the ridge.

Two fat puffs. *Attack.*

Eight thousand horsemen were mounted and moving in moments. Hanno had split Machoba's two thousand Red Falcons in two. One thousand would take the Volkai base camps under Machoba's command. The rest under Akdar would join Hanno and seven thousand horses would descend upon the Volkai from the top of their own ridge, pinning them against the river. The squeeze of the vise would be absolute.

Hanno's signalmen launched one fat puff to signal that they were ready too. They waited. Then, removing the char that produced white smoke, they replaced it with wet softwoods and quelled the signal fire with a huge quantity of water all at once, sending a great deformed cloud into the air. Carthaginian Command at the river would see it and read the rising plume of unruly smoke correctly. *Position abandoned.* Hanno's horses were coming.

Hannibal gave the order for general attack.

———

Up and down the Spanish coast, edicts rained down from Carthaginian Headquarters at Cartagena: Ports were closed; vessels were seized; Roman sympathizers were put in chains. Rumors were flying all over the Mediterranean; one had Hannibal marching out of Spain back to Carthage itself in order to proclaim himself king. Hannibal officially declared the eastern coast of Spain off limits to commercial shipping. The busy port of Saguntum was closed to all but the five hundred Carthaginian military ships gathered there. These were sure signs of impending naval action and Roman Command responded by activating twenty-four thousand citizens for naval reserve and deploying them to ports for ship preparation.

Chapter 14

*F*or the night cavalry, the time for stealth had passed. The weapons that had been muffled so carefully were unleashed and at the ready.

At the beaches, the rafts set off once again. This time, the Balearics flanked the archers and new rafts finally entered the water ferrying true swordsmen, mostly Celts. Ox and Barbestro were among them. Battle cries hurtled from every throat. Behind them, twenty thousand Iberian swordsmen entered the water without aid of raft. They waded as far as they could and then began swimming. The Rhône choked with armed humanity as the force advanced across the river.

The Numidians were still not visible.

Of the night cavalry, Machoba's contingent would be the first to draw blood. As they burst through the trees and crossed a wide meadow, the geography of the area became clear. Meadow, forest, meadow, forest. Hilly. Excellent terrain for horse versus man.

While the rest of Hanno's cavalry steered toward the river, one thousand Red Falcons thundered toward their assigned target: the Volkai's base camps. The camps rambled for nearly a league, spread haphazardly along the plateau that led to the Alps beyond.

While Ribas rode near the front of the column, Nargonne, Strabo, and Tourek were in the middle and Nargonne had told them to make poorer time than the rest and thus fall back gradually. This posed no difficulty for Strabo. At full gallop, he could scarcely stay on Castaine's back. This frustrated the horse. Surrounded by the excitement of the rumbling herd, he wanted to run!

Nargonne watched him flop around on the back of Castaine like a landed fish, and despite the gravity of the situation, he fought the urge to laugh. Tourek saw him too, and the two Asturians shook their heads.

The Red Falcons crested a hill and saw the first of the Volkai's ramshackle shelters sprawled across the hillsides. Without a single horse missing a step, they stormed over the camp.

There were few people to fight. The only Volkai left were a few sickly stragglers and these men scattered like mice before birds of prey. Most were slain in the first seconds. Horse and blade caught man after man. The hooves of a thousand horses pounded the camp to pieces. Carts and wagons were overturned. Countless water tubs, food baskets, barrels, and cooking pots were upended. Supply shacks tumbled to the ground. The Volkai's cattle, goats, and pigs all fled squealing before the storm.

The Falcons swept through the tents and their swords demolished them in a flurry of shattered posts and tattered tent cloth.

They went for the fires. Soon they brandished flaming sticks with which they set upon every tent and hut. Within five minutes of marauding, four hundred tents were on fire. Machoba screamed orders and the entire Falcon squadron galloped off to the next clearing.

At the far end of the meadow, two Volkai had hidden when the assault began; seeing the Falcons now heading their way, they suddenly broke from the bushes and sprinted toward the safety of the trees and their army at the river.

Thirty Falcons took off in pursuit.

Ribas had stayed close to Machoba, as he and Nargonne had discussed so many times.

"Let them go!" Ribas shouted to Machoba.

Machoba had a look of incredulity on his face. What was the man thinking?

"Let them spread the word," Ribas continued, "that their camp is overrun."

Aha! Machoba grinned widely. "Yes!" he cried, and his officers called the pursuers back. The refugees vanished into the trees. Machoba blessed his luck that the heady Usson had joined his unit, and the Falcons galloped on. The next clearing full of tents awaited their fate.

Behind them, the first camp burned. Nothing moved but the remains of smoldering tents flapping gently in the breeze and a gritty haze of smoke and dust hung over the place. Three riders cantered quickly into the mist. They were dressed as darkly as Hanno's night cavalry, but they rode Asturian horses. They were Molena, Marinne, and Souk Mallouse.

On the Carthaginian side of the Rhône, the lithoboli and catapults that had slumbered all day woke violently, erupting in a synchronized series of low, reverberating thumps. The sinewy lines that provided the source of their energy unwound with a *whoosh* and the clunky instruments twanged loudly with each round. A flock of iron bolts, each the length of a man, flew high over the advancing rafts and showered into the Volkai forest, shattering trees and throwing up clumps of soil. Hundreds of rocks also blasted in and a few Volkai were pulverized upon impact, though most of the missiles were ineffective at killing. They were, however, completely effective in unnerving the enemy. The Volkai scattered screaming into the trees.

Fifty thousand of them huddled there, regrouping. They watched the advance of the enemy rafts stall on the river. On the opposite shore, the Carthaginian support force strained against the raftlines and the rafts' pole men labored to hold them in place. The thousands of swimmers had slowed. The Carthaginians had halted yet again!

The whole of the Volkai shouted in triumph from the trees. Every leaf shook as their horns blared.

But the rafts did not turn around. They waited, hovering in formation in the swiftly flowing water. And from the south, the blaring horns of the Volkai began to fall off. The earth began to tremble and the Volkai stared down the shore.

Two thousand Numidian horses roared up the shoreline on the Volkai side of the river. The Numidians had ridden hard to the south all afternoon, skipping lunch, in fact. They had crossed unopposed and ridden even harder back to the fight.

As the Volkai took in this unexpected development, they were startled by the sudden detonation of a hundred earsplitting horn blasts rolling down their slope and echoing through *their* trees from the ridge above. Those were the high-pitched assault horns of Carthage! *Behind them.*

Up and down the entire length of the river, Carthaginian signalmen could be seen furiously flashing brightly colored flags.

The raft support group released their hold and the rafts advanced again. The swimmers surged forward and the river went white with the splashing of their strokes.

The ridge above the Volkai shook with the clamor of Hanno's seven thousand horses, which swooped down the slope, an angry deluge of armor and sword and death.

A league inland, Machoba's thousand hit the second camp and then the next. The results were the same. The disciplined Red Falcons were not distracted by the sounds of battle coming from the river. The squadron understood that the riverfront was a task for other squadrons of Hannibal's army. Their assignment lay here in the hills.

In the confusion of Machoba's raid, Nargonne and Tourek found Strabo and bade him continue with the Falcons.

"Find Ribas," Nargonne said. "Bring him." Strabo watched Nargonne and the Souk turn and race their horses back the way they had come.

The Falcons finally met some real resistance at the fourth camp, now that the advantage of surprise was lost. There, three hundred Volkai had formed a tight circle, hurriedly forming a loose and amateur phalanx against the Carthaginians. Strabo thought it a foolish course, but they stood their ground as the Falcons bore down upon them.

Machoba was in the front. So was Ribas.

As they neared the phalanx, Machoba shouted orders,

the horse-borne signifiers flashed red flags, and the Falcons accelerated directly into the Volkai line.

The impact of the armored horses driving into the crowd caused the entire phalanx to stagger back. A chorus of loud shrieks erupted from the Volkai as man after man was crushed by horse and skewered by blade. They fought back with the strength of panic, swinging battle-axes wildly over their heads and stabbing their spears blindly at the horses and their riders.

Like the Falcons, Strabo swung and struck at the Volkai. But his actions were clumsy and devoid of his usual effectiveness. He had little skill from the back of a horse and he longed for his feet to be on the ground. He cursed and swung as the Falcons drove the Volkai into the earth. Thirty-two unlucky Falcons were killed by the Volkai's stand, as well as twenty horses.

All of the Volkai perished in minutes.

The Red Falcons, to their credit, were not ones to pause and reflect on success. They torched the camp and tore off for the next.

Far behind them, the three ghostlike Asturians were combing through the first Volkai camp as Nargonne and Tourek galloped back in to meet them. Tourek smiled at his brother as if meeting on market day.

"Hail, Souk," he said.

"And to you" was his brother's reply.

Nargonne squelched the hellos as soon as he could see that everyone was safe. Back to the business at hand. Nargonne and Tourek quickly joined them in collecting any Volkai war gear they could find from the burning tents. Quivers, boots, belts.

Marinne rescued a pile of smoldering cloaks crafted of

the heavy hide favored by the Volkai. And Mallouse found a basket of the ubiquitous Volkai skullcaps. Molena produced a bulky helmet fabricated from the preserved head of a bear.

"Perfect," Nargonne said. He squeezed the hideous thing onto his head.

There was one thing more they needed from here and Nargonne was getting anxious. "Find them!" he barked. "We're running out of time."

They found them; there were few weapons of substance in the camp, but they at last uncovered a basket of Volkai arrows and a single Volkai spear, its shaft broken.

"They'll have to do," Nargonne muttered.

The five of them donned the Volkai hides over their clothes and covered their heads with the caps.

The arrows of the Volkai were feathered with telltale bright white streamers woven from the feathers of swan. They stowed the white arrows in Volkai quivers and slung them over their backs. Nargonne took the spear. He looked at Mallouse and nodded at the coil of rope and chain that hung from his saddle.

"Keep those handy," he told Mallouse. *I might as well keep the ruse going to the very last,* thought Nargonne.

Tourek produced yellow powder from a pouch and mixed it in his cap with water to form a yellow paste. In no time, he painted bright yellow Volkai stripes on each of their faces.

Then the group tied a number of empty baskets on each horse so they appeared overloaded with baggage.

They were ready.

"Wait!" Marinne said.

She dug into the pack she had carried through the long

nights they had followed the night cavalry and produced a scrunched-up bundle of white feathers: the long, bright feathers of an adult swan. She and her sister affixed them to Nargonne's bear helmet.

The last of the Volkai camps was the smallest and farthest from the river. When Machoba's men galloped in, they found it mostly empty, as the camps before it. A few men ran from tents and they were quickly cut down. Again the Falcons leveled the place.

Machoba quickly conferred with his officers until he was satisfied that their mission was accomplished in full. Now they might be needed at the river, but not all of them. He barked orders to his officers and their shouts erupted over the burning camp. They began to pull out.

Then Machoba's men watched as their leader dismounted and walked over to two dead Volkai and hacked the heads from their shoulders with his sword. He returned with the heads and tied them by their long brown hair to the chest harness of his horse. The heads hung there, the faces scowling in death and dripping blood down the forelegs of Machoba's mount. Machoba laughed. "The dead are our playthings, Falcons!"

Strabo at last rode up to the perimeter of the last camp aboard Castaine and pulled up short.

He could see only a dozen Falcons staying behind as the rest of them again tore off in a furious stampede, this time toward the river. Those remaining were bunched together. It was Machoba and his personal security detail. And Ribas. Strabo moved behind the cover of a tree and watched.

Machoba suspected many Volkai would escape south and he hoped to root them out. Just as he was about to order his men to follow him and spread out in scout formation, everyone turned as a single Falcon from the stampede that had just left galloped back toward them. The rider had been on the trailing edge of the horde and had seen something huddling in the tall grass. The man was nearly out of breath. He pointed to the thick grass at the edge of the meadow.

"Volkai," he told Machoba.

As one, the group's hands went to their sword hilts.

"How many?"

The man gasped for a lungful of air.

"A handful. Maybe half a dozen."

Machoba scoffed and yanked his reins. They all spurred their horses and galloped the short distance to the grass. Machoba's horse was the fastest and he got there first but suddenly shouted "Ho!" and slid to a turf-spraying stop. The others followed suit and stood there wordlessly.

They were Volkai all right. Small ones.

Machoba howled with laughter and the earnest rider who had ridden back flushed red with embarrassment.

They were children. Six young boys huddled in the tall grass. They peered up at the horsemen in terror.

Machoba grinned. "Rise, great Volkai warriors, rise!"

The boys didn't move.

"On your feet!" Machoba gestured with his sword for them to stand. They looked back and forth at one another and finally one stood. Then the others. Two were obviously brothers and they clung to each other's coats. None looked older than twelve.

The boys looked ridiculous in their garb. One wore a man-size buckle that covered his entire chest. All carried short wooden swords. Most wore skullcaps far too big for them and one wore the pelt of a fox on his head. The big pelt tilted drunkenly on the small boy's head and the fox's dead eyes stared at the horsemen.

Machoba scrutinized them. He knew they could not understand his language, but he would have his fun.

"Come to see a fight, gentlemen? To earn your yellow stripes and learn the ways of war from your fathers?"

The boys were as still as the trees.

"Your fathers are dead," said Machoba.

One of the boys started to sniff and sob, but his brother hushed him. *Such is war,* Machoba mused. *War is the thing. The only thing. And many will die.*

His men waited silently on their horses. The severed Volkai heads, dangling from Machoba's horse, grimaced at the children. Only Ribas was staring off over the smoking camp behind them, where in the distance a small band of Volkai appeared. They were leading a train of overladen packhorses through a stand of trees far beyond the wrecked camp. One of the horses was hitched to a cart and two of the Volkai looked short. Shorter than men should be. It occurred to Ribas that Nargonne was cutting things awfully close this time.

"There!" Ribas shouted, pointing.

All of the Falcons turned and saw the Volkai escaping. There were five of them and the big one in front excited Machoba; long white feathers hung from his headpiece.

Machoba reacted quickly.

"Follow me!" he barked.

He paused long enough to single out Ribas and three Falcons. "Finish here, then follow."

Ribas stiffened. Dark memories flooded his brain.

Machoba pointed his blade at the boys in the grass.

"Kill them."

Machoba spun his horse around and the other Falcons followed, peeling after the escaping Volkai band.

Ribas and the three who stayed behind watched the others go. The three did not know Ribas, and he did not know them. Warriors they were, all of them; each accustomed to death and slaughter, each accustomed to the ways of their ambitious colonel.

But Machoba's order disgusted them.

No one said a thing. The soldiers listened to the muted sounds of war floating over the wind from the river. The boys only shivered, staring in silence at the dangerous men on horseback towering over them.

Ribas was the most anxious. He must follow Machoba and do so quickly! His heart pounded in his chest and his spine hardened with resolution. Of the troubled men, he alone knew the boys' fate was decided. And the fate of these men. He broke the silence.

"We let them go."

The others gasped.

"Treason!" one Falcon hissed. The man was beside himself with anger and shame, confusion overwhelming him.

"Our blades are bloody enough. No one shall know," Ribas said.

The Falcons considered the thought, as they already had. But there was no safety in this course of action and they all knew it. Machoba surely would discover it and their lives would be forfeit in disgrace. Men drank and men talked. No secret such as this could be buried. The angry one drew his sword. Inside, he cursed his vaunted colonel as he never dreamed he would. But duty controlled him.

He glowered at Ribas, though his rage was not meant for him.

"We'll kill them quickly," he offered. "And your words will be forgotten." The proposition should have offered some relief to the warriors. It didn't.

In the end, it was the boys themselves who sealed the fate of everyone present. One of them broke and ran.

A Falcon instinctively yanked an arrow from his quiver and put missile to bow in an instant. But the little boy would never feel the shaft tear through his back. The archer's bow hand separated from his arm so quickly, the amputation was at first bloodless. The arrow fluttered impotently to the ground while the man stared in wonder at the sudden vacuum at the end of his arm. The sword of Ribas had sliced it clean.

Ribas spun to face the other two.

"Treachery!" they cried, and they descended upon him in a cyclone of whirling swords.

The armored horses' bodies crashed into each other, Ribas backpedaling and repulsing blows with rapid cross strikes.

The wounded man's fresh stump pumped blood in a rush. He awoke from shock and threw his sword desperately at Ribas and it shuddered off Ribas's helmet, the concussion squirting a spray of angry sparks behind Ribas's eyes.

The man stared furiously at his stricken arm before finally crying out in pain. He seized the bloody end in panic and, cursing Ribas, lost his balance and tumbled from his horse. The remaining boys turned and raced away like rabbits through the grass.

Strabo saw none of this, but he had seen the escaping Volkai when Ribas had pointed them out. He discerned the identities of the two shorter Volkai and realized Nargonne's plan immediately. He watched the Volkai suddenly cast away all of the bags loaded on their horses and take flight, the beat-up cart spinning bravely after them.

As soon as he saw Machoba and his Falcons start after them, he kicked Castaine forward and gave chase as best he could. Impressed as he was by Nargonne's clever ploy to lure prey to snare, one large snag was apparent. A dozen hungry Falcons pursued them and one of these Falcons was the deadliest man in all of Hannibal's army. The "Volkai" were only five.

"Ya! Castaine, ya!" and the horse took off, Strabo shaking violently in the saddle. His nose bounced off the horse's neck and cracked painfully. Soon blood poured from his nostrils and drained away over his face in frothy streaks. Still, he hung on. Now Castaine had eyes only for the horses galloping away in the distance and his mind fired for the chase. Ahead, the warhorses of the Falcons crested a grassy ridge and were gone.

Castaine raced over tall grass and took a shortcut through a bundle of lonely trees rooted on the rolling meadow. Their branches whipped Strabo angrily. The chase possessed Castaine, but the horses ahead held a distinct advantage: Their partners could ride.

Machoba and his men descended the hill and made for the next hill looming before them. The dead Volkai heads tied to Machoba's horse loosened and fell, tumbling away and rolling to a stop in the grass. Their vacant eyes watched the Falcons ride on. As the Falcons galloped up the rise, the meadow made way for stiffer ground and they could see the line of the forest ahead. Before them, at the edge of a long tree stand, they saw the Volkai disappear around a bend.

"After them!" Machoba shouted over the sound of the hooves. They sped for the kill.

As the other "Volkai" galloped on, one of them dived from his mount. Souk Mallouse. He slid to position behind some thick elms and stretched arrow to bow in a heartbeat.

Ahead, Nargonne and the girls abandoned the cart, which had been slowing them down. Molena sliced the cart harness from the horse's neck and bade the cart horse stay as they galloped on. The dilapidated cart sat in their wake, hay drooping crazily from its outboards. The cart horse stood at the ready. The bags on the horse's flanks were stuffed with assorted potions, bones, and rune stones, as usual. The cart horse was Tourek's.

Machoba roared past the trees without a glance. Mallouse was careful to avoid Machoba and take the riders just behind him. In rapid succession, two of Machoba's security detail took long iron arrows directly in their ribs and were launched from their mounts to spill on the ground in front of the Falcons just behind. The group was disrupted as they dodged unsuccessfully around them. The life of one of the fallen was crushed away by the errant hooves of a six-hundred-stone war animal on the run. The other lay in the grass clutching his chest as the rest of the Falcons thundered on. The stricken men's horses cantered away in confusion.

In the trees, the Souk remounted and charged off. Now

there were ten Falcons, two less than before. When Strabo finally came to the trees and saw the Falcons on the ground, he bade Castaine hold, dismounted ungracefully, and, wasting no time, dispatched the wounded Falcon with a single sword thrust. He relieved the Falcons of some weapons, remounted, and followed the rest.

———

Ribas had two able Falcons all over him. His helmet rang loudly and his breastplate clanged. He spun and reared, but they would not be denied. The outrage of the whole experience only served to fuel their fight and they vented a hostility upon him they had rarely felt before.

Ribas was unable to land a significant blow on either of the two. In desperation, he spied an opening and thrust his sword without hesitation into the throat of one of their horses right above its chest plate. The horse squealed and faltered and its rider rode the dying animal to the ground.

The other continued hammering at Ribas and they wrestled and hacked at each other in tight quarters. The experienced Falcon freed one hand and sank his dagger into Ribas's shoulder. Ribas seized the man's arm and yanked him close, twisting him from his saddle, and as the man struggled to stay atop his horse, Ribas brought his sword around and through the man's neck.

The man slid off his horse, dead.

Ribas turned just in time to see the Falcon he had dehorsed on the ground next to him—and in full swing with his sword. The slashing blade took Ribas directly between his two fingers and sliced straight up his left arm, splitting his forearm in two before the sword arced away.

The knife in the shoulder he barely felt in the heat of the fight. This pain was different. The pain shot through his body and paralyzed his arm. The Falcon was in full swing again and another blow caught Ribas deep in the thigh. The wounded Ribas clumsily reared his horse at the man, but the man stepped away and then charged again. He delivered a full swing again at Ribas's feet and the force of the blade pushed Ribas's greaves aside, the sword slicing deep through his calf. Ribas howled.

He struggled to stay in the saddle, to fight back. He still had his sword and that arm remained untouched. But his opponent was good. A single deathblow need not be delivered. The man would wear down the helpless Ribas with a multitude of wounds.

Galloping over the meadows, Nargonne urged the girls on and struggled to keep his beastly headpiece in place. He should not lose it too soon, he thought, lest the deception be exposed.

The Falcons were closing fast. Where was Ribas? his mind shouted. And Strabo! "Show yourselves, warriors!" he cried, but his words were lost in vain to the wind. He thought of the brave girls in front of him. He had put them in harm's way to achieve the aims of his people. *Such is the way of things,* he thought grimly. *This affair may go badly, and then what?* The girls had reluctantly agreed on his code word; if he cried "Usson!" they were to flee. Run all the way home. And they promised him they would. But would they? He doubted it.

Machoba rounded the trees and spotted the fleeing Volkai disappearing into the rugged woods on the other side of a wide clearing. They had abandoned their hay cart to the field. The ten Falcons charged on, and as soon as the first riders passed the hay cart, the hay came to life. A man covered in hay had a bow in his hand. The Falcons had not time to think. Was that an arrow?

It was. A long iron. It thudded into the chest of a Falcon and he fell.

Now there were nine.

Tourek leaped from the cart to his horse without touching the ground and quickly galloped off in another direction. The Falcons had had enough of this trickery. This time, two of them spun and followed Tourek. He rode straight into the trees and they followed him at full speed, but not for long. Their training took over. The Falcons figured that the Volkai would, of course, know their own country well, where they knew it not at all. Besides, their officer required them. They shouted to each other and turned around to follow Machoba.

Tourek cursed and turned to follow them. When he broke into the clearing, he met his brother galloping at full speed through the meadow.

Mallouse shouted, "How many?"

"One, brother."

"Ha! I got two!"

Together they raced after the others.

Molena led with Marinne right behind. Both girls were as comfortable with saddle as any horseman and their lighter weight gave their mounts added speed. Nargonne followed them through a break in the trees and down a steep gully.

Moments later, Machoba and his men thundered down the gully. The hooves of their horses pounded over a

Volkai tribal leader's headdress fallen to the ground. Three feathers of swan were crushed into the dirt.

Nargonne could hear the Falcons' horses over the clatter of his own mount. Where in the heavens was Ribas?

Ribas told his legs to kick the horse hard and away, to run! But his wounded leg did not respond and his horse was confused and frightened. The man kept coming. Barely in the saddle, Ribas held him at bay with weak swings of his sword. He had no leverage with which to strike, whereas the Falcon had his feet firmly on the earth.

The man feinted and feinted again. Ribas considered dropping to the ground but knew he could not stand. Then the man lunged and drove a swift thrust through the thigh of the horse and the horse reared awkwardly; horse and Ribas toppled over backward in a shower of armor and blood. The force of the earth when he landed knocked the wind out of Ribas and the crushing weight of the horse rolled over his leg. The Falcon leaped at the fallen twosome and brought his sword hard down through the horse's throat and the horse went still.

Ribas lay trapped beneath its body. The warrior in him reminded him he still had his sword. And one good arm and one good leg, though that leg was pinned beneath his horse.

His opponent had suffered only a few cuts. The man advanced on him with sword at the ready. Ribas brandished his weapon with as much bravado as he could.

As Nargonne and the girls crashed through thinning brush, Nargonne smelled it first. No! he thought. The sprawling Rhône was fed by a multitude of tributaries, large and small. This one was large. Another river.

The three spilled onto its sandy bank and came to a stop in water, just a few fingers deep. The shallows ran wide, but the center of the river was dark. Nearly black. The river was deep there. Too deep to ford in a hurry. The other side beckoned, but it may as well have been a league away. Nargonne and the girls backed into the river in the shallows and turned as Machoba and his men thundered through the brush and pulled up on the beach.

Machoba stared at the three in disbelief. The furious ride had dislodged their phony Volkai headgear. Sweat had joined the wind in washing the yellow from their faces. Nargonne's eye patch had long been cast aside and even his unruly beard could not disguise him. And the girls. Who could forget those two?

Everyone was breathing heavily from the ride, especially the older Nargonne.

Suddenly there was the sound of hooves and crackling of brush and the two Souks emerged. Despite the obvious odds against them, Mallouse double-checked that the rope and chain were still at his saddle. The Souks drew their swords.

Machoba looked at his men with a bemused smile and laughed. "These are no vicious Volkai." Then he leveled his eyes at Nargonne. "These fools are Asturians."

Nargonne chose not to respond. He had no interest in engaging Machoba in conversation. He kept his hand on the hilt of his sword. Three swords against nine. Nine blades, each more powerful than theirs. The girls bravely brandished Volkai clubs as the Souks cantered up and held a position next to them.

Machoba laughed at the sight and held his hands wide. "Well, Asturian, your little trick worked. Here I am."

He leaned forward in his saddle.

"So what is your business?"

Now Nargonne laughed, but it was feigned levity. He was as serious as he ever would be.

"*You* are my business, Machoba."

"Over these paltry girls? Surely you joke." Machoba was in no mood for banter either. He had business back at the Rhône. "You will pay for your impertinence with your life."

"Is that so?" said Nargonne.

Machoba nodded his head. "Yes, that is so, Asturian, that is very so."

Machoba's guards grinned.

"I'll tell you something. I will let the girls go if you kneel before me so I can hack your head off without mussing my uniform."

His men laughed at their leader's jest. For it was a joke and a joke only. These upstarts would die. All of them. Several of Machoba's men wondered if the colonel would let them have their way with the girls before they killed them. Doubtful, they knew. There was still battle behind them.

The river babbled beneath the Asturian horses. Nargonne's mind raced. He and the Souks could fight and fight hard. But there was no Ribas. *He should be here, damn him!* How to get the girls free? He might die and the Souks too, but the girls must escape. *Damn the gods! Think. Think!*

Machoba turned businesslike. "Fan out," he said to his men.

The Falcons fanned out, flanking their leader, four on a side. Each pulled his sword. Machoba drew his with a smile. "Who shall be first?"

Nargonne had planned to use the speed of the Asturian horse to separate the Falcons over a long distance, but the cursed river thwarted him. He felt bereft of cunning at last.

Machoba scowled and raised his sword. He would take the impudent man's head himself.

He never got that chance. The brush behind him burst open and a man on a horse charged onto the beach and the memory of the *pankration* match flashed through Machoba's mind.

It was Strabo on the back of Castaine.

Ribas's helmet was dislodged, crowding his brow and his view. His fighting shield lay on the ground nearby, out of reach. His thoughts leaped to Nargonne. Machoba would find them and he had his finest warriors with him. Strabo had better be there. He would be, Ribas knew. And Strabo would die with the rest.

The Falcon loomed over Ribas, studying him and his impossible position. The man was satisfied that Ribas was helpless. The Falcon stepped out of Ribas's sight. Ribas struggled to turn his head.

He heard the man laugh. "Fool," the Falcon said. "You are dead!"

A blast exploded in Ribas's skull and his helmet spilled away. The man had kicked him. Ribas's wits swirled from the impact. He craned his neck to see the man over him, sword upraised. Ribas flailed his sword at the man's legs, but the man pranced over the blade and then kicked

Ribas's hand. Ribas felt his fingers crunch at the blow and his sword went skipping away.

So this is my death, thought Ribas. He felt strangely content that his end had come in battle, more or less. He knew the final impact would come hard and fast. His killer was a professional.

The Falcon initiated the downstroke that would finish Ribas at last. Ribas saw the sun glint off the Falcon's blade, but the man lurched forward without lifting his feet—just as the point of a sword materialized through the center of the Falcon's chest and the man tumbled lifeless to the ground.

The hilt of a Carthaginian sword protruded from the man's back, the blade out from his chest on the other side. He had been run through with professional precision.

Ribas strained his neck to look behind him.

A man stood there, wavering; the Falcon whose arm had been severed by the sword of Ribas. The handless arm dangled uselessly and pulsed bright red streams to the ground, which splashed his sandal and coated it in crimson.

Despite the camouflage from nights of riding and the filth of today's raids, Ribas could see the brave Falcon was pale from loss of blood. The man bent to his knees behind Ribas, put his good arm beneath Ribas's shoulder, and pulled. Ribas groaned. The horse's body still pinned his leg. The man tugged again, harder, and Ribas squirmed his way free. His rescuer dropped to his knees, his breathing shallow. He stared at the ground, seemingly considering a great sin.

Each man had one useless, badly bleeding appendage. With his good arm, Ribas hacked a length of rein from the horse and crawled over to the man. With the aid of his teeth, he tied it tightly around the man's severed stump. Then he tied his own arm and watched the Falcon struggle to his feet—as if he were leaving.

At the tributary, Machoba's personal guards turned in surprise as Castaine clattered to a stop just twenty paces away. Strabo sat on Castaine's heaving back and ignored the Asturians, eyes only for his foe.

Strabo, as Nargonne had observed, still had a few things to learn. But no further development was required when it came to combat. The man was born to the blade.

He certainly looked the part of a warrior, thanks to his nose's encounter with Castaine's surging neck. His face bore red swaths of blood from his nostrils to his ears. And Strabo brandished new weapons. His left arm bore a Falcon battle shield lifted from one of the fallen. The shield was painstakingly engraved with the sign of the Falcon and the sight of it made Machoba's men bristle. Had Strabo been a more dramatic warrior, he would have held it aloft and shook it in their faces. But he was not given to such display. He was all business.

His inadequate Saguntum blade lay in the grass back on the meadow, for Strabo had freed another weapon from the grip of the dead. He now brandished high-grade Falcon iron with a fine battle handle that fit to his palm like a glove. Strabo had found a sword.

The Falcons looked to their leader for instruction.

Machoba grunted. "Kill the fool."

But before Machoba could finish speaking, Strabo had surged forward. He drove the snorting Castaine directly into the Falcons' midst.

The river erupted in a flurry of shouts and hooves and clashing metal. Strabo attacked the three Falcons nearest him. Machoba charged Nargonne. The other Falcons charged the girls and the Souks lunged to intercept them.

Three Falcons raised sword high to swing at Strabo in the saddle as Castaine slammed into them. They swung at air. Taking a page from Nargonne's book, Strabo had thrust Castaine into the men as a diversion and leaped from the saddle.

A horseman versus a man is no match. The horseman possesses too much height, too much mass, too much reach. And the horseman had a partner armed to the teeth and weighing six hundred stone. Strabo knew the Falcons had every advantage.

He had only one: He was off that damned horse.

He charged.

The girls backpedaled into the river, their frightened horses kicking up a spray of froth and stone. Only one man made it to them, for the others were set upon by the Souks. Their women under attack, the Souks struck with a viciousness they had not known they possessed.

The Falcon that set upon the girls would soon learn they were truly branches of the same tree as Nargonne. They could not handle weapons, but they could handle a horse. Better than he.

Machoba and Nargonne clashed traditionally. The two men squared off and hacked at each other, swinging sword and shield. Machoba was younger and stronger, but Nargonne parried him. And as he himself had learned from Barbestro, Nargonne held him off and stalled with defensive maneuvers.

Strabo dodged the lunging head of the first Falcon's

steed and slapped it aside with his shield. The surprised rider stabbed at Strabo, but Strabo stepped to the side and yanked the man from his saddle. The other two tried to strike, but the swirling horses got in their way. Strabo ducked, drove his blade through the fallen's throat, pulled the sword away and, in the same motion, brought the sword's backswing through the exposed hamstring of another Falcon. The man's leg kicked impossibly forward and he cried out. The last's blade met Strabo's in a loud clang and Strabo used the opportunity to dive beneath the horse's legs, emerge on the other side and plunge his sword through the man's stomach before the Falcon could react. The man's face went wide in shock, but Strabo did not see it. He was already upon another Falcon.

The two Souks and their opponents seemed a single mass of straining man and animal and bronze. Blades knew no friend or foe. Six swords clashed in a noisy symphony of arcing metal. The horses shoved and heaved against each other and their armor sawed at their flanks.

Molena was prancing around the Falcon, keeping their horses' heads nose to nose.

"Swim, Marinne!" she shouted.

Marinne broke for the deep and the Falcon chose not to follow. *One at a time,* he thought.

Nargonne bobbed and weaved, his horse kicking spray in the shallows. But Machoba was no amateur. He ignored the false openings, refusing to strike unless the blow would be sound. He snarled beneath his helmet and worked Nargonne deeper into the river.

Strabo waited for man and horse to turn and they did. Strabo dodged left and allowed the horse's momentum to turn past him. Then he lunged, but the practiced Falcon parried and reared his horse in Strabo's face. It was the opening Strabo was waiting for. A horse can't rear forever, even Strabo knew that. When the horse brought his feet back toward earth, Strabo jumped forward and stuck the horse below the breastplate.

The horse shrieked and its rider swung futilely as Strabo's blade flashed between shield and sword. The man's ribs splintered from the passing of the sharp metal en route to the center of his chest; then dead Falcon and wounded horse tumbled to the ground.

The water rose rapidly to Marinne's waist. She was in the deep of the river behind the battling Souks.

Nargonne was outmatched. Machoba had Nargonne's mount backing into the deep, where the horse could not react. *Higher ground wins,* thought Machoba. He feinted this way and that, until Nargonne's efforts to evade him left the Asturian vulnerable on the side opposite his sword. Machoba struck, but the blow was only glancing. Another blow followed and this one connected to the leather of the horse's strappings. It gave Machoba an idea and his capable sword slashed through Nargonne's saddle strappings, releasing the saddle pad from the horse's back.

Nargonne slipped backward into the water and went under. In an instant, he surfaced, gasping for air, but Machoba's horse had reared and all Nargonne saw was a set of plate-size hooves plunging toward him. He ducked but not in time. Nargonne was bashed into the river bottom with a great cry of triumph from Machoba. Marinne saw it and screamed.

Machoba eyed her next.

Molena's Falcon grew tired of toying with her. He had

seen what his colonel had done. He reached out, sliced her harness, and she slipped into the water.

Her sister screamed, "Molena!"

Molena struggled for her feet and made for the water's edge as her Falcon reined his horse after her and leaped in for the kill.

His last thought was only of surprise. Something gleamed in his eyes and then there were sparks and darkness. And water. And then something skewered his body. Then death.

Strabo had hurled his Falcon shield through the man's face and run him through when he hit the water. Strabo turned to the Souks. The Falcons were overcoming the Souks at last.

While Mallouse dodged one way, another Falcon took him in the side with his sword. Another bore down on him and Tourek abandoned his two to strike at the man, round-housing the Falcon with a passionate blow to the head that sent him into the water, his armor pulling him drowning to the riverbed.

One horseman stabbed at Mallouse as he struggled to the riverbank, crawling desperately along the rocks in the shallows. The strikes pierced deeply, but Mallouse struggled on. Tourek set upon the Falcon attacking his brother, when another Falcon intercepted him. A sword raked across Tourek's back and Tourek pitched off his horse into the river.

Now three Falcons were descending on the beleaguered Mallouse, so Strabo threw himself before them and drove them back. But the Falcons were undeterred. They would run Strabo down.

Machoba immediately took stock. Most of the upstarts

were down. The girls were no threat. Five of his men lay still on the bank. He could not fathom how that had come to be, but he still considered the situation well in hand. There was only one man left, the latecomer, now horse-less, with three Falcons closing on him. It would be over soon enough. Machoba was considering pursuing Marinne into the deep water; then he saw Molena wading ashore without a horse.

The obviously faked death now burned at him. This rowdy band of Asturians had duped him, made him the fool, he thought. Disgraced his Red Falcons. The vile rebels would die, this time for certain. And the little bitches he would dispatch himself.

His eyes darted to Marinne and then back to Molena. He could not tell which was which. He could only re-member that he had enjoyed the virgin's tight loins. She struggled and bit at him, and that had only fed his lust. What did she weigh? Fifty, sixty stone? She was no match for him, pigheaded girl.

Look alike, die alike. He bolted for the girl on the bank.

Molena saw Machoba coming and would have pan-icked—had *he* not been waiting there just a few paces away: *Castaine.*

In two fleet steps, Molena was on the horse's back and he whinnied in delight at the familiar weight and smell of the woman. The softness of her heels. The exact place she clung her calves to his ribs. He would know her in a cave. He was not surprised by the urgent pitch to her voice today.

"Run, Castaine, run!" She squeezed her legs into him and Castaine took to the bit with fire. His limbs rushed into motion and horse and rider accelerated down the river.

Machoba was just a few strides behind.

The two horses flew through the shallows, spraying water in sheets behind them. Machoba was so close Castaine's spray had not yet fallen by the time Machoba rode past.

Molena glanced over her shoulder in terror. "Run, Castaine!"

The shallows were giving way to deeper water and both horses slowed. But only for a moment. Molena looked for an opening and saw it just ahead. She waited until the last, hoping to catch her pursuer off guard. Then she bolted to her right through the brush and in a flash she was in the woods.

But Machoba had matched her move. The horses rocketed through the forest so close together they appeared as one. Trees blurred by like the stakes of a stockade.

Machoba's armor flapped loudly but did nothing to slow man and horse. Machoba's horse was the fastest horse in Hannibal's army and he, raised on horseback, one of the finest riders. Possessed of the chase, the animal's nostrils flared and steamed.

But he was not as fast as Castaine. Castaine's shoulders that flopped and jerked in such odd fashion when he trotted suddenly straightened at speed. His low chest hung close to the ground. His shoulders and flanks rippled with power.

As they flashed through the trees, the mischievous Castaine's eyes flickered back and forth. He seemed to let the pursuing horse get near, only to burst forward again and widen the gap in a matter of a few strides.

But the seasoned pursuers would not succumb. Machoba stayed close.

Molena did not know the ground, but she prayed that her instinct would be right. She led the chase far from the river—then turned and doubled back. Back to the water.

In the shallows there, Strabo now faced three determined Falcons. Strabo killed the horse nearest him with a swift jab, and as the rider fell, Strabo rammed his sword through the man's chest armor and the man fell, bawling.

He turned to the others but too late. Their swords clashed with his and Strabo's sword was knocked away to sink uselessly in the river.

Now two Falcons fell upon him and he was without sword or shield. Strabo had only one weapon left. Water.

He dodged a blow and yanked one of the men to the water. The Falcon was, of course, well trained on horseback. He was skilled with horse and bow and sword. But there was no training for hand-to-hand fighting burdened with a horseman's armor in water. His movements were slow and Strabo spun him around and hurled him to the deep, where he struggled to get to his feet. Strabo punched him hard in the face. The stinging blow snapped the man's head back and he stumbled backward into deeper water. Stunned and without footing, he sank and was gone.

Then the last Falcon's horse boomed into Strabo's back and dashed him beneath the surface. Horse and rider leaped and pounced and pounded him into the riverbed. Strabo reeled beneath the water. No air! He rolled and clawed at the river bottom. Hooves exploded the gravel around him.

Strabo's eyes were open and the river water clear. He rolled on his back. He could see the animal's underbelly as clearly as if he lay on open ground. He reached up and grabbed the horse's understrappings. The Falcon felt it and charged his mount forward, dragging Strabo through the shallows.

The river bottom raked Strabo's back and the horse's hooves hammered at him from all sides at once. He felt weakness coming fast. His fingers began to slip. The thought suddenly occurred to him that even if he was released now, he would be in no position to defend himself. He was spent.

Then the horse above him jerked sideways and Strabo lost his grip, and horse and rider tumbled away from him. Strabo pulled himself above water and gasped for air.

He saw the Falcon. And Marinne!

She had driven her horse into the Falcon and he, as weary as the rest, had lost purchase and been dumped from his saddle to the water. But the man fought on. *Admirably,* thought Strabo. *A pity.*

The Falcon took a step toward Marinne with thrusting sword and died. He lurched forward and sank face first into the water. The long iron arrow in his back sank with him.

Strabo and Marinne looked to the beach from where the arrow had come. Mallouse knelt there unsteadily. He was painted red by the blood of his wounds, only his face a mask of bloodless white. Then he toppled over lifeless, his bow still clutched in his hand.

Only the forest and the meadows witnessed the meteoric contest of horse versus horse, rider versus rider. The flight was long, but when most horses would tire, neither of these would. *Keep him from me, Castaine,* she prayed.

Castaine had walked and trotted and cantered for weeks with Strabo like a boulder on his back. But now he could run. Run! Castaine widened the gap and Machoba silently cursed. *What animal is this?*

Molena was breathing as hard as Castaine. She burst out of the wood and through a familiar meadow at last. The gully to the river lay ahead.

Machoba was behind by many horse lengths, but the chase was anything but done. *The stupid girl has taken us back to the river,* he thought. He grinned and drew his sword.

Molena and Castaine stormed down the gully. The ground flattened, the low brush parted, and they arrived in a flurry back at the beach.

Bodies lay everywhere and Molena could make no immediate sense of the scene. Machoba burst to the beach behind her. He charged with sword raised for the kill, eyes only for his prey. But it was *he* who had fallen to trap.

Molena hadn't seen the figure in the trees. Neither had Machoba. The figure lunged out and took Machoba full in the face with a raging swing of a heavy Volkai war club.

Machoba was ejected from the saddle by the force of the blow and his mighty horse ran on into the shallows before stopping. Confused, the horse turned and stood there, panting.

Machoba lay on the ground stunned, the breath blasted from his chest. His face was ruined. A dozen teeth were gone and the bridge of his nose bent unnaturally into his eye socket. A man's bones are no match for a weapon swung in vengeance.

Dripping wet, Nargonne stood over him, war club still in hand.

The rest of the Falcons were already dead. Tourek cradled his brother at the water's edge. Brother pressed cheek to brother and the shoulders of Tourek shook and heaved. Strabo felt the pit of his stomach twisting. Mallouse was gone.

Death was death and Strabo had witnessed more of it than most. But he had slipped through life knowing no one well. There was no one to care for—until now. The beach had changed. It was no longer a place where men had clashed. Another place to move on from when the action was done. To Strabo, the beach had become a holy place. *The man had fired an arrow past my ear in jest.* In the company of ghosts, Strabo felt the power of the man's life seize him.

Molena and Marinne ran to Nargonne, but they were afraid to embrace him, such was the look on his face. Strabo stepped to their side. He and Molena nodded grimly at each other.

"I'll fetch the chains," Strabo said.

"There is no need," said Nargonne.

He did not look at them. He only stared down at Machoba. The man who had murdered his brother and his brother's wife. The man who had whipped and defiled the girls who were like daughters to him. The man who would kill them all if he could.

He couldn't and he wouldn't. It was done, thought Nargonne.

Machoba was coming to life. He mumbled something through his broken mouth, but Nargonne ignored him. Nargonne retrieved the broken Volkai spear from the sand.

Strabo put his hand to Nargonne's chest.

"The chains," said Strabo.

Nargonne did not respond.

"The ransom," Strabo said. "The gold."

Nargonne smiled drunkenly.

"There is no ransom, warrior."

Strabo gasped. "What?" His mind reeled. All this? The march? Mallouse! For what? Revenge? A killing? Killing could be done anytime, anywhere. A killing was a simple matter.

And most killings were. But not this one.

Machoba's body convulsed in the sand. His skull had been crushed by Nargonne's blow, but his brain still functioned. His monstrous face stared defiantly up at Nargonne.

He mumbled through his broken mouth: "You dare to murder me."

Nargonne felt the man not worthy of conversation. The disciplined Nargonne called an evil turn to his lips.

"Not me, Machoba. The Volkai."

Nargonne lifted the Volkai spear, kicked Machoba's breastplate aside, and plunged the broken spear deep into the man's chest. Machoba's body jerked from the impact and he died.

Ribas's breathing was growing shallow. He sighed and wondered: Would the brave Falcon leave? Would he strip the military bearings from his person and flee this place? Flee forever this profession of glory and gore? It struck Ribas that the man was a better man than he, and the realization depressed him.

But the loss of blood was taking its toll on both men and the Falcon wasn't going anywhere. Overcome, he keeled over and lay weakly on the turf.

On the ground, the two warriors could only stare at each other. The Falcon stared in resignation, Ribas with gratitude and an impossible understanding. Ribas nodded his head at the man and attempted a smile. He could glean no response from the Falcon, though the man held his eye for as long as he could. Then Ribas uttered the only words that would ever pass between them.

"We were ambushed," Ribas rasped at last.

With great effort, the man nodded his head. Then the Falcon's eyes rolled white and closed. He passed out in the dirt.

Over the man's shoulder, Ribas saw a boy's head peering over the tall grass a hundred paces away, watching them. The boy flinched when he realized he had been seen. He turned and ran away. Then thought left Ribas too; he fainted into darkness.

At the remote river, Tourek was incapable of speech. Each Asturian touched him carefully, as if he might shatter, so that they could press their love and grief to him in some way. Tourek thought not of runes or signs. He thought not of the gods or visions indecipherable. Entombed in a fog of grief, he felt nothing. He only imagined his brother by his side.

The Asturians trussed Mallouse's body as carefully as a newborn to Castaine's back. Then they bound each other's wounds as best they could and stripped all sign of the Volkai from their bodies. Nargonne urged them to hurry and told Strabo to lose a fine blade he had again lifted from another of the fallen Falcons. Strabo looked at the weapon, reluctant to let it go. Nargonne barked at him.

"Don't be a fool."

The obvious blade would, of course, give them away. Still, he hesitated.

"Throw it," insisted Nargonne.

Strabo cast the sword into the river with a sigh.

Another sword followed it. Machoba's. Nargonne flung it to the river and the ivory hilt disappeared beneath the running waves.

They impaled the dead at the river with Volkai arrows, on their way back to the Rhône, they did the same with the dead Falcons along their route.

Behind them, they left Machoba's body in the sand, the Volkai spear standing in his chest. A single white feather of swan protruded from his broken mouth.

———

Rumors reached Rome that the Carthaginian elephant pens in Gades were empty. The Roman intelligence officers scratched their heads. Where were the dangerous brutes? In southern Italy, Roman sentries captured a squad of Carthaginian spies scouting out beaches on the western coast. Despite their denials, the spies were executed on the spot. It was now clear to Roman Command that Carthage was preparing a seaborne assault based from Saguntum. Roman warships were recalled from North Africa and all ports were emptied as every available Roman vessel was ordered to defensive positions along the western coast of Italy.

Chapter 15

*T*he pounding hooves of a single warhorse can shake the ground. Thousands of them on the run will shake the very trees. With devastating suddenness, Hanno's night cavalry had plunged into the Volkai and swept them aside as if they were children. The desperate Volkai struggled to fight up slope, but there was no hope there. Nothing but death.

The archers and the slingers unleashed shower after shower of missiles and cleared the beach as the thousands of Carthaginian swordsmen swarmed ashore, Barbestro and Ox among them.

The Numidians rolled up the opposition on the banks to the south and those few Volkai left fled to the trees.

Few battles were desperate fights to the last man. The object was almost always advantage, not annihilation. Most were over when it became obvious that one side had gained the upper hand. The courage of the individual Volkai would never be in dispute. But as a fighting force, they were finished.

The disorganized Volkai broke and ran in all directions at once.

Hannibal's army chased them, but not far. There was little to be gained here by superfluous killing. These weren't Romans, after all. The officers recalled their troops. Still, a certain amount of wanton slaughter was inevitable.

By nightfall, Nargonne and his people descended back to the main camp through the Volkai forest. They trod carefully down the ridge, picking their way through the bodies that littered the forest floor. The stench of human waste assaulted their nostrils; for men gutted by sharp blade had their insides spilled to the world.

No one spoke.

The dead Volkai stared in all directions and Molena closed her eyes more than once when she found a corpse staring into hers. Marinne sobbed softly. The dead were on their backs, on their faces, slumped over fallen trees. Some were in pieces, some bent in unnatural postures, some looked as if they were merely sleeping. Blackened blood was splattered across tree trunks and bushes and gathered in puddles, congealing before it could seep into the loamy forest floor.

Nargonne and the others visited the Carthaginian hospital tents. They were nearly empty. As Hannibal had intended with such elaborate preparations, Carthaginian losses were minuscule, while the Volkai had lost over ten thousand men. Tourek was left to be tended to. Nargonne promised him they would be back soon. At their campsite, Santandar's joy at seeing his father overcame him and he wept. The women covered their heads with hoods and stayed close to their fire ring. The closest Marinne came to injury was when Barbestro hugged her tight and held her for a long time, until the tears in his eyes subsided.

For Hanno, his night cavalry, and the Red Falcons, Machoba *was* a loss, but such losses, although unfortunate, are to be expected. Carthaginian officers prided themselves in leading their troops, as Hannibal himself often did.

Akdar and the Red Falcons had followed the trail of Machoba's fallen security detail. They couldn't miss the signs of pursuit and struggle they found everywhere. The signs of the Volkai. The insult of the feather in the mouth of their hero.

Machoba's body was burned at the edge of the Rhône with two thousand Red Falcons in attendance. Akdar seethed. His mentor was dead and he had not been there when his leader needed him. The failure tore at him and he felt the looks of the other Falcons upon him, though no one said a word.

One Red Falcon missed the funeral. In the exclusive cavalry's own hospital tent, the healers poured a great deal of wine down his throat and then plunged his amputated wrist into hot pitch. That painful moment would save the man's arm, at least. As to the other that had been found with him, the foreigner, the last two fingers of his left hand had to be snipped off and the unconscious Ribas cried out when they put his raw wound to the pitch as well. His mutilated appendage was wrapped and his other wounds stuffed with leaf and herb, then wound tightly. The man would heal in time, the physicians knew, and most likely fight again.

By dusk the next day, the groggy man limped painfully from the tent, promising his concerned healers he would return.

Ribas missed the private funeral of Souk Mallouse. Nargonne had sent Barbestro to locate Ribas, but he could not get past Red Falcon security and so Nargonne still knew nothing of Ribas's fate.

At daybreak, the Asturians bore Mallouse's body to a clearing in the hills they found suitable. The clearing had an open view of the Rhône far below. They dug the grave.

Souk Tourek took off his cloak and he and the women gently wrapped his brother in it.

"I will always embrace you, my brother," Tourek said. He cried unabashedly and the women with him.

"You will be safe here," he whispered. "My coat will keep you warm."

Tourek squeezed his brother's hands around several of his favorite rune stones and crossed the dead man's hands across his chest. Strabo watched and felt the man's death in his bones. He felt as lifeless as he.

Tourek then bent to the ground and scribbled many circles and arcs there and muttered his chantings. At length, he held a twig of yew aloft and then lit the twig with flint stone. The twig burned down to his fingers and he barely grimaced as his own flesh extinguished the flame.

Tourek placed the ashen twig gently beneath his brother's chin and pressed it into the whiteness of his throat. Then Tourek turned his tearstained face to Nargonne.

"That is my farewell."

Nargonne had been stone-faced, but now the memories of the man washed over him like a creek in springtime. He stood over the grave and spoke at length, invoking their mutual ancestors and thanking Souk Mallouse on behalf of their people. Then he said his final good-bye.

"You, my noble Souk, you have gladdened our hearts and made our way soft. You have warmed us and guided us and kept us safe. Know this now, Souk. You have given all."

Nargonne unclasped his necklace and placed it on the man's body. "You are forever cherished, brave friend."

One by one, the Asturians kissed him.

Sargonne shook with tears.

"I love you," Santandar told the dead man.

Strabo stepped forward. He knew no rituals, no ceremony. He only had what he had and that was his devotion. He bent his face to the dead's and kissed the man on the forehead.

They covered Souk Mallouse in Asturian blankets and buried him deep. They gathered plants and flowers and replanted them on the bed of soil they had made.

They each touched the mound a last time before returning to the camp in silence. They left Tourek there alone. The remainder of the day was filled with the mundane, as it was for the rest of the army. Eat. Rest. Heal.

At the first hint of sundown, the exhausted Asturians bedded down and Barbestro lay discreetly near Marinne, who kept a hood about her face. Molena caught Strabo's eye and rolled her eyes in the direction of Barbestro and Marinne, and Strabo's face flushed.

He smiled back at her and she closed her eyes and dreamed. They all slept heavily.

All but Nargonne. He steamed. The man had failed him, he thought, and Mallouse was dead. Had the Souk not perished, Nargonne's heart would be soaring because he alone knew they had pulled off the impossible. But the beloved Mallouse was dead and Ribas had not shown. *Ribas! Damn you! Damn your soul to the dark gods who burn and enslave. If you are dead, then so be it. If you are not, you soon will be.*

He closed his eyes, but they kept opening against his will and he stared blankly into the black sky. His daughters were so very far away. His twin nieces were his family now too. He thought of his wife. By all the heavens, she had been the most beautiful of women! How lucky he was to have found her and to have had her for so long. He missed her now. Missed her eyes and her laugh and her touch. Madly. But she was gone and so now was Mallouse. Nargonne was consumed with love for the dead and his affection crossed the realms of the dark. Death was no barrier. It was a gateway.

He heard someone stir. Strabo was sitting up in the dark. From his bed, he had suddenly produced a sword as only a warrior like he would. It was the old Saguntum sword he had retrieved begrudgingly from the meadow.

Nargonne looked where Strabo looked and saw a man emerge limping from the shadows. *So you have come at last, Ribas.*

Nargonne and Strabo rose softly so as not to awaken the others. Nargonne did not glower, he only motioned for the men to follow him, and the three walked silently up the hills into the night.

To the Souk's grave.

The climb was an ordeal for Ribas, who limped heavily. But it was nothing compared to the ordeal that was to come.

Ribas stared silently at the flower-covered heap of earth. There was nothing wrong with Ribas's eyes and he had recognized each sleeping form in the camp. He knew who lay in the soil. Ribas knelt there and prayed. Strabo and Nargonne watched silently. They could see Ribas had been badly injured, his left hand swathed into a club of cloth. They could smell the medical man's herbs.

Nargonne took his time constructing a small fire near the Souk's grave. Strabo helped him.

"Sit," Nargonne finally said to Ribas.

Ribas came and sat by the fire. He watched Nargonne fan the small flames to life. Nargonne spoke without looking at Ribas.

"There he lies."

"He was a friend," said Ribas.

"Oh yes, he was that," said Nargonne. He still would not look at Ribas.

But Strabo could not take his eyes off the man. He was stung by the searing heat of betrayal but held his tongue. *Be smart,* he thought. *Listen and learn.*

At length, Ribas spoke. "I was delayed."

"Delayed," Nargonne repeated.

Ribas did not reply.

The fire blazed in Nargonne's eyes.

"Please tell me what could be so important. What would stay you from the duty for which we have labored a thousand leagues?"

Ribas looked past them into the night, his eyes gazing into the darkness of the trees at something not there. His answer caught Nargonne and Strabo off guard.

"Africa," he said.

Strabo looked surprised, but Nargonne's face revealed nothing. Ribas stared back at the older Asturian. He shifted his painful leg.

"If you must know about me, then I shall tell you," he said. Ribas heaved a heavy sigh. "Perhaps I should have told you long ago."

Nargonne said nothing. He and Strabo only waited. Ribas adjusted his belts.

"There was a time that I thought I was not a soldier, but I am cut from the same cloak as you, Strabo. More than you know. The difference between you as soldier and me as soldier is simple. And wicked."

Ribas drew in a labored breath.

"I soldiered with Carthage," he said.

Nargonne didn't react, though the news hit him like a blow to the head. Strabo instinctively inched his fingers for the handle of his weapon. *I knew it!*

Ribas eased his sword from its sheath and set it on the ground in front of him. He closed his eyes and gathered his strength.

"That was long ago. Our troops were skilled and well financed. We had the finest schooling, the finest horses, the finest weapons the swollen vaults of Carthage could buy."

Ribas spun the end of his sword sheath in the sand.

"I entered my military service at ten years of age. A sword my pillow, a shield my bed. I was sent to the African provinces and spent many years there training. I became good with the blade and the lance. I learned many things a soldier must know to survive.

"When I was of age to kill, I entered the foot regiments and waged war on any African tribe that opposed us. We marched through desert and mountain and jungle. My battles were many and we killed many, but some tribes succumbed to our superiority and pledged allegiance to Carthage without a fight."

Ribas tallied the years in his head.

"Twelve winters ago, I was dispatched to Egypt. I learned to ride a horse well on that journey and I'd be dead by now, had I not."

He smiled a sad smile at Strabo.

"Journeys are as good a place as any to learn to ride, don't you think?"

Strabo thought of Castaine but only briefly. Molena flooded his mind. *Yes, thank you, Molena, poor student that I am.*

"We took boats up much of the great Nile River. An easy trip. The rich banks of the Nile are filled with all manner of new things for a young man."

Ribas paused.

"I knew a woman there."

Ribas gazed off into space again. It was plain that he could see things there in that hazy place that records a mans life for him and him alone.

Ribas looked back into the flames.

"But that is a tale for another fire."

A weary look came over his face, as if he were about to drop into sleep. He swallowed painfully and went on.

"In upper Egypt, we came against a ferocious tribe. They fought like tigers. Their numbers were small so they would ambush us at night. They poisoned our drinking water and set disease upon our animals. They set primitive traps for us.

"But in the end, we overcame them. And then the order came."

Now Ribas stared at Strabo.

"A soldier will get such orders, Strabo. 'Leave no one alive' was the command. Not the old. Not the young. Not the women. No one. We killed their herds, their livestock. We even killed their dogs. It was annihilation."

The memory made Ribas grip the handle of his sword, though he was unaware he had done so.

"We entered their town on horseback. Killing is easier on horseback. You are farther from the dead, up there in the saddle.

"They just watched us, helpless. Some of them began to weep and many beseeched us with loud prayers. Mothers held out their children so that we might spare them."

Ribas suddenly glared and smiled at the same time at the two men, as if ready to fight.

"We butchered them. I butchered them. I swung my blade and I slashed and I killed them. I wouldn't have believed I was capable of such deeds, but I did as I was told. They told me it would be difficult, but to kill anyway. As I was trained. *Do as you are trained!* And after the first few bodies fell, I was taken by the hellish trance of it, and it was as if I were in battle. Strike, strike, strike, or die!"

Ribas gulped hard and his breathing became more labored. A look of hate and horror descended over his face.

"The saliva sprayed from my mouth. It was mindless. A rage. I ran them through, all. The little ones, the women. The wounded elders, until they breathed no more. No more!"

Ribas was seeing it again.

"One woman slit her daughter's throat right in front of me so I would not! She spat on me, spat on my shield and my horse. Then she took her own life with the blade that had taken the child's.

"It was I who killed her, just as surely as if it were my own blade. She, with more courage than an entire army.

That I should dispatch such a heart to the world beyond. The heart of a lion!"

Ribas stared again at nothing. He breathed in shallow bursts. Tears overcame his eyelids and flowed steadily down his cheeks into his beard. He did not feel them.

"I hated them."

Ribas's breath came in tight gasps, as if he were dying himself.

"I hated their screaming. Their wailing! *Sit still and die, damn you! Do you not understand? Die!*"

Nargonne and Strabo leaned forward as if to aid him but did not. He who had been one of them.

Ribas glared at the fire.

"Soon we were ordered to erase another town. But that is not soldiering."

Ribas shook his head.

"Annihilation." He spat at the ground, but little came out. His mouth was dry and his body spent.

"I spoke to no one. I abandoned my regiment in the middle of the night like a wretch. I told the watchman I had to piss."

He scoffed at the thought.

"And now I am here."

Ribas slid his weapon back into his belts and straightened his posture, trying to look dignified again.

"You know me as Ribas. But that is not my given name. That name you shall not know. Not ever. For I am born of the house of Mahalcat."

Ribas paused as the significance of this revelation sank in. Strabo knew the house. And by the look on Nargonne's face, so did he.

Mahalcat was the legendary Carthaginian warrior clan.

Ribas turned and lifted his torn tunic to the top of his shoulder blades. There, in the middle of his back, was an angry scar the size of a fist. Strabo knew all too well the type of scar he saw. It was a vicious burn. Ribas tucked his tunic back in place.

"I made a fire and stoked a stone to red. I obliterated the dove." He spat that last word from his lips.

Ribas had borne the tattoo of the dove, the dove of Carthage.

Nargonne rolled from his bedding and looked about. The still-smoking embers of their campfire tossed winding streaks of dusty white into the early-morning light. Everyone was still asleep, save Strabo, who looked as if he hadn't slept a wink. He hadn't. They had left Ribas up in the hills. Next to Mallouse.

Nargonne rose and brushed himself off. He took a swig of water from a water bag, rinsed his mouth, and spat. Strabo watched him. Nargonne motioned for him to stay and Strabo nodded.

The Asturian strode through the camp and climbed into the hills again. He found Ribas as they had left him. The small fire there had died and was smokeless.

Ribas sat in the same place, his weapon on the ground in front of him. He looked up bleary eyed at Nargonne as he approached.

Nargonne stood over Ribas and looked down at the wounded warrior. Ribas unsheathed his sword painfully and handed the weapon, hilt first, to Nargonne.

"I have deceived you. I have deceived all. If you wish to end my life, I will not prevent you. You may use my sword, if you please."

Nargonne twirled the sword in his hands and looked at his reflection in the blade. The grave of Mallouse loomed behind him. *The world is full of wonders,* Nargonne thought. *Ribas is one of them.*

"Do you wish to die, Ribas?"

Ribas did not answer. Nargonne knew what the answer was.

"That time is not yet come," said Nargonne. "You are needed yet."

He bent to one knee and looked Ribas in the eye. Then he pointed a stubby finger to his own eyes and bade Ribas look back at him.

"Listen to me, youngster, listen! You are at home with us, Ribas. Your journey has been a hard one. Harder than most men. But you are home now, Ribas. That is all. No more need be known or said. The past is the past and doesn't belong to us. Not to you, not to me. Not to anyone."

Nargonne laid the sword in Ribas's lap and stood.

"The future, however, is another matter. Only the future. And you shall share yours with us."

Nargonne turned around and walked back down the hill. Ribas would either accept things as they were or he would not. Nargonne hoped with all his heart that he would. *Spare yourself, Ribas,* he thought.

When Nargonne returned to camp, he found his brother brushing a scrawny pack pony and oiling the pony's desiccated harness. Nargonne sat heavily on the ground and watched his brother work with proficiency and care on the insignificant animal. Sargonne cooed to the animal and it patiently allowed him to plait its mane.

Up and down the river, the Carthaginians were waking

and beginning preparations for the final crossing. Hannibal's gold had purchased many boats and supplies from tribes all over the area. The army must move on. Harvest season was waning and no host of this size could stay in one place for long.

Nargonne watched the others in his camp preparing for the day. The women kept their hoods tight and stirred rabbit in a pot on the fire. Santandar handed out small loaves of bread. Strabo had gone to the river to wash and Souk Tourek sat by himself. He had spread the entrails of a rabbit in the dirt and was poking at them with a stick, studying them. He had not foreseen his brother's death, Nargonne thought. That man must be kept busy.

Barbestro sat on the ground clutching his jaw and grimacing while Marinne poked gingerly about the inside of his mouth. *A toothache is a nagging nuisance,* Nargonne thought.

"Smithy come," said Sargonne, nodding in Barbestro's direction. It seemed Sargonne's smithy friend was also something of a dentist, or so he claimed.

They all took notice of Nargonne's return and he noticed them all casting glances Molena's way. *So she will speak for all of them,* Nargonne thought. *She would be the one. She should be.* Nargonne's heart swelled with pride. *How lucky I am. My brother's daughter. My kin and blood. She is a strong one.*

Nargonne watched Sargonne patiently refit the pack pony's harness. Nargonne smiled at his brother.

"You care for this miserable creature as if he were the finest of warhorses."

Sargonne scowled. "Pony not miserable. Only pack animal, yes, but deserves attention."

He tucked the harnesses gently into place and tightened them. He patted the pony on the muzzle.

"Only important horses get special treatment." Sargonne sniffed, clearly opposed to this philosophy.

The horses! Of course! How stupid of me, thought Nargonne. He slapped himself on the knee and the weight of uncertainty lifted from his shoulders like a falcon to the hunt. *We have found it, Mallouse! We have found it! Aha!*

Nargonne jumped up and grabbed a surprised Sargonne by his shoulders.

"You are a wise fellow, brother," he said, and turned to the others in camp.

He strode into their midst. The mourning of the dead would have to wait. He was seized now by purpose and the course that had just come to him. Molena immediately confronted him as he stepped to their fire.

"You must speak to us. All of us."

Nargonne sighed. He knew what was coming.

"Very well," he said. "First, breakfast." His niece handed him a wooden bowl of rabbit stew and a loaf of bread.

Nargonne ate as the others gathered around the morning breakfast fire. They watched him eat in silence. Finally he finished just as Strabo arrived, freshly cleaned by the river. He noticed the glance of approval that Molena gave the man and Strabo's shy grin. *Good. The two of them make a good pair. Surely their children would be strong and wise, if as stubborn as their father.*

But Molena's thoughts were far from romance. She turned her attention to her uncle.

"What of our people now?" she demanded.

The others bowed their heads, uncomfortable with this

affront to Nargonne's authority, though they all felt the same. They were happy that Molena was leading the charge. She lowered her voice in challenge.

"What of ransom, Uncle? Our boats stay chained. Our people owe a heavy tithe. They await our duty, Uncle. How do we pay the fine now?"

All were silent and Nargonne simply looked coolly at Molena, which only angered her.

"You have your revenge. I hope you are content. It is my father and mother who have been murdered."

Nargonne stared into the fire.

"They are avenged," he said. "This is true. As you have been avenged. You and your sister. This vengeance is just, Molena."

"It is arrogant." Molena struggled to control her voice. "Do you not think I wanted him dead? Do you not think I would set fire to this whole damned army if I could? I put myself aside for our people, Nargonne, as you should have done."

Barbestro and Marinne exchanged nervous looks. Tourek sat blankly, but Santandar grew anxious at the attack on his father. The whole group was taken aback by this naked offense to Nargonne's character. But not Nargonne. He was more proud of her than ever, despite her fighting words. *Yes,* he thought, *the brave and able will do such things. Will commit all and sacrifice all. As I intend to do, sweet niece.*

Molena didn't let up. "It was supposed to be a kidnapping, not a killing."

Strabo knew their faith in Nargonne was wobbling. So was his. Where was his reward going to come from now? Had Nargonne not betrayed them all? Time after time, he had put them all in danger, including the man's own son! And Mallouse was dead. For what? Vengeance, it now seemed, and no more.

Like Nargonne, Strabo was proud of Molena too. She was the boldest among them.

Nargonne was silent, thinking.

Molena never shifted her eyes from her uncle. He would answer her!

Nargonne lifted his eyes to hers.

"Do you know what would happen to us if we kidnapped a Carthaginian officer? Do you have any idea what that means to them? It is the greatest affront, the greatest insult, the greatest assault on their pride and their culture."

Nargonne stared at Strabo and Strabo nodded that this was true.

"They would hunt us down, niece. When a Libyan tribe murdered one of their officers in a robbery, the Carthaginian army descended upon their hills and slaughtered them all. They slaughtered their livestock and burned their lands to the ground. Then they covered the very ground in inches of dirt to rid the world forever of that tribe, and they did just that. Those people are extinct.

"Such is the retribution of Carthage."

Nargonne's explanation had impact for everyone but Molena. She was unimpressed. "That only means that kidnapping was a foolish course in the first place, while our people face disaster."

"I couldn't agree with you more. It would do nothing to rescue our people. Nothing."

Nargonne's eyes held Molena's before Tourek finally

spoke. He had been politely listening, but his mood was understandably short.

"Who will deliver us now?" he asked. "We would need the sword of Hannibal himself."

"Ahh, but we have that sword," said Nargonne.

Then he smiled a smile that Molena knew well. That smile was the knowing look of his that never failed to delight her as a child and it extinguished her fury like water on a campfire. He had something up his sleeve. Of course he had! He always did. Relief surged through her veins.

"The sword of Hannibal is not of damascened bronze or hardened iron," Nargonne said. "Neither is it a strong horse or a clever flanking maneuver. The sword of Hannibal cannot be seen by man."

Nargonne had all of their attention now.

"I will remind you that Hannibal has been preparing this expedition of his for years. Years! Has the man not demonstrated his commitment? He has mobilized half the continent. He will cross the very Alps, in winter no less. All for his cause. All to lock horns with Rome. Sleep will not be his until his aims are achieved."

Strabo noticed how Nargonne locked his eyes on his son. Nargonne thumped his thumb to his chest.

"The sword lies here. It is not metal born from the earth but rather it is mettle born from your heart. It is a devotion so great that you throw everything into it."

He involuntarily glanced up into the hills where Mallouse lay eternally quiet.

"Everything."

He looked at Molena and was pleased to see they understood each other. He set his eyes on hers and lowered his voice to a whisper.

"The Carthaginians are responsible for our plight and it is the Carthaginians who will pay."

She nodded at him and Strabo was surprised to see she seemed satisfied. Nargonne turned to Barbestro.

"Are you assigned to the raft works today?"

"I am."

"The heavy rafts?"

"Yes."

"Good. Then go."

Nargonne turned to the others.

"Marinne, you and Santandar help Sargonne with the animals. The rest of you, come with me."

He abruptly stood up. "Molena, bring a fat quiver of arrows."

Everyone did as they were told.

Nargonne was soon leading Tourek, Molena, and Strabo in a circuitous route through the sprawling camp. They meandered through the thousands of Iberian foot soldiers camped all over the rolling banks of the great river. They made their way past the elephants and the cavalry. Finally they ascended a hill to settle near the back of a group of blacksmithing wagons. The smoke from the blacksmiths' fires obscured them, yet they could still make out the scene below, where thousands of men worked steadily at the river's edge.

Nargonne bade them sit and make as if they were repairing arrows. Backed up to the river sat the treasure wagons of Hannibal. Behind these sat the bread train.

As usual, there was much activity around the area. Hundreds of guards on foot and horse circulated about the treasure wagons, and as usual, only a few attended the bread train.

A few soldiers were even sweeping the area, cleaning it of leaves and debris. Nargonne watched as the cleaning crew moved from wagon to wagon, going so far as to sweep beneath each wagon as well.

Nargonne fiddled with one of the Souks' long-iron shafts and spoke softly without looking at the others.

"Molena, you see the treasure train, how well it is guarded."

"I do."

"It makes a tempting target for thieves, no?"

He smiled at her.

"But the bread train is in disrepair, isn't it? Look at how sorry it is."

The bread train did appear dilapidated. The siding of the wood on the wagons was peeling and dry. The upper carriages of the vehicles leaned drunkenly and their corners were not true. Bakers were loading flour and grain into the backs of some of the wagons. Then Strabo noticed something that even Nargonne had missed.

"The bakers bear weapons."

"So they do," mused Nargonne.

Even from this distance, they could all see the sword sheaths protruding beneath the aprons of the baking crew.

"All of the bread wagons look the same, don't they, Molena?" Nargonne smiled mischievously at her.

"A riddle," she said.

"A riddle," he answered. "But a horseman such as yourself should discern that ten of the wagons differ from the others."

It wasn't the wagons themselves, it was the horses that pulled them. Ten of the bread wagons were pulled by some of the finest horses she had ever seen. They were disguised somewhat, but not enough to fool the horsemen of Asturias.

They were northern bred, a horseman such as she could see that clearly. Their forelocks were thick with rough fur and their manes were long. They were not tall, but their necks and legs were huge. A thick coat covered them from wide shoulders to wide hips. *A man can sleep comfortably on those backs,* she thought. *They are big and they are strong.*

Their coats were perfect and shone in the morning sun. Their hooves were trimmed meticulously. Their tack was oiled and in perfect order. Only their obvious manes had been allowed to fall to tangle and neglect.

"Strabo, you know your metals. What kind of wagons do those look like to you?"

Strabo studied the wagons and their thick, oaken spokes. Each wheel was reinforced with wrought iron. The hubs themselves gave them away. They were of wide and sturdy iron, each the diameter of a small tree. He knew at once they supported extraordinarily thick iron axles. He could see minute stains bleeding from the centers of the hubs. The stains of a well oiled wheel.

"Those are mining wagons."

Nargonne nodded. "Is flour so heavy?" he asked.

Even the heavyhearted Tourek managed the hint of a smile.

"And if they are so heavy, why not oxen?" asked Nargonne to no one in particular. It was Molena who answered him.

"Horses can run if need be."

Again Nargonne nodded. "My thoughts exactly. Ever see an ox run, Strabo?"

He had not, but he laughed with the rest of them.

Nargonne gestured to the gaudily decorated treasure train.

"Would Hannibal, the master of deception, bear his gold in such obvious fashion?"

Molena smiled. "Only if he wants you to think there is gold where there is not."

"But we've seen them dispensing moneys daily from the treasure trains," Strabo observed.

"Look carefully at the ground beneath those wagons," said Nargonne. "Note how dutifully they sweep there."

Strabo realized it.

"They transfer the gold at night. From bread train to treasure train. Underneath the wagons."

Under cover of darkness, the subterfuge would be complete.

"There must be hatches below," gushed Molena.

"Clever boy, Hannibal," said Nargonne.

The group marveled at the endless ingenuity of the Carthaginians. Now they all knew. The deliverance of their people sat waiting for them in the back of a baker's cart. Nargonne began packing up the arrows.

"Soon those wagons must cross the river. My guess is they'll make the crossing at night. Perhaps even tonight. We must make ready. All we need is a man who can swim like a fish."

All eyes turned to Strabo.

After a day of rest and recovery following the attack against the Volkai, the army was in full gear again. The day was spent first ferrying animals and then supplies across the river. The hastily constructed heavy rafts, towed by a multitude of local boats, carried many horses. Smaller rafts ferried support crews. These were towed by rough canoes the Carthaginians had quickly created, copying the design of some of the local craft.

Nargonne and his group were assigned to the water crews and ferried across the river, where they filled barrel after barrel with fresh water from the Rhône. Thousands of water bags were also filled. They loaded the barrels on carts and set aside a mountain of bags for the draft animals to carry when the army set off.

Nargonne, and particularly Strabo, spent their time well. They got a chance to cross the river and perform the mental calculations they needed; heavy rafts, they noted, took about thirty minutes to cross. Those would be the rafts used to carry the gold.

The only excitement of the day came when the elephants went across on their earth-covered rafts. Upstream, the handlers had positioned a long line of boats far out into the river as a breakwater of sorts, in order to slow the current before the elephants.

Despite all their preparations, some of the elephants panicked from the unfamiliar motion of the river beneath them and their drivers lost control. Two of the rafts toppled and all were thrown into the river. Two drivers were swept away and drowned, but the elephants, good swimmers, eventually swam ashore and were recovered, although not all of them emerged on the intended side. Still, over half of the thirty-seven elephants would be successfully ferried over by the end of the first day.

News of the Volkai debacle traveled fast, and by late afternoon, word circulated through the officer corps that emissaries from the Keltoi, another group of tribes related to the Volkai, had guaranteed safe passage for Hannibal's army through their lands.

Hannibal was pleased and much business was done. Grain was purchased, as well as many boots and furs capable of withstanding the ice and snow that awaited them. For additional payment, the Keltoi agreed to follow the army as rear guard all the way to the foot of the mountains, the extent of their lands.

Tourek worked quietly all day and Nargonne and Strabo left him to himself. Despite the welcome revelation about the bread train, no one was in a celebratory mood.

At day's end, the great rafts had been moored close to the bread train. What's more, their guard had been reduced by nearly a third and Nargonne didn't have to look far to locate the rest. They were assembling inconspicuously on the other side of the river.

The crossing would be tonight.

When they returned to their camp at sunset, they were joined by the quiet smithy who had befriended Sargonne. The smithy had a bundle of sharp bronze instruments in one hand and a bucket of water in the other.

Barbestro and Marinne were waiting for him. Barbestro reclined against a leaky water barrel, his ungainly hand jammed in his mouth in a vain effort to ward off the pain there. The big man's thunderous toothache would soon come to an end.

Another man was there; the Celt, Ox. The man looked as concerned over his new friend as the rest of them. Barbestro had convinced Nargonne that Ox was a good man and trustworthy. Even so, Nargonne insisted that the man was to know nothing of their plans.

They all gathered to watch the surgery. Barbestro listened suspiciously as the smithy assured him he knew what he was doing. The tradesman patiently plied the big man with wine and made him rub a jellylike mixture of lard and herb into his gums. Then the smithy produced his instruments and looked Barbestro sternly in the eye.

"Vow you shall not hurt me."

"What?" said Barbestro.

"Vow it," the man commanded.

"Why?"

"Because I am about to hurt *you.*"

Everyone laughed. Save Barbestro and Marinne. Barbestro frowned and made the vow.

"How much will it hurt?" mumbled Barbestro.

"A lot," the smithy said.

Marinne grimaced, but Barbestro only shrugged. The deed must be done.

Light was waning fast, so Tourek fabricated a crude torch and Ox held it steadily nearby, appropriate enough, as it was he who was responsible for the tooth's demise in the first place.

Marinne helped hold Barbestro's mouth open and the smithy went in without hesitation. Barbestro groaned as the smithy poked around, painstakingly surveying the wreckage inside. He emerged at last and told Barbestro to close his mouth and relax. Blood seeped from the corners of Barbestro's mouth and Marinne gently wiped the man's beard clean with a wet cloth.

"Soon your foul breath will be gone and my sister will kiss you again," Molena joked. Marinne blushed and Barbestro flashed a smile through bloody teeth.

The smithy produced a thin set of pliers with shovel-shaped ends. The blades of the tiny shovels sported two tiny prongs that curved menacingly. The smithy made no effort to hide the evil-looking instrument and Barbestro's eyes widened at the sight of it.

"Good for horse and pony," offered Sargonne.

Ox grinned at Barbestro. "Close enough," he said.

The smithy leaned Barbestro back and opened the man's mouth. They watched as the smithy patiently positioned the tool. He stared away from Barbestro's mouth and up into the growing dusk, working the tool to the correct spot by feel alone.

Now the smithy asked for assistance. He looked at Ox.

"Put your foot to the man's chest and hold him," he said. The look on Barbestro's face widened and Nargonne chuckled. Ox did as he was bid and put most of his weight against Barbestro's chest. Barbestro groaned.

Then the smithy squeezed the pliers and twisted deftly. Barbestro yowled and jerked, but Ox held him firmly. The smithy yanked out the wounded tooth with a triumphant flourish, and when Ox let Barbestro free, the big Asturian rolled to the ground, clutching his bleeding face.

Eventually he rose, glaring violently at the smithy despite his vow. The smithy held the dripping tooth before him.

"Would you rather have it back?"

"You are lucky the horses don't bite your head off!"

"Many have tried." The smithy grinned and he tossed the guilty tooth to the fire.

He and Marinne cleaned up Barbestro and stuffed an herb-laced feathery wadding in his mouth. Tourek had concocted a potion just for the occasion and made Barbestro gulp it down. He spat out half of it.

"Delicious," said Barbestro.

"Now sleep," said Tourek.

The smithy packed up his equipment and made ready to leave.

"Thank you," Marinne told him. Barbestro finally grinned crookedly at the man.

"You are a butcher."

"And a good one," the smithy answered. "Eat nothing for two days." The suggestion outraged Barbestro, famished from the day's work.

"I will not skip dinner!"

"You will," said Marinne, and she led him groggily to his bed. The potion of Tourek was already taking effect. Nargonne thanked the smithy too and the man made his leave. Nargonne took Ox aside and thanked him as well. Then he whispered in the huge man's ear. Ox thought for a moment before nodding and leaving for his own fire.

Sargonne beamed. The smithy and the tooth had been his personal project. He went to bed happy.

Nargonne, Strabo, Molena, and Tourek waited until the rest were in bed and then gathered quietly around the fire to plan the night's course of action. Barbestro snored peacefully, Marinne at his side. They had already decided on the place from which Strabo should set out. There was a fleet of small fishing vessels parked on the beach. Strabo should be able to slip into the water there undetected.

"There will be soldiers there," said Strabo.

"Leave that to me," said Nargonne with a wink.

The spot was necessarily upriver from the wagons by a treacherously long distance. They discussed his entering the river from a half a league farther up but dismissed the idea; should he spend that much time in the water, Strabo would be too cold even to move his fingers, let alone do the work required. Nargonne had had Santandar fetch heavy oil from one of the many vendors following the army. Tourek dyed the oil black with the contents of one of his clay jars. Strabo would cover himself in the oil as protection from the cold.

"You'll have to swim naked, of course. Clothing would slow you down and soak up too much water. We can't have them finding a great puddle in the middle of their vault," Nargonne told him. Strabo nodded.

Barbestro had been feeding Nargonne detailed information as to the design and construction of the heavy rafts. Short walls were secured to all four sides of the raft and lined with tar. The Carthaginians would be taking no chances with waves dashing over the sides. One wall was hinged so the wagons could roll on and off.

The rafts themselves were a simple ribwork of wide yew trunks interlaid and crisscrossed on top of each other, then lashed together at many joints, half a span apart. A man could squeeze through from the water below. "As long as it isn't me," joked Barbestro, patting his wide belly.

Nargonne scanned the moonlit sky. The moon was half full and the sky slightly overcast. *It will have to do,* thought Nargonne.

Their biggest obstacle was time. The wagons would make the trip in just over thirty minutes. With the current of the river behind him, Strabo could arrive at the wagons within five minutes of their leaving the bank. Five minutes to get in, Nargonne calculated, five minutes, maybe less, to get out. That gave Strabo only fifteen minutes at best in the floating vault itself.

He told Strabo he would have to count to nine hundred

in his head and exit immediately when the count was finished.

"Immediately," reiterated Nargonne. "Do not tarry."

"What if I lose count?"

"Then the Carthaginians shall spear themselves a very big fish."

Strabo smiled at the man grimly. So did Molena.

"Get some sleep," said Nargonne. "I will wake you when it is time."

They went to their beds and Strabo did not sleep at first. He lay practicing. He held his breath for a minute. Then two. He practiced for over an hour and at best could only hold his breath for just less than three minutes. And he wasn't even swimming. He would have to come up for air. So be it, he thought, and he slept.

He slept two heavy hours, until shaken awake by Nargonne. Strabo found the slavers' crimpons next to his bed. The crimpons could be used to seal, or unseal, not just chain, but iron lock sets. Santandar had oiled them and attached them on loops to a wide leather belt as his father had told him. Embedded in the belt were two thick nails. *Good boy,* thought Strabo.

He threw on his cloak and soon Molena was next to him, dressed in black and ready. He was glad she was to go with him, even though this was as dangerous an affair as they had yet undertaken. He should be insisting she stay here by their fire, safe. Instead, he wanted her by his side. He needed her. *Let her be safe,* he prayed.

They walked along a well-worn pathway through the fires and tents of Hannibal's mercenary army. There were no sentries here. The Carthaginians concentrated on the river.

In less than an hour, they had wound their way upriver, past the camp, and into the heavy wood. They turned and made for the waterline.

They reached a suitable spot along the river that was overhung with heavy branches and brush. Silently Strabo stripped his clothes from his body. He hesitated when it came to removing his underclothes.

"You've seen *me* naked," Molena said helpfully. She was smiling at him in the dark and Strabo thought her the loveliest sight in the world, that the deepest of shadow could not veil her beauty. Not for Strabo.

"That was different," he said.

Both knew it mattered little.

He removed the cloth and Molena tried bravely not to take in the view, but, of course, as a woman, she did. She adored his body. All of it. *It will be soon,* she thought.

"You will need to keep your hands clean of the oil," she whispered.

She rubbed him all over with the black oil, careful about his privates. She giggled and he shushed her. Then he giggled and she shushed him. He stood as still as a man could, under the circumstances. Her hands ran over every inch of his body. She was particularly careful with his back when she felt the scarring there. Even in the low light, she could make out the ridges of deformed skin. *Your back, my back,* she thought.

"I didn't get to do this with you," he complained.

"Stay alive and maybe you'll get the chance," she murmured. He felt her warm breath on his neck and then she kissed him there. It was a long, gentle kiss. The kiss of a lover.

Then she covered that hallowed place with the oil and

covered his head and face until she could make out only the whites of his eyes and teeth. She stood back and looked him over. She thought him beautiful.

"Hello, dark creature," she said.

His teeth formed a wide grin in the dark.

He took Santandar's belt and cinched it about his waist. Molena giggled again. He looked silly indeed, naked except for the belt and the crimpons tied there. Strabo rolled his eyes.

"Shush."

She gathered up their things in a bundle and slung it over her back. They were ready.

They stared into each other's eyes for the longest of moments, for as long as they could afford. She was the stronger of the two, he knew, and she proved it.

"Go, black fish," she whispered at last. She blew him a kiss and disappeared into the trees.

Strabo stood alone on the bank until he shook his thoughts of her. Then he crept downriver along the bank under the cover of the overhanging forest. He held the crimpon set tightly to prevent them from clinking together. He eventually ran out of forest cover and crawled along the tall grass like a snake in the night.

He came at length to the fishing boats and crouched in the darkness.

There were guards there. Fewer than a dozen. He couldn't be sure because some dozed against the boats on the beach. He counted six standing and making bored conversation. Two more paced the area. One stood directly at the river's edge, scanning the darkness all around. Damn the Carthaginians, he thought. They were a disciplined lot.

What was worse, another obstacle floated in front of

him, something Nargonne had not anticipated. The floating breakwater of boats the Carthaginians had employed to suppress the current above the elephant rafts had been redeployed to assist in the treasure transfer and it stretched before him several hundred paces downstream. There were few tenders and no torches aboard the dark line of boats and all was quiet.

Strabo would have to swim beneath and past them. His first swim would be a long one.

He peered past the makeshift breakwater downriver. Four wagons had already made the crossing and another was nearly across. An empty raft was making its way back to the starting point. The bend in the river prevented his seeing the loading point, but he knew another raft must soon be disembarking.

The guards nearby were alert and he could not get past them to the water. The minutes passed and he made himself take great lungfuls of quiet air, preparing himself for the swim, as he had as a child. That was another river—a gentler river and far from here.

Strabo needed to time his departure perfectly so that he swam downstream just as a "bread wagon" was loading aboard the raft. That way, he would reach the raft far enough from shore to elude detection of the guards there, but still with the maximum amount of time required to perform his task.

Then he heard voices and they were not the voices of the sentries. Two men were stumbling along the path near the boats. They bumped into each other and argued as they walked. They appeared stone-drunk and they barked at each other stupidly.

Strabo could make out only two large silhouettes as they approached.

Barbestro and Ox.

Downriver, the returning raft could no longer be seen. It was being loaded. Time was short.

As the two big men walked by the sentries, the sentries told them to quiet down. The two men argued drunkenly with the sentries. Barbestro did not require much acting skill as he was still woozy from the medicine Tourek had given him. And he was already quick to anger, thanks to the pounding pain in his mouth that had returned the moment Nargonne had rousted him.

As for Ox, he was a master. He wobbled on his feet and issued loud and incoherent threats. He even paused to produce a loud belch that would have knocked a man to the ground all on its own.

The guards gathered near them, but the one at the river's edge staunchly stayed put. Strabo's eyes darted to the group and back to the man at the water. *Move, damn you.*

The sentry held his post.

The big men knew it too, so Ox suddenly cursed Barbestro and took a misguided swing at him, missing him and stumbling forward. Barbestro leaped back at him and the men exchanged blows. Real blows. The guards leaped into action and surrounded the men, but the two fell to the ground and began driving each other around in the dirt with loud cries and groans.

Strabo watched in amazement. Had they practiced this?

The sentries raised their voices and the ones previously dozing jumped up and joined them. The soldier at the water's edge watched his fellow sentries scurry around the two combatants and try to gain control of them. Strabo held his breath.

The sentry bolted from the water to assist.

Strabo slunk fast and low through the boats, blacker than shadow. The boisterous row of the drunks behind him now, he reached the water and slid to the sand.

He crawled forward, and as he slithered into the current, the shock of the cold hit him like a club. He shook it off and was neck high in the water in seconds. He took a deep breath and dived noiselessly below. "I shall knock out the rest of your damned teeth" was the last thing Strabo heard before his ears submerged and he heard only the surging of the river as it raced along the bottom to the sea far away.

No one saw him slip in. No one—save for Nargonne, and he only saw a faint blur pass between the boats. He watched safely from behind a merchant's cart up the hill.

Nargonne looked downriver.

The raft was emerging around the bend.

Strabo was a full pace below the surface and pulling himself through the water with powerful strokes. He told himself to conserve his strength. The river was carrying him fast. Good. *By the gods, it is cold!*

Nargonne now feared the two men had overdone it to lure the sentry from the beach. Finally the two men allowed themselves to be pried apart. They sat on the ground hurling insults at each other.

"Vermin of cesspool!"

"Motherless whelp!"

Strabo's lungs cried for air and he knew he had to surface soon. He urged himself beneath the shadowy bulk of the breakwater boats and they passed harmlessly above him. Denying his lungs, he swam farther before he finally emerged cautiously. He knew that it would do no good to come up gasping loudly. He exhaled underwater, and when he broke through, he floated and filled his lungs.

He turned to see the floating breakwater of boats far behind him. The current was more powerful than he had estimated. He was too far to the middle of the river and the raft was still near shore. A spark of panic stung him. He was in danger of being swept past his target!

Had anyone been looking, they would only have seen a black blob floating with the current before the water swallowed it again. Strabo had sucked in a lungful of air and submerged, this time swimming hard to his right. Toward the riverbank. He fought the current that was pushing him along too fast.

Nargonne was stuck. The sentries were binding the two and he heard one of them call for irons. *Irons!* One of the sentries dashed off.

It would be disastrous to have the two put in irons. Questions would be asked and Nargonne could not afford that kind of scrutiny. But what could he do?

The river surged over Strabo and he pulled and stroked as hard as he ever had. He kicked his legs furiously and he could feel them losing strength. He was out of air.

Nargonne watched the beach sentries yank Barbestro and Ox roughly to their feet. The sentries were in a foul mood. Nargonne briefly thought of running back to the fire and evacuating the rest. *Some of us shall survive,* he thought, not for the first time.

*   *   *

Strabo swam and prayed he would not fail. He exhaled again and surfaced at last just upriver of the towboats when, washed silver by the moonlight, the great raft suddenly loomed before him. The cold was forgotten. He sneaked a breath and pushed himself below again.

Nargonne left his post by the merchant's cart and started toward the river. He would think of something to say by the time he reached the sentries. Which would be in no time at all.

Then he stopped in his tracks.

A black figure walked up to the group of sentries and their unruly captives. He wore the flowing cape of a Carthaginian officer. Even in the darkness, Nargonne could see the red crest of the Falcons on his breastplate.

The frigid water stung his eyes, but Strabo could see the unworldly black form gliding over him. He lunged upward for the bottom of the raft.

He broke through the water and struggled to get a grip on the wide yew beams. The oil on his arms may have saved him from the cold water, but now it made everything slippery. His legs flailed beneath the water against inexorable current. He pushed one forearm over a log and then, with a mighty heave, he brought the other up and locked his hands.

He was on.

The guards rowing the towboats had all been ordered to silence. Still, the gnawing of wood against the iron oarlocks and the splashing of their oars covered any watery noise Strabo might make.

Strabo pulled himself along the yew beams and reached up to one of the wheels of the wagon. He pulled a nail from his belt and scratched a deep gouge along one of the spokes. Then he lowered himself and peered frantically in the darkness for the hatch. There!

The space between the beams was indeed tight, but here the oil saved Strabo again. He clenched his eyes to the pain and squeezed his body up. The oil served to squeeze him through and he yanked himself up between the beams and swung himself crosswise across two of them.

He lay on his back and breathed heavily. The hatch was there, just fingers above him, and it was well oiled. He heaved a sigh of relief; the hatch was locked with a simple set of irons. He freed the crimpons from his belt. Santandar had tied each instrument to the belt with a long leather cord so that Strabo could still work with them, and if one was dropped, it would not be lost. *Like father, like son,* thought Strabo.

The Red Falcon officer limped up to the sentries and Nargonne stepped back out of sight. The sentries stiffened and Nargonne heard the officer demand, "What ruckus is this?"

The Red Falcon officer was Ribas.

Up in the hills, Souk Mallouse rested in his grave and his brother waited on horseback in the stillness there, rolling his stones in his fingers. A shadow stepped from the darkness, panting for breath. Her clothes were tattered and torn from her run through the heavy woods.

The shadow whispered to the Souk.

"All is well, so far," Molena said. She gave him Strabo's clothes. The Souk already carried two heavy blankets. He nodded silently and turned his mount toward the higher trees above. Molena set off back for their fire. In order to avoid camp scouts, Tourek rode a full league directly west before turning south.

Strabo's frozen fingers struggled with the crimpons. The first would not work. The second was too large to fit the iron clamps. The third was the right size, but Strabo could not fit it to the iron clasp. It wouldn't go in! In desperation, he dragged the tool through his armpit, covering it in the black oil. He pushed it into the body of the clasp. It slipped in and the clasp fell free. He slid the hatch along its runners and pulled himself up into the darkness of the bread wagon at last.

Ribas demanded to speak to the officer of the watch and one man stepped forward.

"They are drunken fools, sir."

Barbestro cursed the sentry and Ribas kicked Barbestro in the ribs. Hard. The big man groaned in pain and the sentries grinned. Barbestro mumbled another drunken curse and Ribas kicked him again. Harder. Barbestro shut his mouth at last. Ox glared at Ribas and Ribas returned the favor.

"A word from you and you shall taste my boot as well!"

The sentries were impressed with the fearlessness with which the Falcon officer abused the two huge men.

Careful to conceal his bandaged left hand, Ribas knelt

painfully and tugged at the ropes that bound the two prisoners' hands. Satisfied, he turned to the sentries.

"These men have served beneath me and their strength
is needed tomorrow, though they may lose their tongues."

Ribas spat on the ground between them. The sentries
could plainly see the officer was disgusted with the
drunken louts.

"On your feet!"

The sentries yanked the two drunks to their feet. Ribas
lectured the two. "Tonight you'll enjoy the hospitality of
the Red Falcons."

The sentries all laughed.

"Tomorrow you will enjoy the lash."

This brought more smiles to the soldiers; praying the
two would forgive him later, Ribas shoved Barbestro in
the back and kicked Ox in the rear.

"March!"

The sentries grinned and mocked the prisoners as Ribas
led the men away.

Nargonne sighed in relief. *The man is a wonder,* he
thought. Then he turned his attention to the raft on the
river. It had cleared the bend and was on its way. *Is he inside?*

All was peaceful on the river again. The beach sentries
were back at their posts and the raft moved silently in the
distance. *Our course is set,* thought Nargonne. *Let all to
their tasks.*

He strolled calmly back to his fire.

The interior of the bread wagon was as dark as the
night outside. Tiny shards of moonlight filtered in through
cracks in the oaken ceiling and the open hatch itself al-

lowed muted moonlight to reflect from the water below. The river's feeble reflections glowed and swam about the walls of the wagon.

Strabo hovered in the hatch, half-in and half-out of the wagon. His hands were on the floor of the wagon and his arms held his body suspended in the center of the hatch so that his legs dangled through the opening and the water dripped free from his body to the river below. He waited and watched the last of the water drop away. His eyes adjusted to the weighty darkness. Then he pumped his arms and rolled himself in.

The walls of the wagon were lined halfway to the ceiling with built-in oak cases, creating a thin corridor running the length of the wagon. Everything was heavy oak and every surface was covered with bags of flour of various size.

The sounds of the night he had left, the sounds of the oarsmen and the river, all were muted in here. Outside, the river shoved and lapped against the raft. Strabo began silently counting: *One, two, three. . . .*

Pushing aside the flour bags, he flung open a case and was greeted by a gleaming rack of bricks whose golden cast was unmistakable even in the weak light of this place. The man knew his metals and he hefted a brick in his hand. He inspected the brick closely and judged the weight of it in his hand. He smelled it. He licked it. He scratched it deeply with a crimpon. It was the real thing, through and through.

Strabo got to work. Brick after brick he carried and cast through the hatchway, where they *plunked* quietly, one after another, into the water below.

In the depths far beneath the surface, the first of the gold spun through the deep and thudded softly to the floor of the Rhône. A second brick landed next to the first. Then another . . .

When Strabo finished the first layer, he came to a heavy board. He removed this shelf from its stays and started in on another layer.

Plunk, plunk, plunk, went the gold.

And Strabo counted not the bricks but the passing of time. *Ninety-eight, ninety-nine, one hundred. . . .*

Strabo tore at the treasure like a dog after a bone. Layer after layer disappeared into the depths.

Strabo replaced the top shelf of the empty chest and, using the shelf as a false bottom, reassembled the top layer with bricks. To a cursory inspection, the chest would appear full, though the layers below held nothing but air. Then he closed the chest and opened another.

On shore, another man counted in his head on the way back to his fire: *210, 211, 212. . . .*

Strabo's arms begged for relief, but he urged himself on. His breath came so heavily he huffed and blew as if he stoked the fires of a forging furnace with his very lungs. His back felt numb and broken, but he carried on.

He completed a second case and disguised it as he had the first. He ripped into a third. The river had stolen much of his black oil coating, but some still streaked his body. Strabo looked like a brindle-sheened animal. The naked man pounced and leaped about the dark wagon like a panther. The only fluid on the floor was the sweat streaming off his body. He hoped the Carthaginians, if they discovered it, would think the moisture came from the crossing: *573, 574, 575. . . .*"

Nargonne arrived at their fire just as Molena did. She rushed to speak to him, but he gestured for silence. He bade her lie on her bed and she did. He lay on his and counted the stars above.

Strabo finished another case and began the next: *591, 592, 593.* . . . Outside the small confines of the dark wagon, the raft was approaching the end of its trip across the water. In its wake, it was disgorging a fortune in unmarked gold in a long line across the river bottom below. The bricks came to rest in the depths, one by one.

Six hundred forty-six, 647, 648. . . .

Far from the river, the Souk rode hard to the south. His thoughts were dark and lonely. He rode alone after all these years. Alone in a strange wood in a strange land. Alone in a world forever cleaved in two.

He made the turn back toward where he knew the river must be. Alone on his horse in the deep of night, the spirits seemed to take him and the tears came again. The wind whipped them back over his ears and they flew from his hair to light on the forest floor. Those droplets of grief seeped into the earth behind him, swallowed by the world.

He finally reached the river's edge and found himself a rocky outcropping jutting defiantly into the current far downstream from the mighty military camp. He dismounted and waited, scanning the water.

Despite the cold outside, the interior of the wagon had become a simmering box. Strabo steamed and sweated:

888, 889, 890. . . . He was only midway through a case, but all the time spent with the wise Asturian had its effect. *Nine hundred.*

Molena was wide awake and watching as Nargonne suddenly sat upright. He said nothing, but she could see the concern written on his face. Nargonne stared in the direction of the river. *Get out!*

Strabo quickly dispersed the flour bags back over the cases and headed for the hatch. He took one last look about the wagon when one case caught his eye. He hadn't noticed it before. There was something about its general size that drew him.

He bolted to it, wiped the bags from its surface, and lifted the lid. He was sweating and panting and exhausted, but even in his frantic state, he recognized what lay within. The case was constructed in the same fashion as the others, each layer separated by an oaken board on stays. Except this case smelled of oil and was filled with a dozen long, narrow mahogany boxes packed tightly together. Each box was completely sealed in Egyptian wax, which shimmered translucent yellow. Protection from moisture, he knew.

The mahogany boxes themselves were each just five fingers wide and a little longer than a man's arm, their weight unmistakably familiar to a swordsman like Strabo. He knew what lay in each box. What was so special about them that Hannibal would treat them like treasure?

Strabo extracted a single box from deep within the case. He slid the flour bags back, tossed the box through the hatch into the water below, and slipped through the hatch just as he heard voices raised outside.

Thump! The raft jerked to a stop.

He had waited too long.

The raft began rotating and he heard the soldiers outside barking for lines and ties. His heart pounded and he slid crossways across the yew logs and slid the hatch home again. He fumbled furiously with the crimpons. Which one was it? Footsteps of men coming aboard sounded on the raft above and he froze. Had they heard the tinkling of his tools?

He breathed as quietly as he could, but his lungs sounded to him as if they were roaring. He felt for the crimpons underwater and one of them slipped greasily through his fingers. *That was the one!* He fit it to the latch and the latch responded, spinning cleanly home.

Strabo could see the shadows of a dozen soldiers' feet all around the wagon on the raft. They made more noise as they harnessed the wagon to a team of horse waiting on the bank.

He waited.

He heard the soldiers curse the horses as they backed them up onto the raft and the raft swayed as the big animals backed aboard. Then a dark shadow fell across him and he looked upriver. It was the two towboats passing as they went to rehook to the other side of the raft and haul the thing back again.

He knew the dockage area and the beach were lined with sentries. He couldn't risk a deep swim for it from here. In his exhausted state, he wouldn't make it far enough to escape detection. He listened as the last of the horse harnesses were hooked up.

Then a solution occurred to him. He would ride the raft back! He would spend more time in the water than planned, but it was a chance. But then he realized how that answer was a fleeting one. There would be no wagon to shield him and he had no idea if any sentries would make the trip back aboard the raft. He would soon discover that it didn't matter.

The horses moved off to the "Hai!" of their handlers and the raft rocked as the animals pulled the groaning wagon to shore. He lowered himself into the water, below the big yew beams, to get a look at the towboats that would pull the raft back.

They were gone. This raft wasn't going back!

He could see the towboats oaring smoothly away, back to the other side, moving fast. Fast because now they towed no load. Strabo cursed himself for his stupidity. He had wanted the mahogany box and now he would die for his blindness and greed. He would die and end up at the bottom of the river with the very box he cherished.

Think like a wise man. He watched the oars of the disappearing boats sweep the current. He realized he had but one chance left.

He took in a huge breath and slipped beneath the biting water. He kicked and he pulled and kicked and pulled and his lungs swelled in pain. There was no way he could risk coming up for air. He fought his own body now and stayed below. *Swim!*

He pulled hard, back toward the opposite shore through water as clear as it was icy. He pulled and yanked at it, urging his strokes to efficiency and speed.

Then he saw them. Two blurry, whalelike shadows came into view. The oars on each side of the boats dipped through the water in unison. There was no time left; his lungs were done. He swirled for the boat nearest him and swam directly beneath it, kicking furiously for its prow. Its dark mass grew in his eyes as he kicked toward the surface. The current tugged and pulled at him. Strabo kicked back.

He came up just in front of the boat and exhaled slowly with the last of his will. The bow of the boat met his hands and he thanked the gods for the short line of rope that dangled there. He clutched it between his frozen fingers and held on. Then he carefully drew in a long breath, though his lungs howled for more. But he kept his head and forced his body to breathe evenly, quietly.

He clung to the prow of the towboat as it plowed through the water. Concealed there in the shadow of the boat, the rowers could not see him and neither could the treasure regiment soldiers on either shore.

The rowers had felt the extra weight but attributed it to the river's finicky current. The boat moved forward, and though the men were mostly quiet as ordered, Strabo listened to the whisperings of the rowers as they pulled back toward the other side. Theirs was the common grumbling one would expect from soldiers laboring hard through the night. Strabo held on and told himself to rest.

The unforgiving temperature of the river dug deep into Strabo and he winced at the thought that he would not be escaping it soon. It was cold, so cold! Finally the rowers reached the center of the river.

Strabo prepared himself with another series of deep breaths. Then he relaxed, took a final big gulp of air, and released his hold on the rope. He slipped beneath the water to as deep as he could stand and began swimming away with the current.

Swimming again. Freezing. He pulled and pulled as before. His muscles were weaker now. Much weaker. They responded sluggishly, but still they toiled on. He fell as if into a trance beneath the waves. *I am safe here,* he thought. *Safe in the water. It has always saved me.*

When he first came up for air, he dared only a single breath before submerging again. *Swim.*

When he came up a second time, he did the same.

The third time, he chanced a look about him. To him, the bank itself appeared to be flowing past and he as still as a boulder in the water. He recognized the feeling; fatigue was bending his mind. *Swim.*

He swam and surfaced and swam.

When he finally paused again, he turned to see he was far downstream and the great camp of the army flowed away in the misty distance. *Swim.*

He floated and kicked weakly along the surface now. He hadn't the strength to stay under. He hadn't much strength left at all. All he knew is he must begin making his way now to the other side and he ordered his finished body to go there.

The cold river would not tire. It swept him through the darkness.

Strabo's lungs began to give out. He cursed them. *My legs still work, why not you?* His legs did work, barely, and gradually he pushed himself toward the opposite bank. But his mind was failing him too. He began to be confused as to which way was up and which was down. The stars above joined their dancing reflections on the water, until it seemed he was struggling through the ether of space itself. He choked and spat when he breathed water, where he thought there was air.

The hallucinations came. He was floating through the narrow streets of Sigeum. Carthaginian soldiers floated along with him. Were they Red Falcons? He could not tell. None had faces. He saw racks of unfinished spear and felt the heat of the iron furnace. The nickel and plating vat floated by and he reached for it, though he knew that it must scorch his hands. His back blazed with the pain of hot iron. He moved his arms and legs by habit alone.

A horse head rose from the water and stared at him, eyes wide and white. *You are death,* Strabo thought. *A horse is death.* Strabo's mind and body failed him at last and he felt the water take him. He blacked out.

Tourek turned his horse in the deep and urged the animal to swim quickly. He had desperately looped a line around the only thing he could: Strabo's neck. He feared he would kill him if the water hadn't already. He dragged the man out of the water. It occurred to him they were always dragging the man out of the water. Satisfied that Strabo was still breathing, Tourek heaved the deadweight of the man onto the horse, rolled up his rope, and mounted. Then he spurred the horse away from the river and deep into the forest.

———

In the Spanish port cities of Gades and Saguntum, the Carthaginians made a great show of the multitude of troops assembling at the dock areas. Roman spies reported the number of troops was so large they marched for hours just to enter the city. Reality was another thing entirely: These troops were exceedingly small in number, but they marched through the front gates with much fanfare, then surreptitiously slipped out of the city, only to march back in again. They kept up the act for days on end.

Chapter 16

*W*hen the camp awoke, both the treasure train and nearly half of the bread wagons were safely across on the other side of the Rhône. The rest of the bread train transfer proceeded smoothly, taking only until noon. Lighter than the others, these rafts moved faster. After all, those wagons contained only flour.

The Numidian cavalry had suffered negligible losses against the Volkai, and Hannibal sent thousands of them up and down the Rhône to reconnoiter. Hannibal valued intelligence, as much as he could gather. Far to the south, they unexpectedly encountered a Roman cavalry contingent. The resulting skirmish there left nearly two hundred dead Numidians, though they pressed the Romans away.

Hannibal had not known it, but the ambitious Roman general Scipio and his navy had paused at the mouth of the Rhône at the Mediterranean Sea en route to the Spanish Peninsula. The encounter was an accident.

Wisely, the Numidians headed away west before doubling back at all pace to the Carthaginian camp on the Rhône. When the cavalry returned to camp in the late afternoon, Hannibal cursed his luck. He had not only lost many capable Numidians, but the Romans were near. The last thing he needed was their having any knowledge of his unexpected presence. The news spurred Hannibal to action. Not that he needed prompting. The winds grew colder every day. The order was given to move out at dawn.

Hundreds of Carthaginian fires burned on the shore where the Volkai had so recently opposed them. All of the heavy equipment was across the river and only a few dozen fires remained for the night on the western bank. Nargonne's was one of them.

Ox had returned to the Celts. Ribas had spent the day with the Falcons but returned at nightfall. The wounded warrior was quiet, but his drawn face revealed his pain. Nargonne demanded to see his wounds, not from distrust but out of care. Ribas's many injuries would heal, Nargonne could see. But he winced when Ribas unwound the bandage that protected his shattered left hand. All that was left was the claw of his thumb and his two lead fingers. Nargonne and Molena re-dressed the wound and Ribas clenched his teeth against the pain.

"The Souk has medicines," Molena told Ribas.

"I will use the hand again, Nargonne," Ribas said.

"Yes, you will." Nargonne sighed. But not soon.

There was no sign of Tourek. Or of Strabo.

The Asturians paced about aimlessly and prepared their horses. Nargonne told everyone to bed down, but none save Sargonne could sleep. He and the smithy had had a busy day with final preparations of pack and draft animals of every description. The smithy had said good bye and crossed the river at last light, and like everyone else, he prepared himself for the cold journey ahead.

Just before midnight, a horse stepped from the darkness. Tourek. Like a child, Strabo clung to the saddle behind him. Molena sprang from her bed and helped Strabo from the saddle. His leaden legs hit the ground with a thud and Nargonne watched as she hugged him before the others, unembarrassed. Nargonne wanted to hug the man too. Maybe. If he had been successful. Tourek wore an expression of stone that told Nargonne nothing. The Souk looked as exhausted as Strabo.

They led the men to the fire and the others gathered close. Santandar looked at his father with the excitement they both felt. Nargonne put his hand to his son's head and tousled his hair.

"Sit still."

Nargonne saw that he could not prevent everyone from eagerly hearing the news, any news. Sargonne rubbed his tired eyes to life as everyone made themselves comfortable in quiet anticipation.

Nargonne studied Strabo. *The man has the constitution of a bear,* he thought. Molena covered him in extra blankets and he accepted them without a word.

Strabo looked better than he felt. The shiver had still not left him completely. He had slept like a dead man next to a roaring fire Tourek created far back in the thickly forested hills. Tourek had tended it ceaselessly to keep it from smoking. Strabo's spent body had demanded he sleep the whole day away without dreams, without thought. Now here he was, another soul returned to the world by the Souk.

"Can you talk?" asked Nargonne.

"I can," said Strabo.

"Were you detected?"

"No."

"Never?"

"Never."

"Are you sure?"

Strabo paused, then nodded his head.

Nargonne sighed and looked about the largely abandoned camp. There were no other fires near. *It is time they all knew,* he thought. Everyone had demonstrated their worth and their mettle. *I could not have done it without them.* His heart rose with hope. They would need to know.

"Tell me," said Nargonne.

"Everything?" Strabo looked around their fire at eager faces.

"Why not," said Nargonne, and everyone was relieved to see the man allow himself a smile. *Let them smile now,* he thought. *Let us all enjoy for a few moments. They have earned it; by the heavens, they have!* For all cheer would soon evaporate, as only he and Strabo knew.

Strabo described the events of the night with a minimum of elaboration. He began with the breakwater and the sentries on the beach. He grinned at Barbestro. "The Celt bested you at last."

"That was only pretend, Strabo," Barbestro reminded him.

Strabo made little of the cold, deciding he would rather not think about it. And he kept the secret of the mahogany box to himself. Nargonne listened intently as he described the interior of the wagon and the construction of the cases. He told them of the hatch and winked at Santandar. "Your belt saved us."

Santandar beamed and the moment did not go unnoticed by Nargonne.

"Any silver?" Nargonne asked.

"No. All gold."

"Coin or brick?"

"Brick."

The group went wide-eyed when Strabo indicated the size of the bricks with his hands. He told them of the tossing of the bricks through the hatchway, the close call at the opposite dock, his escape on the prow of the towboat.

"Then I swam away and the Souk pulled my freezing carcass from the river." The heavyhearted Souk managed a thin smile.

Nargonne turned to Tourek.

"And you?"

Tourek shook his head. "Undetected" was all he said. No one spoke while Nargonne blankly watched the fire. He poked the blaze with a branch of spruce and looked around cautiously again. He returned his eyes to the flames.

"How many bricks?" he asked at last, without looking up.

Like a flock of swallows in flight, all their eyes turned back to Strabo. But Strabo shook his head slowly.

"Too numerous to count."

The group shifted in their seats.

"Hazard a guess," said Nargonne, smiling at the others.

The group chanced a chuckle and waited.

"I don't know."

"Did you count to nine hundred?"

Strabo nodded.

"How many were in a case?" asked Nargonne.

Strabo considered this. He had not thought of numbers. He had been too busy. But while his bones were still numb, his memory was not. The image of the rows of bricks were tattooed in his brain forever.

"There were two hundred forty bricks in a case, but I never emptied one completely," he finally announced.

Nargonne nodded.

"How many cases did you get to?"

"Seven. My guess is there are over a thousand bricks at the bottom of the river."

The revelation struck the group as if the freezing Rhône itself had reached out and slapped them. Everyone was speechless. Nargonne only nodded solemnly.

"A productive night's work" was all he said. The fortune was greater than he had ever imagined. Just a handful of the bricks would be sufficient to pay the fine that oppressed his people. No one dared dream of such riches. Not even he.

Molena studied him. She studied Strabo too and was unsettled that neither man seemed to share the elation of the rest of them. *It must be the weariness,* she thought.

Nargonne cleared his throat.

"It is a simple matter, then. We return in the spring and fish the bricks from the river."

He gazed over each of them and spoke pointedly. "Wait until spring. By then, Hannibal and his thousands will be warring the Romans in Italy. They will be busy."

They all stared back at him in silent acknowledgment. It was the wise course, they realized. Then he repeated himself again.

"Wait until spring."

He looked them all over and they each nodded.

"Do you understand?"

Molena could contain herself no longer.

"We understand, Uncle, we will wait until—"

Nargonne interrupted her. "Good!" The interruption was a rebuke and it puzzled them. Molena felt a chill run through her.

"Say nothing. Nothing!" Nargonne said.

Everyone nodded.

Nargonne took a deep breath and straightened his tunic. Ribas stared back at him with a face that mirrored his. *So now you have realized it too, Ribas,* Nargonne thought. Nargonne looked at Strabo.

"You marked the wagon?"

Strabo's look went cold and he dropped his gaze to the fire.

"I did."

A shadow passed over Molena's thoughts. "Uncle," she said, "mark the wagon? What do you mean 'mark the wagon'? Whatever for? We will never see it again."

Nargonne stared only at Strabo.

"One task remains," Nargonne said.

Molena was stricken. *No!* she thought.

"What remains?" she said. "We are done! Done! We quit this place, Uncle."

But the sober look on Nargonne's face quieted her. The chill she had felt coming enveloped her now. Dread settled upon the group. Nargonne still stared only at Strabo.

Strabo's eyes had returned to the fire and he broke the silence without looking up.

"The wagon must be destroyed," he said.

Barbestro leaped to his feet. "What?"

"Why?" Molena demanded, but as the word escaped her lips, a shudder shook her.

"No," she whispered. But she now knew too.

Strabo's eyes met Nargonne's.

"It must be done," Strabo said.

Nargonne only nodded and Molena's shoulders slumped.

"Why, Father?" Santandar did not yet understand as the adults did. Molena turned to him.

"They will discover the deed, Santandar. On the other side of the mountains, the Carthaginians will regroup. They will inventory everything. Troops, horses, weapons . . ."

She stared at her uncle. "Gold."

Santandar blinked his eyes to ward off the danger he felt press upon them.

"Perhaps they will never know," insisted Tourek. "It could have happened a thousand ways."

"Listen to me," said Nargonne. "It is true it could have happened a thousand ways, but they will investigate those thousand ways, all of them. Hannibal will leave no stone unturned. Wouldn't you? They will think. Listen to me. They will *think*! We have ridden with them and fought with them. They are the ablest of people."

He was looking at Ribas, who hung his head grimly. Molena felt the spirits of her weary people sink. All appeared done, yet now they were in greater danger than ever before. Her eyes turned dark.

"They will come back to the river," she whispered. "We will be found out."

The reality of the statement hit them as surely as a missile hurled from one of Hannibal's catapults. They sat brooding in silence until Barbestro spoke. "We set the blasted wagon to fire."

Barbestro had not quit. He could be wearied and wounded but never broken. "We burn the whole lot of them!"

Strabo looked grim. "Gold does not burn."

Again the group was silenced. The cold wind swirled around them and spun the sparks of their fire to die on the night air. Nargonne spoke.

"Think no more of it. You go home at dawn."

"I will not," Barbestro protested, but Nargonne's nerves were frayed to the breaking point.

"You will! I say you will and so you shall! You will return to our people, Barbestro. My son—my brother—you will take them safely home!"

Nargonne stood before them, his hands on his hips in defiance. He knew their wishes well, but he would not accommodate them. Not in this.

"I will go alone," he said. It was an order.

"And what?" Tourek asked. "What will you do?"

"Leave that to me."

"Not alone!" Marinne jumped up next to Barbestro.

"Alone," Nargonne insisted.

"What will you do?" demanded Tourek. He would follow Nargonne into the darkest of pits, but this was more than he could bear. "Enough of your mystery. Tell us. Haven't we followed you well enough? Have we not earned the right to know now? Tell us!"

The Souk was right, thought Nargonne. He of them all had paid for their success with the greatest of loss. They all waited, but Nargonne would not answer him. The wounded Ribas stared blankly at Nargonne. Then he spoke.

"He will look for a way to destroy the wagon, and if it cannot be done, he will confess to the crime."

The revelation took Molena's breath away. Nargonne said nothing still.

"As an Usson," Ribas said.

They all understood at last. The defiant Nargonne did not move a muscle.

Another throat cleared and a bleary eyed Sargonne stepped into their circle. He had been listening and understood only what was needed.

"Strabo," he said.

They all turned to Strabo and he struggled to his feet. Molena watched him avert his eyes from hers and she stared at the man she might love. Had he championed them time and again only to abandon them now? Disappointment joined the anger in her heart. How could he?

He could and she knew it. He had found them alone and he would leave them alone. Capable as he was, he could not embrace them. She had always known it and had not wanted to believe it. Suddenly she hated him for it. Hated him for his insular ways, for his quick sword, for his disdain for their beloved horses. For everything.

She loved him and she cursed him for that most of all. He had looked them all in the eye—save her. *Coward!* she wanted to scream. The man was not afraid of spear or sword or warrior, but he was a greater coward than any. Her mouth trembled from the effort to keep her lips sealed.

Sargonne looked beseechingly at his brother.

"Strabo will wait for the army to leave, Sargonne,"

Nargonne said, "then he will take another swim. He will pack as many bricks on his back as he can and be gone."

Strabo had turned away from the group and he felt the heat of the fire on his back. Again the heat of the fire. And the heat of all their eyes on him—save two.

Now it was she who would not look at him.

Molena turned her face from him and Strabo knew at that moment that she was lost to him. *And for what?* he thought. *For pay. And for a mahogany box. Is that all there is for me? What then will I leave behind? Nothing. Nothing but gold and death.*

The thought of it made him spit on the ground and he stepped away. Away from the Asturians. Away from Molena. Away from Nargonne and his endless, impossible tasks. *I cannot live with these people. I am not of their stock. Not of them. Then of whom?*

Of no one was the only answer he had. *Their fate is theirs and mine is mine.*

I am not like Nargonne.

Strabo stepped away into the shadows.

Nargonne did not bid him stay. *A sword is only a thing,* thought Nargonne. *A blade of metal forged by men.* Still, Nargonne fought the urge to cry out to Strabo as if to a petulant child: *Have you learned nothing?* But he held his tongue. Each must make his choice. As Nargonne had. As Ribas had. As Molena had.

"Leave, then!" Sargonne suddenly said.

It was the first time in memory anyone had seen Sargonne angry and Strabo jerked to a stop as if hit by one of Mallouse's long-iron arrows. Despite Strabo's love for Molena, Sargonne was the only one who could strike him so. Sargonne glared at Strabo's back and then angrily turned from him and announced to the rest, "I go."

Strabo knew the man had little idea of the undertaking he was volunteering for, and then, that the man had every idea what he was volunteering for. It did not matter to Sargonne.

What does it matter? thought Strabo.

Nargonne shook his head. "No."

"I go," replied Sargonne.

He stepped back to his bed, rolled it over, and produced a bundle of rags. He carried the bundle to the fire and unwrapped it. Inside was a battered iron sword. The sword was bent and rusting and had no sheath. Its hilt was cracked. Sargonne thrust the point of the feeble weapon into the dirt and stared defiantly at his brother. The events of the last twenty-four hours overcame Nargonne and tears welled in his eyes, brilliant tears of pride and devotion. Sargonne understood death no better than anyone else, but he understood it well enough.

The group was silent and watched the two brothers face off. Nargonne's brain swirled with emotion and a battle raged there. Pride versus fear. He looked at his brother and saw only the iron of a man.

From behind the fire, Strabo saw it too, and he cursed his own stupidity for the hundredth time. He might not know what he would leave behind, but by the gods, he knew what he would not. He stepped from the darkness and pulled the useless sword from the ground. He put a hand to Sargonne's shoulder and looked him in the eye.

"The horses need you," he said to Sargonne. Strabo's mind spun fast and in desperation he invoked the dead.

"Mallouse needs you to care for the horses that will

take your people home." Strabo swept his arm across the group.

"Do you understand, Sargonne? The horses take them home."

Sargonne did understand but was not moved. He thought only of his brother alone in the mountains and set upon by hordes of angry Carthaginian soldiers.

Strabo locked eyes with the man.

"Your brother will not be alone, Sargonne. I will be with him." Strabo held Sargonne's crude sword reverently between them before tucking the pitiful weapon into his belt with a flourish.

"And so will you."

Then Strabo turned from them all and stalked off into the night.

It was late, very late, and Nargonne bade everyone sleep. Molena waited until all were settled, then took her uncle aside and begged him.

"I know where he is," she said.

Nargonne sighed. "Take Castaine, then."

She found Strabo crouched at the grave of Souk Mallouse. He had heard the horse ride up and was surprised that he recognized the uneven patter of Castaine's feet. Strabo knew it was Molena. She dismounted nearby and hastily unrolled blankets beneath the protection of a towering oak. She went to him.

"I doubted you," she said.

"I gave you every reason."

"Let the Souk rest." She pulled Strabo to the oak, where he collapsed in her arms.

He buried his face in her chest and the world swirled

through his head. Darkness. Water. Horses. Pain. She comforted him and soothed him in silence. At length, his deepest sorrows passed and he felt the strength of her lift him.

He took her face in his hands and gazed at her. *What metal is she made of?* She smiled back at him and her strength was his.

He pulled her to him. Their mouths touched at last and he passed his love to her and she gave hers to him. They kissed breathlessly.

"I am a fool," he whispered.

She shrugged. "You are a man."

They smiled and their lips met again.

The two of them were one brightness. One joy. And they partook of each other slowly and gently, feeling their way tentatively through each warm region of passion, giggling shyly when tickled too close. They lay there together for hours, exploring each other and guiding each other and learning of each other. They revealed themselves to each other through their mouths and their thighs, as lovers do. When their passion finally subsided, they lay together in an exhausted heap, limbs tangled together and mouths pressed softly somewhere, anywhere into the other.

When dawn came, the Asturians moved about the fire as if stone boots clung to their feet. A bitter wind blew in from the north and they tightened their cloaks against it. They silently heaped winter supplies on the broad back of Corcell, an extra mount for those who would go on.

Nargonne instructed Santandar to climb the trees near the treasure dockages and secretly mark the place. Then he announced that Tourek alone would stay, entrench himself near the grave of his brother, and build a snow camp. There he would await their return.

"It won't be long," Nargonne promised them all.

For his part, Nargonne was not much for long good-byes. He hugged each of them and kissed his son. He pulled a thin gold ring from the third finger of his right hand and pressed it into the boy's palm. The ring bore the engraved head of a horse. "Your mother's ring," he told his son. "She will be with you, as I will—always. Now listen to your elders, boy." He hugged his son and hoisted him onto a horse.

Ribas limped up to Nargonne, but Nargonne bade him keep silent. "You are in charge, warrior," Nargonne said. "Get them home." Then Nargonne lowered his voice to a whisper, "In a couple of months, we'll take a swim together, you and I." Nargonne nodded toward the river and Ribas could not suppress a laugh.

Nargonne took two more of the strongest among them: the horses Castaine and Archon.

Strabo and Molena had said their good-byes up in the hills, but when Nargonne gave the command to mount up, he noticed Molena blow a kiss to her sister. In that moment, Nargonne knew the woman's mind was set. Covered head to foot in winter furs, Molena sat on the back of Tundra with her arms crossed. The stare she leveled at Nargonne was as familiar to him as if she were his own child.

Nargonne sighed. "There will be death in the mountains, Molena."

But she didn't waver, as he had known she wouldn't. The woman would tackle a firestorm, he thought.

"So be it," he said.

The other Asturians parted from them and headed west. Nargonne, Molena, and Strabo watched them go. Molena held Strabo's hand and winked at him and Nargonne laughed.

He relished the look of embarrassment on Strabo's face and told the two of them, "Whatever plans you two have, you'll need my permission, of course." Strabo only nodded in resignation and the three of them turned for the Rhône and made one of the last ferries over the river.

———

Far to the south, Scipio's two Roman legions at the mouth of the Rhône grew anxious. The cavalry regiment that had discovered the Numidians had chased them back west, back to Spain, or so the Romans assumed. There were no other signs of enemy activity to be found anywhere along the coast. And the open seas, according to all reports, were empty. General Scipio dispatched half of his force onward to Spain and requested new orders from Rome. In the meantime, his remaining legionnaires constructed defensive stockades along the shoreline and waited it out on the lonely beachheads.

Chapter 17

*H*annibal's army numbered slightly less than before. A handful had deserted at the Rhône, but this mattered little. His crack troops were still with him. On the other side of the Alps waited the Ligurians and a host of other tribes hostile to Roman rule. He would gain more allies.

The marching army again broke into three manageable columns and proceeded as before. On horseback, the Asturians had little trouble regaining their former place in the column among the Celts and other horsemen, and Molena kept her face hidden beneath her hood. The Red Falcons knew the foreigner Ribas had been wounded badly and so did not miss him. Only Akdar was suspicious, but still burning from his failure at the Rhône, he held his tongue. The column marched without incident for two weeks to the very feet of the mountains. And where the slopes of the Alps began, so did the leaden weather.

It began to snow.

There was no rain or sleet to herald its arrival. The heaping snow simply began with fat flakes one afternoon.

The way grew slippery, and though they were slowed little at first, the whole column had come to a stop before dusk. The snow fell heavy and wet and the supply train was busy distributing warm weather gear courtesy of Hannibal's gold. Thick boots, fur overcoats, fur blankets, horse blankets, leather trousers, and thousands of hastily sewn fur hats.

The cavalry tried to affix leather boots to their horses, but the southern animals kicked them off as soon as they had been put on. The tents and coverings of the army proved worthless beneath the weight of the snow and most men bedded down in groups for the night with their tents pulled over themselves like blankets.

By the next morning, the snow had accumulated halfway up a man's thigh. That, combined with the steady uphill climb, made the going slow. The army in the rear began to spread out because the footing in front of them had been churned to a quagmire of mush that made forward motion almost impossible. The Campaign Escort tried in vain to rein them in.

The Carthaginian command was worried now. They had been escorted from the Rhône thus far, at great expense, by the Keltoi tribes and by assorted tribes of the Segovellauni. But as Hannibal plowed into the Arc Valley, which marked the threshold of the Alps, those temporary allies made their leave, as had been agreed. Intelligence from Carthaginian emissaries and scouts told Hannibal that a hostile reception lay ahead. They were entering the lands of the Allobroges.

The Allobroges were a Gaul-like conglomeration of tribes that cherished their verdant highlands, which served as the source of wheat for much of the continent, including Italy. They were also accomplished raiders and had grown wealthy exacting heavy tolls from centuries of trade passing through their mountains. They had demanded a huge payment from the Carthaginians. The Carthaginians had deemed the demand excessive and had promised the Allobroges death instead.

The mountain tribes were assisted by others. The Ambares and Aedui to the north. The Sequani and the Helvetii to the east. And the Ceutron, who inhabited the very ground the Carthaginians marched over.

At length, the army came to a flat river, where warehouses processed grain throughout the fall. The river facilitated the gathering of grain from all over and sent it south to markets in the Mediterranean. But as the Carthaginians approached, they could see smoke rising in the distance. Soon they would pass through settlements completely abandoned. The smoldering winter storehouses had been stripped of grain by the hostile locals and put to the torch in front of Hannibal. The soot from the fires joined the snow and wind to create waves of gray drifts that rolled away downwind.

The freezing column passed a tall stone statue of Sucellus, the hammer god of the Gauls. His war mantle and helmet of granite were capped with snow as he stood there standing guard at the gates of a settlement. His crudely hewn face watched the interlopers pass until a group of Celts slung ropes over his shoulders and pulled him to the ground. They laughed. There was to be rare sport on this journey.

The Carthaginians conferred day and night. They learned that the various chieftains of the Allobroges and the other tribes had collaborated and would be waiting in ambush in a multitude of high positions above the Carthaginians as they passed. The elephants were moved next to the treasure wagons. A contingent of Red Falcons was assigned there as well and Strabo was sure he spotted Akdar among them.

By the fourth day, the slopes steepened and snow turned to ice. The army wove slowly through tall canyons with vertical walls that soared above them. The wind whistled and sang through the rocky wasteland. There were few in Hannibal's army who had ever experienced such conditions. Certainly Strabo had not. The frozen landscape was a far cry from the salty warmth of his Mediterranean Sea. Nargonne seemed comfortable, or at least he didn't complain. He only clenched his teeth to the biting cold and steadied on. He had insisted they be swathed head to toe in wool, for which Strabo and Molena would thank him for the rest of their lives. Nargonne added heavy fur pelts and boots. "Warm as a lamb," he had said. They covered their horses with wide woolen blankets, which itched their flanks but helped them ignore the cold. Castaine and Archon stayed strong. Tundra and Corcell marched as if they had been born in the snow. So Strabo learned yet another thing about Nargonne. The man had mountain experience; others did not.

Soon the army had scaled to the heights where the relentless winds began. It didn't matter that snow wasn't always falling from the sky. It was always in the air. Whipped up everywhere by the wintry blasts from high mountains, it tore at the army without rest.

Days passed and the men began to fail. Their feet suffered frostbite and sores, which would not heal beneath the pounding pace of the march. Head colds turned fatal and fires were unable to heal the sick. Many were destined to die here. They were afraid to go back for the justified fear that weakened stragglers would be easy prey to the hostile tribes that shadowed their passing.

Animals failed too. Their baggage, if it could not be carried, was left to be buried by the mountain weather. But a horse is a hardy beast and most would make it through. The elephants also fared surprisingly well. They each wore crude sets of thick shoes, which they took to easily, and their battlements were removed so that they suffered no load.

Not so the pack animals. Their burdens proved too great and they succumbed by the thousands. Nargonne and Strabo picked their way past mound after mound of frozen animal.

They found a familiar face in the blowing snow, tending to a stricken mule. Sargonne's smithy looked up at them through a thicket of ill-fitting hide and a flopping fur hat that covered his face like a beast. He was busier than ever, though the mule was a lost cause. They could see that half of the smithy's face was covered with a frozen splatter of blood and snow. He had been kicked hard by some struggling animal. An inevitable injury, given that the man was forced to work on the ground amongst their legs as they died. Still, the smithy greeted them with a smile.

"How is my dental patient?" he asked.

They told him Barbestro was doing well and then the smithy asked of Sargonne. Nargonne told him he had sent him home. The smithy looked thoughtful. "That was wise," he said. "I hope I see him again."

"Will you go all the way to Italy?" Nargonne asked.

The man shrugged. "Look at all these animals."

Nargonne liked the smithy a great deal and spoke to him sternly. "Listen to me. From here on out, there is nothing you can do. If the animals falter now, they die. You can't nurture them back to health in these accursed hills. All you can do is what any man can do and that is slit their throats quickly."

The smithy gulped at Nargonne's candidness. He knew it was true. Then Nargonne surprised Strabo by dismounting and stripping their extra baggage from the back of Corcell.

"Your gifts are for the living. Now go back."

The smithy turned and looked up the mountain before them.

"You can't help them," Nargonne said again. "This is a solid horse. Take care of him."

The smithy hesitated. Then he laughed.

"I have nowhere to go," he said.

"Yes, you do," answered Nargonne. "We have need of you back in our lands. In Asturias."

The man nodded at last. "Sargonne has told me much of your people." Still, he stood there, thinking, deciding.

"The women are beautiful," added Strabo. "Prettier than the horses."

"So I noticed," the man said with a sly grin.

Molena blushed and the four of them laughed there in the howling weather. "Can you find your way there?" asked Nargonne.

The smithy nodded and they picked through their baggage for the bare necessities and cast the rest to the ice. The smithy took the Asturian horse and thanked them before disappearing behind them in a fog of blowing whiteness.

Strabo and Nargonne and Molena trudged on wordlessly. Castaine kept his nose to the snow.

At one point, Nargonne paused to peer up at the crags that reared over the pass in front of them and turned to Molena. "They'll be coming soon."

The Allobroges lived here. All year. They knew well the mountains, whereas the Carthaginians did not.

No sooner had Nargonne's words escaped when a band of Numidians thundered past them going downhill. A Carthaginian officer was shouting for all horses to follow. That meant them and they did.

They galloped over the slippery ice and snow with nearly one hundred other riders to the rear of the column, past panicky bands of stragglers who shouted at them as they passed. At last they rounded a towering corner of granite and came to a stop.

Hundreds of their army lay dead, their baggage either demolished or gone. Broken weapons protruded from stiff bodies. There had been many carts here pulled by both animal and human and they were each afire. The cavalry looked about helplessly. The canyon was still, save for the smoke and snow. Hoofprints disappeared into a multitude of crannies and cracks. They scanned the canyon walls. Nothing. The attackers had escaped.

Orders were given to follow the prints and they tracked them for hours, but they only led through an endless maze of high granite and stone until they were obliterated by the wind.

At nightfall, the dejected cavalry climbed back up and did not reach the main body until midnight. It was a long, cold march. The difficult going had spread the column over many leagues. Too many. When they finally did reach the main cavalry camp, they learned that the front of the column had also been attacked with similar results.

The Carthaginian command conferred and the Campaign Escort was angrily dispatched to shore up the march. The chastised escorts ruthlessly harangued the entire column throughout the next day, but despite their best efforts, the column continued to move ahead in fits and starts. It could not stay together.

Carts broke down. More animals and men grew ill. And weak. The impossible terrain made it difficult to disseminate proper food. Warmth was a memory.

The Asturians slept in a heap against the big body of Castaine, who rolled into a ball and dozed like Cabo. Archon and Tundra stood over them, quiet and sleeping, dreaming of the sun.

Something woke Strabo in the middle of the night and he reached for his sword. Nargonne was out of his bedroll. He held a finger to his lips. Strabo ignored the gesture. "Where are you going?" he whispered.

"Looking for an ambush. Stay here."

Nargonne left, heading uphill on foot. Strabo watched the wind billow his dark cloak against the white all around them. The man returned before dawn. "We must reach the bread train by nightfall" was all he said.

The three of them pushed hard that day. They made steady headway and strode past a long length of the column. Snow was falling lightly, but the endless stuff was stirred by the wind until they and their mounts were painted white. Snow and ice clung to every piece of fabric, every inch of fur, every inch of exposed skin. Nargonne's beard had become a wobbling chunk of ice.

They forced themselves to ignore the very worst: dying men in the snow. Some spoke to them and weakly begged for help. Most just stared. A doom of white patiently waited for them to breathe their last.

Then came the first of the great gray humps. The elephants were failing. The young ones first. The beasts looked pitiful lying on the ground. Snow billowed about them and filled the nostrils at the ends of their trunks. Their tusks had been scavenged by their own handlers and their mouths hung open, their wide tongues frozen to the ice. Then came more heaps of the thick gray hide and snow. The weaker of the older elephants were failing as well.

The army's plight was turning ugly. Strabo had to threaten a grain cart with his sword to get a meal for their horses. The Campaign Escort was no longer a threat to anyone; they were dying too. As for the Asturians, they munched rock-hard jerky from their packs until Strabo swore he'd never put the stuff to his lips again.

His lips were bleeding as well. At least they wanted to. Blood congeals quickly in the cold and all three suffered from it. Their mouths became ghoulish red gashes surrounded by pale, wind-blistered skin.

The entire army was woozy now from fatigue, and from all things, wine. Potable water was a rare commodity up here, though the stuff surrounded them in frozen form. Fires burned feebly in the snow and wind. Fuel was scarce. It was an achievement to warm a frozen water bag and eke out a drop or two of the life-giving liquid. The army turned to wine, for the fermented stuff did not freeze.

Food was a problem too. Everyone on the mountain simply stuffed their mouths with coarse grain, sucked it into a pulp, and swallowed hard. Tired as he was, Nargonne grinned through the cold at Strabo and Molena. "You can tell your children you ate like horses in the mountains," he said.

As the day wore on, the grade steepened. The paths into which the army squeezed grew narrow and all was ice: the ground; the walls of rock; the precipices threatening from above.

Any movement was a treacherous one. Horses and men slipped and fell. They took care in these desperate straits to fall carefully. This high in the sky, a broken bone meant death, as surely as a spear thrust to the heart.

Then they saw them. Half a dozen of the great pachyderms. The handlers were having a difficult time with the animals, now more skittish than ever. They tried blindfolding the beasts against the sheer drops and alien landscape, but that only frightened the elephants further. Their handlers had taken to lining the path before them with shattered pieces of wagon and cart to firm up their footing. The handlers and drivers scrambled back and forth, snatching with numb hands the planks the elephants had stepped on and ferrying them back to the front again for use as steps once more.

The Asturians moved on and came to another troop of elephants enduring the same procedure. Beyond these elephants, they came to what they had been pushing so hard for. The rear of the bread train.

Then horns blew and the procession ground to a halt.

What was this? They picked their way past the elephants and the bread train. The three eyed the bread wagons carefully, but none could discern the telltale mark. It occurred to Strabo that he could not remember which side of the wagon he had marked. Was his mind failing him?

Beyond the wagons, the canyon broke open to their right and revealed the slimmest of paths winding past the craggy peak beyond. The start of the path was blocked. Several giant stones that dwarfed the largest elephant lay crashed there, barring their way. Nargonne looked up. The peaks above were a jumble of icy overhangs and outcroppings of rock that reached out in defiance of gravity itself.

To their right, the mountains exposed themselves in a sheer openness that rattled their nerves. They squinted to take in the view. Through the high mists, they could finally see just how high they had come. Impossible, thought Strabo. The whole world stretched out before them beneath the palest sky he had ever seen. He could make out hundreds of snowcapped peaks that stretched to eternity. Some lay in shadow, but the setting sun glinted off the very tops of many of them. Brilliant yellow tinged with orange glowed at their crests. Not the color of gold, Strabo thought, but the color of flame. The frozen peaks looked afire.

Nargonne casually pulled a frozen chunk of rabbit jerky from deep within his pack. His numb hands clumsily hacked it to pieces, nearly taking a freezing finger with it. He gave some to Strabo and Molena and they put the stuff in their mouths and tried to suck the things warm.

They came to the landslide and halted. The small mountain of rock barred the army's way on the narrow pass. It might have been an act of nature, Nargonne thought. He looked up. Could the mountain tribes get so high above them? He shivered. They could.

The Carthaginians were shouting into the wind and listening for distant shouts from the other side of the landslide. The forward scouts had returned and found themselves trapped on the other side. They were trying to shout descriptions of the quantity of stone to their comrades, but all was in vain: Everyone's words were lost to the wind. Nargonne watched as a Carthaginian engineer scribbled notes in chalk while another blunted the tips of a few arrows. They tied the notes to the arrows and shot them over the impasse. Soon those same arrows came lofting back over the rocks. Two of them were lost to the wind. One of them *thumped* at the engineers' feet.

More notes and arrows shot up and away and returned in high arcs through the wind and snow as the engineers communicated. If the arrows whistled as they struggled through the gusts, their sound reached no one. It was eaten by the wind.

The engineers conferred. They gathered men, lumber, and elephants, and set to work prying the rocks apart and pushing them off the mountain. "We help them," Nargonne said. They worked wordlessly with the corps of engineers as the glow of the peaks in the distance gave way to darkness. They worked through the night, hacking at the mountain of rock. The steady wind Strabo had become accustomed to picked up and snow began pouring into the high canyon. Strabo had never witnessed a true blizzard. He would see one now and wish he hadn't.

Finally the last of the rocks plummeted off the edge and disappeared into the white maelstrom below—the way was clear. Molena shivered and sighed in relief.

The scouts on the other side rejoined them and the Carthaginians exchanged grim smiles. Congratulations were brief. All agreed that while it was dangerous to proceed through the blizzard, it was more dangerous to wait. Every minute in the mountains weakened the army.

The procession moved on.

The Campaign Escort directed a long contingent of Celts and Iberians over first, followed by twenty-five hundred Numidian cavalry. "Be wary" was the order. The blizzard was only half the threat.

The engineers confirmed and reconfirmed that the narrow ledge was sound and finally began sending the heavy wagons over at midday. They spaced them far apart and placed the remaining elephants among them. Elephant. Wagon. Elephant. Wagon. There was room for little else. Only a handful of men could negotiate the winding ledge, sometimes only four abreast. The scouts had reported that the ledge wound up and down for two leagues until another peak converged upon it and ledge became pass. That pass would lead them to the summit and a descent could be had at last.

The three Asturians watched the wagons roll by. They took turns watching the wheels so as not to draw attention to their inspection. It was Strabo who spotted the marked spoke.

A slight nod of a head was all that Nargonne needed. Night had returned by the time the last wagon lumbered and skidded its way past. Strabo, Molena, and Nargonne followed with the engineers.

The slick ledge was indeed treacherous, but there was one saving grace. The blowing snow obscured the dizzying height and thus the elephants were less inclined to spook.

The order came down through the ranks via a series of muffled shouts: "We march all night." The Campaign Escort was justifiably leery of the extreme jeopardy the procession faced. They were stretched to a needle-thin line along a slippery ledge that gave no purchase and provided no cover. The position was essentially indefensible.

And the Allobroges knew it. They would wait until the army was stretched out and clinging to the side of the mountain, then strike.

The procession was mired again and again as portions of the outside of the ledge gave way beneath the unaccustomed pounding of hooves and feet and wheel. Elephants had to be coaxed over carefully. Chains were attached to the big animals and they dragged the heavy mining wagons over the low spots of failed rock.

Nargonne brought up the rear as Molena and Strabo were keeping their eyes on their wagon. Suddenly, from far ahead in the mist, came a sound so unearthly it penetrated even this unforgiving wind. It was the terrified scream of an elephant slipping off the mountain and it sent shivers down the spine of everyone who heard it. The sound faded and the elephant was gone. It wouldn't be the last to perish that way.

Clefts in the mountainside appeared on their left, and horses and men gathered there, resting. The Campaign Escort urged them on. The clefts grew more numerous and larger as the mountain began fracturing into a series of peaks separated by crevice after crevice. The steep rise of the mountain wall on their left presented a multitude of hiding places and icy cover.

They came to the widest cleft yet and Nargonne squinted, inspecting it. The mountain formed a wide bowl above them, studded with hundreds of spires of rock and ice. To their right, the edge and oblivion below. He could see a band of fifty Numidians at the ready at the far end of the ledge before it turned the corner. They were assembled with one hundred Carthaginian regulars. Hardened veterans all. The Celts and Iberians had mostly passed. Where were the Red Falcons?

Nargonne knew what the Campaign Escort knew. This would be the place. But there were still three wagons to protect. Nargonne's wagon, the one with the mark Strabo had made, was in the lead chained to an elephant, but bogged down. The drivers were slowly pulling the wagon free.

The rumbling began ahead of them and behind them at the same time. Then came shouts of alarm from everywhere at once. The mountain began to rain rock and ice, and Strabo saw a storm of white rocks explode from the hills and descend upon two stamping elephants just ahead. The beasts took the rocks directly and were swept off the edge. They screamed as they fell. Like the other had.

The ground shook beneath Strabo's feet and he looked to his left.

"Move!" shouted Molena as an avalanche of loose rock thundered down the mountain. The horses screamed and bolted and Strabo nearly lost the reins, but Molena grabbed them and pulled Castaine forward as the landslide tumbled by in a cloud of powdery debris. The three Asturians spurred for the wagons ahead.

All was chaos and it was suddenly every man for himself, as it seemed the whole mountain cast itself upon the column. Many of the rocks were as big as a man. Some were the size of horses. Their shapes were ugly and gnarled; their velocity and power unstoppable. Man after man was taken from his feet and washed from the ledge by the raging flood of Alpine stone.

"Nargonne!" Molena saw a stone glance off the man's side and rip him from Archon. Strabo dived from Castaine and tackled the tumbling man to a stop just shy of the edge.

Strabo looked back at the mountain and ducked as a boulder leaped past his ear.

The Numidians were in disarray. Their horses bucked and shied in terror, but the veterans dispersed along the edge of the wall and drew their weapons. Strabo pulled Nargonne to his feet and the man clutched his side but pulled his sword. Strabo did the same and helped Molena from the saddle.

"Stay behind me!"

Horses up and down the ledge stampeded down the path in panic. Molena slapped Castaine: "Hai! Run, run!" The Asturian horses followed the others and galloped away down the mountain.

And then the mountain tribes came.

They sprang like wild mountain animals from the crags above and jumped in long leaps down the snowy bowl. Fur capes flapped about them like evil wings. They were as numerous as the rocks and bore clubs and axes. That was all that was required up here. No sword or spear. The slightest blow upon the weak meant death in this harsh environment, so far from succor. In their experience, no great skills in the sharp arms were required, so they never bothered with the sword. It was an omission Strabo would make them regret.

Hannibal's trespassing army had their backs to the precipice and they spread out and faced their attackers. The ambushed were less than two hundred men and outnumbered. This time, they had no clever plan, no meticulously prepared tactics, no advantage. Nargonne knew the tribesmen would be the most vulnerable when they hit the ledge and tried to regain their footing. He cried out to all.

"Hit them as they come!"

As the mountaineers came screaming to the bottom of the slope, the Carthaginians struck into them with fury.

The Numidians launched their javelins and the mountain men fell. Then the Numidians surprised Nargonne by dismounting. Their animals' poor footing had become a liability in the tight space. They took to their swords and fought as bravely on their feet as they had in the saddle. But for each mountain man that fell, another leaped over to attack.

Strabo surged forward to the foot of the slope and drove his sword at them. The strength of combat had found him and his movements were easy and fluid. Now the attackers' momentum worked against them as Strabo dodged their swinging clubs and stabbed, dodged and stabbed.

Still they came.

The Carthaginians were overcome by sheer number and the veterans began to drop to the ice. The ledge was a mass of swirling bodies and swinging weapons. The Numidian horses stampeded in confusion and many ran screaming over the edge. The rest disappeared in a stumbling mob around the corner ahead.

Then the pandemonium intensified as three terrified elephants tossed their drivers, broke free, and stampeded through the throng. They jerked in berserk circles and crushed friend and foe alike. The bodies piled up.

The terrifying war screams had ceased, replaced by the urgent grunts and groans of exertion and injury. This was battle now, and all energy was delivered to weapon and weapon only.

Nargonne and Strabo fought side by side, protecting each other's flank. Molena hovered behind them and clubbed every mountain man within reach. Their only thought was survival. They did not care if the wagons were taken. The Carthaginians and the Numidians soon reached the same conclusion. The few survivors turned from the fight and ran toward the corner ahead, abandoning two wagons behind them. The third wagon was nearing the corner up ahead. The elephants were trying to tow it to safety—Nargonne's wagon!

Then fire came to the mountain.

The Carthaginians regrouped by Nargonne's wagon and put flint to pitch. If the last two treasure wagons couldn't be saved, at least they wouldn't fall to the enemy; dozens of flaming arrows buzzed over Molena's head like a swarm of fiery hornets and thumped into the two wagons left behind. The dry mountain air had sucked the desiccated wagons dry and they burst into flame.

Then puffs of smoke also appeared high up the slope. The mountain men produced fire arrows of their own and the smoking shafts rained down upon Nargonne's wagon and the few defenders gathered there. The wagon began to burn. Only three elephants remained on this whole stretch of the ledge: Two were free and one was pulling Nargonne's wagon. The terror of the two animals on the ledge overwhelmed them and they ran screaming up the path and scattered the Carthaginians there. The two animals bumped their way past the elephant towing the wagon and thundered around the corner. The last beast would have followed and did try, but he was chained to Nargonne's wagon. When the elephant glanced back and saw that the wagon he pulled was now on fire, he trumpeted in panic, desperate to escape. The animal yanked at its chains and stamped. The flaming wagon jerked forward.

Only a pocket of fighting remained and the three Asturians were in the thick of it. Nargonne saw his wagon slipping away.

"Strabo!" he cried, and Strabo turned to see him running from the fight. Strabo and Molena could not follow. They were set upon by two Allobroges, who wisely backpedaled and dodged Strabo's sword, but kept him at bay with swinging axes.

Molena watched Nargonne make for the wagon. The rest of the Carthaginians had abandoned it, leaving only two drivers struggling to free the thing from where it had bogged down dangerously close to the edge.

Then Strabo lunged between his attackers and whirled to split them up, but they kept their distance from his sword. Strabo chanced a look over his shoulder to check on Nargonne. Nargonne had thrown his sword to the ground. Strabo's mind screamed, *Not your weapon!* But Nargonne had found the only weapon he required. Fire.

Strabo turned to Molena and shouted, "The horses!" She took to her heels and sprinted across the ice to the far end of the path, where dozens of horses stampeded about. Strabo's attackers were momentarily distracted by the fleeing woman and one of them started after her, but Strabo cut him down from behind. He then spun on his heels and took the other in the midsection and both men were finished.

Few of either side were left alive on the narrow ledge. There were only a handful of mountain men crawling painfully on the ground and Molena was far down the path, where the horses had fled.

She was safe for the time being, so Strabo raced after Nargonne and the wagon just as three men on horseback suddenly appeared from up the mountain. Strabo easily identified the big man in the lead, his red cape flapping behind him: Akdar.

They bore down on Nargonne, who only saw them at the last second and stumbled out of their path. But three horses were too many to dodge and one of them struck him and he sprawled savagely to the ice.

Akdar had seen Molena running, her hood dislodged from the fight. He recognized the Asturian woman immediately and cursed. *What trickery is this?*

He and his horsemen turned on Nargonne, weapons drawn, and now Akdar had his heavy long sword swinging high above his head, circling for a kill. They surrounded Nargonne but had made one misjudgment in the excitement: They had ignored Strabo who, sword in hand, rushed them from behind.

He leaped up and tackled the first Falcon from his saddle. Akdar and the other turned to see Strabo take the Falcon to the ice in a blur of flailing cloak and blade. Strabo rolled free and the first Falcon lay dead on the ground. Nargonne saw his opportunity and rushed for the wagon as Akdar and the other turned their attention to Strabo.

Akdar gasped when he recognized him. The Asturian woman and now this—the man from the *pankration* match! The bold fool nearly drew a sword against him then, thought Akdar. *Let him try his luck here and now!*

"Crush him!" roared Akdar, and they reared their horses and drove upon Strabo, who dived and rolled to keep from the pounding hooves.

One driver was on the back of the panicking elephant, while the other urged the animal forward with a staff. Nargonne rushed the driver at the foot of the elephant and slammed into the man, sending him beneath the big beast and the driver was kicked and crushed beneath its feet. Ignoring the driver who screamed at him from the back of the elephant, Nargonne ripped the flaming canvas from the side of the burning wagon and leaped in front of the elephant, waving the smoking sheet in its face. The elephant bellowed and the driver threw a javelin at Nargonne. It missed. Nargonne howled at the animal and flapped the canvas in its eyes. The elephant's trunk whipped like an angry snake while its sharp tusks lashed out to spear its attacker. It reared and kicked its huge feet, but Nargonne darted in and thrust the flames to its mouth.

Behind him, Strabo unbalanced the Falcon horses by rapidly thrusting his sword in their faces and the Falcons found their mounts difficult to control on the slippery slope. Akdar swung his long sword at Strabo, who managed to stay just out of its lethal range.

Strabo did not give the men room to maneuver. He kept his body close to their mounts, where the horses could not trample him and the Falcons could not get a clean swing.

This was a dangerous course as the horses spun and danced, but Strabo grabbed the nearest by its harness and hung on. Then he yanked himself up on the Falcon's horse, smashed his fist into the man's face, and shoved the rider off. As the man fell, Strabo swept his sword across the man's neck and the Falcon crumpled to the ground.

Akdar cursed Strabo and swung again but missed. Now the two of them jostled their mounts into each other, neither able to position a blow upon the other. Strabo knew he couldn't outduel the seasoned horseman this way. He kicked the horse into Akdar's and jumped from the saddle at the big man, who tried to bring his long sword around. Strabo, however, was too close, too fast. Momentum took them both from the horse's back and they crashed to the ice.

They wrestled for a moment before Strabo felt the big man's arms trying to lock his head in their viselike grip. He squirmed free and rolled away, but Akdar was back on his feet as quickly as Strabo. Both squared off with weapons in hand.

Akdar scowled at Strabo. "You are no Usson."

But Strabo only unleashed his battle snarl and circled him.

Nargonne straddled the very edge of the cliff, threatening the elephant with the flames, forcing it back. High atop the elephant, the driver readied another spear and urged his animal forward and the elephant responded. A massive foot struck Nargonne in the chest, sending him reeling to the ground. He looked up just in time to see another javelin whistle his way and the thing plunged clear through his leg. Nargonne hardly felt it. There was little pain now. Only thought. The thought of one thing. *The wagon must go.* He struggled to his feet and limped forward.

Akdar's long sword had the advantage on open ground and he knew it. He advanced on Strabo with wide, wicked strokes, but Strabo fended him off, not going for a kill but buying time and keeping his distance, waiting for his chance.

A guttural howl erupted from Akdar and he charged with a series of overhead strikes, as if he meant to cleave Strabo like firewood. Strabo deflected the blows, but the big man's heavy sword took its toll on Strabo's frigid Saguntum blade. It failed under the onslaught, fracturing to pieces. Strabo cursed and somersaulted away from Akdar's attack.

Strabo's sword was finished, though Strabo still brandished it. There was nothing left of it, just the handle and a hand's length of jagged bronze remained. Akdar eyed the broken weapon. It was a pathetic thing against the might of his long sword. Akdar grinned and the canines in his mouth showed yellow against the whiteness of the ice and snow all around. He lunged forward.

At the edge, Nargonne had harassed the elephant and the wagon to the very edge of the cliff. The shouts from the elephant's driver alerted the Falcon whom Strabo had taken to the ground; the man suddenly came to life. The man was mortally wounded and could only raise himself to one knee. He bled heavily from Strabo's sword, but the trained veteran managed to pull his bow from his shoulder. He quickly put arrow to string, let fly, and the arrow found its mark.

Nargonne shuddered at the impact. The arrow drilled him through the side, shattering his ribs before settling deep in his chest. Nargonne felt the air hiss from his lungs but pressed forward. The driver kicked the beast at Nargonne and threw another javelin from close range and this one pierced Nargonne's left shoulder. Nargonne groaned and waved his sheet of flame. His lifeblood poured to the snow and he felt his legs weakening fast. *The wagon must go!*

Behind Nargonne, the Falcon had another arrow to bow and had pulled the bow taut. He drew a deadly bead on the unprotected back of Nargonne just in front of him. His last thought was that the man was dead; then a flash of light blazed across his brain and his body was dashed to the snow. The arrow sailed harmlessly away. Horse and rider had returned and the man never knew that he had been crushed to death by an Asturian horse.

Molena and Castaine had ridden him down. The two of them turned for the elephant.

Akdar attacked but met no defense this time. Strabo turned and ran—he needed a sword and he knew where to find one. He slid on the ice between the heavy wheels of the burning wagon and found the frozen trapdoor beneath. Akdar saw that the driver was holding off Nargonne and paused, then made his choice. He went for Strabo.

Strabo hacked at the icy hasp of the trapdoor with what was left of his broken blade, ripped the door free, and clambered into the belly of the smoking wagon. Akdar dived beneath the wagon in pursuit.

Strabo was in the wagon again. This time, it was filled with smoke and lurching wildly, thanks to the efforts of Nargonne outside. Coughing and sputtering from the fumes, Strabo quickly found the rear of the wagon, where he knew the mahogany boxes were stored. He tore the top off the case and seized one of the long boxes inside. He heard the scraping of boots behind him and whirled around just as Akdar charged him, swinging his long sword. But the Falcon's weapon found only the wagon wall as Strabo spun away. Strabo thrust the end of the box in Akdar's face and clubbed the Falcon with it. But Akdar recovered and now the two men stared at each other just a pace apart. Strabo could see the Falcon's black eyes gleaming in the light that filtered in through the burning holes in the cabin. Strabo had looked a warrior in the eye before, and so had Akdar. Neither flinched.

Strabo heard a cry from outside. "Strabo!" It was Molena!

But at that, Akdar charged and Strabo twisted out of the long sword's path. Using his box as a weapon, Strabo knocked Akdar's blade aside and drove his shoulder into the Falcon as he passed. The two of them smashed against the side of the wagon and neither noticed the wagon shake and begin to slip. Strabo pounded Akdar with his fist and the two men grunted and gasped, but Akdar slipped free, turned, and thrust his sword again at Strabo. Strabo again used the box to parry the blow.

Outside, Nargonne flapped the canvas furiously at the elephant, and the driver flung more javelins at him. The elephant backed away in terror as suddenly a new threat arrived—Molena on the back of Castaine. She urged Castaine at the elephant and Castaine gamely lunged at the giant animal.

The elephant stepped back again and the wagon began to slide over the edge.

Inside, the floor of the wagon lurched and upended and the two combatants were thrown to the floor. Strabo landed painfully on his back. Akdar was the first to his feet and now he knew he had Strabo. Without hesitation, he raised his long sword and brought the heavy thing down on Strabo, who raised the box in front of him like a shield just in time. The blow blasted into the box in a shower of splinters. Akdar seethed but stirred with energy. Even a good blade was no protection from his heavy sword, let alone a flimsy wooden box! *The fool was finished.*

He rained down blow after blow upon Strabo; the box splintered and crumbled in Strabo's hands with every strike. Akdar was possessed by the kill now. Relentless. He would finish him!

He hardly noticed that his unending blows began to produce sparks as the box disintegrated in Strabo's hands.

Strabo knew the trapdoor's opening was just behind his head. Pressed by the crushing blows of the determined Falcon's heavy sword, he knew he couldn't escape and he couldn't last much longer. Then he heard Nargonne's shouts from outside.

"Fall, beast! Fall, you!" Nargonne cried, and as his failing knees buckled, he threw the flaming fabric over the head of the elephant with the last of his strength and collapsed to the ice.

Strabo felt the wagon lurch again. The floor lifted even higher this time and the groan of the wagon against the rocks below filled his ears. The wagon was going over. And Akdar's blows kept coming.

Then the decisive blow came. The blow blasted the box to fragments at last and revealed what only Strabo knew was inside: a sword of gleaming blue, which shimmered with menace in the smoky light of the wagon. Akdar raised his long sword for the killing blow as the wagon floor rose up sickeningly. The Falcon hissed, "Time to die, whoever you are!" But, the handle of the blue sword had found Strabo's hand. In an instant, he drove the point of the precious weapon deep into Akdar's chest. Akdar stiffened and gulped in bewilderment as Strabo pushed the blue blade deeper.

With his opposite hand, Strabo took the man by the throat, locked his eyes to Akdar's, and growled in his face, "I am Asturian."

The wagon rose on its side and Strabo shoved Akdar away. He abandoned the prized blade to the Falcon's dying body and tumbled for the trapdoor.

Outside, the elephant felt the searing heat of the flame. Beneath the smoking sheet, the huge beast's eyes bulged wide in panic and the shrieking monster could take no more. It reared back, kicking frantically for hold. But it lost its footing and the ledge gave way under its enormous weight and crumbled. Another unearthly bugling rocked the mountainside as the elephant slipped backward and plunged head over heels off the edge.

The driver fell with his animal as the chain rattled by in a flash. The chain swallowed what slack there was and the other end held tight to the axle of Nargonne's wagon. Chain followed beast and wagon followed chain. The massive wagon jerked away.

The trapdoor!

It was rising out of Strabo's grasp. He put his boot against a case of Hannibal's gold, launched himself for the door, and yanked his way through to the light outside just as the wagon crunched loudly over the rocks and slid away beneath him. The wagon rumbled and roared as it broke up and toppled over the cliff at last. The cry of the elephant rang in Strabo's ears and he felt himself sliding, slipping, falling off the mountain! Panic seized him and he only thing he could grab onto was . . . a leather rope. He snatched it and wrapped it around his arm as the wagon plummeted away from him in a cloud of smoke and ice and snow.

Strabo clung there on the cliffside, his head spinning, his feet dangling in midair. He watched the wagon disappear into the mist below and the wagon was gone. And Akdar. And the sword.

Strabo felt a tug on the rope. The rope tightened and Strabo held fast as he was pulled roughly up the cliffside, scraping painfully off rock and ice until he was pulled up and over the edge and onto flat ground, where he slid to a stop.

He rolled over and his lungs pumped for breath. Above him was a familiar sight: Molena on the back of Castaine. The other end of the rope was tied securely to Castaine's neck.

Strabo blinked in disbelief at the horse. "You devil, Castaine."

Molena dismounted and helped Strabo to his feet, but there was little jubilation at his escape.

"Nargonne," Molena whispered.

They ran to where Nargonne lay still on the snow and bent to him. Blood ran from Nargonne's mouth and wounds, his icy beard was soaked in blood. Strabo looked about frantically, but there was no aid up here. The forsaken spot was deserted, the soldiers either all slain or run off.

Molena wrapped Nargonne's cloak tight around him and Strabo cradled the man's head in his arms. Nargonne gasped weakly, his breathing shallow and failing fast.

Molena pressed her cheek to Nargonne's. "You are loved, my uncle," she whispered.

Strabo knew from his wounds that Nargonne's body was mortally broken. He was afraid to move him. Afraid that the slightest touch would finish him.

"What should I do?" he asked the doomed man at last.

Nargonne managed only a weak laugh. "Take her to wife, you fool," he said. His eyes twinkled at Molena as tears began spilling down her cheeks.

Strabo smiled back, faint and grim.

"I will," he promised.

Nargonne took his eyes from them and stared blankly into the vast paleness above. He saw that the snow still whipped and the wind still blew.

"My son," he said.

Strabo hovered over him, his heart beating thickly in his chest.

"I will care for him," said Strabo.

Nargonne nodded weakly and spoke no more. They watched life leave him and Nargonne was gone. Strabo looked into the face of the dead man for a minute, an hour, a lifetime. Then he closed Nargonne's eyes. Molena pulled Nargonne's head to hers and prayed.

Strabo and Molena looked about the mountainside littered with bodies and the patches of red snow, which speckled the place.

All was death. All was over. Strabo wrapped his arms around Molena and she wept in his embrace for the longest of times.

The weeping warmed them both and at length they found themselves moving again. Ever so carefully, they plucked the lethal barbs from Nargonne's body and stuffed the wounds with fabric torn from their own cloaks. Then they wrapped the dead man safely in cloak and hide, tied him to Archon's back, and started back down the mountain.

They stumbled mindlessly and few words passed between them. Then thought left them. Anger and emotion had abandoned them too. They only walked.

They passed others on their way down; stragglers struggling after the army. Only one man spoke to them, a man who looked earnest and grave. The man gestured at the body borne on Archon's back. "Leave him," the man said. "Save yourself."

Strabo glared at the man. *Fool*, he wanted to say. They ignored the man and continued down.

By sunrise, the blizzard had abated and the Asturians turned to take in the peaks behind them, where so much had been lost and so much gained. The Alps had claimed Nargonne. They would tower as his tombstone, but not his grave.

———

Hannibal eventually broke the opposing mountain tribes and made the summit, exhorting his men to the floor of Italy, waiting below. There were riches there, and glory. His army emerged from the mountains with far fewer men than had started. Fifteen thousand had been lost and two thousand horses. Only fifteen elephants survived. Treasure and gold had also been lost, though how much could never truly be known.

All was of little matter to Hannibal as now the fertile Italian plain of Lombard lay unprotected before him.

Back at the mouth of the Rhône, Scipio learned of Hannibal's crossing. He raced back to Italy, but he was too late. The Romans had been caught flat-footed and Hannibal quickly commandeered the rich lands of the Po valley. The Roman Senate panicked and recalled nearly every soldier in their far-flung empire back to Italy. Roman concern was well founded: Hannibal now controlled all of North Italy and was hero to the multitude of oppressed tribes there. He gathered them around him as allies and pointed his rejuvenated army south. Toward Rome.

Chapter 18

Strabo and Molena found the going down no easier than the ascent. They led Archon and Castaine and Tundra as best they could and leaned on them often. The animals were far more surefooted than they and descended steadily, day after exhausting day. Strabo scavenged the dead for grain and pried the frozen millet from their stiff packs. He and Molena settled each night by fires fueled by an endless supply of wooden hafts from discarded, frozen weapons. Castaine slept beside them in the snow.

The ice seemed always the same, but the air grew thicker. The winds slowed, and the horses and their riders recovered their strength. Unmolested by any Allobroges, they were alone in the heights.

When at last they descended back to the plains of the Arc Valley they found that winter now had the lower world in its icy grip too. Snow had piled high, but they were able to dig through it where they saw soft spots that told of running streams beneath. They drank when they could and the twelfth month of the year drew to a frigid close.

The snow seemed part of them now, no longer the alien force it had once seemed. It swathed them in its embrace and caked the horses from fetlock to mane. Archon bore Nargonne's body from sunrise to sunset over the unending plateau.

Three horses. Three riders.

It was deep in the first month of the new year by the time they reached Tourek waiting at the Rhône. Hearts leaden, they carefully exhumed the grave of Mallouse and set out for home with their dead.

They paused at a bluff that overlooked the Rhône and stared long at the river below, its banks frozen and white. The cloudy haze of winter shrouded the sun, but their future was as clear as a summer day. They would return in the spring, as Nargonne had instructed, and recover the gold, which would pay the crippling fine and favor the Asturians for generations to come.

The river held much for the Asturians, Strabo knew, and for him. The secret swords of Hannibal had all been lost to the mountains. Save one. It waited for Strabo in a mahogany box at the bottom of the slumbering river. He had held the blade for only a few seconds during his struggle with Akdar, but in those seconds he had recognized the spectacular nature of the weapon. The unfamiliar blade had mesmerized him. It was not of rough iron or of hardened bronze. It gleamed a brilliant blue and black and flashed silver when it caught the light. The metal had withstood the punishing blows of Akdar's long sword without suffering a nick. *Steel.* Strabo vowed to retrieve it and unlock the secrets of its making.

He looked at Molena and she smiled back at him across the stiff winter wind. She didn't look tired or worn. She shone like the finest of metals and Strabo felt her energy surge through him for the hundredth time. He knew that the two of them together were as powerful as that secret prize resting on the floor of the Rhône.

Strabo climbed aboard Castaine and smiled at the thought of the man who had carried him so far. *"What will you leave behind?"* Nargonne had asked him that. Strabo's spirits soared, nearly lifting him from the saddle. He would leave behind what Nargonne had—a world changed, and everything forged anew.

The Sword of Hannibal
Glossary

Cubit	Distance from elbow to finger tip
Digit	Width of a finger, not *length* of a finger
Fathom	With arms outstretched, distance from right hand finger tips to left hand finger-tips
Hectare	"Hekaton" in Greek. Roughly 10,000 square meters
Jar	The Greek version held nearly five liters
League	Roughly three modern miles
Pace	A fast double-step—a little more than a modern meter
Palm	Width of a man's hand
Rod	Roughly a modern meter
Span	Distance from tip of little finger to tip of thumb, with hand outstretched
Stadia (stade)	One eighth of a kilometer
Stone	The Phoenician version equals just over four kilograms, though many cultures have used "stone" to define a variety of weights.
Talent	The amount of weight a man could carry on his back

About the Author

Terry McCarthy lives in Michigan with his wife, two children, and various animals too numerous to detail here. He studies ancient history and listens to loud music. This is his first novel.